← TO TOWN   ROAD

HEATER'S
House

PASTURE

PERFECT'S
House

B
G

CANAL

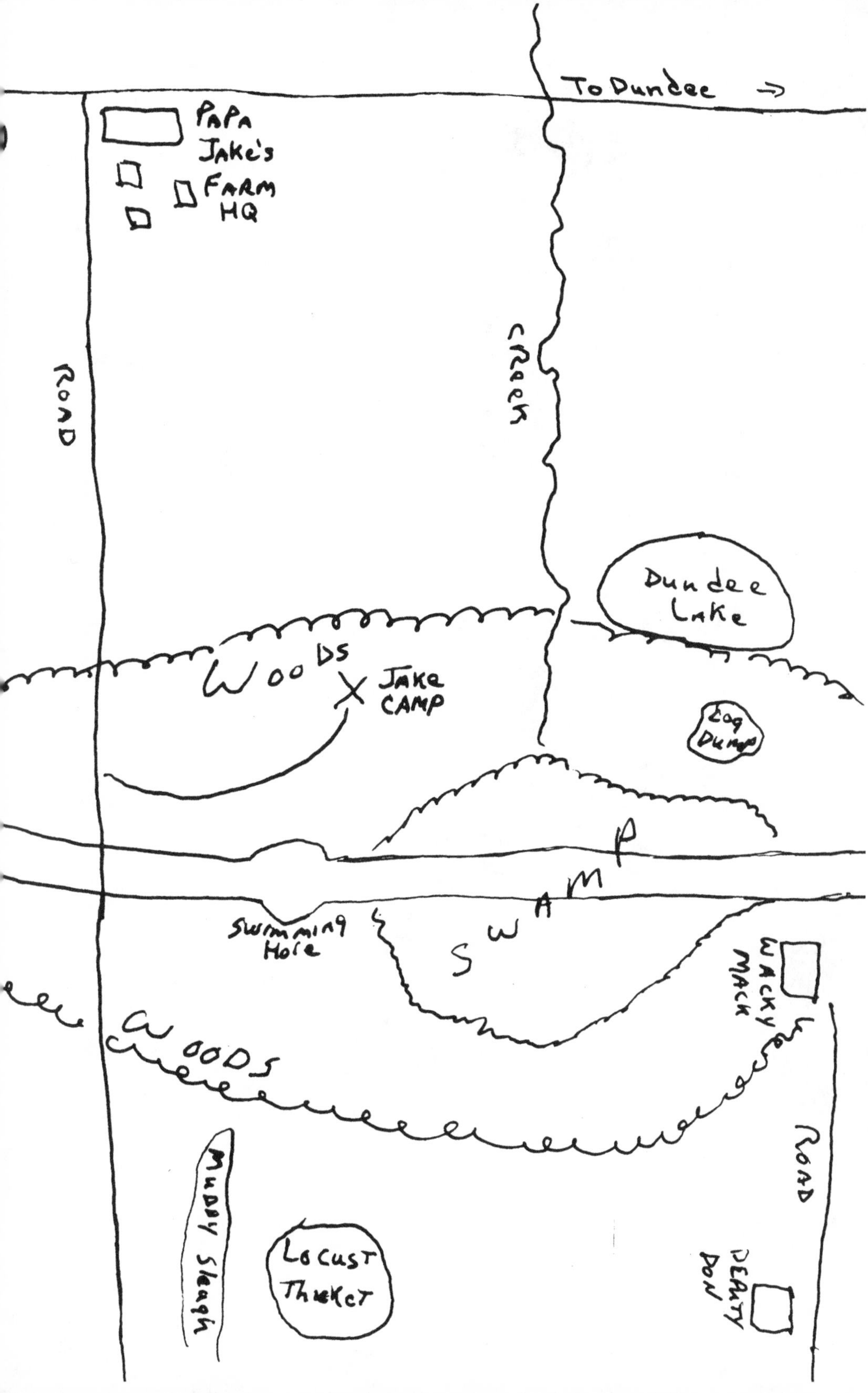
To Dundee →
PAPA JAKE'S FARM HQ
ROAD
CREEK
Dundee Lake
WOODS
JAKE CAMP
Log Dump
SWAMP
Swimming Hole
WACKY MACK
WOODS
ROAD
MUDDY Slough
Locust Thicket

THE JAKES!

THE JAKES!

definition: a JAKE is a young immature male turkey

by

Robert Hitt Neill

Mississippi River Publishing Company
Leland, Mississippi

Illustrations by

Sam Beibers, Mickey Kyzar, Beau Neill

Jacket Design by

Sam Beibers

Published by

MRP

Printed in the USA by

Lightning Source

Other Books by Robert Hitt Neill:

THE FLAMING TURKEY

GOING HOME

HOW TO LOSE YOUR FARM IN TEN EASY LESSSONS AND COPE WITH IT

THE VOICE OF JUPITER PLUVIUS

DON'T FISH UNDER THE DINGLEBERRY TREE

BEWARE THE BARKING BUMBLEBEES

OUTDOOR TABLES & TALES (compiled & edited)

THE MAGNOLIA CLUB (compiled & edited)

THIS BOOK IS INSPIRED BY AND DEDICATED TO....

WHO ELSE ?

BUT...

THE JAKES!!

Adam Neill
Mark Ethridge
Coo Collins
Bryon McIntire
Tommy Burford
Joe Bernardi
Tommy Borgognoni
Robert Brunstetter
Cliff Lusk

AND THE GIRLS...

B. C. Neill
Christie Neill
Melanie McCrory
Denise Lee
Lena Beth Burford

Contents

Part I: Age 13

TRIALS BY FIRE 15
A SUNDAY DRIVE 25
BUCK FEVER 31
SUGARPIE'S BATH 33
HOOKED! 37
THE BEST DUCK HUNT 41
THE GREAT RABBIT HUNT 45
BREAKING BULLIES 49
THE LOST JAKE 52
HOW TO FIND JAKES 57
THE JAKE PHILOSOPHY 61

Part II: Age 14

WATER SKI LESSONS 65
GEORGE, THE PET TURTLE 68
FROG GIGGING 73
HEIGHTROPHOBIA 77
SNAKEBIT! 80
HORSES AND HORNETS 87
THE GREAT HAILSTORM 89
THE LAST CARTRIDGE 95
RABBIT RUNNERS 97
"HAINTS!" 101
THE JAKEFEST 105
THE LONG RIDE DOWN 109

Part III: Age 15

TICKS 115
DEADLINES 119
THE ROOKIE 125
THE TEACHERS 129
PANTHERS 134
THE LAST LESSON 139
THE MAULING 143
WAR! 148
AFTERMATH 154
A CAMPFIRE VISITOR 156
DWI 159
METEOR SHOWERS 164

Part IV: Age 16

DYNAMITE! 171
CHICKEN TO DATE 176
GIRLS IN THE JAKECAMP 180
PLAGUES 184
HOG HUNTING 193
STORMY NIGHTS 199
JAKES VS. SENIORS 201
THE WRECK 205
THE QUITTER 208
THE DEER RESURRECTION 211
THE JAKEFIGHT 214

Part V: Age 17

SKINNY DIPPING 223
TROLLING FOR PIRATES 235
THE EXPLOSION 243
THE READING PROGRAM 246
ALIENS: THE SET-UP 251
ALIENS IN THE JAKECAMP 255
COACH ROACH 261
THE COACH'S TROUBLES 264
THE PROM 274
TORNADO! 278

Part VI: Age 18

THE BIRTHDAY PARTY 287
DOVE HUNTING 293
DRIVING CRAZY 297
THE DEATH OF OLE COW-FOOT 301
THE SINKING OF SNEAKY PETE 305
THE HAUNTED HOUSE 307
GIVING 312
THE WILL OF WACKY MACK 314
THE LAST SEMESTER 318
THE GRADUATION PARTY 324

PREFACE

The last of the boys finally arrived at our home six miles out in the country, and all the other boys were already loaded up, waiting, when his mother's car turned into the gravel driveway. The late youngster was opening the car door as it braked at the edge of the garage, where I was standing. With a grinning nod to me, the boy tossed a "Bye, Momma" over his shoulder, gathered up his gear, and trotted to the jeep. As he handed his stuff up to his noisy comrades and vaulted in himself, the lady stepped from the car and walked over. I knew her vaguely, but knew her boy well. "Good evenin'," I greeted her.

The thirteen year old at the wheel cranked the jeep and backed carefully out of the garage. Five boys were packed into the open vehicle. Each one had a shotgun, a .22 rifle, a belt knife ("scabbard knife" we used to call them), and a pocket knife. A couple had deer rifles, and one wore a .22 pistol. Two had hatchets, and an axe handle stuck up from behind the back seat. They laughed, waved, and yelled good-byes as the loaded vehicle roared out of the driveway and turned toward the woods.

"Good Lord!" the city mother exclaimed. "Aren't you worried about them?"

I grinned. I had taught every one of those boys gun safety, usually in behind their own fathers' intructions, and had for years watched them shoot and hunt. They all could use a compass, sharpen a knife, clean their own fish and game. They knew poisonous snakes from harmless snakes, could draw a rough map of the tract of woods where their permanent camp lay, and had

11

learned rudimentary first aid. Not a one of them drank, smoked, or took drugs. They would return in thirty-six hours, and I would not even check on them unless I decided that I wanted to hunt a while with them tomorrow.

"No ma'am," I drawled. "But I'd be worried about 'em if they were gonna be ridin' around town half the night!"

"Papa Jake"
Brownspur, MS
November 1982

THE JAKES!

(definition: a jake is a young, immature male turkey.)

PART ONE: AGE 13

Hell!

Into the darkness of those endless depths plunged The Heater, feetfirst, the flames singeing both his soul and his soles. He tried to draw his legs up, cringing from the Devil's fires. He tried to lash out at his tormentor; but alas, he had been bound with chains before being cast into the fire. It was just as Revelation had warned. The Heater cried and pleaded with his Maker.

"God! I'm saved! I'm saved!" his muffled moans besought the Creator's ear, but only seemed to arouse the ire of demons, who began to howl, drowning out his prayers.

"Eeeiiiyyy!!!" Boateater screamed. "Heater's on fire!"

"I'm saved!!" Heater tried to shout. Well he remembered that Sunday night when he had felt the Savior pulling at his heartstrings and had spoken of his conviction to Mr. Tate, the third-and-fourth-grade Sunday School teacher. After talking with his parents and the pastor as well, The Heater had "walked the aisle" that next Sunday morning, proclaiming his decision to the congregation and the world.

So why was he going to Hell?

The flames leapt upward, and the Imps of Satan began to dance around him, pummelling him, shrieking hideously as they tortured and pulled his burning body to and fro in the eternal darkness.

"Roll 'im!! Roll 'im!!" cried Boateater.

"Beat 'im!! Beat 'im!!" bellowed Birdlegs.

The Heater's past sins began to flash before his consciousness as the fiends continued their agonizing devilments. "I'm sorry!! I'm sorry!!" *he repented. Then, in answer to his prayers, he heard an angel's resounding peal:*

"Pull him out!" *came the Heavenly order.*

"Pull 'im out!!" yelled Perfect.

Holy hands gripped the Heater's shoulders, yet still the hellish darkness enveloped him. "I'm saved!!" *he declared again desperately, writhing as the burning persisted. Acrid smoke stung his nostrils.*

"The zipper's stuck!! The zipper's stuck!" roared Deadeye.

"The viper's struck! The viper's struck!" taunted the Hounds of Hell, urging on Satan's serpents. The Heater's back arched in agony as he felt the deadly fangs stab like fiery darts into his legs and ankles.

"Use your knife!!" ordered Perfect, dragging the Heater from the fire, as Boateater and Birdlegs beat at the flames and Deadeye jerked at the zipper.

"Lose your life!" The Heater recognized the angel's voice, dooming him to the pits. He gave one last violent wrench to break the binding chains. "But I'm saved!!" *he shouted, and suddenly he was free, tumbling backwards in the angel's arms.* "I'm saved!"

"I know you're saved! But get those jeans and socks off!" Perfect hollered in Heater's ear, snapping his friend to consciousness. Birdlegs, Boateater, and Deadeye joined him in stripping the smoldering clothes from Heater's body, hurling the garments toward the torn, smoking sleeping bag. Deadeye quickly dragged the ice chest over, dumped the food out, and tilted the chest to allow Heater's feet and ankles to be jammed into the ice. The wounded one exhaled explosively in relief and collapsed back into Perfect's arms.

"Boy!" Birdlegs exclaimed, reaching for a canned drink that rolled toward him. "No more sleeping that close to the fire again! You scared the *Hell* out of us!"

"Hey!" croaked the Heater. "No kiddin'. We're goin' to *church* tomorrow!"

And sure enough, they did. All except the Heater hunted squirrels for a couple of hours the next morning, but they came back to camp early, with Deadeye dragging in last as usual. After the game had been cleaned, they loaded everything into the jeep and Birdlegs drove the three miles back to Heater's parents' house, where each Jake kept at least one change of clothes.

Papa Jake and Other Mother were surprised to see the youngsters returning so early, but wisely did not pursue the subject after initial inquiries brought unanimous "Aww, nothin'" replies. Though only Heater and Perfect were Baptists, all five Jakes attended Mr. Ballentine's seventh-and-eighth-grade class, then sat in the balcony for services, where all but Heater and Boateater slept. The latter slid down the pew to sit directly behind Crazy Sharon where he periodically leaned forward, obstensibly to gently pull her pigtails, but really to smell her perfume. Puberty calls early for some.

This group attendance was to become a pattern for the Jakes on at least a once-a-month basis, generally on rainy Sundays when the ducks weren't flying or the fish weren't biting. Except during April, of course. The Jakes subscribed to Uncle Bubba's theory, which had been expressed to Father Phil one time as, "Phil, if the Lord had wanted me to come to church in April, He wouldn'ta set turkey season in April!"

This was not the first, nor would it be the last, near-tragic encounter the Jakes would have with "The Fire Monster," as they came to call it. Indeed, the last time it had really been cold enough for a fire the spring before had resulted in the destruction of their tent. Birdlegs had the firewatch that night — the Jakes always organized, you had to give them that. They took regular turns on different details: firewatch, cook, clean-up, and KP.

When Birdlegs awoke shivering that late-March morning, he considerately tried not to disturb the other boys, all of whom had retreated into the depths of their sleeping bags. Clad in moccasins and one-piece longhandles, he stepped through the tent flap to discover that it had showered during the night. Not a live coal remained of their campfire.

Not to worry; that's why God made gasoline, and the Jakes kept a contingency can of it against the big sweetgum tree at the edge of the Camp clearing. Birdlegs piled a gracious plenty of damp wood on the dead fire site, and retrieved the gallon gas can.

Birdlegs and the Heater shared a certain engaging degree of precipitousness, which usually was tempered by the natural caution of Perfect and Deadeye. The former pair, left to their own devices, could prove logically that, for instance: if one pill was prescribed, then two would get one well twice as fast; if eight hours was the norm for a certain job, then one could work twice as hard and finish in four (giving four extra hours for hunting and fishing!); if Papa Jake said to drive the jeep at twenty miles per hour, they could arrive at their camp deep in The Woods in half the time by driving forty miles per hour (as long as they waited until they were out of sight of the house before speeding up); and, in the present circumstance, if a quart of gasoline would get a decent campfire going again, a gallon would be infinitely better.

Birdlegs emptied the can onto the pile of dead branches.

Sadly, the same shower that had killed the campfire had also soaked the box of matches in previous use. The firewatch Jake realized this only after he had replaced the can at the sweetgum tree. No matter; there were dry matches in the huge blown-down hollow cypress log that served well as the Jakes' storage facility and lay opposite the fire from the tent. Birdlegs leaned into the cavity, found the fruitcake tin with dry matches inside, and removed another box. At this point, all the activity had bestirred a certain call to nature in his innards and the boy stepped over to the nearby latrine to relieve himself while he was close to the source of dry toilet paper, which was also kept in the hollow cypress. A couple of minutes later he returned, flap down, to replace the roll of paper in its cracker tin. Then, yawning, he stood between the log and the pile of dead branches, struck a match, and flipped it toward the pile.

"Faaahh-WHOOOMMPP!!"

Gasoline fumes had of course seeped into the tent, but fortunately all the other boys were completely encased in their sleeping bags, so no one was hurt in the initial explosion. The flash and concussion was certainly sufficient to awaken them, however, and rip three grommets out of the tent fabric. The rest didn't last long.

The Heater was well known for his fast reactions; he had batted over .400 the previous summer. He was in a dead run before his bag's zipper was halfway down, and also before he realized which way the tent flap was. It is doubtful that his initial surge would have torn the tent, but only a second later Boateater hit the opposite wall at full steam. The canvas was not strong enough to restrain two Jakes going at full speed in opposite directions simultaneously. Both sidewalls ripped out, but at some cost. Boateater tripped on a tent peg and sprained his ankle and Heater's momentum carried him into a low branch. He suffered a stick jab in his eye; not crippling, but certainly painful.

Deadeye was at the opposite end of the spectrum from Heater, reactionwise. He didn't walk, he ambled; he didn't speak, he drawled; he could drift into a dead sleep at the drop of a hat; and usually, when he woke up it took him at least five minutes to stretch and find his glasses. Thus, his reaction to the explosion was to sit up and reach for his horn-rimmed spectacles. It was unfortunate that he was outboard of the Heater.

Heater's shin caught Deadeye squarely in the face, and though the nose was not broken, it was severely bent. Blood spurted spectacularly, to such an extent that afterward the Heater thought he had cut his leg, judging from the amount

19

on his jeans. Blinded and bleeding, Deadeye scuttled out the back of the collapsing tent, where some grommets had already been blown out by the initial explosion.

Perfect was the only Jake to exit the tent at the flap, and he splintered the tent pole, some of which Heater had to remove from his shoulder after the excitment died down. He was greeted by the sight of Birdlegs, on the other side of the fire, trying desperately to step over a five-foot-high cypress log without putting either foot on the ground. Apparently the log had prevented an outflowing seepage of gas fumes, resulting in a build-up exactly where Birdlegs was standing when he struck the match.

The firestarting Jake was minus most of his eyebrows and lashes, but the old Navy surplus watchcap he slept in had protected his head. There had not been much hair on his legs before, but now there was none up to the mid-calf point where his long johns ended. Not only was the hair singed from his exposed skin, but he was also flash-burned. His unprotected epidermis positively glowed.

Including the portion most revealed to Perfect at first glance: where the long john flap had been dropped. For years after, whenever the subject of Birdlegs' moral fiber was brought up, the other Jakes would harken back to this day in the Woods, with the time-worn expression "he ain't got a hair on his ass!" Of course, this observation was never used before adult ears.

Much later, after first aid had been administered to all wounds, Deadeye removed the bloody tee shirt he was holding to his clotting nostrils and asked his standard question: "Are we gonna get in trouble for this?"

The tent had been a tenth-birthday present to Perfect from his parents. That worthy surveyed the carnage and turned a baleful eye upon the firewatch Jake.

"Birdlegs is!" Perfect promised.

For two years, Birdlegs did an extra KP tour and the others split his firewatch between them. And, though he had outgrown his youthful appearence of two-thirds legs and one-third body by the age of seventeen, Birdlegs had to endure during stories-around-the-fire-time for fifty-five years the acting out by the other Jakes of his mad dance trying to step over a five-foot-high cypress log while exposing a bright red, smoking rear to his audience.

Some fame is not so fleeting.

*   *   *   *   *

Oddly enough, it was less than two months after the Heater's profoundly religious experience that the Jakes underwent a third trial by fire. This one was occasioned to a large degree by Lady Luck.

The Jakes, as usual, were the recipients of extra tickets to the annual Ducks Unlimited Banquet and Auction, bought for them by Uncle Bubba. These events are marked by donations from most businesses in the community of free products, some of which are auctioned, some raffled, and some drawn as door prizes. This year was a lucky one for the Jakes, as all of them won at least one prize. The Heater got two boxes of shotgun shells, an insulated vest, and a camouflaged boat cushion; Perfect received a case of Gatorade and a pair of hunting boots; Deadeye won a carton of .22 cartridges and a pair of insulated mittens; Birdlegs got a pair of waders, a framed print of three Labrador puppies, and from a raffle ticket, a camouflage flotation coat; and Boateater won a boat heater.

"A boat 'eater?" was his pained exclamation when his name was drawn. "I ain't even got a boat!" The words were meant only for the ears of his tablemates, but were uttered during one of those impossible-to-predict silences that sometimes occur in crowded rooms, inevitably when something embarrassing is spoken. The whole audience burst into laughter as the red-faced Jake rose to retrieve his prize.

"But I ain't even got a boat!" became a standard expression around town when a gift relative to another piece of equipment was presented. The fun with the saying reached a high point three years later when the Duke of Dundee won a free vasectomy donated by Doc McClendon. The Duke's meticulous, exaggerated drawl boomed out from the corner where the bar was set up: "But Doc! Aye ain't even *got* a boat!" It almost broke up the meeting.

The Jakes made use of the boat heater by converting it to a Camp heater, but it got very little use that fall because the weather was exceptionally warm until after Christmas. The first real cold snap arrived between Christmas and New Year's, and the Jakes met it with enthusiasm, decked out in all their new gear. Perfect had even gotten a new tent from Santa Claus, one of the new-fangled geodesic designs. He proudly showed the other boys how to assemble it, pointing out that not only was it windproof and waterproof, but it even had a floor and a zipper-sealed flap.

Yet so few things are truly Jake-proof.

The Jakes made camp before noon in their usual style. Just opposite the huge hollow cypress log, the Heater and Perfect set up the new tent, while Deadeye dug a latrine hole in the Woods behind the log, and Boateater and Birdlegs gathered firewood. The jeep was parked on the other side of the big sweetgum tree, at the base of which the boys unloaded the ice chest, two cases of canned drinks, a two-gallon cooler of water, the boat heater and a gas can (a new gas can: Deadeye had given it to Birdlegs for Christmas. It was a square, one-gallon can, on each side of which Deadeye had glued a picture of Birdlegs. He had then carefully painted a large "X" across each picture.)

With Camp set up, the boys retrieved from the hollow log their cooking utensils and sleeping bags. While Deadeye and Heater rinsed out the old cast-iron skillet and dutch oven, the other three carefully shook out the sleeping bags before laying them down in the new tent. Boateater had once found a chicken snake in his, and since that evening all bags were checked thoroughly.

Chores done, the Jakes went to the Woods for the afternoon, looking for deer sign. One by one, they returned to camp around dark, Perfect being the only one to see a buck. He had jumped "Ole Cow-foot" out of a honeysuckle patch, but had been unable to get a shot. Heater had come in early to get the fire going and to start supper. A pot of chili prepared the night before by Other Mother bubbled on the bricks next to the campfire.

Before he sat down to eat, Boateater had one final chore.

He fired up the boat heater and sat it on a couple of bricks inside the tent. "We'll sleep warm tonight with my ole boat heater," he promised.

After supper, while the others were cleaning up, Deadeye also had one final chore. This Jake was deathly afraid of wasps and other stinging insects, and had formed the habit of spraying the tent with insecticide about an hour before bedtime. He had once entered his sleeping bag in company with a live red wasp, and never intended to experience that again. He got a can of spray out of the hollow log, walked to the tent, inserted the can, and began to spray.

To his credit, Deadeye probably could not have read the fine print on the can, even with his glasses. It said: "DO NOT USE NEAR OPEN FLAME!"

It was a good point. The tent suddenly seemed to swell, briefly glowed, and then went "poom!" in a soft explosion. Luckily, Deadeye not only had his head turned, but had his new mittens on, so his hand was not badly injured by the can's blowing up. The tent itself protected him from the fragments of the boat heater, except for a piece of glass which the Heater dug out of his wrist. Birdlegs' new "mummy"-style sleeping bag proved to be not nearly so flame-retardant as advertised; it, like all the other bags, was a total loss.

In the aftermath, Perfect, true to form, didn't lose his temper. Rather, he seemed sadly resigned to the destruction of his second tent in less than a year. Birdlegs, on the other hand, was furious at the loss of his new mummy-bag, but knew he couldn't afford to say anything after his own troubles so recently. It was Boateater who made the remark to restore perspective. As Heater was probing Deadeye's wrist for remaining fragments, the Jake who had lost his DU prize turned to the Jake who was eyeing the remnants of his tent.

"You got fire insurance?" Boateater asked.

*   *   *   *   *   *

When a boy reaches his teens, it is like a type of graduation. Indeed, some schools follow a practice of having a formal graduation ceremony upon the completion of sixth grade,

which usually coincides with a kid's entering the teenage
ranks. For some kids, puberty begins to call. Some prep
schools test children at this age and begin to push them into
the areas of interest and talents indicated. Less fortunate
youngsters are sometimes taken out of school when they become teens to join the adult work force. Children who a year
ago were playing with dolls, square their shoulders and begin
to set goals: "I'm going to be a doctor!" But for all who enter
their teens, there is that one burning question:

"When can I drive by myself?"

Driving by oneself is not to be misconstrued as driving
with a valid license, you will understand. Especially with
country kids, there is a tendency to learn to drive early (fifteen
is the legal age in the state under discussion), and therefore, to
be allowed to "drive around the place" or even to be sent to
town on small errands. The first boy in his age group to be
allowed to drive the family car on a date in modern times has
achieved roughly the same amount of social status as did the
boy David when he slew Goliath. Kingdoms cheer, and chari-
ots await — preferably convertibles.

Upon reaching their thirteenth year, the Jakes understood
all this, and two of them had a headstart on the others. The
Heater and Perfect, being country cousins, had seized every
opportunity to commandeer a vehicle and drive the turnrows
or the fallow fields — so little to run into, don't you know.
This driving was usually parentally sanctioned, but that summer the two boys found a way to do some driving on their
own.

Papa Jake had gotten a new pickup truck, but instead of
trading the old one in for a nominal sum, he had decided to
keep it to haul seed and chemicals to the fields. Actually, he
had the Heater in mind when he made that decision, but not
for the way it later happened.

The Heater had a second key made for the old truck,
which stayed parked under the tractor sheds about a half-mile
from the houses. On Sunday afternoons, when the grown-ups
were involved in their Sabbath naps, the two cousins would
hop on their bikes, pedal down to the sheds, and borrow the
truck to practice their driving. They even grew confident

enough to venture onto the nearby gravel and blacktop roads where the danger of them being recognized was about as slight as the traffic they encountered.

One Sunday each summer the older country churches would declare a Homecoming, complete with dinner on the grounds, gospel groups singing, and an evangelistic revival preacher who held services each night during the week at different surrounding churches in preparation for the all-day meeting at the Brush Arbor.

The Brush Arbor was an open-air structure with cut cane on top for shade, and pews to seat two hundred people. It was situated in a beautiful grove of moss-hung oaks next to a creek, and seemed relatively cool all summer. The road by the Brush Arbor had recently been blacktopped, and a new elevated bridge had been built, high enough to span both the creek and the railroad track that paralleled the creek on the side opposite the Brush Arbor. Though the road still had wide gravel shoulders, the asphalt on the right-of-way greatly improved conditions in the pews. The Arbor was so close to the road that worshippers had had to endure the dust of passing cars, especially those which gained extra momentum coming down the bridge and were wont to "fishtail" making the curve by the open-air meeting place.

The blacktop also had the advantage of muffling the sounds of the approaching cars, which had previously disrupted the preaching on occasion. But sometimes, as in this incident, a warning might effect less disruption than the alternative.

The Heater and Perfect had attended Homecoming services with their parents but after lunch, when the preaching resumed, they slipped out the back and made their way to the creek. Removing their shoes and socks and rolling up their britches legs, they waded the creek and returned to the road on the other side of the railway, where they thumbed a ride back to Heater's house with Boy Chile Meadows. Though nearly seventy-five years old, Mr. Meadows had been the only male of eight children, six of whom were older than him. No one in town knew his real name; he had simply been "Boy Chile" from the word "go."

"Y'all do like me and get about an hour's nap, and I'll pick y'all up to go back. I can't understand a lot of what that preacher's sayin', but he sure gets het up about it, and that's what counts in preachin'!" The old man remonstrated in his high wheezy voice as he let the boys out, "Now y'all be sure we're goin' back down there this ev'nin'!"

"Oh, yes, sir! We will!" answered Heater.

He did not really intend to keep this promise; certainly not as gloriously as it turned out.

The two Jakes changed into jeans and, creatures of habit, climbed aboard their bikes and headed for the tractor sheds and their Sunday afternoon drive. There was no way they could have known that a brake line had split on the pickup, and that Papa Jake intended to fix it on Monday. For several weeks they had been noticing that some pumping of the pedal was required anyway.

Driving slowly around the turnrows was boring, and the Heater proposed a new venture. "Hey, everybody's at the Homecoming anyway; let's get on the blacktop an' go check 'em out!"

Perfect happened to be driving, and was naturally cautious about any suggestion of Heater's in any case. "Not hardly," was the calm reply.

"Aw, c'mon, man! If you're worried about it, let's jus' ease up to the toppa the bridge an' stop. We'll see if anybody's cars have left, see when they look like they'll be ready to cut the watermelons, an' jus' drive around 'til it's time to go back." He added as an afterthought, "I can't tell halfa what that preacher's sayin' anyway."

That swung Perfect to Heater's side. "Yeah, I don't know how come Father Phil hadda get a Yankee to preach."

"Prob'ly a missionary to the North," the Heater observed without a trace of sarcasm, as Perfect turned the pickup down the gravel road toward the blacktop and shifted into second.

Luckily, there were no other cars on the blacktop, for Perfect was unable to stop when he reached the turn. "Hey, this blame thing doesn't have any brakes!" he exclaimed.

"Aw, you gotta 'member to pump 'em," the Heater snorted. "Don't make any difference; nobody was comin'."

26

That remark rather summed up one of The Heater's Important Philosophies of Life.

By the time they reached the creek bridge, Perfect was tooling along in high gear. As they got about halfway up the incline he reached to shift into second, but Heater stopped him.

"Let it coast up by itself so they won't hear us," he instructed. "Nobody's comin' behind us, so we'll jus' stop on top and watch."

The truck coasted to the top, but only barely. Just as it made the last few feet, the engine chugged and died. Perfect put his feet on the brake and clutch, both of which went all the way to the floor. "Son of a three-toed, bare-backed berry picker!" the Jake muttered through clenched teeth. He had a premonition.

Elroy Jernigan's house was set well back from the road, directly across from the Brush Arbor. Elroy raised poultry, and he raised a lot of it. He did this cheaper than most farmers, because his brother worked as janitor and night watchman on weekends at a large grain elevator fifteen miles away. Every Saturday night, Elroy would drive down to the elevator after it had closed, and he and his brother would sweep up the loose grain and load it into Elroy's old truck. Wheat, soybeans, milo, corn, oats, and rice were all mixed together, along with an occasional busted sack that found its way into the truck with masking tape over the hole. The Saturday night before Homecoming, Elroy had been going a little fast coming down the bridge, and had spilled a good bit of grain in the road when making the turn to his house. His flocks, which usually roamed loose, had found the feed about noon.

When Perfect and Heater topped the bridge, they were greeted by the sight of several dozen fowl scattered across the road at the base of the bridge just before the curve. There were turkeys, ducks, chickens, and guinea fowl busily pecking — but quietly, for the preacher was praying right beside the road, in the Brush Arbor. One hundred sixty-two men, women, and children had their heads bowed reverently, their backs to the bridge. Only the evangelist was facing the pickup, but his eyes were closed tightly as he besought his

God; the same God that the Heater and Perfect were beseeching.

For the truck began to roll forward, in spite of all the pumping Perfect could do.

"Oh, GOD!!" entreated both Jakes.

The heavy old pickup gathered speed quickly, and it gathered it silently, for Perfect had not re-cranked the engine and his foot was still jamming the clutch to the floor. He desperately pumped the brake pedal, shoving with all his strength, which unfortunately required that his head descend beneath the dashboard, so that he could no longer see the road. Nor could he be seen from it. Heater, realizing the predicament, leaned across from the passenger side to help steer. He also was doing all he could to help stop: "Whoa-whoa-whoa-whoa-whoa-whoa-whoa-whoa!" chanted the Heater.

Which was not enough to alert the population at the bottom of the hill. The poultry flocks were used to the sound of engines heralding an approaching danger, so even the guinea fowl were pecking unconcernedly. The pickup reached the bottom of the hill at fifty miles an hour and engaged the unsuspecting flocks just as the Yankee evangelist concluded his prayer and opened his eyes to see the descending driverless truck.

"JESUS CHRIST!!" bellowed the Man of God.

Now, to Southerners, this expression must not be used as a profanity, and a Northerner's habit of doing so is sorely frowned upon. Therefore, when the evangelist, having just invoked the Savior's presence, proclaimed the same in a mighty voice, the whole congregation erupted into awed clamor and spun to witness the Second Coming.

However, the Bible specifies Clouds of Glory, not clouds of feathers. Chickens, geese, guineas, ducks, and turkeys flew or were thrown into the Brush Arbor, where their cackling, gobbling, quacking, squawking, and shrieking blended with the shouts and screams from the congregation. Eight chickens and two ducks, plus a gander and a gobbler who valiantly stood their ground to protect their flocks, were killed instantly. At this point the right wheels left the pavement and the truck began to fishtail, bowling over three guineas, two geese, another duck, four hens, and a Dominicker rooster, all of which were thrown full force into the Brush Arbor. For all the panicked people and poultry, anyone trying to get an accurate identification of the silent vehicle was foiled, but everyone could be reasonably certain that it was headed for the Brush Arbor. The Yankee evangelist led the stampede for the safety of the oaks.

The Heater was unable to turn the wheel enough to make the curve, and couldn't see from his position anyway. He bellowed in Perfect's ear, "Sit up and steer, dammit!"

At which point Perfect jerked himself upright, cut the steering wheel hard aport . . . and let off the clutch. The truck was still in gear. High gear. In which it cranked.

The old engine roared to life, and the wheels spun madly on the gravel, giving the truck enough traction to make the curve. It also threw enough dust and gravel to further disguise their getaway, though flying stones dispatched two more chickens and a turkey hen. The old pickup careened around the curve and down the road, and not one of the congregation had gotten a good look at the runaway vehicle.

An hour later, Papa Jake and Other Mother entered the house in a high state of excitement, to find the Heater and Perfect watching a baseball game on TV.

"How long you boys been here?" Papa Jake asked, dying to spring the story.

"Aw, we left right after lunch," the Heater yawned. "Took a nap, an' then cut on the ball game. Braves're winnin'. We were gonna go back down this ev'nin' with Mr. Boy Chile. That okay?" he asked in perfect innocence. Perfect was engrossed in the game.

"No siree! We fired that Yankee preacher on the spot! Lemme tell you what happened. . . ."

In the shop the next afternoon, June Bug and Big Gus jacked up the old pickup to repair the cracked brake line. The former, being younger and slimmer, scooted under the vehicle on the roller and instantly observed, "Hoooo, Boy! Cat musta caught a chicken up under here! Or maybe a pigeon."

*   *   *   *   *   *   *

Perfect was so called by the other Jakes not only because he had a naturally cautious streak, but because when their inevitable devilment did occur, his perpetually innocent look caused him to never get blamed for anything. As a pure matter of record, the Heater and Birdlegs had such a wonderful propensity for getting into trouble, and so little of their deeds saw the light of adult discovery, that they richly deserved all the blame that accrued to them. And they hardly ever resented Perfect's being perfect; "it's just that every now and then we oughta get some stars in *our* crowns, too," Heater said one day. "After all, we do *some* things right *once* in a while!"

And Perfect never put on airs, to give him credit. He never bragged about being an all-A student, or getting more Sunday School pins for memorizing Bible verses than any other kid in history. He sang, played guitar well, and second base better. Cuddly Carrie had had a crush on him since nursery school, and all the other girls went through various stages of being madly in love with him. He never cussed, seldom got angry, and mechanical things always seemed to work for him. Yet there was one thing all the other Jakes could consider themselves better than Perfect at.

No one, anywhere, ever got buck fever worse than Perfect.

He was always the first to his stand, which was always the best stand. He always saw bucks, and they were always big bucks. He always got good shots at the deer; unlike the other Jakes, his bucks never stopped behind cypress trees or pawpaw thickets, never spooked at the last second from a wayward gust of scent, never turned off the trail for a tempting young doe.

Yet Perfect had never killed a deer — never even bloodied

one. It became such a matter of course that the Jakes automatically assumed that a series of shots were Perfect's, and even started to feel sorry for him. They began to plan drives for his benefit, and once Birdlegs, the best rifleman in the group, even tried to synchronize his shot with Perfect's when they were hunting the Hammer Stand together. It was almost a point of pride for Perfect to dig the .270 bullet out of the buck's shoulder and compare it with his 30.06. "See?" he said. "Toldja I missed."

Late one evening, the Heater and Birdlegs watched "Ole Cow-foot," a huge twelve-point whitetail buck, canter across a wheat field and into a locust thicket of only a couple of acres. They had been hunting wood ducks, and therefore had only their shotguns. But tomorrow was another day.

"Hey, if we drive that thicket in the mornin', I know right where he'll come out. Let's put Perfect by that old log dump. We can circle the field early an' look for tracks comin' out," Heater suggested. It was drizzling at the time, and they knew fresh tracks would be easily discernible.

Sure enough, a search the next day revealed no exit trail. Perfect was carefully coached and sent to the log dump while the others crossed Muddy Slough from the east on a beaver dam and spread out to enter the thicket. Within fifteen minutes Boateater jumped the big deer but was unable to get a shot. He yelled a warning as the buck followed the Heater's prediction, bolting straight toward Perfect.

"Boom, Boom, Boom, Boom, Boom!" five shots rang out.

"Boom, Boom, Boom, Boom!" the second clip was emptied.

The other Jakes emerged from the Locust Thicket at a run toward the log dump. "He *had* to of hit 'im!" Birdlegs ventured. "No one could miss a buck that big that many times!" He pointed out the huge fresh tracks as he ran.

They rounded the decaying pile of logs to see Perfect standing on the ground, shaking like a leaf. "Did you get him?" yelled Boateater.

"BIIG BUCK!!" babbled Perfect, holding his arms up, rifle in one hand, to indicate how big the deer's antlers had been.

"Where is he?" exclaimed the Heater, first to reach the shooter.

"Biiig Buck!!" repeated Perfect, glassy-eyed, still swinging the rifle over his head. Deadeye ducked and took it from his hand.

"How far away was he?" Birdlegs asked excitedly. The tracks passed less than ten yards from the log dump littered with 30.06 shells.

"Biiig Buck!!" chanted Perfect, holding his arms out over his head to indicate a spread of at least forty inches.

Birdlegs scampered up to the top of the log pile, from whence he could see the tracks of Ole Cow-foot continuing uninterrupted across a half-mile of wheat. "You missed 'im!!" he proclaimed in an agonized voice.

"Biiig Buck!" Perfect assured him.

"Well, I'll be durned!" Heater said disgustedly.

Deadeye had laid the guns down and was shaking Perfect by the shoulders. "Biiig Buck!" was heard again, but this time rather tiredly, like a record winding down.

Three Jakes split up to look for signs of blood, as they had been taught to follow up each shot no matter what. They slogged half a mile across the wheat field without seeing a spot of red, nor any place where the buck had even missed a stride. Trudging all the way back in silence, they found Deadeye with a recovered but sadly dejected Perfect. His raised eyebrows were met with shakes of three heads, and still in silence the Jakes made their way to the beaver dam. Rifle reloaded just in case, Perfect started across first.

A small water snake, sluggish at this time of year, was sprawled across the dam at its narrowest point. Perfect stopped five feet from the reptile. He raised his rifle. "I bet I couldn't hit that damn snake!" he snorted in disgust. "Boom!"

He missed!

Perfect lost control. He pumped four more shots into the beaver dam, and while he never did hit the snake, he did a marvelous job on the dam. It was not a very substantial structure anyway, and five 30.06 explosions at its narrowest and lowest point was too disruptive. The dam burst, and the Jakes barely made their way back to the bank. From where they now stood, the jeep was less than a hundred yards away, but on the opposite side of Muddy Slough.

However, it was a half-mile to the nearest place where they could cross the water. Birdlegs and Heater looked fit to bust, but the laconic Deadeye got the first word in.

"Yore problem," he drawled to the crestfallen Perfect, "is that we let you carry too damn many shells!"

Deadeye had gained his nickname, not from anything to do with his poor eyesight, but from an incident involving his own shooting prowess. He and Boateater had wandered nearly all the way across the woods squirrel hunting one morning when they encountered a small pack of wild dogs.

These canines were beginning to graduate from nuisance to problem. Strays, unwanted litters that town folks drove to the country to turn loose, and mongrels that a nearby small-town dog catcher brought to the woods to release, had resulted in a buildup. Wild dogs turn vicious quickly, and have no innate fear of man like wolves or coyotes, who usually avoid contact with humans. Sometimes, when a bitch was in heat, packs of up to thirty-five dogs had been seen. They preyed upon not only wild game but livestock as well, and posed a serious danger to unarmed humans in such numbers. The Jakes had been coached by their elders to shoot wild dogs on sight.

Therefore, Boateater and Deadeye cut loose with their shotguns at the pack of five that came their way, killing two outright and crippling two more. Boateater chased one cripple down and finished it off, but Deadeye couldn't get close enough to the other. The dog made it to the edge of the woods and lit a shuck for Deputy Don's homeplace.

Deputy Don owned about eighty acres on the backside of the Woods, and his holdings sat astride the only other public-access road besides the road through Papa Jake's place. The Duke of Dundee had a private turnrow that entered the Woods from his farm, and Wacky Mack used the road by Deputy Don's. Matter of fact, since the gravel ended at his log cabin, Mack had even installed a gate at Deputy Don's line. These four adults owned the whole eight hundred acres of Woods, Swamp, Canal, and the small lake. The Jakes went to great lengths to keep a good relationship with all four.

Therefore, Deadeye and Boateater had no intention of letting a crippled mongrel remain loose on Deputy Don's. At best, the dog might crawl under a building unseen and die, creating a horrible stench. At worst, it might attack some of the livestock, or even Deputy Don or Sugarpie, his wife. The two Jakes pursued the cripple and saw it crawl under the main house. Though Deputy Don's patrol car was not in evidence, Sugarpie's red Buick was, and Boateater elected to warn her of the impending execution.

"Crawl up under the house an' see if you can see the mutt," he instructed Deadeye. "Lemme go tell Sugarpie we're gonna be shootin' around here."

Deadeye obediently got on his hands and knees, gun as ready as possible, and started under the house while Boateater leaned his shotgun against the wall and stepped up on the porch to knock on the door. Deadeye paused, barely under the home, to let his eyes get accustomed to the darkness. He didn't know he was right under the bathroom.

The hot water heater had been acting up for a couple of days, and Deputy Don had promised Sugarpie that he would fix it after his weekend duty. It gurgled, made ominous rumblings, sometimes heated and sometimes didn't, and occasionally when the thermostat clicked on, it flashed two feet away when it lit. It made Sugarpie extremely nervous; she had once had an aunt who had burned to death in a house fire, and a faulty hot water heater had been the culprit.

Sugarpie had just settled her bulk into the tub for her morning bath, though the appliance behind her made her uneasy the way it was kind of roaring. She hurriedly shampooed her hair, and had just submerged her head to rinse the lather out when Boateater knocked politely on the front door. Naturally, she didn't hear him.

Deadeye heard him, though, and resumed his crawl, for he now saw the crippled stray. However, the dog also saw Deadeye, and realized he was cornered. The canine took the only course of action left open to him: he charged his would-be assassin.

Any way you consider it, a shotgun blast is an explosion. The more an explosion is confined, the more dramatic the effect. Deadeye had a double-barreled twelve-gauge, and was being charged by an angry, wounded, toothed animal in seriously confined quarters. He couldn't run. He only had two choices: one barrel, or two.

The Jake pulled both triggers simultaneously and dispatched the charging dog forthwith. The barrels were right under the bathtub.

"WHOOOMMM!!" sounded the explosion, and the house seemed to lift and tremble violently. Sugarpie jumped slap out of the bathtub and hit the floor running. She never looked back.

Boateater had just lifted his hand to knock again when Deadeye's shot caused him to pause. Scant seconds later, the front door slammed open, catching him right between the eyes and literally bowling him head over heels off one side of the porch. The naked woman in a dead run never noticed him. She jumped off the other side of the porch, jerked open the car door, had the Buick cranked before the door was closed, and threw gravel as she screeched out of the yard and down the road toward Widow Trammel's house, from where she phoned the fire and sheriff's departments.

Deadeye had observed her exit in an awed silence, still under the house. Though he didn't know all of the factors involved, he quickly made the decision that the sooner he left, the better it would be. Somebody was going to get blamed for something, and he didn't want to be around when it happened. He grabbed the dead dog by the tail, dragged it almost out from under the house, then trotted to the nearby corn crib for a croker sack. He wrapped the dog in the burlap bag to minimize any traces of blood, then ran to check on the silent Boateater.

That Jake was still seated on the ground with his head in his hands, moaning. When Deadeye helped him up, he was woozy but able to walk. Both eyes were black, his nose was swollen, and a knot bulged right in the middle of his forehead. Deadeye threw the bag over his shoulder, grabbed both guns, and urging his friend on, headed for the Woods. It was several hours before Boateater fully recovered.

The fire chief was quite put out by the false alarm, for it was nearly nine miles from town to Deputy Don's house. The Deputy arrived shortly after the fire truck, and was severely upbraided by his wife, Widow Trammel, and the chief. The Sheriff allowed him emergency leave for the rest of the day while he installed a new hot water heater. Though it was obvious that the old one had not actually exploded, it was also very obvious that Sugarpie was convinced that it had, and she refused to re-enter the house until repairs were completed.

Deputy Don was totally mystified by his wife's insistence on a large explosion, of which there was no evidence. He even checked with Wacky Mack to see if someone had been dynamiting beaver dams. It was over six months before the Jakes deemed it safe to explain things to the lawman.

Around the Jake's campfire that night, Boateater glumly held ice packs to his face while Deadeye related what he knew of the incident from his rather limited vantage point. The boys had to speculate about most of the happenings, since Boateater couldn't remember anything after walking up the porch steps.

The campfire was beginning to die down when Deadeye drawled contemplatively, "You know, that's the first nekkid lady I ever saw!" He paused, then plaintively continued, "An' I didn't even get to see *her* very long!"

There was a short silence, and then Birdlegs ventured, "Was she black all over?"

Deadeye considered the question judiciously, well aware that he was about to add quite measurably to the accumulation of knowledge previously acquired by the assembled Jakes. Finally, he pursed his lips and drawled, "Waaalll, some spots more'n others."

With the exception of the suffering Boateater, the other boys nodded wisely, silently staring into the fire while visions of nude Negresses danced in their heads. Not one of them was willing to reveal his ignorance by asking what spots.

*   *   *   *   *   *   *

That fall and winter, there was an abnormally large teal migration, both the early blue-wing and the later green-wing varieties. As previously noted, it was also unseasonably warm until after Christmas. So warm, in fact, that for several weekends the Jakes hunted blue-wing teal early in the morning, and fished for bass later on. Most of this activity took place on the small lake at the Duke of Dundee's end of the Woods.

The Duke allowed the Jakes free access to his land, as long as they minded their manners, didn't rut up the turnrows or do any crop damage, and kept an eye out for trespassers. In return, the Jakes supplied the Duke with game for his solitary table and allowed the older man free access to their campfire on his forays into the Woods. The Duke was an inveterate coon hunter and pampered a pack of registered bluetick hounds. Less charitable folks were wont to say that the Duke's all night hunts were really just an excuse for his drinking, but this was not so. The man really loved hound music. But as the saying goes, he was "bad to drink."

On a morning when the Duke's turnrow was dry, Boateater, Deadeye, and the Heater drove the jeep around to Dundee Lake to catch the early teal flight and then fish for a while. They killed a half-dozen teal, retrieved by Heater's black Labrador, Windy, and after it was obvious that the ducks were through flying, they drew the teal and hung them in a willow to drain. They returned to the jeep to trade their guns for rods rigged for bass, and were soon back at the lakebank casting for largemouth. The Heater threw toward a stump with his Jitterbug, and was rewarded by a short strike from a big fish. He quickly reeled in and flipped his rod tip back to cast again. He gave an enthusiastic heave toward the stump.

"Shhhiiii-zick!!" said the reel, backlashing to an abrupt halt. At the same moment, there was an ear-splitting scream from behind the fisherman. The Heater looked in exasperation at a backlash as big as his English teacher's hairdo and turned to see the source of the screaming.

Boateater had stepped behind the Heater to select another plastic worm from the tackle box. The rod tip, with a two-treble-hook Jitterbug close behind, had touched him at the juncture of neck and shoulder. The boy had reacted with a jerk just as the Heater had cast forward, and one gang of hooks had sunk deep into the side of his neck, while the other gang settled firmly into his shoulder. When the Heater turned around, his first impression was that Boateater looked like the guy who played the hunchback in *Young Frankenstein*.

"Gaaakkk! Get it out!!" The hooked Jake would have spoken much louder, but his initial scream had convinced him that any use of neck muscles was painful, and yelling used those muscles.

But the Heater could still yell, and he did so. "Don't walk behind me, dummy!" This was a moot point, from both the backlash's and Boateater's standpoints. "Deadeye!" the boy yelled again. His move to turn and locate their companion, while still holding the rod attached to the Jitterbug, elicited another squeal from Boateater.

"Cut the line, dammit!" he rasped.

The Heater did so, just as Deadeye trotted up. Together they examined their comrade-in-agony. The Heater had removed hooks from the other Jakes before, but he considered this particular situation to be beyond his medical talents. He shook his head. "Those hooks might be into the neck tendon. I think we better get him to Doctor Mac."

Deadeye collected their fishing gear and went ahead to the jeep, while the Heater helped the hunched Boateater in a crablike manuever up the Lake bank. Just as they reached the top, there was a cheer from Deadeye. "Here comes the Duke!" he shouted. The Heater scared Deadeye with his normal driving; the boy certainly wasn't looking forward to a trip at emergency speed.

The Duke took in the situation at a glance and assumed immediate command. He had the Jakes deposit their gear in the jeep; boosted Windy into the back of his pickup with the Heater; and arranged Boateater as comfortably as possible in the cab, head on Deadeye's shoulder and arm extended with hand clutching the dashboard. Driving as carefully as possible on the rough dirt road, the Duke soon had them back at the Heater's house, where Other Mother calmly took charge. The Duke promised to take care of their jeep, so all three boys climbed into the car with Other Mother and headed for Doc McClendon's. The Heater was fully as interested in this operation as Boateater.

Nearly two hours later they returned to the house, Boateater erect at the cost of six stitches, to see the Duke just pulling into the driveway in the jeep, followed by Big Gus driving the Duke's pickup. The farmer's face seemed more florid than usual. He dismounted from the jeep and stalked deliberately to the young trio in the driveway.

Grabbing the Heater by one shoulder, the Duke spun him around and delivered a swift kick to the boy's rear. "Now, that is for not looking behind you when you cast!" he declared.

Boateater was working up a pretty good smirk at the surprised hook-er when the Duke grabbed his uninjured shoulder just as abruptly, and administered the exact same treatment to the hook-ee. "What's that for?" Boateater burst out plaintively.

"That is for walking behind someone who is casting!" the Duke said forcefully, still behind the boy. Then he stepped back and kicked Boateater again, this time so hard that the Jake was lifted completely off the concrete and had to be steadied by a nonplussed Deadeye.

Tears of pain and outrage sprang to the boy's eyes as he cried, "Now what was *that* for?!?!"

The Duke's face was flushed with anger, and the veins in his neck and temple stood out as he shook his finger in the hurt boy's face. "That," he enunciated through clenched teeth, "is for being a damn fool! When Aye went back to get that jeep, Aye checked your shotguns out of habit. AND YOUR GUN WAS STILL LOADED!!!"

He turned on his heel and stomped halfway to the waiting pickup, then suddenly turned back to the stunned boys and bellowed, "Aye do not mind picking you up with fish hooks in your neck. Aye *do* mind picking you up with a hole in your head!!"

Doc McClendon removed the stitches after school the next Friday, so it was late when Papa Jake brought Boateater down to the Camp where the rest of the Jakes were roasting teal for supper around the fire. The succulent little ducks had been simply seasoned, wrapped in bacon, and held over the fire on a green stick like a hot dog. Although the man had already eaten, he accepted a couple of the delicious-smelling birds and joined the boys at supper. In the distance, they could hear the baying of bluetick hounds.

"Oh, by the way," Birdlegs said to Boateater as he rose to begin KP, "the Duke came by about dark an' left a package for you." He held out a plainly-wrapped box.

They could tell that the boy was still put out at the Duke. However, his curiosity got the best of him. "Prob'ly a bomb," he muttered darkly.

But it was a belt knife. A beautiful belt knife. Inlaid with silver on the bone handle was Boateater's real name. It was obviously the work of an artisan, and the other Jakes' feelings ranged from awe to jealousy. There was a short note in the box in the Duke's elaborate scrawl. Boateater read it silently.

40

Perhaps I over-reacted last week in my anger. I am quite sincerely sorry if I hurt you, physically or otherwise. I hope you will accept this gift as my apology.

However, I also hope this knife will serve as a reminder to you to *always* unload your gun when not actually hunting. You Jakes are the only boys I have, and your safety means a great deal to me.

Your Friend,
The Duke

P.S. — It may help your feelings to know you were not the only one hurt. I broke my toe. May we both learn from this.

Just after New Year's, a cold front came screaming through during the night and sent temperatures plummeting. In anticipation of the forecast being accurate, Other Mother had put her foot down about the Jakes staying in the Woods that night. No amount of pleading could sway her, and the compromise that was finally reached involved the boys staying down the road at Uncle Bubba's house and duck hunting with him the next morning, weather permitting.

Uncle Bubba was addicted to duck hunting and turkey hunting. He had taught Perfect to hunt and fish for 'most everything available, but didn't really give a hang for deer hunting, or any type of fishing. He enjoyed the sociability of a dove hunt; the taste of quail, rabbit loin, and froglegs; the hound music on nights when he accompanied the Duke of Dundee; and the excitement when Birdlegs brought his pack of miniature beagles out to run rabbits; but fellowship was the real reason he joined these types of outings. He "wouldn't walk across the street" for a squirrel hunt, which was probably Perfect's favorite sport; but during December, half of January, and April, his law office was not even open on mornings or Fridays.

Uncle Bubba had left a spread of almost two dozen decoys on the little lake at the Duke's end of the Woods, and with five boys to get rolled out and ready, he decided to hunt there this frigid morning. The Duke's turnrow was frozen solid, so they had no trouble reaching the lake in Uncle Bubba's Bronco. As they approached, they could see that the lake was iced completely over, two inches thick.

The man reached into the back of the vehicle for a couple of gallon jugs. "Boys," he said, "this is somethin' I've read about, but never had occasion to try. With everything frozen over anyway, we have nothin' to lose. Come on!"

Shouldering their guns, the Jakes followed Uncle Bubba with his mysterious jugs to the blind, in front of which nineteen decoys were frozen-in solid. The man shook each jug vigorously in turn and then heaved them out onto the ice encasing the decoys. The glass burst, and a bluish liquid splattered onto the frozen surface around the blocks. The boys regarded Uncle Bubba quizzically in the dawning light.

"Laundry bluing," he explained, grinning. "The theory is that from the air, it'll look different from the rest of the frozen lake, and with the decoys in the middle of it, any ducks flyin' over will think it's a patch of open water." He shrugged a trifle sheepishly. "Nothin' ventured, nothin' gained."

It obviously looked different to the ducks, for the early flights of mallards and pintails did drop down and circle. Yet no flocks came close enough for shots, though Uncle Bubba was an expert caller and used all the duck language he knew. "Must not look like enough open water or something," he panted, after another flight of mallards had circled for ten minutes before departing for the river.

The first flight of teal slipped in from the sun, coming in low at full speed, as teal are wont to do. Heater hissed a warning just as the front four hit what they thought was water. But it was ice. Very slick ice.

If the little ducks had been coached by a choreographer, they could not have performed better. Their feet hit the ice, slipped, and four green-wing teal landed flat on their backs doing probably forty miles an hour on the ice at exactly the same time.

Only one drake had a clear lane through the decoys. He zipped right down the middle of the blocks, feet spread, wings braking, head up to see where he was going. He fetched up against a log fifty feet beyond the spread.

A hen bounced off two of the solidly-encased decoys and slammed to a stop against a plastic pintail drake. Another hen ricocheted through the spread like a ball in a pinball machine, ending up close to the log that the first drake was now climbing onto. The final drake glanced off a mallard decoy, caught the tip of one wing on another, and went into a spin that finally stopped in the middle of the lake. When he regained his feet he staggered dizzily for several minutes before tentatively trying his wings.

Not one of the astonished hunters had even raised a gun. Birdlegs began to giggle. Uncle Bubba grinned. The Heater and Boateater started to snicker. Perfect pointed at Deadeye, who was adjusting his glasses owlishly, unable to believe what he had apparently just seen. The whole group then burst into laughter.

Uncle Bubba was wiping tears from his eyes when he saw another small flock of teal approaching. "Hhhsssss! Come some more!" Next to him someone clicked a safety. "Uh-uh!" he hissed, "Don't shoot."

This flight buzzed low over the blocks, zoomed almost straight up, banked, braked, and whipped into the supposedly open pocket. The antics of the two lead drakes warned the rest. One duck somersaulted twice before regaining flight status without a stop; the second bounced off one decoy before skidding to an upside-down stop against the log. He climbed up onto the log and walked up and down it, shaking his head and occasionally reaching out with his toe to test the solidness of the surface. An outburst of laughter from the blind finally flushed him.

One lone hen dipped in next, obviously intending to just check for liquidity first. Though she slipped and slid on first one foot and then the other for a stretch of twenty yards, she never stopped flapping frantically and eventually become airborne again, quacking reproachfully.

For nearly an hour, the teal flew like that, and not a gun-shot came fron the concealed hunters, though there was many a burst of laughter. When it was obvious that the ducks were through flying, Uncle Bubba stood and stretched. "Boys," he spoke around a yawn, "I b'lieve I'll go make a pot of coffee."

"Daddy, would you mind carryin' us around to our Camp first?" Perfect asked. "We might slip up on some squirrels or rabbits later on."

The weather was clearing behind the front, so Uncle Bubba agreed and the Jakes piled into the Bronco. As Deadeye squeezed in between the bucket seats, he drawled, "Ooooweee, Uncle Bubba! I b'lieve that's one-a the best duck hunts I was ever on!"

Only minutes after they arrived at the Jake Camp, the boys had a roaring fire going and water heating for hot chocolate. When Heater got out the tin from the hollow cypress, he checked to be sure it contained coffee as well as hot chocolate mix. Before his uncle could get back into his truck, the Heater called, "Uncle Bubba! If you wanna stay awhile, I'll make you some coffee."

The man considered briefly, then nodded. The other Jakes ran to make him comfortable with an old canvas folding chair from their log, and a wooden drink crate for his feet. Then they all gathered around the fire to re-enact the antics of the ice-struck teal. As the Heater handed out mugs, Birdlegs exclaimed in repetition, "Uncle Bubba, that's the best duck hunt we ever had!" He paused, then continued wonderingly, "And we never fired a shot!"

Uncle Bubba nodded, grinning as Birdlegs laid back kicking in imitation of the teal. He sipped from the mug.

It was the worst coffee he had ever tasted.

He drank three cups.

*   *   *   *   *   *   *

The ground was just thawing out from that hard freeze when a second front moved in more slowly, dumping an unusually heavy six inches of snow. Of course school let out, and Boateater's dad brought the three city Jakes to the country before the roads got too slick that afternoon. Once again, Other Mother ruled it to be too inclement to spend the night in the Woods; however, the prospect of hunting in the snow the next day, plus snow ice cream, VCR movies, and popcorn, kept the Jakes in a good humor.

The morning dawned cold and gray, but without precipitation, and the plan of battle called for a walk-'em-up, kick-'em-out rabbit hunt. Papa Jake had assured them that even the big swamp rabbits, locally called canecutters, stuck tight on days like this. Each boy carried at least a box and a half of shotgun shells in his coat and pants pockets.

The Jakes' normal rabbit hunt was to walk from the Canal bridge east to the old plantation cemetary, tromping the banks of an old slough and the connecting fenceline. From the cemetary, nearly a mile from the gravel road where the bridge was, they then turned north along the small creek that separated Papa Jake's farm from the Duke's. It was a little over a mile to the gravel road connecting the two properties; thus, the boys generally hunted nearly two and a half miles, collecting three or four rabbits apiece.

But this day proved different. Papa Jake had been right; the rabbits were sticking tight. By the time the Jakes reached the cemetary, their halfway point, they each carried a half-dozen rabbits. They piled their kill under the old live oak at the corner of the graveyard, and with renewed enthusiasm, attacked the switch cane thickets and briar patches that grow up around abandoned country cemetaries. Within twenty minutes they had accumulated their limits of eight rabbits apiece, most of them large canecutters.

This meant that each thirteen-year-old boy had about seventy-five pounds of rabbit, plus a shotgun and remaining shells. They stuffed three or four canecutters in the back game pockets of their coats, and followed their usual custom of carrying the rest. Slitting the skin between the hamsting tendon and the bone, they threaded their belts through this hole in the rabbits' back legs, and re-cinched their belts around their waists. The heads of the rabbits almost dragged the ground on everyone but Birdlegs. Triumphant, laughing and joking, they began their long walk to the road where Papa Jake had promised to pick them up.

But now they found another problem. With their loads, they proved to be too heavy for the frozen crust to support. At nearly every step, their feet would break through into the sucking, ankle-deep mud underneath the blanket of white. Within a quarter-mile, they had to call a halt, panting and sweating under their heavy clothes. "Gotta be a better way to do this," gasped Birdlegs.

But no one could come up with one, and the cold soon

began to seep through to their wet skin. "Let's go, troops," ordered the Heater. "We better walk awhile and rest awhile."

They were still over a half-mile from the gravel road when Perfect, in the lead, stumbled and fell headlong. Birdlegs and Boateater helped him to a sitting postion while Deadeye picked his gun out of the mud. "Prob'ly oughta unload these guns," he panted, shucking the shells from Perfect's pump, then breeching his own double-barrel to remove the shells. The other Jakes copied his actions as they rested. No one cared that they were sitting on the freezing ground. Within minutes, both Perfect and Deadeye were shivering.

The Heater knew a little about hypothermia. "Hey, let's go, gang," he coaxed, trying to keep his voice calm. He took Perfect's gun from Deadeye, and helped that Jake up as the others stood wearily.

They slogged in silence for another hundred yards before Deadeye collapsed. "Y'all jus' leave me here an' I'll catch up later," he heaved.

Perfect flopped down behind him, and the two boys leaned back-to-back. "Me too," he sighed.

The Heater motioned to Birdlegs. "Tell you what we better do," he said grimly. "Let's pile these durn rabbits up an' get our tails on over to that road." He began to pull rabbits out of his coat.

Birdlegs followed his lead, but Boateater balked. "Think *I'm* a candyass?" he protested. "I killed these canecutters, an' I'll carry 'em out!" Boateater shouldered his gun and began slogging toward the road again. "Leave the sissies here!" he called back.

The Heater and Birdlegs divested themselves and Perfect and Deadeye of their rabbits. It took some fussing and pulling, but they finally got the two exhausted Jakes on their feet, just in time to see Boateater fall and lie unmoving only one hundred yards ahead. By the time all the Jakes reached that spot, only Birdlegs and the Heater were capable of walking farther. Boateater was shivering violently.

"One of us has gotta get on out to that road an' get help," the Heater spoke levely. "It's still durn near a half-mile, an' these guys could die out here."

47

"Can you make it?" Birdlegs asked, breathing hard.

"I don't know," the Heater spoke frankly.

"Then we both better try, 'cause I don't know, either,"
puffed Birdlegs. Both Jakes laid their guns across the others'
laps.

"We're goin' for help. You guys better try to walk after you
rest a little, understand?" The Heater patted Perfect's cheek as
he spoke. "You can't stay here. You gotta get up an' try,
okay?"

Perfect shook his head as if to clear it and looked wearily at
the Heater. "Go ahead; we'll try. Promise." He clutched
Heater's shoulder.

Birdlegs and Heater were still several hundred yards from
the road when Papa Jake drove up. The man gaped momentarily at the scene that met his eyes. Five boys were strung out
across the snow-covered field for nearly half a mile. The farthest away was crawling on hands and knees, while the closest
two were supporting each other. None had guns. Only one
still had a cap. Papa Jake grabbed his radio microphone and
called Other Mother back at the house.

"Get Bubba and Dundee on the phone ASAP and tell 'em
to get up here to the county line road! And tell Bubba to stop
and pick up Big Gus. And get ready for five boys, cold as hell
and exhausted! Got it?"

"Got it!" came the reply, and the man bolted from the
truck and began to slog toward the nearest two boys.

Late that evening, Other Mother entered the Heater's
room and shook him gently. "Hey, buddy. You've been asleep
six hours. Feel okay?"

The boy was still groggy, but replied drowsily, "How're the
rest of the Jakes?"

"They're okay. Y'all were really whipped and Doc gave a
couple of shots, but everybody will be fine. Bubba, Big Gus,
and your daddy brought y'all in, and the Duke walked all the
way down in the field twice to bring out your guns and rabbits.
He and Big Gus cleaned all those rabbits for you. Matter of
fact, I've fried up some of the loins for supper. Want me to
bring you some?"

The Jake shook his head. "Mama, thanks a lot, but right
now I don't even wanna see th' Easter Bunny!"

Early that spring, a couple of weeks before turkey season, Papa Jake was a guest at the Jakes' campfire one Friday night. He and the boys had been out in the Woods scouting for wild turkey sign, and they had invited him to stay for supper, which was venison stew from his own house. Other Mother had formed the habit of making big pots of things like stew, hash, gumbo, chili, and squirrel or chicken and dumplings, then freezing a large enough portion for the Jakes.

The man noticed in the firelight that Birdlegs seemed to be sporting a black eye. "What happened to your eye?" he asked the boy.

"Aww, nothin'," came the expected reply.

"Hamburger hit 'im," volunteered Perfect.

"What for?" asked Papa Jake.

"Jus' 'cause I was there!" burst out Birdlegs. "That fatso's always pickin' on somebody. Did you see the lump Heater had on his noggin last week?"

The Heater gave a lopsided grin. "I kept my cap on."

"Wha'd you do to him?" his father wanted to know.

"I didn't do nothin'!" the boy persisted. "He jus' walked by and whacked me."

"Wha'd you do *after* that, I mean?" was the question.

"Daddy, what *can* I do?" the Heater asked plaintively. "He's about three times bigger'n I am!"

The man leaned to refill his stew bowl. "Well," he observed, "looks like you Jakes have got to get together and break 'im. With a bully, it usually doesn't take but once."

"All of us? That wouldn't be a fair fight," Boateater put in.

"Boys, I don't b'lieve in fightin' if you don't have to, but sometimes you do have to." Papa Jake instructed. "I've got two rules about fightin': number one, don't fight; and number two, don't fight fair. You can't just keep on lettin' yourselves get pushed around. I've heard y'all talk about Hamburger and that other big kid all year. If they're startin' to give folks black eyes and knots, it's time to do somethin' about it."

"Whadda we need to do?" asked the Heater.

"First, they've gotta know that if they fight one-a you, they'll have to fight alla you. Second, I'd take 'em by surprise.

Hit 'em hard and fast, and for gosh sakes, don't let 'em get back up!"

Monday on the school playground at lunchtime, the Heater marched purposefully up to confront Hamburger as four other Jakes approached nonchalantly from the sides. The fat boy sneered at Heater, "What's your problem? Need another knot on your head?" He reached out to snatch the Heater's cap from his head.

The Heater swung from the heels, and surprised himself nearly as much as Hamburger. His fist hit the bigger kid right between the eyes with a splatting sound. Blood spurted explosively from Hamburger's nose, and he hit the ground like a pole-axed ox. The Jakes moved in quickly to insure the victory.

But Hamburger started crying.

Hands over his gory face, the fat boy rolled in the dust, gushing tears. Smaller kids began to gather and stare in wonder at the fallen Goliath, as his conqueror stood over him, also in wonder at the power of that one blow.

The Heater blew across his fist much as the surviving cowboy in a gunfight blows the smoke from his pistol barrel.

Birdlegs was ecstatic. "Hey, let's go get The Gaper now. We're on a roll!" The Gaper was a long, tall boy who also had a tendency to be a bully. His latest delight was to sneak up behind Deadeye and jerk his glasses off, taunting the smaller boy and staying just out of his reach with the spectacles. The Gaper had a prominent set of front teeth but a receding chin, which combined to make him appear to always have an open mouth.

Birdlegs found the Gaper in one corner of the schoolyard tormenting the girls. Crazy Sharon had her long dark hair in braids that day, and the tall boy was behind her, holding a braid in each hand. "Giddi-yap, horsey!" he was ordering when the Jakes approached.

"My turn," Birdlegs said to his comrades, who nodded encouragement. "Hey, horse-face, let her go!" Birdlegs yelled.

The Gaper was two years older, and thereby bigger, than his classmates, and was totally unused to such disrespect. He released Crazy Sharon and spun around open-mouthed in disbelief. "Wha'd you say?!?"

Bouyed by the earlier victory, Birdlegs almost pranced in front of him. Deadeye moved in too, and other children began to gather in anticipation. It was Deadeye who answered for Birdlegs. "He said 'Let her go, horse-face!' What're you gonna do about it?"

The Gaper was furious, and readied his fists to meet Birdlegs' challenge. "Outa the way, four-eyes!" he exclaimed.

Deadeye was slower to anger and much shorter than the two rivals, but he hated that epithet with a passion. As Birdlegs started his swing at the Gaper's left eye, Deadeye tossed his glasses to Crazy Sharon and went in low.

The Gaper blocked Birdlegs' blow, and countered with a right to the temple. But he had not anticipated an attack in force. Deadeye's first blow took him in the stomach, and the second about six inches below the belt buckle. Deadeye had not struck foul purposely; he was just swinging blindly at his own level.

White-hot pain shot through the Gaper's loins, and he bent over, breathless, just as Birdlegs' left took him full in the fore-head. Almost immediately, Perfect's fist glanced off his ear, and Boateater slammed him in the shoulder blade. The Gaper dropped to his knees, retching. The Heater bent down and lifted the tall boy's head by a fistful of hair.

"We want you to understand that next time you bother us —" he paused, "— or anybody else littler than you, you're gonna hafta fight all of us. You hear?" There was no answer, and he shook the Gaper's head. "Understand?" he asked again.

The miserable boy finally nodded, and as the Heater re-leased his hair and stood, the Gaper rolled over with knees drawn up and vomited all over himself. The crowd drew back in disgust.

All except for Perfect. He grasped the victim by one arm and motioned for Boateater to take the other. "C'mon. Let's help 'im up an' take 'im to the bathroom so he can clean up." Boateater was not nearly so compassionate, but reluctantly nodded agreement. They lifted Gaper to his feet and steadied him as he shuffled toward the school building.

As the crowd of kids began to move away, Crazy Sharon handed Deadeye his glasses, then quickly kissed him, Birdlegs,

51

and Heater on the cheek. "Thanks," she smiled gloriously, and turned and ran, braids bouncing.

"Yuck!" the three Jakes exclaimed simultaneously.

But none of them washed their faces that week.

Deadeye was dead beat that afternoon of the opening Saturday of turkey season. There had been a junior-high tennis tournament seventy-five miles away on Friday afternoon, and he and The Space Ace had gone all the way to the finals in mixed doubles before losing in straight sets. Then Coach Fuzzy, who was driving the bus, insisted on going in to eat hamburgers on the way back instead of getting take-out orders, even though he knew that turkey season was opening in the morning. It had been eleven o'clock before the tennis team got back to the school, and it was midnight when Deadeye's father had dropped him off to hike the muddy road to the Jake Camp. It had been spooky walking the half-mile in by himself, even with a flashlight.

Boateater had roused everybody at four a.m.; too early, but understandable on opening day. Both Uncle Bubba and Papa Jake had joined the boys for the morning's hunt, when Birdlegs had killed a big gobbler while Uncle Bubba and Perfect, hunting together, had missed one that had come up behind them. They had all come to Camp for lunch and a nap, then returned to the Woods for the afternoon hunt.

Deadeye had heard a couple of gobbles early, but nothing since, and had not seen a turkey all day. About four-thirty, he leaned his gun against the tree, slumped down until he was comfortable, and dozed off for a catnap.

He was jerked back to consciousness by a series of shotgun blasts that frightened him so badly that he had jumped to his feet and run several steps before he remembered where he was. He felt for his glasses and took several more steps before he realized that he had them on and that this blackness was night. He had slept nearly four hours; but he could only guess that, because his watch did not have a luminous dial. Even holding it directly in front of his face didn't help. However, his flashlight was next to his cushion and gun under the tree.

One hand in front of him, he tried to retrace his steps to his blind, but the tree that he first felt was not nearly as big around as the one he had been sitting against. He blundered farther, and almost tripped over a grapevine. The tree that this vine was attached to was bigger, but was not the one he was looking for. He stopped to try to remember which direction a viny tree might have been from his blind.

Now that he thought about it, he couldn't even remember a viny tree. He tried to recall which way and how far he had moved from his blind. His gun, flashlight, cushion, and bugspray were within thirty feet, he knew. But in which direction?

He closed his eyes and relived the previous few minutes. He had run several steps — say five — before he had stopped, and then taken three more short steps before he realized that it was night. That made about twenty feet away from his blind. But he had walked farther than that looking for it, so he figured he must have walked by it a few feet away. He carefully pivoted, turned maybe ten degrees back right, and paced off five steps with his arms out.

No tree.

He paced off five more, then two more, before he touched a sapling. His heartbeat was beginning to race. He almost stepped on an armadillo, and the animal flushed noisily to his right, scaring Deadeye so badly that he ran blindly left until he fell over a log and lost his glasses.

He scuttled about on hands and knees for several minutes before he found them, but couldn't see any better in the darkness with them on. Just as he picked them up another shot boomed, farther away than the original shots that had awakened him. He heard a faint yell and realized the other boys were searching for him.

Deadeye started to answer, started to go toward the shot, but pride interfered. Did he dare to face their ridicule, not only for being lost, but for losing his gun? No, he had to find his stuff first. He resolutely decided on the direction his blind must be, and again paced forward with hands outstretched.

He found a big tree and circled it, searching. Nothing.

In circling the tree, he lost his sense of direction, and could only guess which way he had been walking. He took his best guess, paced off ten steps without touching a tree, and stopped. Fighting down his panic, he finally decided he'd better yell for the others, pride or no.

"Heeeeeyyyy!!" he bellowed.

There was no reply. In a bottomland swamp sound doesn't travel far, and none of the other Jakes were close enough to hear him. As a matter of fact, they were making their way back to the campfire.

Deadeye yelled again. "Whoooo-EEEE!!"

"If I could find my gun, I could shoot an' they'd hear me!" Deadeye exclaimed aloud. The sound of his own voice startled him, and he made a rush forward, as if he could find his gear by taking it by surprise. He stumbled into a clump of palmettos, and their clatter not only frightened him but reminded him of the danger of snakes. Deadeye gave in to his panic and charged headlong into the darkness, arms flailing in front of him.

He headed directly for the Swamp.

At the fire, the other Jakes were also thinking of snakes. "What if he got bit an' is lyin' out there dyin'?" Birdlegs asked.

Perfect voiced all their thoughts. "We better go get help."

He and Heater drove out, leaving the other boys in case Deadeye showed up. They found Papa Jake already in his bathrobe, watching a TV movie. Their elder immediately assumed command.

"Call your daddy," he told Perfect, "and tell him to call the Duke. They can go in from the Duke's side — to heck with his turnrow gettin' rutted up. Lemme get my clothes on and I'll call Deputy Don and have him go down and roust out Mack."

Ten minutes later, three adult-supervised search parties were readied. Deputy Don drove down the gravel road to

Mack's log cabin, for Mack didn't have a telephone. The lawman tooted his horn to alert his neighbor of his presence. He liked Mack well enough, but wasn't exactly sure about him. Without ever having actually seen any, he was nevertheless certain that the quasi-hermit probably had his homestead booby-trapped with claymore mines or something. "It's just me," he called.

Wacky Mack materialized next to his shoulder. "Trouble?" he rasped.

Deputy Don jumped and banged his head on the car door. "Dammit!! Make some noise! You always scare the *hell* outa me just appearin' like that!" he grumbled.

The younger man, bearded and dressed in camouflage fatigues, just shrugged. Papa Jake had once said, "Mack never uses two words when one will do." The truth was that Mack had suffered a throat wound in Vietnam. Speaking was a real effort for him. A full beard covered the scars, but he received a one-hundred-percent-disability pension for his wounds.

"One-a them damn boys done got himself lost an' they called for us to help hunt for 'im. You wanna go with me?"

"Nah. Better alone," came the reply. "Radio th'others. Fire two three-shot series if he turns up. Patrol th' edges 'case he makes it out. If he's in th' Woods, I'll bring 'im out." Mack turned on his heel and walked to his cabin, emerging seconds later buckling a pistol belt. He beamed a flashlight at Deputy Don once in signal just before disappearing into the trees like another shadow.

Deadeye had floundered waist-deep into the dark Swamp waters before his panic subsided. He waded back out and stopped, shivering, to consider. Since he had not crossed the Canal that ran through the middle of the Woods, he knew he must be on the north side of the Swamp. Therefore, if he walked directly away from the water, he should come out in Papa Jake's open fields, or else on Dundee's Lake. He steeled his nerves, stood with his back to the Swamp, pointed with his finger, and began to walk.

In ten minutes, he was back at the edge of the Swamp.

"Aaaaaaarrrrggg!!" he roared in frustraion, and the sudden noise startled a beaver ten yards away, which slapped the water with a splash not unlike one an alligator might make. Assuming the alligator was coming after him, Deadeye headed away from the water again, this time at a dead run. Within twenty steps, he slammed into a persimmon tree and fell, momentarily stunned and losing his glasses again.

He was searching for them on hands and knees when a beam of light suddenly illuminated the ground in front of him. It frightened him, appearing so silently, and he bolted again, almost stepping on the spectacles. Wacky Mack had to catch the boy and hold him. Rasping "Quit, dammit!" the man hauled him back into the clearing and retrieved the glasses. Finally, Deadeye quit struggling and surrendered to being found. Tearfully, he hugged his bearded rescuer.

"Where's your gun?" asked Mack.

"I don't know!" wailed Deadeye, and began to spill out his story to Wacky Mack.

Soon the man nodded and grunted, "We'll pick it up on th' way back. I know 'bout where it is." The boy almost broke and ran again when Wacky Mack pulled his pistol and fired two series of shots. There was an answering boom to the west. "C'mon," rasped the veteran.

Deadeye started forward, then stopped abruptly, gripping Mack's sleeve. In concerned tones, he asked, "Am I gonna get in trouble for this?"

The expression was as close to a grin as any of the Jakes had ever seen Wacky Mack come. The man considered briefly before nodding his head just once. "Some," he responded.

The very next Friday afternoon, when the Jakes made their way into Camp, a surprise awaited them. Five military-type compasses hung from the limb of a tree by the cypress log, and five hand-drawn maps in plastic folders were spiked to the log. There was also a "treasure" map, complete with instructions in Wacky Mack's distinctive handwriting.

All of the Jakes knew the principle of a compass, but they had never used one in the manner the treasure map described. However, their curiosity had been pricked, and they were quick to learn. It didn't take long to figure out how to take a proper bearing, and on the first try they paced off the four hundred feet from the cypress log and got close enough to the designated stump to see the small orange marking flag on it. They hurried too much on their first bearing from the stump, and had to backtrack and make a more careful sighting, but soon they found another orange marker on a hollow cottonwood tree. In the hollow was a two-gallon cooler filled with obviously homemade peach ice cream. The Jakes had a feast that night, but never saw a sign of Wacky Mack.

The following Friday when they drove into Camp, another map was spiked to the cypress. This trail was a little harder to follow, but eventually Perfect figured out the leg that required a crossing of the Creek, and they found five cartons of one thousand rounds each of .22 ammo. With spring snake- and frog-shooting coming up, this was nearly a month's worth of cartridges for the Jakes.

For the next several weeks, the Jakes began to eagerly anticipate these exercises and the prizes left by their mysterious benefactor, who never showed his face. The Heater and Perfect even drove all the way around to his cabin one Sunday afternoon to thank him, but Wacky Mack was apparently not home; their knocks went unanswered. It was the first time Perfect had ever been to the cabin, and he was surprised at the newness and neatness of the homestead.

Wacky Mack had appeared on the scene almost fifteen years before, and had obtained permission from Papa Jake, Deputy Don, and the Duke of Dundee to trap in the Woods, Swamp, and Canal. In return he kept the poachers out, looked out for loose livestock, mended fences, and left frequent gifts at the landowners' homes of game meat, wild fruits or berries, sassafrass roots for tea, and an occasional cord of firewood.

Unbeknownst to anyone but Uncle Bubba, Mack had un-covered an obscure homesteader's law on the books, and put up a fence around eighty acres at the east end of the Woods. Seventy years before, a now-defunct drainage district had bought the land for a bridge and right-of-way, but scrapped the plans at a later date. For five years, the veteran kept several cows, sheep, and goats on the isolated acreage, as well as building himself a rough one-room shanty. At the end of the required period, Uncle Bubba had recorded the legal work and title, whereupon Mack had paid the taxes and become a land-owner. That summer he had ordered a pre-fabricated log cabin home, and with Deputy Don's and Big Gus' help, had built on a high spot where the gravel road ended, in a grove of oaks and sweetgums. His neighbors seldom saw him.

Neither did the Jakes during the compass training, which they came to realize was a result of Deadeye's traumatic experi-ence. Over the next few weeks, they sometimes had as many as three exercises a weekend, and their "treasures" ranged all the way from a case of shotgun shells to tickets for a new rock-'em, sock-'em movie.

The final hunt was different. Not only did the instructions specify that the boys must wait until dark to begin their hunt, but there were five maps, one in each of their names. Deadeye wasn't the only Jake who was a little nervous about a night exercise, but the enthusiasm of Birdlegs and the Heater carried the day. As dusk fell over the Camp, the Jakes built up the campfire; gathered flashlights, compasses, and guns — in case of snakes or distress; agreed on signals if necessary; and left Camp on five different bearings.

Deadeye's pulsebeat was almost audible, at least to his own ears, but he screwed up his courage and bravely ventured forth. His map showed only two bearings, and by concentrating on his compass and his paces, he found the first marker with no trouble. However, he had to detour around a huge fallen hackberry trunk on the second leg, and missed the mark.

He had a moment of panic and almost ran when a deer blew noisily at him, but forced himself to calm down. Using the compass, he took a reverse bearing to the hackberry blow-down, sighing with relief at regaining a familiar point. Calculating carefully, he sighted again along the dial and began to pace.

Once again, his flashlight beam failed to reveal any markers after the required number of paces. His breathing became faster, and he fought down panic again. "Where am I wrong?" he growled.

A stick popped to his right, and when he looked that way he had a faint impression that he had seen a brief ray of light. "Hey!" he called, thinking it might be another Jake. There was no answer, but again he caught a brief wink of light about forty yards away. "Hey!" he repeated. No answer.

Deadeye carefully shined his beam around him, and kicked a space smooth of leaves to mark the spot. He took a bearing toward the suspicious wink and slowly counted his paces, out loud. ". . . thirty-one, thirty-two, thirty . . ." and suddenly he spied the little orange marking flag. His mouth dropped open. "Gah-lee!" he whispered.

Hanging from a persimmon sapling on a wire coat hanger was a brand-new leather jacket, with his name embroidered over the left breast pocket. With awed appreciation, he sniffed the new-leather odor of it and ran his fingers over the rough surface before trying it on. It was a little big, but he liked the weight of it, and squared his shoulders a bit more. With a bull whip instead of a shotgun, he might look a lot like Indiana Jones in *Raiders of the Lost Ark*, he imagined. He wanted to run back to Camp, but just in time remembered to take a bearing. He spooked another deer on the way back, but this one didn't scare him at all.

The Heater was the only Jake back at Camp when Deadeye arrived. He also had on a new leather jacket, a twin to Deadeye's and Indiana's, except for the name on the pocket. He too was in a state of awe. "Can you believe this?" he greeted Deadeye.

One by one the others returned, similarly clad. Only Boateater admitted having experienced any trouble with his bearings, as he related during a late supper. "I was about to hit the panic button, but then I saw a flash of light a couple of times. I figured it was one-a y'all's I saw through the Woods, so I started toward it an' like to tripped over my last marker."

He paused. "Wonder which one-a you was that close to me?"

Deadeye's heart suddenly swelled to fill his chest, and he pounded one fist into the other palm. "That was Wacky Mack!" he exclaimed to himself, barely audible to the others.

"Do what?" Birdlegs asked.

"Nothin'," Deadeye ducked his head and busied himself cleaning his glasses.

It was Perfect who found the last message from Wacky Mack when he entered the tent. It simply said, "If you ever forget your compass when you go back into the Woods, I get your jacket back. Otherwise, we're even. Mack."

On the last morning of turkey season, Uncle Bubba took both Perfect and the Heater to the Woods with him. Neither of the boys had bagged a gobbler that season, though Perfect had missed two. This was to be their last chance of the year.

Uncle Bubba's owl hooting had induced a tom to gobble in the pre-dawn darkness, and the three hunters were able to get within a hundred and fifty yards of the bird, which was roosting at the edge of the Swamp. The man put one boy on each side of him with their backs against a large cypress tree, stuck a few branches up in front to break their outline, and gave a couple of clucks on his call. The turkey sounded off again from his roost, a peculiar throaty gobble.

"That's Garglin' George," Uncle Bubba whispered. "I've hunted him before, and he's T-U-double-uff tough! But maybe we'll get lucky. He's got to fly back toward us when he comes down, 'cause he's out over the water."

Sure enough, as day began to dawn they heard wings flapping. Uncle Bubba immediately cackled, following with a series of yelps. The throaty gobble responded lustily from the ground, less than a hundred yards away. A second gobble sounded closer. The Heater began to ease his gun up.

"Hold still," his uncle whispered. "This one isn't gonna come in fast. With all these trees around, you'll have time to get it up when he's within range."

And Garglin' George didn't come in fast. He gobbled nearly forty times in the next hour, and several times the hunters glimpsed him moving along the Swamp edge, out of range. Then he shut up for thirty minutes, and both boys thought he had departed. They began to fidget, but were sternly shushed by Uncle Bubba.

Sure enough, the big gobbler stepped into a clearing directly in front of Perfect, in full strut. He pirouetted majestically, but the range was fully sixty yards. "Too far," warned Uncle Bubba. "Wait."

The turkey paced back and forth in the clearing, occasionally gobbling in response to the caller's soft clucks and purrs, but refusing to come closer. Then in the distance a short gobble sounded, followed closely by two more.

"Jakes," whispered Uncle Bubba.

Garglin' George bellowed back his own challenge and popped into strut again. A series of gobbles was the answer, one on top of the other and getting closer. The Heater glimpsed movement way off down the Swamp edge and hissed at his uncle. "Be ready," the man breathed. "Maybe when Garglin' George sees these young birds comin', he'll move into range."

Garglin' George never had a chance. Three young gobblers sprinted into view along the water's edge, and they never slowed down. They ran right up to the blind and braked only when the Heater raised his gun. "Okay," Uncle Bubba whispered, "each of you get one. . . . Go!"

The young turkeys stood and stared inquisitively while the boys raised their guns. One of them actually had started another gobble when the two guns roared in unison. The surviving jake was seemingly reluctant to retreat even when his comrades went down flopping, and he only ran when the Heater burst out of the blind to finish off his crippled prize with a second shot. Garglin' George was long gone.

As the boys hoisted their trophies proudly, Uncle Bubba decided to try to make a point. "Now, you two need to learn a lesson from this," he instructed. "You saw that old turkey was cautious and smart. He took his time comin' up, and wanted that hen to come part of the way to him before he committed himself. But those young gobblers were just like young boys are sometimes. They go through life full-speed, balls to the walls; runnin' here, there, and yonder; just lookin' for girls, or trouble, or whatever. See, you Jakes need to learn to think about what might happen before you go chargin' in. Or," he concluded wisely, "somebody's liable to end up holdin' *you* by the neck!"

The Heater thoughtfully fingered the inch-and-a-half-long beard on his bird. "But Uncle Bubba, if there had been a girl turkey here, wouldn't these jakes have had a lot of fun with her while that old gobbler was standin' off out there showin' off?"

The man paused to consider his reply, reflexively rubbing the deep scar on his chin. He had acquired the scar during his college days when he had gone to the defense of a pretty coed who was obviously trying to reject the advances of an inebriated freshman football player. The boy had broken a beer bottle on Bubba's jaw before being subdued by his teammates. Three years later, Bubba had married the coed. The football player flunked out, got drafted, and was sent to Vietnam.

"Uncle Bubba, were you ever a Jake?" asked Heater.

"Yeah," the man replied slowly, smiling. "Fun, ain't it?"

Heater said to Birdlegs, "Better swing by the beach an' let 'im off. He's beginnin' to get tired."

As the boat neared the gravel where the other two Jakes waited, Heater motioned for Boateater to let go of the rope handle, but there was no response. Birdlegs made another circle. Again, Heater held his hands up and made a throwing motion, but the skier's hands seemed frozen in their grip.

"Let goooo!" the Heater screamed, his words lost in the wind.

Irritated, Birdlegs cut the wheel hard aport. "He gonna ski all day?" he asked.

The boat made a tight turn, swinging the skier wide in another pop-the-whip maneuver. Once more, the Heater indicated that Boateater was to release the rope. Finally, on the outside of the turn and making forty miles an hour, Boateater did so. Of course, even without the means of propulsion, his speed kept him atop the water in his crouched position.

Headed right for the gravel beach.

Perfect, standing in waist-deep water about ten feet from Deadeye, was the first to realize the problem. "He doesn't know how to stop!" he spoke in amazement. "Fall back!" he yelled, startling Deadeye, but having no effect on the rapidly-approaching Boateater.

Knees bent, eyes glazed, arms at his sides, the skier skied speedily onward. "Fall back!" once again fell on deaf ears. Boateater's present course would take him about six feet to Deadeye's left. Perfect, on Deadeye's right, yelled, "Catch 'im!"

"Are you nuts?!?" Deadeye exclaimed, and dived right. Boateater flashed by.

Water skis are sanded, varnished, and then waxed, so as to glide across smooth surfaces with a minimum of friction. The process was never intended to be of any help on gravel roads, however. Boateater was still doing upwards of twenty miles an hour when his skis left the surface for which they had been manufactured.

As the Heater later pointed out, it was probably a good thing that Boateater was going so fast, for he only hit three times in crossing a thirty-foot-wide gravel road. He was also lucky, Perfect assured him, that the farmer had just plowed the soybean field on the other side of the road, providing plenty of fresh dirt for a cushioning effect. Birdlegs made the helpful observation that his pupil would probably have suffered much more "if two-a the bounces hadn'ta been on his head."

Deadeye absorbed most of the blame, however, for not tackling the skier as he went by.

Doc McClendon made all necessary repairs without stitches, and after listening to their story, ushered the Jakes out with one observation: "From now on, when you're teaching somebody how to do something, also teach him how to quit!"

They are not nearly so plentiful as they used to be, but huge snapping turtles are still fairly common in Southern waters. A "loggerhead" as big as a washtub is not unusual at all, and sometimes they get as big as the hood of a jeep. Which was exactly what Birdlegs pointed out to the rest of the Jakes when he spied the huge turtle sunning on the beaver dam.

"Gaahh-lee!" he exclaimed. "That ole loggerhead's bigger'n the jeep hood!"

The Jakes had just stepped into an opening on the Canal bank from whence they could see the dam, seventy-five yards away. The boys immediately crouched to observe the monster.

"Sonuvagun," Deadeye drawled. "I could take a bath in that shell. If the turtle was out of it," he added.

"Let's shoot 'im and see!" Boateater whispered.

This was a normal boy reaction, and would usually have been suggested first by the Heater or Birdlegs. However, these two had only a week before viewed a National Geographic special on TV about the South Seas. As one voice, they both suggested enthusiastically, "No! Let's catch 'im an' ride 'im!"

Perfect rolled his eyes. "You're outa your gourd! That thing could take your leg off in one bite!"

"We ain't gonna ride his head!" the Heater pointed out. "We'll lasso his neck an' put a muzzle on 'im."

"Yeah, an' get a bridle an' bit," enthused Birdlegs. "We'll tame 'im an' ride 'im all over town! I'm gonna call 'im George."

"A turtle named George?" questioned Perfect.

"C'mon, we gotta get back and find some rope for lassoes," urged Heater. He and Birdlegs began to double-time back down the trail to Camp.

As they turned to follow, Deadeye asked Perfect, "Are we gonna get in trouble for this?"

"Prob'ly," was the rather grim reply.

The excitement of Birdlegs and the Heater was catching, though, and soon all the Jakes were headed back for the Canal carrying fifteen-foot lengths of half-inch rope. They crept up to the bank and peeked over. The huge loggerhead was still on the beaver dam.

The Heater had a plan, based upon the fact that there was a series of seven beaver dams within a quarter-mile along this stretch of the Canal. "Me an' Birdlegs'll try to slip up on 'im an' lasso his neck an' one leg. If we do, the resta you gang up an' lasso his other legs. But in case he sees us an' tries to make a break for it, Boateater, you go upstream to head 'im off at the next dam; an' Perfect, you an' Deadeye go downstream in case he goes that way."

"Once we get a noose around George's neck, we got 'im!" chortled Birdlegs.

The boys all headed for their assigned stations, and the Heater and Birdlegs began their stalk. They actually crawled within twenty feet of the big turtle undetected. As they paused, they could clearly see leeches on the great, rough, mossy shell. At this range, the project seemed a little more ambitious than they had previously thought. "This is gonna be like lassoin' an Army tank," whispered Heater.

The two conspirators decided on a rush, and burst from the ragweeds toward their intended victim. The Heater's rope landed just short of the loggerhead's neck, and Birdlegs got so excited he forgot his rope and actually grabbed the turtle's tail. But George spun on his belly and dived off the dam, headed downstream. Birdlegs was pulled into the Heater, and both Jakes tumbled into the water. Birdlegs' hold was broken.

"Here he comes!" shouted Heater.

Perfect was in the center of the next dam, crouched. George either never saw him, or didn't care. The huge snapping turtle burst out of the water, head extended, and flounced quickly across the dam. Perfect dropped the noose perfectly over his head, and the rope tightened as the loggerhead dived into the next pool. Perfect wrapped the line around his wrist and yelled, "I got him!"

He certainly did.

Like the Heater had pointed out earlier, it was somewhat akin to lassoing an Army tank. As the turtle surged downstream and the other Jakes cheered, the rope suddenly tightened, and Perfect had only a moment to react and try to brace himself.

It wouldn't have made any difference if he had had a half-hour.

Perfect's right arm jerked straight out, pointing downstream, and the youngster wasn't far behind it. With his left he made a futile grab for Deadeye, who at the last second realized his friend's predicament and reached out, but it was too late. Head-first, Perfect dived in behind George. The other Jakes stood transfixed.

Boateater, the farthest away, was the first to break the trance. "Head 'im off at the next dam!" he yelled, and began running.

Deadeye, being closer, made it to the next dam just as the loggerhead flopped across it. Perfect — muddy, dripping, and gasping for breath — managed to get to his knees at the dam, frantically fumbling at the rope around his wrist. Deadeye got

close enough to grab his
friend's left shoulder
when the slack was
taken out. Both
hands on the rope
this time, Perfect
was again jerked
into the water
behind George.

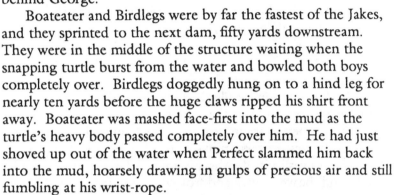

Boateater and Birdlegs were by far the fastest of the Jakes,
and they sprinted to the next dam, fifty yards downstream.
They were in the middle of the structure waiting when the
snapping turtle burst from the water and bowled both boys
completely over. Birdlegs doggedly hung on to a hind leg for
nearly ten yards before the huge claws ripped his shirt front
away. Boateater was mashed face-first into the mud as the
turtle's heavy body passed completely over him. He had just
shoved up out of the water when Perfect slammed him back
into the mud, hoarsely drawing in gulps of precious air and still
fumbling at his wrist-rope.

The Heater galloped determinedly along the bank toward
the next dam, Deadeye not far behind. From the corner of his
eye, he glimpsed his cousin surfacing briefly, both hands still on
the rope, gasping for breath. Yelling "Hold on!" Heater
turned onto the dam just ahead of George, and reached into
his pocket for his knife.

The loggerhead was almost across the dam when Heater
caught him, for the boy had slowed slightly to open the blade.
As the rope started over the mud and sticks, with an almost unconscious Perfect attached, the Heater lunged for it, grabbed
hold, and began sawing. As he was being pulled into the
water, the lasso parted, just as Deadeye arrived to grab
Perfect's heels. He and the Heater dragged the

wheezing boy, scratched and covered with mud, back to the bank where all three collapsed. Birdlegs, blood oozing from deep scratches on his chest, and Boateater, just as muddy as Perfect, came staggering up.

"You okay?" the latter gasped to the expert lassoing Jake. Perfect barely managed a nod.

The five boys lay on the bank for several minutes catching their breath, reflecting on their close call. It was Birdlegs who finally broke the silence.

"Dammit!" He punched Perfect lightly on the shoulder. "You let my turtle get away!"

*   *   *   *   *   *   *

The Canal wound lazily through the middle of the Woods and the Swamp, and was the source of a lot of enjoyment for the Jakes. They swam in its waters; duck hunted over them; watched beavers, otters, minks, and other aquatic denizens make their lives in its depths; caught fish (and turtles) from its banks and beaver dams; and frog-gigged in it.

Frog-gigging, as practiced in the South, generally involves at least two people in a flat-bottomed "john" boat. The front man in the boat wears a headlight, spots the frogs, and gigs them; the back man runs the motor, steers the boat, and deposits the gigged amphibians in an ice chest. Both men, and any others accompanying them in their craft, participate jointly in one other activity: they all watch carefully for snakes. Moccasins are the best reasons for gigging from boats.

It is a given premise that any Southern sportsman worth his salt will boast that his canal, or swamp, or lake, or neck of the woods, has more snakes per square foot than anybody else's. It's the same obligatory philosophy as "my dog's better'n yore dog!" and usually applies equally to young wives, old shotguns, and kids — "except the dumb coach's got somethin' against 'im!" The encounters that the Jakes had with the reptiles insured that they truly believed down deep in their hearts that their Canal was the "snakiest" in the world.

There was the night, for example, that the Heater, Birdlegs, and Perfect had been wading the Swamp in hip boots, frog-gigging. Each boy had a burlap sack attached to his belt into which he deposited his frogs. They were quietly moving through knee-deep waters about fifty yards apart when suddenly there was a commotion from the Heater's side, closest to the bank. The other two Jakes heard, "Hey! Hey! Get outa here! Get! Shoo!!!" then there were some surging, splashing, and crackling sounds, followed by the Heater's cry of "Yiiiii!! Help! Help!"

Perfect and Birdlegs had come together during the course of this commotion, and now they began sloshing hurriedly toward the faint beam of Heater's headlight, which seemed to be directed upwards into the trees. Birdlegs pointed this out. "What the heck is he lookin' at up there? Reckon he's got a bobcat treed or somethin'?"

"No tellin'," Perfect rejoined.

And neither of them could have foretold the Heater's present situation. As they rounded a cypress tree, they became aware of a high-pitched moaning: "Huuunnng! Huuunnng!" They traced its source to the beam of light shining up into the trees. The headlight that the beam emanated from was itself nearly ten feet above the water. The two Jakes stood open-mouthed at the tableau that met their eyes.

The Heater hung upside down from the limb of a locust tree, arms and legs encircling the thorny branch. Locust trees are well-known for their ornaments of clumps of two-inch-long thorns, and these projections were one cause of the Heater's moans. The other cause was a huge, angry, four-foot-long stumptail moccasin, whose thrashing tail could barely touch the water. "Huuunnng!" whined the Heater from his perch.

The serpent's fangs were snagged securely on the burlap sack, which hung straight down from the Heater's belt. The weight of the wet sack, frogs, and mad snake was putting quite a strain on the boy's midsection as he hung in turn from the fanged branch.

Birdlegs was the first to recover. "This is gonna be fun!" he remarked to no one in particular as he strode forward, reversing his gig. The handle of this weapon had been fashioned from a cotton hoe handle, and was quite sturdy. Birdlegs stepped up like a batter to the plate and took a practice swing, measuring an intended stroke right behind the big moccasin's ugly head.

"Just hang on a minute longer," he remarked with a great deal of anticipated satisfaction, though Perfect wasn't sure whether he was speaking to snake, sack, or the whining Heater.

Birdlegs drew his bat back into a stance not unlike that of a major leaguer, eyed an imaginary opposing hurler, muttered "Kiss that'un good-bye," and swung for the bleachers.

"All hell broke loose," Perfect later testified.

The batter hit his target all right, but with such force that his bat broke slap in two. The follow-through dislodged his headlamp. The blow also split the sack, and fourteen gigged-but-lively bullfrogs poured forth into the shallow water on top of the thrashing snake. In addition, the powerful swat also dislodged the Heater from his limb.

Though he had not particularly enjoyed his prickly perch, it was infinitely better than being on the same level with the stumptail, which the Heater now assumed had jerked him down. In flailing frantically for another limb, his forearm struck the pivoting-to-run Birdlegs in the back of the head, plunging them both into the dark waters with the frogs and the snake. Perfect wisely kept his distance from the melee.

Fortunately, Birdlegs' blow had almost literally knocked the moccasin's head "clean off." The viper was beyond ever biting again. Back at the Jake Camp, the Heater, almost naked, was submitting to the efforts of Perfect to remove a score of thorns from his body when Birdlegs, holding an ice pack to the back of his head, asked, "What in the world possessed you to climb a thorn tree?"

Occasionally one of the Jakes made A Wise Statement, and tonight was the Heater's night. "When a snake that big is after you," he growled, "a tree is a tree is a tree!"

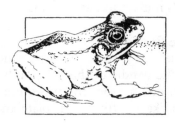

For a while thereafter, the Jakes did all of their frog-gigging from the safety of an old wooden john boat that Deputy Don let them have in return for ten percent of the frogs for that summer. "I love froglegs, but I hate snakes," he remarked to Sugarpie. "If them boys is crazy enough to mess with 'em, maybe they'll be crazy enough to bring us some!" And the Jakes did so, faithfully, even though the cypress craft was not fated to last beyond the dog days of August.

Boateater, Deadeye, and Birdlegs were out in it that night. The Heater and Perfect were off in the northern part of the state playing in a baseball tournament. The trio had reached a bend in the Canal where one of their favorite swimming holes was. The water was nearly ten feet deep here, and a cypress tree overhung the hole, complete with a "diving limb" and an old rope swing.

Birdlegs, who had just rotated to the front of the boat to gig, directed his headlight beam at the base of a big elbow bush about twenty feet from the cypress. "Big frog!" he exclaimed. Deadeye, who was running the little six-horse-power outboard motor, slowed and turned toward the indi-cated bank.

The middle man in the boat, in this case Boateater, had the job of using a hand-held spotlight to check the surrounding bushes for snakes. Both lights were connected to an automo-bile battery, so there was plenty of illumination. "Wup!" he now warned suddenly, as Deadeye started in under the bushes. "Snake!"

About six feet up in the elbow bush was coiled a large water moccasin, obviously regarding them as intruders. Deadeye slipped the motor into reverse, backed up, then shifted to neutral. Birdlegs studied the situation. "That's a mighty big ole frog," he observed. "Tell you what. Ease in kinda from that side an' lemme lean way up an' gig. Jus' keep an eye on the snake an' back out quick as I get the frog," he instructed.

Deadeye reluctantly agreed, mainly because he was in the end of the boat away from the moccasin, but also because he was in control of the motor and therefore of his own destiny. Birdlegs got as much slack as he could in the cord from the battery to his headlight, leaned over the bow, and signaled that he was ready. Deadeye shifted to forward.

The gigger held his weapon as far out as possible, concentrating on the bullfrog. Boateater concentrated on the snake. Deadeye concentrated on being in immediate readiness to get the heck out of the vicinity. As Birdlegs drew his gig back slightly in preparation for his strike, the moccasin began to uncoil and Deadeye shifted to neutral.

The next three things happened simultaneously. Birdlegs lunged forward, the snake dropped from the bush, and Deadeye roared into reverse.

The combination of his powerful surge forward, successfully gigging the big frog, and the boat's powerful surge backward, successfully dodging the big snake, suddenly left Birdlegs without a tangible base of operations. He simply lay face-down in four feet of water. Boateater's beam shone on a scene mindful of Neptune: a trident rising from the depths, and finally a head and shoulders appearing above the water. Then, "Snake in the water!" yelled Boateater.

Birdlegs' headlight was dangling from the bow of the boat, still attached to the battery, but there was enough light coming from Boateater's beam for the gigger to see. With the boat twenty feet away and a snake in his immediate vicinity, Birdlegs took the obvious choice and charged up the bank, still holding his gig and trophy.

Boateater was laughing and could not resist his next mischevious impulse. "He's right behind you!" he bellowed to the boy on the bank.

Even in the dark, Birdlegs knew this place. The Jakes had swum here for years. By instinct, he sprinted for the cypress tree, reached it in four bounds, and swarmed up the steps nailed to the trunk that led to the diving limb. He inched out on the limb as the boys in the boat followed his progress with the light. Noting the desperate expression on Birdlegs' face, Boateater turned laughingly to Deadeye. "Watch this," he chuckled.

"Snake in the TREE!!!" he roared.

Birdlegs never hesitated. He launched himself from the diving limb for the safety of the light. Feet-first, arms in the air, from a height of twenty feet, he descended on his suddenly petrified comrades. It had to be one of The World's Truly Great Jumps.

At the last second, Boateater rolled backwards off the middle seat into Deadeye's lap. Birdlegs had leapt for the light, and his aim was true. He hit just forward of the middle seat and hardly slowed down.

Cypress is a fairly soft wood anyway, and this cypress was old and water-logged. The floorboards burst completely out of the john boat and Birdlegs plunged all the way to the bottom of the Canal, not even spraining an ankle. On his way back to the surface, he passed Boateater and Deadeye, headed down. The former was still clutching the battery-anchored spotlight and the latter was holding onto the motor.

When they finally reassembled on the opposite bank, they faced a long walk in the dark, but without the burdens of their gigs, Perfect's battery and lights, the Heater's ice chest, or Papa Jake's motor. Miserably, Deadeye nodded, "We're gonna get in trouble for this!"

And they never told anyone, especially Birdlegs, that the snake had not climbed the tree.

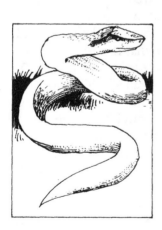

This same swimming hole was the Jakes' favorite skinny dipping spot, and had been for several years. Other Mother used to worry about them, but finally was resigned to the fact that they were going to do it whether she approved or not. She settled for a once-a-summer round of tetnus and typhoid shots, and made up her mind not to ask too many questions.

Actually, the very same swimming hole, with its rope swing and diving limb, had served Papa Jake and Uncle Bubba when they were boys, and the two men laughed at her fears. At the same time, though, Papa Jake did ask Wacky Mack to keep an eye on the Jakes during swimming season, if he happened to be in the vicinity. Somehow, the older man got the idea that the seldom-spoken veteran knew an awful lot about the Jakes' antics anyway, and suspected that Mack made opportunities to observe the boys from afar. He didn't know how right he was.

For instance, Wacky Mack had watched with amusement the incident when the other Jakes found out that Perfect was scared of heights, yet he had been prepared to go to the rescue if the boy panicked. Fortunately, he had not.

The Heater and Birdlegs were of course the first two Jakes to climb all the way up to the diving limb. Certainly they were headstrong; but most men will admit that it takes no little bit of courage to climb, naked, twenty feet up into a cypress and jump out feet-first into the water, even if one is only fourteen. Boateater was quick to follow, and Deadeye eventually was persuaded to try it; his main hang-up was that he certainly couldn't jump with his glasses on, and couldn't see where he was jumping without them. But Boateater climbed up with him the first time to hold his glasses while he leapt. After that trip, Deadeye decided that he was better off jumping blind.

But Perfect consistently declined to try out this new thrill, and it was weeks before the Jakes discovered that he wasn't particularly afraid to propel himself out into space — it was being high up in the air that bothered him. As he continued to demur to even make the climb to "see that it wasn't all that far," the others, being boys, began to taunt him. Boateater's teasing hurt the most. "Candyass!" he called. "C'mon, candy!" Soon the rest of the boys, not thinking about being malicious, took up the chant. "Candy, candy! C'mon, candy!"

Wild boars are mean; stumptail moccasins are mean; ground bumblebees are mean. But boys can be meaner than these three rolled into one. "Candy, candy! C'mon, candy!" shrilled the hated chant.

Finally, the Heater realized that the teasing really was bothering his cousin. Putting his arm around Perfect's shoulders, he whispered, "Hey, no sweat. C'mon, I'll go up with you. We'll dive off together and shut these guys up!" At the end of his rope, Perfect nodded agreement.

When a person has a phobia and decides to meet that fear

78

head on, that is raw courage. To hell with charging machine gun nests; to hell with sticking one's head into a lion's mouth; if a man is deathly afraid of spiders, it takes more guts for him to let a common, garden-variety, green-eyed jumping spider walk across his wrist than anything else he could possibly do. When Perfect was halfway up that cypress, climbing hand-over-white-knuckled-hand, gritting his teeth, and staring straight ahead at the rough bark six inches from his face; somehow the other Jakes realized they were witnessing just such a test of courage. To a boy, they vowed to cut their tongues out if only that dreaded taunt could be recalled from Perfect's ears. There was an awed silence.

The Heater reached the crotch and stepped nimbly out onto the diving limb. Turning, he offered his hand to Perfect, who stood gingerly erect, back against the tree, hands behind him clutching the trunk. Having come this far, he could neither advance nor descend. He froze.

"C'mon," coaxed the Heater, reaching out, "the hard part's over. It's easy to get down."

White-lipped, Perfect glared at his helpful cousin. "If I ever do get down from here, I'm gonna kill you!"

But three hours later, when he finally did jump, he had forgiven him.

    *   *   *   *   *   *   *

The old rope swing hung not so high in the tree as the diving limb, and the Jakes would swing out from a small bluff bank and drop into the cool water of the swimming hole. Depending on how high he swung, which in turn depended on how much of a running start he got, a Jake might even attempt flips or other aerobatics from the swing. But no one ever did as many things on one swing as the Heater did the day he got snakebit.

Generally, the swing was kept secured in the fork of a small hackberry tree fifteen feet from the edge of the bluff. A boy would reach up to grab the handle and dislodge the swing from the fork, lean backward until the rope was taut, then run breakneck toward the water, propelling himself as far as possible with his final step. About six inches below the edge of the bank, a ball of willow roots jutted out from the clay bluff.

This day, the Heater was the first Jake to shuck his clothes, and happily sprinted to be the first one to the swing. He jerked the handle out of the fork, yelled "Whoopeee!" to attract attention, and charged the water. Just as he bunched his muscles to leap from that final step, he glanced at the edge of the bluff. Coiled on the top of the root ball was a four-foot moccasin, preparing to strike the charging boy, who could not stop charging.

The Heater made a last-second attempt to draw his legs out of reach of the snake, then realized instantly that this would place other, less desirable, appendages on prominent display as targets. Changing his mind, he directed a desperation kick at the viper. Truth be known, that's what caused the snake to strike.

As the Jake launched himself off the bluff, the energy of his kick caused his feet to fly upward, and therefore his head and shoulders swung downward. Holding the handle, he almost turned a complete somersault. The snake was re-coiling when the Heater's head passed directly over it, but there was no time for a second strike.

However, the moccasin apparently realized it was going to get another chance. It turned outboard and readied itself.

The Heater recovered from the somersault, boosted his upper half up over the handle, and jerked his legs forward to try to examine them in flight. He was still outbound at probably twenty miles an hour. He knew the moccasin had struck, but wasn't sure whether it had been accurate. Leaning over the handle so that his nose almost touched his knee, he was able to observe a trickle of blood from a puncture on his leg just to the side of his shinbone, which sported a long scratch that was also oozing blood.

His mouth was suddenly dry as cotton, and he momentarily froze in position, mind racing. The swing reached the outermost limit of its journey and, as swings do, started back from whence it had come.

The Heater reflexively started to drop, then thought better

of it. He wanted to be on dry land to do whatever was called for on the snakebite. Yet just after he made the decision to stay for the ride back to the bluff, he remembered that the snake was also back at the bluff. In mid-air, he reversed his grip on the handle like a trapeze artist and turned to check on the whereabouts of his no-legged adversary.

Who was, for the first time in its life, seeing a victim return for seconds. The snake reared up cobra-like for a better look. The Heater took this action as indicative of more planned hostilities. He had two choices: up or down. Visualizing veritable beds of squirming vipers beneath the surface of the water, Heater, in mid-swing, swarmed up the rope and stood on the handle.

The rest of the Jakes were at first in awe over the feats being performed by their comrade, but then Boateater, next in line on the bluff, moved forward to catch the returning swing and glimpsed the moccasin rising from the root ball for another strike. "Snake!" he yelled, grabbing a limb and charging to the rescue.

Boateater was so intent on the reptile that he forgot about the swing, and the Heater was also too intent on the snake to focus on his friends. The Jake with the stick bent over to slam a killing blow at the striking viper, and was in this position when the swing handle hit him right on the top of the head. Normally this would have been only a minor distraction, but this time there was an extra hundred and twenty pounds perched on the handle, plus some residual velocity. Boateater, having just dispatched the snake, was knocked head over heels down the dry side of the bluff.

The impact also dislodged the Heater, who tumbled down behind Boateater. The other three Jakes, still not exactly certain of the cause of all the ruckus, ran to their wounded buddies' aid.

Boateater had obviously been knocked silly, but it was just as obvious that the Heater had been scared just as silly. Ignoring the pain of his rescuer, Heater grabbed Perfect and Deadeye forcefully by the arms and stuttered, "I-I-I b-b-b-been snakebit!!!"

"You what?!" Perfect exclaimed.

With trembling finger, the victim pointed to his shin. Sure enough, twin trickles of blood had reached all the way to his ankle.

"Son of a three-toed, bare-backed berry picker!" breathed Perfect.

Deadeye blinked owlishly at the wounds. "Holy sh . . ."

"Don't say it!" interrupted Birdlegs, rebuking in all seriousness. "What if he were to die, an' you cussin'?"

"G-G-G-Gimme m-m-my jeans," the Heater requested weakly. "I don't wanna die nekkid."

"I'm 'bout to die an' nobody cares!" moaned Boateater, sitting up and feeling his skull tenderly.

"You'll be all right," Deadeye drawled. "It hit you on the head. But what're we gonna do for a snakebite? Cut it an' suck it?"

"I think you pack ice on it," Perfect said thoughtfully, reaching for his own clothes.

"Uh-uh! I saw a cowboy show where they cut it, poured gunpowder on it, then set the gunpowder on fire!" Birdlegs was waxing enthusiastic. Here was a chance to try something new. "That pulls the poison right out!" He went to his jeans, too, but not to put them on. He began emptying his pockets of .22 cartridges.

It was at this point that Wacky Mack made his appearance. One moment he wasn't there, the next moment he was kneeling next to the Heater. "Lemme see," he rasped.

Over the years, these sudden appearances by the bearded, camo-clad woodsman had become so common that the Jakes were hardly startled by them. Mack never smiled and seldom spoke, but the boys had subconsciously come to count on his presence. Once, when Other Mother had refused to let the Jakes head for their regular Friday night campout because of tornado watches, the Heater had burst out, "But Mama, even if there is one, Wacky Mack will help us!" He had not convinced her.

The Heater had already donned his jeans, and had one leg rolled up past the bite. The bearded man looked closely at the puncture, which was already beginning to swell and turn red, and reached into his pocket for his knife. He raised his eyebrows in an apology of sorts to the Heater, then slit the pants leg all the way past the knee.

"Other Mother's gonna kill you!" Boateater muttered to Heater, still resentful about the lick to the top of his head.

Wacky Mack pulled a bandana handkerchief from his fatigues and quickly fashioned a tourniquet just above the victim's knee. Looking up at the boys, he gently tugged on the bandage and instructed, "Not *too* tight."

Next he produced a cigarette lighter and passed his knife blade through the flame several times. "Sterilizin'," he rasped. That done, he stretched the Heater's leg out and prepared for surgery. Even the bite victim was becoming absorbed in the operation.

The veteran tapped the Heater's shin with his fingernail, producing an audible sound. "Too hard; no pentration," he indicated of the fang that had hit the bone and just made a long scratch. Then he pressed the knife gently just above the one puncture wound. "Watch," he rasped.

The blade only moved a half an inch, and cut less than a quarter-inch deep. Blood welled up, yet the Heater never winced. He watched in fascination, obviously taking mental notes. Mack handed him the knife.

"Never do this with mouth or lip sores," cautioned the man, and the Jakes all nodded their understanding as he lifted the leg to his mouth. The Heater's first indication of pain was a sharp intake of breath as Wacky Mack bent slightly, put his lips to the wound, and began sucking. From where he was kneeling, Perfect could see horrible scars on the man's neck as the full beard fell forward.

Alternatively sucking and spitting, the veteran kept up treatment for fully fifteen minutes. He then rose and said "Get dressed" over his shoulder as he strode to the Canal, where he bent to scoop up some water with his hand and rinse his mouth several times. Boateater, the only boy still nude, threw the Heater his shirt and sneakers from the willow tree where they hung, and dressed quickly. By the time all the Jakes had their shoes on, Wacky Mack had boosted the Heater onto his back. The man nodded to Deadeye. "Lead the way to Camp," he ordered.

They had traveled less than a hundred yards when Heater began to tremble and moaned miserably, "I'm gonna throw up!" His carrier barely had time to put him down before he vomited explosively. The retching lasted several minutes and left the victim limp. From the depths of another pocket, Mack produced a pint flask, which he uncapped and held to the boy's lips. The Heater grimaced in anticipation, but it was only water. He rinsed, spat, then sipped. The man returned the flask to his pocket and stooped to lift his burden again.

Thrice more on the way to Camp, nausea spells overcame the victim and the group had to pause. The Heater was ghostly pale, breathing shallowly, and so weak his head lolled on Wacky Mack's shoulder. Each time they stopped, the woodsman silently showed the Jakes how to check the tourniquet, as the wounded leg was swelling rapidly. When they neared Camp, Birdlegs and Boateater ran ahead to start and turn the jeep. Wacky Mack lifted the Heater into the back seat between Boateater and Deadeye, and turned to Perfect.

"Tell Doc it's been about two hours since he was bitten by a moccasin. Only one fang punctured, an' it wasn't too deep. Got it?"

"You're not goin'?" Perfect asked.

"Nah. Worst is over. Be okay in a coupla hours. Li'l skin'll rot at the bite. Tell his folks not to sweat." The veteran seemed to be making an effort to get the unaccustomed words out. He turned to Birdlegs sternly. "Now you drive careful! I didn't go to all this trouble for you t' break his neck in a jeep wreck!"

"Yes, sir," the driver said meekly.

Wacky Mack reached out to touch Boateater lightly on the head and nodded. "Good job killin' that snake so quick. Prob'ly saved Heater." Boateater sat up straighter and his chest seemed to swell with pride. The man stepped back and tapped Birdlegs on the arm with a fist. "Go. Slow," he rasped.

As the jeep was turning into Papa Jake's driveway, the driver spoke, breaking the Jakes' awed silence. "Usin' the gunpowder woulda been more fun, I bet," he speculated.

84

*　　*　　*　　*　　*　　*　　*

Early that fall Baby Sister turned twelve, and Papa Jake gave her a pair of ponies for her birthday. Supposedly, she would care for them herself — her father threatened to sell them back if she fell through on her promise. Realistically, he lined up Big Gus to check behind her. It soon became apparent, though, that she intended to live up to her responsibility, at least until the new wore off. "Lawd, Bossman!" Big Gus complained. "That chile treats her hosses better'n folks!" Soon Baby Sister graduated from riding in the ten-acre cow pasture to riding the turnrows by herself, as long as parental permission was obtained beforehand.

Neither the Heater nor Perfect had much use for horses; the heroes of their generation had gone beyond cowboys and Indians. Perfect intended to be an astronaut, and Heater had set his sights early on doctoring. Birdlegs, however, was a Jake with old-fashioned values, and rode with Baby Sister whenever possible.

Despite the two-and-a-half-year age difference, not to mention the sex difference, the girl got along fairly well with all the Jakes, and often was invited to accompany them on their adventures. These were limited to day-time, dry-land excursions, however; she was not permitted to tag along on their campouts or swimming activities. Several years before, when she was seven and the boys were going on ten, they had introduced her to the sport of strip poker, and Papa Jake had walked in on the upstairs game at a point when it was obvious Baby Sister had not mastered all of the skills required. The man had chased, caught, and whipped girl and boys until he was exhausted and Other Mother was afraid he would have a stroke. As the result of his enthusiasm, the Jakes were among the last in their class to mature sexually.

For a couple of months, Birdlegs worked closely with Baby Sister in caring for the ponies. While not neglecting his time with the Jakes, he helped put the finishing touches on Pal and Polly's saddle training. Polly was the gentlest and Baby Sister's favorite; Pal, perhaps because he was the equine counterpart to a Jake, had his wilder moments. Sometimes, however, these moments were completely understandable.

One pretty Sunday afternoon, Baby Sister and Birdlegs had gone for a ride around the Woods, and were on the back of Deputy Don's property when they spied a huge hornets' nest about nine feet off the ground in a persimmon tree at the edge of the Woods.

"What's that?" pointed Baby Sister, reining Polly up at a distance of twenty yards.

"That's a big ole hornets' nest!" exclaimed Birdlegs. "An' it's right where I was gonna bow hunt for deer next month." In the South, persimmon thickets are prime deer-stand areas when the fruit drops during the early bow season. The boy dismounted and respectfully walked closer to investigate. The nest was obviously occupied. "I gotta take care-a this thing," remarked Birdlegs.

He searched the area around the horses, and came up with a twelve-foot-long chinaberry pole, light enough for him to swing, but heavy enough to do the job. Speculatively, he looked from the nest to the grazing Pal and back, finally nodding that he had a plan.

"Yonder's Deputy Don up at the toppa the hill in his garden. You ride on up there," Birdlegs ordered, "an' I'll take care-a this ole hornets' nest." Baby Sister nodded dubiously, clucked at Polly, and trotted toward the garden, two hundred yards away. They both heard Deputy Don yell a greeting, and Birdlegs waved in that direction before mounting Pal with the chinaberry pole.

Pal was a little headstrong today, and to give him credit, he probably had never seen a hornets' nest in his life. The boy had a little trouble getting the pony to the exact spot he had chosen, but finally they were positioned. Birdlegs stretched out the pole carefully in one hand to measure his distance. Satisfied, he dropped the reins over Pal's neck, drew the pole back, took a deep breath, and swung.

His aim was true. The hornets' nest was knocked ten feet.

Instantaneous with the impact, Birdlegs dropped the pole, grabbed the reins, whooped, and slammed his heels into Pal's flanks. "Go, Pal!" he bellowed.

Incensed by such treatment, Pal stood his ground, turned his head, and looked the boy in the eye. Who did this kid think he was, anyway?

A buzzing ball of yellow-and-black hornets rose from the destruction of their home and only took a moment to assign responsibility for the deed. At the same time that a second series of kicks was being imparted by his rider, several score of stinging insects disclosed their fury by attacking Pal's soft underbelly and private parts.

The pony initially attributed this assault to Birdlegs, and began to buck, crowhopping and sunfishing in one place. That was enough for the Jake, as yet unstung. He kicked free of the stirrups, bailed off, and lit running. Luckily for him, the hornets stayed with the horse. At least at first.

Pal — snorting, kicking, and bucking wildly — suddenly caught a glimpse of his ex-rider racing away on foot and realized Birdlegs was not the source of his torment. The pony made haste to follow, streaming hornets.

Deputy Don later related the scene to Papa Jake, as witnessed from the safety of the top of his hill: "That hoss got flat out, an' catched th' boy; when th' hornets started on th' boy, then he catched th' hoss! They was back an' forth fer two or three times, then that fool boy outrun th' hoss at full gallop an' got back on 'im!"

It was a tribute to Birdlegs' speed that he was only stung

eight times. Deputy Don annointed the stings with chewing tobacco. Pal, however, "swoll up like an elephant," and the lawman put him in his own catch pen until Papa Jake could get the veternarian out to look at him. The doctor prescribed an antibiotic and two weeks' rest for the pony.

But after that, he minded explicitly when Birdlegs rode him.

Only a couple of weeks later, on a Friday afternoon, Baby Sister came in from school to an empty house. Papa Jake was out on the Place, and Other Mother was in town. The Heater had gone home with Boateater, whose dad had agreed to take the Jakes to the River with him, jugfishing and camping on a sandbar.

Baby Sister wrote a note to her parents, notifying them that she was going riding for a couple of hours on the south side of the Woods. Though technically she was supposed to have prior permission, leaving a note was deemed okay if no one was home. She grabbed a handful of cookies and a canned drink, dropped the note on the kitchen table, and hurried out to the pasture to saddle Polly.

The kitchen window was open, and unobserved by the twelve-year-old girl, a line of thunderheads had built up in the west. Fifteen minutes after she slammed the door, Baby Sister's note had blown off the table and into the pantry.

Since she was riding east, the girl never noticed the fast-moving front slipping up behind her. Even the approaching thunder did not alert her, for once she crossed the Canal bridge and reached the south side of the Woods, Polly had warmed up enough to run, and Baby Sister let the pony have her head. Alternatively galloping and trotting eastward in the shadows of the Woods, the pair never suspected that the weather was worsening behind them until they reached the gravel road at the far end of the Woods, the turning-around point.

Though she was close to both Deputy Don's and Wacky Mack's places, Baby Sister had but one thought when she turned Polly and glimpsed the dark, fast-moving, ominous clouds: to get home as fast as possible. Her mount was not particularly thrilled with this choice, and became less so when the lightning began. Polly became increasingly harder for the youngster to control. Just as the first cold raindrops began to splatter them, a bolt struck a nearby cottonwood tree with a deafening blast. Branches and pieces of bark flew around them, and Polly reared straight up, pawing with her forelegs. Baby Sister had never experienced this manuever before, and slid backward to the ground, unhurt. The pony came down and headed for the pasture.

Birdlegs, veteran horserider and watcher of ninety percent of all western movies made, had once warned Baby Sister that some homing inclination was apparently included in The Horse Ten Commandments. This observation had been made after he had dismounted from Pal on the bank of Muddy Slough in order to look more closely at a set of deer tracks, and the pair had had to ride Polly double the two miles back to the pasture, where Pal waited for them outside the gate.

Any chances Baby Sister might have had to catch her steed were dashed by the brief band of hail running in front of the storm. Polly, to give her credit, had paused in her flight about a hundred yards away from the girl, who was trotting toward her and calling soothingly. Then the hail hit.

When one is in the middle of an open field without even the shelter of a hat, a hailstorm is, at best, a painful and down-beating experience. The pea- to marble-sized bits of ice, coming from the west, hit the horse first and reinforced her initial inclination. Polly went home.

Baby Sister realized that she was a long way from where she needed to be. The Woods was two hundred yards to her right, and she spun and made a mad dash for the shelter of the trees. She had covered maybe a fourth of the distance when the storm broke.

Though she suffered no visible or lasting damage, she later told Heater, "It was kinda like standin' in the middle of the basketball court durin' assembly and lettin' the whole school throw marbles at me!" Baby Sister dropped to all fours, covered her head with her arms, and turned her jean-clad rear to the stinging bits of ice.

The hail lasted less than five minutes, which probably doesn't seem too long unless one is caught out in it. Then with a rush, the rain was upon her — huge, cold, splatting drops. She could not walk into it; yet she could not stay where she was, with lightning bolts flashing around her. Baby Sister began a stumbling trot toward the Woods, quartering east again.

Papa Jake and Other Mother, not finding a note, assumed their daughter was either down the road at Uncle Bubba's or else had taken shelter in the barn when the storm caught her doing her chores. It was not until Polly came plodding up to the pasture gate saddled but riderless, that the adults hit the panic button. They had no idea which way to look. Since she usually rode the turnrows, Papa Jake left, oilskin-clad, in the open jeep to check the open spaces for her while Other Mother got on the telephone to alert the neighbors.

In the meantime Baby Sister gained what shelter she could from the trees at the edge of the Woods and moved eastward, within a half-hour glimpsing a gleam of light ahead of her. Thankfully, she finally stumbled up onto the porch of a small log cabin in a grove of oak and sweetgum trees and leaned on the door, thumping with her fists.

Wacky Mack was surprised for one of the first times since he had moved to the South. He had of course met Baby Sister, but this bedraggled, soaking wet, mud-smeared, tearful child who collapsed into his arms seemed like a complete stranger. Dropping to one knee, he quickly reached for his bandana and wiped her face, rasping, "Who're you?" Before she could sob a reply, he answered himself with a surprised "Baby Sister!"

The girl was now shivering violently with a combination of relief, fright, cold, and wetness. The bearded man seemed at a loss for a moment, then shook his head once with an obvious decision, picked her up and carried her toward the small bathroom. There he started running a hot bath and searched through a cabinet until he found a huge fleecy towel, almost the size of a blanket. He also produced a washcloth, a bar of soap, and a bottle of shampoo. By this time the tub was nearly full and Baby Sister, through chattering teeth, had managed to make the veteran aware of her predicament.

"Here," he said gruffly, handing her the items from the cabinet. "You get in the tub and soak 'til you're warm all over, then clean up." Mack's color seemed a little high, she was to remember later. "I'll drive down to Deputy Don's and call your folks. No phone here." He seemed to be apologetic.

He turned on his heel as she began to remove her boots, and closed the door quickly behind him.

Wacky Mack hurriedly donned raingear, for his jeep was also presently topless, and departed for Deputy Don's house to call Papa Jake and Other Mother. However, Don was on patrol and Sugarpie had gone shopping. The woodsman had to drive all the way to Widow Trammel's house, and it took nearly fifteen minutes of pounding before the deaf old woman let him in. Even when she knew who he was, the widow wasn't keen about admitting him.

Wacky Mack knew that his almost hermit-like habits, and the silence and dour manner caused by his scars and their covering beard, gave him a reputation for being somewhat crazy. This suited him, for he had his own reasons for not wanting company. Only occasionally, like this evening, was his reputation an inconvenience.

Baby Sister's normal good humor returned with the warming effects of the tub. After her bath, she dried off and, disdaining her sopping garments on the bathroom stool, wrapped up in the towel and ventured out of the bathroom. She noted that her host had not yet returned. Naturally inquisitive, she began to look around the cozy log home, wondering at its neatness. "Wonder how long it's been since a girl was in here?" she thought.

There was no way for Baby Sister to know that she was the first visitor to set foot inside Wacky Mack's home since it had been built. The veteran had paid off his helpers when the shell of the pre-fab cabin had been completed, and had finished the inside by himself. Until tonight his privacy had never been invaded. True, he occasionally had visitors; but he had never invited them in, and the rocking chairs on his porch had served for short conversations with anyone, including neighbors, who ventured to the end of his road.

The log cabin was simple. There was a large central chimney with three fireplaces, one of which opened into the bedroom, which was adjoined by the bathroom where Baby Sister had bathed. A second fireplace warmed the kitchen, and had a charcoal grill built into one side of it. A much larger fireplace faced out into the other half of the cabin, all one big open room. The young girl's first impression of this room was, "Books!"

Bookshelves covered every wall, and the shelves were neatly filled with volumes. Even the mantel over the fireplace held books. Baby Sister loved to read, and as she moved about, she realized that this room was as well-stocked as most libraries; indeed, she even had the vague impression that Wacky Mack might refer to a cataloging system, the arrangement seemed so neat. She saw authors' names from Plato and Shakespeare to Tarkington and Twain. Just as she pulled out a copy of *Penrod and Sam*, the door opened to the owner's return.

"Gee, you must read an awful lot!" she smiled at the man.

Wacky Mack stood silent for a full minute before he replied, then nodded at the book in her hand. "Yeah. Try that one. I'll make hot chocolate. Your daddy's comin'."

An hour later, when he heard Papa Jake's pickup pulling into the driveway, Mack wrapped a blanket around the girl, picked up the plastic sack with her wet clothes in it, and lifted Baby Sister in his arms to carry her to the truck. She held the book up in his face. "Can I take it home and finish it, if I promise to bring it back?" she asked, her ordeal forgotten.

Wacky Mack hesitated only briefly. "Yeah," he finally rasped, and nodded as she tucked it under the blanket to protect it from the rain. "Jus' come by yourself," he said, striding to the truck.

She did. Somehow she sensed the man's almost obsessive need for privacy. But perhaps once a week, barring bad weather, Baby Sister would ride over on Polly to return a book, bearing also a fruitcake tin of cookies or brownies. After she had come twice while he was away and left the tin at the door with a note, Mack swore her to secrecy and then showed her where he hid an extra key. Sometimes he would come in from the Woods to find her curled up on the sofa, lost in the pages, just a brief smile of greeting for him. They never talked much, and she never told anyone else but her parents.

Not even the Heater.

The Heater wasn't even hunting that afternoon, but luckily he had a .22 rifle with him. It was the week before deer season opened and the Jakes were scattered all over the Woods scouting for deer sign.

Heater had ended up almost at Dundee's Lake following the sign of a buck that either rubbed his antlers on a scrub cedar, or made a "scrape" every hundred yards or so in an easterly direction. As he neared the lake, the buck's tracks led into a five-acre field that had once been a log dump and had now grown into an almost impenetrable mass of briars, saplings, and palmettos. The Jake skirted the tract, noted only one heavily-used trail through the thicket, and decided to walk through it to see if there was a suitable place for a tree stand.

He had only taken a few steps into the dense brush when suddenly a chorus of barking came from the trail ahead. With no room to manuever, the Heater thought to retreat, and had taken one step backward when eight wild dogs came snarling, baying, and barking down the trail toward him.

The boy had not made a sound for the past half-hour, just slipping quietly through the Woods, so his first reaction to the charge was, "Who, me?" He couldn't believe the dogs were intent on him, and yelled to frighten them. "Heeeyyy! Hyar!!"

If anything, the canines redoubled their efforts.

The Heater never had time to raise his gun to his shoulder. Firing from the waist as the snarling, snapping pack attacked, he killed the first three dogs with head or chest shots at point-blank range. The fourth swerved to avoid a sprawling mate, and the .22 hollow-point took her too far back. However, the bitch began "ki-yi-yi"-ing and nipping at the wound, circling and blocking the trail. The other four dogs stopped, growling ominously. Finally, the boy was able to raise the little rifle to his shoulder. "Take that," he muttered, sighting on an ugly yellowish cur and pulling the trigger.

"Click!" said the .22.

"Uh-oh," breathed Heater.

There were more shells in his pocket, and he slowly reached for them; afraid to move to move quickly, but knowing this standoff couldn't last forever. He withdrew a handful of cartridges, lowered the gun cautiously, and was just starting to raise the loading rod from the stock when the crippled bitch flopped down by the side of the trail and went into final convulsions.

The battle was on again.

The yellowish cur bawled a coarse "Raarrk, raarrk!" and renewed his charge. There was no time to run, and no time to load. The Heater flung the shells into the dog's face, grasped the rifle by the barrel, and broke the nylon gunstock across the snarling jaw. The cur rolled, regained his feet, and headed off into the brush, his muzzle just forward of his eyes crushed and hangingly loosely to one side of his intact lower jaw.

The boy had no time to bewail the splintered stock. He barely had time to draw back for another swing. A smallish white shaggy mongrel had begun its jump toward the Jake's throat when the club took it in the side of the head. There hadn't been enough time for the blow to be full-force, but fortunately for Heater, the nylon splinters raked across the dog's face and slashed one eye out. The mutt flipped backward in the air, rolled to its feet, and beat a retreat between its two remaining packmates, yipping and shaking its head from side to side. Splatters of blood flew with each shake. The two survivors skidded to a stiff-legged sullen stop, growling.

Feeling like Horatius At The Bridge in the narrow trail littered with carcasses, blood, and gore, the Heater decided to take the initiative. Brandishing his weapon and bellowing his war-cry, he charged. "RrrrAAARRRgggg!!!" Heater roared.

One of the reasons that wild dogs are so dangerous in areas

where they have built up to pack size is that they have no innate fear of man. However, by definition, "innate" means "inborn; not acquired." The remaining canines in this pack had in the past sixty seconds or so acquired no little degree of respect for, and some fear of, *homo sapiens*. The Heater's charge broke their resolve and they high-tailed it back into their dense refuge.

The boy had sense enough not to follow. In five acres of this stronghold, who knew how many more packs there were? When he stopped, the shudders started, and he had to breath deeply to control the trembling. Ruefully, he examined the remains of his weapon. The little Remington Nylon 66 had been Papa Jake's, and had served the family well for nearly twenty years. Now the stock was gone, and the chrome receiver was bent where it joined the barrel.

Heater picked up the remaining piece of stock and eased back down the trail and out of the thicket. He broke into a trot when he hit the open Woods, only slowing for breath a couple of times before he reached Camp. None of the other Jakes were in evidence, so the youngster busied himself with chores and supper preparation, gradually calming down. By the time Birdlegs and Deadeye strolled into Camp, the Heater was almost back to normal.

"Shoot-a-mile!" Birdlegs exclaimed, spying the remains of Heater's gun. "Was that your rifle?!?!"

By the time the last Jake, Perfect, returned to Camp, the story had been told and retold. All of the boys had been warned, and all realized the dangers of wild dogs, but they had never heard of such an attack in force before. Sitting around the fire, they at first discussed plans for taking the offensive against the non-domestic canine population. These plots ranged all the way from massive retaliation involving automatic weapons, to napalm bombing raids. The fact that none of them owned an automatic, airplane, or a supply of napalm was not a deterrent to the conversation.

As the evening waned, however, the discussion turned toward a more defensive strategy. The Jakes could just imagine that the dogs themselves were planning an attack in force once their Camp was slumbering. It was finally decided, in the absence of claymore mines, that they would stand one-and-a-half-hour watches throughout the night. Birdlegs volunteered for the first watch and began to arrange his arsenal against the cypress log. Finally, he held up a full fifty-round box of .22 cartridges. "My last-ditch weapon," he announced.

The other Jakes were involved in pre-bedtime rituals. The Heater and Deadeye were a few yards out in the Woods at the latrine; Boateater was under the sweetgum tree where the water cooler sat on top of the ice chest, brushing his teeth; and Perfect knelt at the tent, untying his boots. The latter raised an eyebrow. "What're you gonna do with that, throw it at 'em?"

"Naw, throw it in the fire," Birdlegs rejoined. "If I'm outa ammo and ain't got time to reload, at least I'll take 'em all with me." Obviously, he envisioned an attack by many, many dogs.

"They won't do nothin' but jus' pop!" Perfect said scornfully.

Scorn is not an acceptable attitude to a Jake. "Oh, yeah?!" Birdlegs returned. "Watch, smarty-pants!" He pitched the box into the middle of the fire.

"Fool!!" Boateater yelled, spitting white foam as he stepped quickly behind the big sweetgum tree.

"Dummy!!" bellowed Heater, just beyond the firelight, still buttoning his jeans. He dived behind the cypress log.

"Gahhh! Idiot!!" sputtered Perfect, scampering on all fours to take cover on the back side of the woodpile.

Birdlegs vaulted the cypress log to join Heater when the shells began to explode. Coals and sparks flew in all directions as the volley of shots rang out in the night.

Deadeye, still involved in tending to business, assumed the Camp was under attack by someone, and escaped into the night. He was the only real casualty; in his haste, he had jerked his britches up long before he should have.

The shooting seemed quickly over, and the Heater rose to his knees, clenching his fists and gritting his teeth in anger. "What the hell possessed you . . ." he began to rant.

"Wait!!" Perfect interrupted urgently, loud enough for the other Jakes to hear. "Get back down!!"

"Why?" But Heater dropped obediently, as did Birdlegs.

Perfect's voice was muffled as he scrunched down behind

the woodpile, but it was loud enough for even Deadeye to hear him. "I only counted forty-nine!!"

When the harvest season on nearby farms started, the Jakes would stock up on shotgun shells and .22 cartridges, and fill their mothers' freezers with some of the finest of wild meat — rabbit.

The way they acquired the bunnies would perhaps have been considered by some authorities unethical, if not entirely illegal. However, it was a highly effective method, and, as Papa Jake told the Duke, "If the boys didn't get 'em, the wild dogs, foxes, bobcats, and coyotes would."

When the huge harvesting machines began to reap the soybeans from the fields, gobbling six to eight rows at a time, the inhabitants of those fields suddenly found themselves without home and habitat. This is sad, but it is the way of the world. To suggest that a farmer should abandon his considerable investment in a hundred-acre soybean field so that the bunny rabbits can live happily ever after, would be somewhat akin to asking a supermarket chain if they would consider removing the concrete from their parking lots in nine states and planting that acreage in bald cypress for whooping crane habitat. The Wheels of Progress grind on.

On a farm, however, the bunny rabbits (and whooping cranes, too, if there happen to be any in the soybean field) have a choice: most fields are bordered by ditches, treelines, sloughs, or some other form of refuge. When the crops are harvested, thereby denuding the rows, the rats, mice, chipmunks, snakes, skunks, birds, possums, coons, and rabbits vacate their open former homes for the safety of nearby cover. It was at the point of their vacating that the Jakes took unfair advantage of the rabbit population.

As the combines cut around and around the fields, the

inhabitants thereof would turn ever inward, so that when a forty-acre beanfield had been reduced to five acres, that last five acres would literally be teeming with wildlife. Thereafter, on every swath they cut, the combine drivers would see a score of rabbits, as well as all the other creeping, crawling, running living things. However, in harvesting, up to a certain point, speed is time is beans is money; drivers usually only braked for skunks. Big Gus had combined a skunk once, and Papa Jake eventually had to sell the combine. As a matter of fact, had slavery still been in vogue, he would probably have sold Big Gus, too. A bath in tomato juice finally restored the driver to his employer's good graces; but the same treatment for his machine, all things considered, was deemed too expensive.

The Jakes would station themselves at various points around the field, and when the rabbits started to pop out and run for cover, the nearest boy would head the target off. Fields of fire were carefully observed, and the Jakes were always mindful to share with the drivers of the machines. Big Gus would even blow the combine horn when a wise old canecutter would try to slip out undetected.

As with most wild animals, the rabbit population seemed to run in cycles. One year there would be few to be seen. A couple of years later, rabbits would be everywhere. This particular fall, it was a banner year for bunnies. After the first few hunts, the Jakes knew that they needed something to add extra challenge to the sport. Quite by accident, Boateater was the one to discover the solution.

This Jake had walked out into the field to retrieve one rabbit when three more spurted out from under the combine and ran directly toward him. With two shells left in his shotgun, Boateater dispatched a pair, but the survivor never swerved. It raced by the boy less than three steps away, and the Jake did what came naturally. He dropped his shotgun and gave chase.

Now, a rabbit is indeed fast, as is held by tradition — but only for short spurts. As the other Jakes cheered, Boateater came so close to the cottontail that it had to dart sideways to escape his clutch, thereby swerving from the refuge of the fencerow. Back and forth they went, the boy managing to keep the bunny in the open, until finally the exhausted Jake made a flying leap and grabbed his equally-exhausted prey by a hind leg. Both chaser and chasee lay prone for several minutes before Boateater arose and held the rabbit above his head to receive the accolades of his comrades. A passion for imitation consumed them.

An hour later Papa Jake, from his perch atop a cotton trailer a half-mile away, noticed that both combines were stopped down at the Pete Ford Cut. Fuming, he jumped down, stomped to his truck, and sped down the turnrow to investigate the cause of the trouble. His attention was riveted on the big machines, and he drove the pickup right across the harvested rows to the closest one, which was still halted. June Bug's machine had begun to move again. The farmer bounded up the ladder and jerked open the cab door. "What's . . ." he stopped, dumbfounded.

Big Gus, his huge belly resting on the steering wheel, was leaning back in his seat gasping for breath with tears streaming from his eyes. He waved one hand weakly at his bossman, who immediately fell to one knee beside him in concern. "Gus, you okay? Where's it hurt?" He feared a heart attack.

The huge driver shook his head. "Lawd, Boss, I ain't never seen nothin' like this in all my born days!" he wheezed. "Jus' watch them crazy fool boys!" he pointed.

June Bug's combine had pushed several rabbits out of the small remaining plot of unharvested soybeans, and five boys were sprinting, darting, jumping, and diving in different directions after their quarries. As the two men watched, Birdlegs and Boateater collided at full speed while the big canecutter they were pursuing was headed off by Deadeye, turned around, and jumped squarely over Birdlegs' head. That Jake made a grab, missed, rolled to his feet, and rejoined the chase. Soon Papa Jake was laughing just as hard as his driver. The farmer noticed that the other combine was stopped again, too.

"Hold up a minute," Papa Jake instructed. "The Duke is pickin' cotton just across the line. I gotta show him this! Start back up when you see my truck comin' back."

Only ten minutes later, with the Duke at his side miffed because he was being taken away from his own harvesting operations on some mysterious mission, Papa Jake came roaring back down the turnrow in a cloud of dust. As if on signal the two combines started cutting again, and the farm owners watched a half-dozen rabbits dart out into the open, harvested portion of the field.

The chase was on.

Seconds later, the two farmers and the two drivers were in tears, laughing. Yet all had to return to their duties, albeit reluctantly, so soon Papa Jake cranked his truck, swung around, and left the scene, still chuckling. "Worth it?" he grinned at his companion.

The Duke of Dundee sighed and wiped his eyes with a sleeve, nodding. "Good Lord, man!" he exclaimed. "Think of the breeding stock possibilities! We know they will run, now if we could only teach them to bark!"

*　　*　　*　　*　　*　　*　　*

Rabbits were not the only game the Jakes chased. There

were many armadillos in the Woods, and unless they were hunting something else that the activity would disturb, any time at least two of the boys together saw one of the "armoured possums" (as the Duke called them), it signaled a chase. They added a new twist, though, when Birdlegs confiscated a couple of cases of spray paint that his father had decided were not going to sell and had discarded from the lumber yard. It was a greenish-yellow flourescent paint.

The Jakes' rather ambitious goal was to paint every armadillo in the Woods, and that Saturday they made a good start. Rapid Robert was visiting for the weekend, so they divided up into three teams and kept score that afternoon. Deadeye and Boateater won, with twenty-seven armadillos painted. The Heater and Birdlegs were right behind with twenty-five, and the Perfect-Rapid Robert team painted an even twenty. All told, the Jakes had a total record of one hundred eight painted armadillos for Friday afternoon and all day Saturday.

Tired but fulfilled, they lounged around the fire that night eating squirrel and dumplings and retelling tales from the day. In the distance but gradually drawing closer, they could hear the baying of Scotch and Soda, the Duke's current bluetick coon hounds. "Sounds like that ole coon's gonna run right through Camp," observed Deadeye. Sure enough, the chase went by less than a hundred yards away.

Half an hour later, Deputy Don and the Duke of Dundee came rushing into Camp. The two often coon hunted together, and often visited the Jakes' fire; but it was unheard of for them to hurry, and the boys had never seen either of the men agitated, except for the time the Duke had kicked Boateater. "Son," the Duke greeted Heater, "if you would be so good as to prepare a pot of coffee, Aye would be eternally grateful!" Deputy Don nodded agreement, rolling his eyes.

As noted previously, the Duke of Dundee was "bad to drink." Truth be known, he was an on-again, off-again alcoholic whose drinking had caused his wife to leave him years before. He was a happy drunk, and had sense enough to do his heavy drinking either at home or on his frequent coon hunting expeditions.

Coon hunters are generally men who brave the night-time

woods only for the pleasure of listening to the hounds run. Few coon hunters ever carry weapons, and fewer still will kill a coon. The usual practice is to have a .22 pistol for snake protection. The Duke carried only a six-foot oak walking staff and four pints of whiskey — one for each pocket — on his coon hunts. He never went alone, his most frequent companions being Deputy Don, Uncle Bubba, or Father Phil. The Duke was obstensibly Catholic, and it was he who had hung the "Father" tag on the Baptist minister.

Both the deputy and the farmer had obviously been drinking, but the Jakes had never seen them in this shape before, nor had they ever requested coffee. The Heater obligingly put the pot on, as Perfect offered the men bowls of squirrel and dumplings. Deputy Don seemed about two shades lighter than usual, and both men's hands shook as they gratefully accepted the food.

The Jakes were somewhat awed, and a little frightened, of whatever had caused this unusual reaction in the coon hunters. Had they too been attacked by wild dogs? Had they seen a panther? A bear? Rapid Robert, being the most unfamiliar with the Woods and therefore the most perturbed, finally broke the silence as the Heater poured mugs of coffee. "What's wrong?" he asked.

Deputy Don once again rolled his eyes expressively, and shook his head. The Duke glanced sideways at his companion, then he too shook his head. The flushed farmer shuddered as he sipped from the mug, which upset the boys even more. They never considered that it might have been the Heater's coffee that caused that reaction. "Wha'd y'all see?" Deadeye drawled.

The lawman looked at the Duke, who was staring intently at the ground. Deputy Don took a deep breath and spoke shakily. "Haints!"

"Spooks?" Birdlegs asked tenatively.

"Yas," the Duke articulated. "Aye have never seen anything to rival it. Aye have not even had overmuch to drink yet." He pulled the first pint from his pocket and held it up. It was almost a quarter full. Deputy Don reached out to remove the bottle from his hand, twisted the cap, and silently poured the rest of the whiskey into their coffee mugs.

"What kind of spooks?" ventured Boateater, glancing nervously behind him into the darkness. Birdlegs rose to place another branch on the fire.

"Ain't no tellin'," rejoined the lawman, shaking his head moodily, "but fer sure it's haints. All out in the Woods. Everywhere we goes. That fire's th'only thing keepin' 'em off us now." He addressed the Duke, "Reckon it's the Second Comin'? When the graves open up an' folks go walkin' 'round in grave clothes?"

"Aye do not know. Aye only know that for the first time in my life, including when Judith left me, Aye am considering giving up drinking," his meticulous tones contrasted heavily with the deputy's accent. "As a matter of fact," he withdrew three full pint bottles from his other pockets, "could you young men possibly cache these until Aye have made a firm decision?"

"Cash 'em?" wondered Birdlegs.

"C-A-C-H-E. Cache," the Duke spelled absently, "means to put them in a safe place." The Heater rose to accept the bottles and cache them in the hollow cypress.

"If it's the Second Comin', how come we's still here?" Deputy Don demanded broodingly.

"Aye have been a bad man," the Duke stared up at the stars, "Aye have beaten my wife and consumed too much whiskey," he confessed.

"Waal, I do whup Sugarpie ever' now an' then," Deputy Don admitted, "but only when she needs it. Is you boys saved? How come y'all still here?"

The Jakes nodded as one. "Yes, sir," but several of them were having second thoughts.

"Ever beat your wife?" asked the Duke. Despite having handed over the bottles, he was still somewhat under the influence.

"No sir!" Rapid Robert and Birdlegs assured him, while Perfect and Deadeye pointed out, "We ain't married."

"Is y'all been baptized?" Deputy Don was still not sure the Second Coming had not come and gone, leaving him and the Duke. Yet he wasn't prepared for these young innocents to have been abandoned to the Wiles of Satan unless there was good reason.

The Heater, Perfect, and Rapid Robert were able to answer affirmatively, but the other boys were not so sure. "Does christenin' count?" Boateater asked.

"Aye believe so," the Duke sounded reassuringly positive. "Don, Aye do not think that is the most reasonable explanation. However," he admitted, "Aye have yet to come up with one myself. Aye do know several things: Aye do not wish to hunt anymore tonight; Aye do not wish to drink anymore tonight; and Aye do not wish to walk through these Woods anymore tonight." He stood. "Would one of you young gentleman please chauffeur us in your vehicle to Don's house?"

All six Jakes consented quickly, and there was a mad rush for the jeep, leaving no room for the two adults left standing by the fire. Since nominally it was Heater's jeep, he took charge. "Look, all of us can't go. Me an' . . ." he chose the best protection over the kinship of Perfect, ". . . Birdlegs will drive 'em home while y'all break camp, an' then we'll come back for y'all." Birdlegs ran to get their rifles and plenty of cartridges.

On the way out of the Woods, two of the newly-painted armadillos scuttled glowingly across the jeep road at the far edge of the headlights. From the back seat, Deputy Don exclaimed, "Lawd A'Mercy! Duke! Duke! Some more of 'em! They's still after us!" The lawman cringed against his friend, who sat nearly transfixed. "Faster! Faster!" he ordered the driver.

The Heater looked at Birdlegs, open-mouthed. Ever so slightly, Birdlegs shook his head, biting his lips.

Twice more, "haints" scampered into and out of the beams of light, which Heater flicked on low. Finally, at Deputy Don's house, the two adults clambered out of the back seat of the open jeep.

"Thank you, boys," the Duke sounded shaken. "Are you quite sure neither of you saw anything on the way out?"

"No, sir," the Jakes shook their heads solemnly.

"Don," the Duke addressed his comrade, "Aye crave company tonight. Would Sugarpie object to my spending the remainder of this night on your sofa?"

"Tell you the truth, I'd be much obliged if you'd stay, Duke," was the answer. "Reckon we oughta tell Sugarpie what we been seein'?"

"Aye do not believe that would be wise," his guest replied firmly. "Good night, boys. Drive carefully."

Back at Camp, the other boys were ready to leave, but after explanations from Heater and Birdlegs, they re-made camp. Deadeye finally voiced all their nervous fears, for no one had laughed as yet. "Are we gonna get in trouble for this?"

Looking grimly at Rapid Robert, who was a guest at the campfire, the Heater replied pointedly, "If anybody ever tells, I bet we will!"

It was mostly gratitude that spurred the discussion that culminated in The First Annual JakeFest, but there were perhaps a few twinges of guilt for the times that the adults had been "put out" by some Jake activity or other. Variously, each one of the boys claimed credit, but actually it was Perfect who made the original suggestion.

Birdlegs did a little calligraphy, and formal invitations were hand-delivered to Papa Jake, Uncle Bubba, Wacky Mack, Deputy Don, and the Duke of Dundee, all of the landowners of the woods and waters that the Jakes enjoyed so. The Friday night after Thanksgiving was the appointed time, with postponement in case of inclement weather. But that whole weekend was clear and crisp, just cool enough that the campfire felt good.

The Jakes turned to and cleaned up extra well around their campsite. Perfect borrowed some old folding chairs, since, as he said, "Grown-ups don't seem to like to sit on the ground; they have trouble gettin' up." Boateater sneaked an old card table out of his attic; it had been consigned there because one leg had a tendency to fold up by itself unexpectedly. He solved that by shoving the legs about six inches into the ground next to the hollow cypress.

The adults arrived in two vehicles — Deputy Don and Wacky Mack in the latter's jeep, and Uncle Bubba picked up the Duke and Papa Jake in his Bronco. The Duke even took it upon himself to bring a gallon jug of dinner wine. "Aye anticipated that you boys would forget it," he explained.

The Jakes always cooked on a grill over a pit next to the campfire. This night, they had prepared a venison loin marinated in soy sauce; teal and dove breasts seasoned, wrapped in bacon, and spitted over the coals; foil-clad french bread; and baked potatoes. The card table was used for serving from, and even Wacky Mack went back for seconds. Deputy Don, Uncle Bubba, and the Heater had thirds, "to keep from havin' to throw out the leftovers."

At the Duke's request, Deadeye produced the three pints of whiskey that had been cached earlier, to add to the adults' coffee. The grown-ups had already done in the jug of wine. While Birdlegs and Boateater gathered the paper plates and cups for burning and Heater and Deadeye washed the utensils, Perfect pulled his guitar out of the tent and began strumming. Soon he and Uncle Bubba were in the middle of "Ghost Riders in the Sky." Deputy Don then serenaded them with "Swing Low, Sweet Chariot," but this rendition was marred by the Duke's joining in on the last verse and chorus.

"Dawgonnit, Duke!" the lawman complained. "You can't sing no spiritual with a ack-cent like you got!"

"My dear Deputy," was the rejoinder, "Aye was under the impression that Aye was the only one present *without* an accent!"

A round of mimicking followed, and as the guitarist began strumming again Deadeye drawled, "Really, how come you <u>do</u> talk like that, Mr. Duke?"

Unoffended, the Duke grinned in reply, "Aye had a serious speech impediment as a youngster, and was sent to a boarding school in the East for several years. My speech instructor was a former British stage actor. As a matter of fact, my college major was drama and theater. Harken!" the Duke arose and re-enacted "The Charge of the Light Brigade," holding his audience spellbound. He bowed graciously to the applause and sat back down, holding his cup out for more coffee and whiskey.

The Jakes were somewhat relieved that the Duke had returned to his normal drinking habits. Deputy Don held his mug for a refill, too. "That was somekinda fine, Duke," he spoke admiringly. "You coulda been a preacher." He turned to Perfect, "You know 'Just a Closer Walk,' son?"

The Jake nodded and began to pick out the hymn, while the lawman accompanied in a deep bass voice. Uncle Bubba joined in with his tenor, and Birdlegs began to snap his fingers. Then, blending in so softly and subtly that no one knew when it started, came the gentle wailing of a harmonica. Wacky Mack sat in the background against the cypress log with his eyes closed, the instrument almost lost in the depths of his beard. Only the movements of his hands gave his playing away.

As the last notes of the song faded away into the blackness, even the performers seemed reluctant to break the silence that followed. Papa Jake finally spoke, reverently, "Be-yoo-tee-full!!"

"How come you ain't never said you could play a mouth organ before, boy?" Deputy Don demanded.

Mack shrugged, started not to reply, then the mood broke his normal reticence. "Learned when I couldn't talk for a coupla years," he rasped. "Know 'Five Hundred Miles'?" he asked Perfect.

The boy shook his head, but his father reached for the guitar. "You lead," he told the veteran, and after a few bars, Uncle Bubba picked up Mack's rhythm. He strummed and sang softly, then took the lead himself on "Where Have all the Flowers Gone?"

Deputy Don was in tears as they ended. "Y'all oughta go on Tee-Vee," he declared.

Uncle Bubba handed the guitar back to his son. "Y'all do 'City of New Orleans' together," he requested.

The favorite part of any harmonica player is the chance to do a train whistle. Wacky Mack put all the volume he had into the lonesome sounds, and on the second one a hoot owl answered from just beyond the sweetgum tree. Throughout the song the owl joined in, and before it was over another one hooted from the edge of the Swamp.

This precipitated an owl-hooting contest between Uncle Bubba, Papa Jake, and Deputy Don, and soon a dozen owls were answering from different parts of the Woods. The Duke broke it up by giving his version, bringing a volley of derision from his peers. "Ain't never heard an owl with an English ack-cent!" taunted Deputy Don.

"*British* accent, please," corrected the Duke as he retired from the competition and poured another mug of half coffee, half whiskey.

During the interval, a screech owl gave its haunting, shiver-ing cry from the sweetgum, and Boateater's "Spooky!" com-ment turned the conversation to the occult. The recent haunt-ing of the Woods was discussed, and the Heater caught a knowing look crossing Wacky Mack's face. He realized their secret was safe when the veteran caught his eye and nodded slightly, just once.

Deputy Don and Papa Jake vied in the telling of ghost stories, until the Duke upstaged them by quoting the entire "Rime of the Ancient Mariner." Birdlegs and Heater rose to get more firewood, but Uncle Bubba stopped them. "Time to put the chairs in the wagon, boys," he yawned, directing his comment not to the real boys, but to the adults who were acting as such.

The Duke rose and bowed. "My compliments to the hosts!" he said formally. "Gourmet food, top-notch entertain-ment, and fine friends. My acres are yours, so long as you do not rut up my turnrows," he looked pointedly at Boateater, "or be careless with firearms!" Turning to Uncle Bubba, he observed, "Aye hope you are more capable of driving home than Aye am!"

All the men thanked the boys for the JakeFest, but the Heater tugged at Wacky Mack's sleeve to hold him back. "You ain't gonna tell 'em 'bout the 'haints', are you?" he asked anxiously.

The bearded man seemed to consider quite seriously before replying. "Naahh. Not for a few years, anyway." He punched

the boy lightly on the arm and walked to his jeep. As he cranked it, he winked at the Jakes and gave a thumbs-up signal. Heater sighed in relief.

Deadeye glanced at his watch. "Twelve-thirty," he drawled. "Y'know, growin' up might not be so bad after all."

Perfect looked up from where he knelt rinsing the coffee pot. "Huh. They don't have that much fun very often!"

* * * * * * *

During duck season it rained and rained, and rained some more. There was too much water and, though there were a lot of ducks, they quickly became call-shy and difficult to hunt. There were several openings in the Swamp where the Jakes hunted, but unless the weather was bad, they seldom had much luck. On foggy or rainy mornings the ducks decoyed much better.

It was clear the morning that Birdlegs got frustrated at the flocks of high-flying mallards and had an idea that would enable him to even the odds, so to speak. The Jakes were standing wader-clad in waist-deep water only a short distance from the edge of the Swamp, where Birdlegs had a deer stand. Not a single duck had dropped down into gun range, though hundreds had streamed over from the east.

"Okay," Birdlegs declared, "If the ducks won't come to me, I'll just go to them!" So saying, he placed his new .12 gauge three-inch magnum in the crotch of the big hackberry he was leaning against, and turned to wade toward dry land. "Back in a minute," he called over his shoulder.

"What's he gonna do, sprout wings?" wondered Boateater.

Within minutes, the boy re-appeared, carrying his "climbing" tree stand. This contraption boasted foot-straps on a small platform which connected to the tree by a V-shaped serrated metal strap, hinged to fit behind the trunk and re-fasten. The hunter would attach the stand to the tree at ground level, stand on the platform with his feet in the straps, sling his gun on his back, embrace the trunk with his arms, and then climb the tree by drawing his knees up. When the pressure was on the seat, the serrated strap would bite into the wood on the opposite side, holding the stand firmly in place. But when the downward pressure was removed from the seat, the strap released, thus allowing the stand to be moved up or down the trunk. Birdlegs indeed intended to go to the ducks.

The other Jakes nodded respectfully, the Heater and Boateater wishing they had thought of it first. They watched as Birdlegs slung his shotgun across his back and waded about twenty yards out to a long-dead cottonwood tree. The bark had been shed from this tree years before, and the top had succumbed to a windstorm. It was a slick, slim pole maybe fifty feet tall. Birdlegs began to fit the stand onto the trunk of the tree at water level.

"That tree's dead," Deadeye pointed out.

The would-be climber bestowed a withering glance on his comrade, not even favoring this remark with a reply. He boosted himself onto the seat and fitted his wader boots into the straps.

"That thing ain't gonna hold you," warned Perfect.

"Hey, climbin' don't bother me!" Birdlegs rejoined pointedly. So saying, he began to climb.

Even with the unaccustomed bulk of his waders, he went up the cottonwood like a cat. At nearly forty feet he paused, surveyed the area, backed down a few feet, and bounced on the stand, setting the serrated strap firmly into the trunk. He adjusted his gun around to his chest, seated himself gingerly, and reached behind him for the safety belt that is a necessary part of such a contraption. Birdlegs buckled up, unslung and loaded his shotgun, and quacked tenatively on his duck call.

"Eat your hearts out, boys," he gloated. "Jus' get ready to pick up my ducks!"

A flight of wigeons passed by on his right, but he couldn't get around quick enough. From his height advantage, though, he sighted another flock of mallards bearing down on him from dead ahead. "Here they come," he advised his companions below, and gave a feed-call chatter on his duck call.

The mallards didn't drop any lower, but they were within range on their present course, especially for a boy shooting a .12 gauge three-inch magnum. Birdlegs waited until they were almost overhead before swinging his gun up. The first drake folded neatly, and he swung without hesitation on a second.

"Whoom! Whoom! Whoom!" the big gun spoke.

Perfect and Deadeye had been prophetic. The old dead tree had been gnawed by beavers, but that damage was unseen under the present water level. Now, the heavy recoil from the magnum shells thirty-five feet up finished the beavers' job. The cottonwood broke at the base as the force of the shots pushed it backward.

Birdlegs had his eye on the two drakes he had killed, and wasn't quick to realize the problem. The tree had achieved about a ten-degree angle before he knew something was amiss. The other boys, watching from ground level, were aware instantly.

"Son of a three-toed, bare-backed berry picker!" Perfect breathed.

"Good Golly Greenwood!" exclaimed Boateater in awe.

"Not on me!" blurted Deadeye as he began to run to the side. Running in waist-deep water is not recommended for escaping falling trees.

"Timmm-beeerrr!" yelled the Heater; then, "Bail out, dummy!"

But Birdlegs couldn't jump. His initial reaction, when he finally had a reaction, was to lean forward to counterbalance his listing perch. His second thought was to jump. His third thought was to release the safety belt. However, by leaning forward, he applied too much tension to the catch and was unable to trigger it. Leaning out as far as possible, holding his gun outstretched in both hands, Birdlegs strained to help the toppling tree regain its balance. Below him, the prognosis was not favorable.

"He's a dead duck!" predicted Boateater.

"Paaaaahhh-LOOOOSSSHHH!" went the tree.

It missed the desperately-retreating Deadeye by less than ten feet, but the resulting tidal wave drenched him, then lifted and dunked him. Perfect, surging to his rescue, kept his feet but got a waderful of water. The Heater and Boateater, on the other side of the fallen giant, escaped by stepping behind the hackberry trunk.

Fortunately, at the last second Birdlegs had lain back against the trunk, so the impact did no permanent damage, although he later admitted "it *did* rattle my teeth." His back and shoulders were bruised, and subsequent X-rays for chronic pains a month later revealed that he probably cracked his coccyx at this time. Or "broke his tailbone," as Heater put it.

The Jake's troubles were not over, though. There is probably written somewhere a Law of Fallen Trees which states that when a tree falls in water, gravity continues to affect it and the heavier side tends to float down. One side of this tree had approximately one hundred fifty pounds of boy, gun, shells, and stand on it. Gravity asserted itself. The log rolled over.

There was a very brief period when no pressure was on the safety belt release, but Birdlegs failed to release at the strategic time. After the log rolled, the boy was hanging face-down underwater from his belt, still clinging to his brand-new gun.

Part III: Age 15

The Jakes camped out all year long, but of course their favorite time was fall and winter. Hot-weather camping in the South is at times almost unbearable. In the first place, it is so hot! The humid summer heat is like a heavy, moist, steamy blanket carried about on one's shoulders, and makes sleeping in a sleeping bag outdoors well-nigh impossible. The bag itself gains five pounds a night by sweat-soaking, and within a week will send any self-respecting skunk into a state of shock.

A campfire or even a lantern just adds to the heat, and attracts swarms of buzzing, stinging insects. Wasps, hornets, ground bumblebees, and honeybees are common at summer campsites, and once a whole swarm of bees invaded the Jake Camp right at dusk and took up housekeeping in the tent. Mosquitoes, gnats, sweat bees, horse flies, and biting flies also contribute to the camper's discomfort.

And of course, there are the snakes. Even a non-poisonous snake is cause for a great deal of excitement when it shows up in a crowded tent at night. And dread of the poisonous ones is sometimes sufficient reason for staying home, even if the fish are biting. In almost every gathering of Southern sportsmen, someone can heist a pants leg and show a snakebite scar.

Finally, there are the creepy-crawlies: centipedes, spiders, fire ants, chiggers, fleas, and ticks. These pests are more subtle, invading one's privacy undetected and then making their presence painfully known in often embarrassing places. Sometimes the embarrassment is worse than the pain.

The Jakes awoke one late-summer morning after a frog-gigging expedition the night before. As they moseyed about performing their wake-up rituals — teeth-brushing, hair-combing, breakfast root beer, latrine visits — the other boys suddenly heard the Heater shout from the latrine area. "Hey!! Get offa there, you little . . ." His voice became muffled. A moment later, he walked awkwardly back into Camp, several shades lighter than his normal tan.

"Whatcha got?" queried Deadeye.

The Heater hesitated. "I got a problem," he finally admitted, his hands in front of him in a strange position.

"What it is?" Boateater asked lightly.

"Umm, I might need to go see Doctor Mac," the Heater ventured reluctantly.

Now, for a Jake to voluntarily suggest a visit to a doctor is indicative of a serious mental problem, whether there are physical infirmities or not. The others gathered anxiously around the obviously worried Heater. "What's wrong?" Perfect asked his cousin.

"Well . . . um . . . er . . . well . . ." the Heater fidgeted nervously, still in his strange stance. "Errr . . . well . . . look! You ain't gonna b'lieve where I got a tick!"

They didn't.

"I ain't b'lieving that!" Deadeye drawled.

"Believe it!" Perfect said grimly.

"Gaah-leee! He's fixin' to go in!" observed Birdlegs. The Heater gasped and sat down to see for himself.

"Naw, he ain't movin' atall," reassured Boateater. "Y'know, I never hearda one there."

"I think I better go see Doctor Mac," the Heater repeated, "but one-a y'all gotta drive." He obviously was not willing to leave the tick unattended for any length of time.

"Saturday mawnin'," Deadeye pointed out. "Doc's either fishin' or playin' golf."

"'Course, we could always go whuppin' out across the golf course in the jeep," Boateater suggested, "yellin' 'Hey, Doc! Come get this tick offa Heat . . .'"

"Shut up!" the victim interrupted. "This ain't funny!"

"Tuesday night they said on TV that some folks in Wyoming died of Rocky Mountain Spotted Tick Fever," Deadeye informed them helpfully. He considered judiciously. "But I don't think they said where they was bit. Myself, I'd guess a fella would die quicker bitten from the inside, though. An' that's where it looks like yours is headed."

"He ain't mine!" The Heater was getting angry.

"Well, he ain't mine!" Birdlegs assured him.

"If he was mine, I'd move him, though," was Boateater's observation.

"I tried. He's stuck! You wanna try?"

Boateater demurred politely. "I ain't touchin' 'im there. Thanks anyway."

Perfect was serious. "Hey, you guys. We gotta do somethin'. Whadda you do to get a tick to turn loose? I know if you leave the head in, it gets infected an' your . . . whatever . . . rots off." Heater turned another shade lighter and began to breathe audibly.

"Hey, put gas on it!" Birdlegs exclaimed.

"No way!" The Heater was firm. "You 'member when we turpentined that tomcat last month?"

"Yeah. That scoun'nel left at a hunnerd miles an hour an' we haven't seen him since!" Birdlegs looked speculatively at Heater. "I bet you'd outrun the jeep."

"We could tie 'im to a tree first," Boateater was barely holding back a smirk. The Heater made a mental note to avenge himself on this Jake, assuming he survived.

"You put somethin' hot on 'im an' he'll move," Deadeye drawled. "My dad sticks a lighted cigarette to 'em when they're on our dogs."

No one had any cigarettes, but Perfect stepped to the cypress log and procured a box of matches. "How you wanna do this?" he asked Heater.

"Strike one, let it burn for a second, blow it out, an' stick it to his butt!" Heater gritted.

Perfect first offered the matchbox to the other Jakes, who drew back. "Go ahead," invited Birdlegs graciously.

Perfect struck, paused, blew, and held the match toward the tick. Just before it reached its mark, though, the match flared back up. "Hey!" Heater bellowed, more in anticipation than pain. "Blow the durn match out first!" He knocked the burning stick from Perfect's hand. Birdlegs snickered.

Perfect tried again, being sure the match was really blown out this time; but by the time the burnt head reached the tick, it wasn't hot enough to cause a reaction. Except from Heater.

"Hold it still, man!" Boateater directed, noting the problem. "Don't draw back!"

"Durnit, it's doin' it by itself!" the Heater answered.

A third and forth match produced no movement from the tick, but the same scientifically interesting reaction from the insect's perch. "Do that again!" Birdlegs requested, fascinated.

"This ain't workin'!" Heater declared. "Seems like I read that coverin' 'em with Vaseline will make 'em pull their head out to breathe. Try that."

"We ain't got any Vaseline," reported Deadeye after a search of the medical kit in the hollow log. "What can we substitute?"

The Jakes were lost in thought for only a moment before Birdlegs found a solution. "Grease!" he announced. "We'll use grease from the jeep!"

He strode to the vehicle, stooped and reached a long arm under the back, and came out with enough grease to cover a tick the size of a canecutter rabbit. "Got a'plenty?" asked Deadeye.

"You ain't smearin' that black stuff on me!" Heater declared.

"Shoot-a-mile! I ain't fixin' to touch you." Birdlegs added another medical worry to the Heater's troubles. "If you go messin' around with that, you get AIDS! Put it on yourself." He held out the handful of grease to the victim.

"Aw, you don't get AIDS from gettin' ticks off!" Boateater scoffed.

"Well, you could, too. If it's in the blood, it'd be in the tick, wouldn't it?" Perfect didn't help his cousin's feelings.

"Yeah, but Heater would have to have it first!" Boateater insisted.

"Not if the tick got it from somebody else's blood before he bit Heater!" Deadeye pointed out with chilling logic.

The subject of the discussion gave a resigned sigh. "Gimme the grease," he said. He smeared the tick liberally with the black goo and wiped his hand on his jeans. The Jakes gathered to observe the insect's reaction.

"Betcha a buck he moves in...three minutes," Birdlegs offered, glancing at his watch.

"You're on," Boateater agreed. "Heck, I can hold *my* breath longer than three minutes."

"Be ready to head 'im off in case he tries to go in," Deadeye advised helpfully.

Ten minutes later, the tick still had not moved. "Reckon he's dead?" asked Perfect.

Birdlegs pulled out his belt knife and struck a match to hold under the six-inch blade. "Lemme heat my knife blade an' lay the hot steel on his little tail!" he suggested.

Boateater wiped imaginary sweat from his brow. "Whew! Heater thought you was sterilizin' it like Wacky Mack did, to cut it an' . . ."

"I ain't gotta take this kinda stuff!" the Heater suddenly roared, standing. He whipped out a handkerchief, removed the covering grease, grasped the offending tick with thumb and index finger, ripped it loose, and zipped up his jeans. "Let's go fishin'!" he ordered.

Birdlegs was disappointed, having gone to the trouble to heat his knife blade, but the others were somewhat concerned. However, they rose to gather their fishing gear and followed the Heater to the jeep. Deadeye was the last in, as usual, and he was the first to speak as they spun out of Camp.

"If it starts swellin' up, you know it's 'bout to fall off," he instructed their driver.

*   *   *   *   *   *   *

Boateater was the first of the Jakes to obtain his driver's license, as he was the first one to turn fifteen. Armed with this pass to a whole new world of freedom, there was a period of nearly three months when he lorded it over the other Jakes. He could go farther from home; he could get there faster; once he got there that quick, he could go into places with people doing things never experienced by a Jake before. In a world that is often too reluctant to pass judgement, it is nevertheless safe to say that all this came under the general heading of "It's Bad For You!"

The other Jakes reached this conclusion on their own, though their parents would have concurred had they been consulted. As a matter of course, the parents were unanimous about not giving the rest of the boys blanket permission to accompany Boateater — or any of their newly-licensed classmates, for that matter — on unspecified forays into The World. The rules were: "we need to know where you're going, you need to go there, we need to know what time you'll be home, and you need to call if for any reason you can't make it by that time."

Boateater's parents had this same set of rules. (Actually, these commandments are printed in the Bible, but their exact chapter and verse are kept a closely-guarded secret until a couple has a teenage child.) However, the restrictions were

harder on Boateater than the rest of the Jakes simply because it was his vehicle. If six boys went to the picture show, which was over at nine, and they were allowed a half-hour to get a hamburger after the show, then another half-hour to get everyone home, Boateater's parents felt the newly-turned fifteen-year-old should be back by ten. They cut the boy a half-hour's slack to be fair, and carved it in stone: 10:30 P.M.

Naturally, what happened was that the other boys told their parents, "Well, Boateater can stay out 'til ten-thirty." The standard having been set, parents acquiesed to their sons' pleading, and ten-thirty became everyone's deadline.

What the parents did not realize, being so far removed from the situation in their own memory ("Did they have cars when you were a kid, Dad?"), was that they were putting Boateater in the position of having to take his passengers home before their curfews, in order to make his own. Since the Heater and Perfect lived in the country, and Deadeye and Birdlegs in different parts of town, it took even an adult driver a good half-hour to get all the Jakes delivered. By "puttin' the pedal to the metal," Boateater could cut five minutes off, but that was all. Therefore, he needed to head for the country by ten, taking the Heater and Perfect home a full half-hour before they felt it necessary. Boateater's past sins came back to haunt him. "C'mon, candy! We ain't gotta be home for a long time. Don't your folks trust you? Gotta get your bottle and be tucked in? Candy, candy! C'mon, candy!"

Naturally, the young driver rebelled, staying out later, without calling his parents ("You gotta check in every ten minutes?" — this for a once-a-night call). Naturally, his parents got mad and grounded him. Naturally, the other Jakes teased him. And naturally, he became even more rebellious. If his folks said don't go somewhere he went there simply because they said not to. All this is also in the Bible, for those who care to look. It has been so since Cain was handed the reins to the family unicorn. Years later, when Cain got in trouble for killing Abel, it was not simply because of a sacrifice. The root of the trouble went back to when Abel also turned fifteen and was handed the unicorn's reins with the admonition, "Now, for Yahweh's sake, don't go horsin' around like your older brother did!" And Abel didn't, only because he had already observed the friction that such rebelliousness caused.

And so did the slightly younger Jakes learn, at Boateater's expense, the perils of rebelliousness. While never realizing what part their own agitations had played in their comrade's troubles, they all made vows "not to act like that when I get *my* license!" At least, some benefit was gained from the experience.

One Saturday night on patrol, Deputy Don was routed to a reported one-vehicle accident just outside of town. Upon arriving at the scene, he recognized Boateater's truck in the ditch, and was relieved to see the boy perched dejectedly on the side of the pickup bed, unhurt. The lawman left his engine running and lights on to illuminate the scene, and walked over.

"What happened?" he asked.

"Aw, I was goin' a little fast comin' into this curve an' ole Elroy Jernigan was comin' from th'other way. He took a little bit more than his side, an' when my right wheel got into the gravel, it started fishtailin' an' I couldn't catch it."

"What're you doin' out here this time-a night, anyway?" the lawman spoke as a friend, not officially.

"It didn't happen 'this time-a night'!" the boy protested. "I been sittin' here forty-five minutes. Ole Elroy had been drinkin' a little, an' he had to come look *everything* over 'steada goin' to call right away."

"*You* been drinkin'?" the question sounded official this time.

"No, sir," was the glum reply. "But I might as well have. My folks are gonna kill me dead anyway."

Deputy Don rolled his eyes. "We'll git 'em for murder if they do." He paused. "They know where you are?"

"Doubt it," the Jake was low. "Can I go home with you?"

"What's the damage to the truck?" Deputy Don ignored Boateater's question. He walked around the vehicle as the boy boosted himself off the side and followed. Except for a slightly-bent right rear fender, it appeared that there was no major damage. The lawman made a decision.

"C'mon, let's go back to my car an' call your folks. Looks

like everything's awright 'cept a fender, less'n you got a bent axle or tie rod. I know ole Elroy well enough to borrow his tractor. We'll pull it out an' see."

The Deputy had the department dial Boateater's number and then "patch in" so that he could talk directly to the boy's parents. They had never met him, but they knew the lawman by reputation, and were grateful for news of their overdue son. Deputy Don winked at Boateater as he spoke. "Aw, naw, it wasn't the boy's fault atall. Coupla hours ago a drunk ran 'im off the road, but I don't believe the truck's hurt. Know the boy ain't. I'll help 'im get it out, an' if there's any doubt, I'll either follow 'im home, or bring 'im myself." He listened for a moment, then said reassuringly, "Ain't no sense in that. Time you'd get over here, we'd be out an' gone. Y'all go on to bed. I'll take care-a this boy. He's a good friend-a mine!" He listened again. "Yes, sir. Bye now."

Twenty minutes later, the pickup was out of the ditch, obviously all right, and the pair were waving to Elroy Jernigan as he putted away on his old tractor. "How's he keep that ole thing runnin'?" wondered Boateater.

"You talkin' about the tractor, or Elroy?" joked Deputy Don, who had called in his report and now switched his engine off.

During their few minutes together, Boateater had poured out his resentments toward his parents' restrictive and distrustful attitudes, glad of an adult ear. Now as he grasped the door handle, he again voiced his sentiments. "Well, thanks, Deputy Don. Guess I'll go home an' get reamed out again!"

The deputy stopped him, and boosted himself onto the side of the truck, motioning for the boy to join him. "Son," the man said, "lemme tell you a story." He fixed his eyes on the quarter moon, took a deep breath, and began.

"Years ago, I had a boy, about your age. Called 'im Don L. He growed up so fast, an' got to where he was stayin' out half the night, near'bout every night. I came down on 'im mighty hard an' we got to fussin' an' fightin' every time we was around one another. I wanted 'im to come in an' do right, an' he wanted to prove he could drink all the beer an' chase all the women in the world.

"Finally, I gave up; knowin' I was wrong, but not wantin' no more fightin'. Told 'im if he was man enough to do all that, he was man enough to stay out long's he wanted to, even if he did have a job. He'd stood me down an' quit school in the eighth grade." He paused and sighed, looking down at the road now. The cicadas were raising a din in the nearby moss-hung oaks of the Brush Arbor. From the same direction, a screech owl wailed, "wooo-ooo-ooo-ooo-ooo." Boateater dared not speak and break the deputy's train of thought.

The man squinted unnecessarily at the moon again. "Waal, about a week after that knock-down drag-out when I gave up, I got a call around five in the mawnin'; five-seventeen, per-zac'ly. Never forget. Don L had done run offa the ole creek bridge — right yonder —" he pointed, "an' got pinned in the car with one leg cut plum to the bone." Boateater heard the raw pain in the man's voice. "An' Doctor Mac's report said . . . it said . . ." a deep audible breath, "said . . . it took Don L nigh onto four hours to bleed to death."

There was another pause. "Son, your daddy had already called a coupla other Jakes to see where you was. I had 'im call 'em back to tell 'em you're okay. I sent my boy off thinkin' I didn't care whether he came in or not. I didn't call nobody." He pointed again as he finished. "Every time I look at that creek bridge the water looks red to me. Sometimes on a smooth patrol I park on that bridge an' listens. An' sometimes I hear him whimperin' down in that red water." The screech owl called again. "Hear 'im?"

Boateater could barely speak, but forced out, "It's just a screech owl."

"To you, that's an owl. Til I die, that'll be my Don L." In the darkness, the boy could see the whites of the man's eyes as Deputy Don turned toward him. "Son, *now* you know why your daddy wants to know where you are?"

"Yes, sir," Boateater breathed. "Now I understand!"

* * * * * * *

A new gymnasium had been built that summer and, as with

any school project, construction had not been completed before classes started. One afternoon after school, Boateater's truck wouldn't crank, and Deadeye and Birdlegs, the other town Jakes, were pooling their ignorance with the driver's to try to solve the problem. As they tapped this and thumped that, one of the younger members of the construction crew walked over to help.

"Sounds like the automatic choke," he observed, grinning a greeting. He was a tall boy, slim, with overlong hair and a limp, uneven mustache. From ten feet away it looked like the kid had drunk chocolate milk for breakfast and not wiped his mouth.

"Yeah, I thought so, too," drawled Deadeye. Birdlegs shot him a dirty look.

"Got a screwdriver and a pair of pliers?" asked the newcomer.

"Yeah, thanks," Boateater said as he produced the tools. "'Preciate the help. Workin' with these two guys is worse than no help atall."

As the youngster bent over and began fiddling with the air cleaner cover and the carburetor, Birdlegs asked, "You workin' on the new gym?"

"Naw, dummy," Boateater answered for his mechanic, "he's wearin' that li'l ole apron 'cause he cooks and delivers pizza!"

The fellow straightened and looked quizzically at the pickup's driver before Birdlegs could rejoin. "No, I don't," the stranger assured Boateater. "I'm a carpenter's helper. See, this little bag has nails in it . . ."

"I know, I know," Boateater interrupted. "I was just kiddin' these guys. Can you fix it?"

The new kid shook his head. "I never know when you Southerners are serious." He leaned back under the hood and did something with the screwdriver. "Try it now," he said.

Sure enough, it caught. "Toldja that's what it was," drawled Deadeye.

"You never did! You wouldn't know an automatic choke from a hydrophonic boat!" Boateater rejoined. "Show me what you did," he asked the stranger politely.

125

The mechanically-minded youngster indicated how he had placed the screwdriver, and showed them how to remove the air cleaner cover to get to the carburetor. As he finally closed the hood, Boateater thanked the boy. "Much obliged. How much do I owe you?"

The billfold was waved away. "Not a thing. It didn't take but a minute."

"Wouldn'ta taken that long if it hadn'ta been for havin' to put up with these two dummies," the driver indicated Deadeye and Birdlegs. "If you won't charge for fixin' the truck, how much do you charge for havin' t' put up with folks like these?"

"Hundred dollars apiece!" grinned the kid with the mustache.

Boateater stepped into the truck and closed the door. "Right! Pay up, you guys!"

The stranger burst out laughing. Then, pointing to the .22 rifle in the truck's gun rack, he said seriously, "Really, I won't charge you, but I'd love to get to go hunting with you sometime. I've never been hunting."

"Never been huntin'!" the Jakes chorused.

As the kid shook his head, Boateater came forward with true Christian charity. Part of the invitation was gratitude for his now-cranked pickup, but part was genuine concern for one so deprived. "Never been huntin'!" he repeated. "Well, we'll take care of that tomorrow night!"

And The Rookie became a Jake.

The Heater and Perfect were at first reluctant to share their campfire with a complete stranger, especially one who spoke with a Yankee accent. But the Rookie was quick to correct this impression, disclosing that he was originally from California. At this, Perfect turned to Heater in all seriousness and said, "Let 'im stay. He needs our help."

"Well . . . we ain't gonna catch any-a those exotic California diseases, are we?" the Heater asked with a straight face.

"Oh, Golly-Wolly, no," the Rookie assured him. "I had to have a complete physical to work for the construction company. You won't catch anything from me. Unless I catch it here," he added as an afterthought.

"Better watch out for ticks, then," warned Deadeye. The Heater threw a burning glance at him while the others broke into laughter. Since the Rookie didn't understand, that precipitated a round of story-telling. It was nearly midnight when they finally hit the sack.

Early the next morning, there was no small competition to see who would take the Rookie with them to teach him how to squirrel hunt. Boateater and Deadeye finally claimed the honor, and two groups of boys left Camp in different directions just after daylight.

The Rookie had no concept of moving slowly and quietly in the woods, and as a result every squirrel the trio saw was out of shotgun range. Within an hour, the Rookie was beginning to doubt the competence of his guides. "When do we start shooting squirrels?" he asked.

"Waal," Deadeye drawled, winking at Boateater, "first you have to find their homes. Then you have to chase them out so the guys on the ground can get a shot. There's a nest now," he pointed about twenty feet up in a half-dead pecan at the edge of the Swamp. "Reckon we oughta let Rookie have first chance?"

"To do what, exactly?" the Rookie sounded rather dubious.

"Climb the tree, shake the limb where the nest is, and when the squirrels run out, we'll shoot 'em," explained Boateater.

"Nothin' to it," observed Deadeye.

The newcomer seemed reticent to make his admission, but finally did so. "You fellows are going to think I'm a sissy, but, well . . ." he flushed, "this is the first time I've ever been in the woods. I was raised in the city. I've never climbed a tree!" he wailed.

"Never climbed a tree!" Deadeye echoed.

"You show 'im, boss," Boateater encouraged.

Hoist on his own petard almost literally, Deadeye never hesitated. Without a word, he breeched his gun, stood it against the tree, and went up the trunk like the squirrel he was in quest of. In less than a minute he was directly under the limb with the nest, where he hesitated and warned his companions below, "Now don't shoot me!" He looked pointedly at the Rookie. "Watch close, so you can do the next one." He inched out from the trunk, stood on his tiptoes to reach the nest limb, and shook vigorously.

It was a dead limb.

With a loud crack it broke, and the Jake pitched forward head-first.

"Good Golly Greenwood!" whispered Boateater, dropping his gun and heading for the other side of the tree.

He hadn't noticed the Rookie, who stood with gun shouldered and now cried in surprise, "He's bringing it down with him!" Apparently, the custom was to shake the squirrels from the nest once one had it on the ground.

The only thing that saved Deadeye was that he fell into the soggy earth at the edge of the Swamp. Although his companions thought he would land on his head and break his neck, at the last possible second he twisted to take the impact on one shoulder. "Squish!!" was the sound he made, as mud splattered for ten feet.

Boateater knelt, unsure where to start first aid. Deadeye's glasses had not even been dislodged, though his eyes were tightly shut. His breathing seemed little more than normal. Finally, eyes still closed, he tentatively wriggled his fingers; then wrist, arm, and knee. Both arms and legs worked. Still without any help from the two companions who knelt at his side, Deadeye slowly contorted to check hip, backbone, and neck. Only when he was sure nothing was broken did he open his eyes.

He looked questioningly at Boateater, who answered, "Yeah, we're prob'ly gonna get in trouble for this!"

The Rookie observed, "I don't know, but I don't want to do the next one!" He paused, considering. "Matter of fact, I'm not sure I'm going to like squirrel hunting!"

Early on, Papa Jake had taught the Jakes how to care for their game. "If you catch it or kill it, you gotta clean it and cook it!" was the rule. The man had realized that this group of boys showed promise of becoming ardent outdoorsmen at an early age, and he wasn't about to get roped into cleaning all their game. Nor were they allowed to let anything go to waste. The only exceptions were the predators like wild dogs, coyotes, turtles, and wild housecats; the nuisances like beaver, muskrat, nutria, skunk, and armadillos; and the dangerous like poisonous snakes and wild dogs. Though bobcats, foxes, the occasional panther or alligator, minks, possums, otters, and coons fell into some of the above catagories, they were pro-

·tected species in the Woods. Besides, except for panthers and alligators, Wacky Mack kept the populations of the others at controllable levels with his wintertime trapping.

The Heater made the cleaning of wild game almost an educational experience, once he got the hang of it. Of course, that itself took a few years. The first deer that the boy field-dressed by himself was reported by Wacky Mack, who had heard the twelve-year-old's shot while running his trapline one morning. As the woodsman told Papa Jake, "He was so bloody I wasn't sure who had gutted out whom. Looked like he'd cut a li'l hole in th' buck, then crawled in an' pushed everything out in fronta 'im!"

Without being morbid, the Heater would open up the fish, bird, or animal, and examine it for anything out of the ordi-nary in the innards. Simply by observation, he could identify lungworm, liver flukes, intestinal parasites, old injuries or wounds, and diseased organs. If there was an audience, he would explain these problems, as well as the bodily functions often either regarded as mysteries or taken entirely for granted by the other boys.

For several years, it kept Doc McClendon on his toes just to stay ahead of the Heater, as the physician once observed to Other Mother. She was amused by her son's interest also, in later years claiming, "I knew he was either going to be a doctor or an axe murderer!"

The Rookie now became the new recipient of this knowl-edge. The newcomer had absolutely no idea of how the body — rabbit, fish, deer, or human — worked, and was fascinated by the details. Muscles, bones, ligaments, heart, liver, intes-tines, genitals: he wanted to know it all. And in teaching him, the Jakes realized anew many things they had come to take for granted over their years together. Suddenly, they came to the realization that they not only knew, but understood stuff that many people in the world did not.

Fortunately, this new appreciation of their own knowledge and talents did not "puff them up," as The Good Book puts it. Instead, they became eager to share with this new Jake who was equally as eager to learn. Having discovered that they knew something worth teaching, they became teachers —

teachers who genuinely cared that their pupil learn what they could teach — the best kind. Their enthusiasm was indeed catching.

The other Jakes were just as important to the Rookie's education, though at times he sorely tried their tempers and patience. Perfect taught him gun care and safety, and any other Jake would have severly chastised the Rookie when he prematurely released a spring during the reassembly of Perfect's .22 and it took three hours to find all the parts ejected into the dark away from the campfire. Hunter safety was probably the hardest lesson to impart to the newest Jake, who was so happily enthusiastic about his new world.

Birdlegs took it upon himself to make a marksman of the Rookie, and was quickly successful with pistol and rifle. With a shotgun, however, the task seemed almost hopeless; the pupil just could not grasp the principle of "leading" a target. Ballistics was a campfire subject night after night, and finally Birdlegs remembered a story from Robert Ruark's *Old Man and the Boy* series involving a running boy and a water hose. The Jakes returned to the Heater's house and were just beginning to get the idea across when Other Mother interrupted the lesson, pointing out that it was "forty degrees outside and you're all gonna catch pneumonia!"

Deadeye, who had always been able to observe for hours on end without moving a muscle, was a natural choice to reveal the mysteries of wildlife behavior to the Rookie. The discussions on these observations generated a great many campfire semi-arguments. While most of the Jakes knew that wildlife did certain things, their new companion always wanted to know "Why?" and their various explanations often conflicted. Disagreement spurred research, and while teaching, the teachers themselves learned.

Once, when the Rookie took his turn gathering wood and building a campfire, he nearly killed Boateater and Perfect, who were allergic to poison ivy. In his ignorance, the boy had thrown several dead vines on the pile of wood, and breathing the smoke for only a short time resulted in the two victims' fast trip to the hospital emergency room. Perfect was barely able to breathe through swollen, constricted air passages, and both

131

youngsters' eyes were swollen completely shut by the time Doc McClendon arrived. When the two were discharged after two days in the hospital, Boateater grimly resolved to teach the Rookie everything there was to know about camp craft. He even gave written tests, which the pupil guiltily welcomed. Within a month the Rookie could identify every kind of tree and wild vine indigenous to the Woods, and by the end of the year was positve about the woody growth in six Southern states. Boateater was apparently not willing to chance a long-distance wood-gathering operation.

The Rookie balked at learning to cook wild game, however. Indeed, after his first efforts the Jakes were all satisfied that he had no latent talents in this field of endeavor. He had been horrified to watch the Heater frying froglegs on that first weekend when he was invited to Camp.

"Golly-Wolly! They're not even dead yet!" he squealed, as the legs twitched spasmodically in the hot grease.

"Yeah, they are," scoffed the Heater. "You watched me clean 'em."

"Well, I'm not eating any dead frogs!" declared the brand-new hunter.

"How 'bout a steak, then?" asked Boateater.

"Yeah, that would be better," the Rookie sounded relieved.

"Well, steak is just ole dead cow meat," Birdlegs pointed out triumphantly.

"An' po'k chop, sausage, an' ham, sho' is ole dead pig meat," Perfect had his guitar and was strumming a tune for this new litany. "Mutton saddles an' chops of lamb... Is old an' young dead sheep meat!... De drumstick on de plate, an' de fish in de bowl ... Was once scratchiñ' corn, or swimmin' in de hole... An' de shrimp boiled in pots an' de oyster on de shell... Was... "

"All right! All right!" the Rookie interrupted. "I'll try the damn things, but I'm not saying I'll like them."

"C'mon, man," Perfect reproved, "I was just beginnin' to git down! That mighta been a million-seller!"

"Trust me," Deadeye drawled. "It warn't."

"How old are you?" asked Birdlegs of the newcomer. "I bet you ain't old enough to be workin' on that construction crew." Since his father owned the lumberyard, he had seen other youngsters denied employment because of age and liability requirements.

"Don't tell anybody, but I'm only sixteen. I lied about my age to get the job. I'm tall, and I think my mustache makes me look older."

"Trust me," Deadeye repeated. "It don't."

"That a mustache? I thought you jus' hadn't washed your face," observed Heater.

"I figgered that was jus' old snuff stains," Perfect joined in.

"Oh, no, I wash my face morning and night. And snuff goes in your . . . Aw, you guys are just teasing me again!" The Rookie smiled back at the grins of these new-found friends.

"How'dja get outa school?" Boateater wanted to know.

"Just quit. In the big cities like L.A., they don't care. I finished the seventh grade."

"Where're your folks?" Deadeye wanted to know.

"My what?"

"Your folks," was repeated.

The Rookie looked puzzled, glanced around him, and raised his eyebrows in a question at Heater, the cook. "How would I know? You tell him where they are. But I don't mind setting the table, or whatever you want me to do."

The Heater was nonplussed, and not used to having to reveal ignorance on any subject. "I don't have any idea. You oughta know where your own durn parents are!"

"Parents? I thought he was saying 'forks' real lazy. I'm sorry. You Rebels . . ." the boy laughed at his mistake. Then he sobered for the first time since Deadeye had fallen out of the tree that morning. "I really don't know. Never knew my dad. Mom remarried a few years ago and moved away. She said I could come, but I didn't like the guy. She'd been living with him for a while, and he beat both of us."

"So how'd you get here?" The Heater was serving froglegs, pork-and-beans, and toast on paper plates. Perfect got up to fetch some more root beers from the cooler at the sweetgum tree, but his concentration was still on the Rookie's story.

"Got a job, saved money for as long as I could stand the crowds, put back a hundred bucks for food, and bought a ticket on Amtrak to get as far away as I could with the rest of my money. And here I am!" he finished, grinning broadly as he picked up a frogleg.

The Jakes ate in silence for a few minutes, somewhat awed by the tale, and no little bit more appreciative of their own situations. Finally Boateater asked, "Where'd you work?"

"Disneyland," was the rather proud answer.

"Ohhh, yeah," Deadeye wagered speculatively, pointing a frogleg. "I betcha you played Goofy, didn'tcha?"

*　　　*　　　*　　　*　　　*　　　*　　　*

Wacky Mack strolled into the Jake Camp one Friday evening and, without saying a dozen words, accepted an invitation to supper, made himself comfortable, and ate. After the meal, Perfect got his guitar and talked the veteran into accompanying him with his harmonica on several songs. The Rookie was enthralled by this quiet, bearded man, and the Heater finally called the newcomer over to the sweetgum tree to explain things.

"Look, trust me on this. Don't be askin' Wacky Mack any questions. We'll tell you everything 'bout 'im after he leaves, but jus' keep your mouth shut while he's here. Understand?"

"No; why can't I ask stuff? Why's he so quiet? What will happen if I . . ."

"He might jump the tracks an' wipe us out, or somethin'," the Heater hissed. "Hush. Just do what I say, or somebody might get hurt!" He tapped his temple significantly, for once silencing the Rookie.

As the strains of "The Wreck of Old 97" were dying away,

Wacky Mack suddenly held up his hand and cocked his head, listening. The guitarist stopped strumming and the other boys watched the veteran closely.

Way off toward Dundee's Lake there was a wild, lonesome, squalling cry. The Jakes' eyes widened, and the Rookie edged closer to the fire. "What's that?" he whispered to Deadeye.

"Y' got me," was the hushed reply.

The scream sounded again, lingering, hanging in the starlit night, finally dying.

"Son of a three-toed, bare-backed berry picker!" breathed Perfect.

"She-panther," rasped Wacky Mack, his hoarseness adding to the spooky feelings of the youngsters.

"Pan . . . ther?" Deadeye could hardly get the word out.

"Cougar, puma, mountain lion — all th' same," nodded Mack. "Wanted y'all t' hear it."

"A she?" asked the Heater.

"Female in season. Callin' for a mate t' come breed her. Jus' like a she-housecat. Been hollerin' last coupla nights." This was a long speech for the woodsman. "Thought y'all might be int'rested."

"Or scared," Birdlegs suggested.

"Or scared," Wacky Mack agreed. The eerie wail echoed again, farther away. The man stood and brushed his camouflage fatigues. "Don't sweat it. She won't bother you. Jus' wants a mate." Perfect thought he caught a twinkle in the speaker's eye. "Y'all might understand one day. Night." The veteran turned at the edge of the firelight. "'Joyed supper; and playin'." He nodded at the Rookie. "Glad t' meetcha." He disappeared into the darkness as the panther screamed again, far off.

"Shoot-a-mile!" Birdlegs exclaimed. "A panther!"

The Rookie had been raised in a metropolis; he was used to strange sounds. "Forget the panther," he said in little more than a whisper. "Tell me about Wacky Mack."

"Waal," Deadeye was the one to answer, "it's like this: he kinda looks after us, and figured we'd hear that squall and go bananas. So, . . ." The legend of Wacky Mack grew.

During that next week, the Heater, Perfect, and Birdlegs

plotted to play a trick on their mates — this panther episode was too good an opportunity to miss. Birdlegs went down to the public library after school and searched until he found an educational film on video cassette that had a scene involving a panther's scream. He delivered this to Perfect, who took it home, hooked up some of his elaborate recording gear to the VCR, and played with it until he had a pretty good imitation of a panther's scream on an audio cassette tape. He then borrowed one of Uncle Bubba's portable cassette players and made sure it had fresh batteries.

The Heater, meanwhile, removed two red reflectors from Baby Sister's bicycle, snagged a four-foot tomato stake from the garden, glued the reflectors to each end of a ruler, and wired the ruler across the top of the tomato stake. Thursday evening, the three conspirators drove down to Dundee's Lake to check their plan.

With Perfect in a quickly-constructed blind at the base of a big cottonwood just around one bend of the small lake, holding his battery-powered spotlight (recovered from the bottom of the swimming hole), the Heater and Birdlegs walked across a small alfalfa field and lay down in a slight depression. At this distance of nearly seventy-five yards, Birdlegs turned the little recorder up to full volume and pressed "play" while the Heater held up the stake with the reflectors. The panther scream roared out and Perfect's spotlight was immediately shone in that direction. The two red "eyes" glowed like coals of fire in the beam.

"That even scared me!" Perfect yelled.

They experimented with it several more times, until they felt there would be no hitches, and were walking back to the jeep when headlights flashed down the turnrow. As they stopped, the Duke of Dundee drove up.

"What the hell are you all doing down here?" asked the Duke. "Aye thought Aye had caught some headlighting poachers!"

"Oh, no, sir," the boys assured him, and proceeded to demonstrate their practical joke for the Duke's benefit. "Perfect's gonna take the other guys out predator callin' tomorrow night," Heater explained, "an' me an' Birdlegs are gonna tell 'em we're goin' to the football game. But we're gonna be out here first an' when they make that first call we're gonna scare the bejabbers out of 'em!" The boys grinned.

The Duke raised an eyebrow. "You may get your little tee-heinies shot off."

"We thought about that," Perfect informed him. "I'm gonna have the only gun. I'm loadin' Daddy's .38 with blanks."

"Be sure of that!" the Duke said sternly. Then he tipped his hat slightly with two fingers. "Good luck in your subterfuge, gentlemen." He toasted them with a pint bottle, smacked his lips, and drove off with a wave.

Birdlegs shook his head admiringly. "There's a real gentleman!"

"'Cept for his drinkin'," observed Heater, and Perfect nodded agreement.

"Aw, cut 'im some slack!" Birdlegs protested. "Gentlemen drink!" His companions shrugged.

Friday evening, while the other Jakes where in Camp, Uncle Bubba drove the Heater and Birdlegs down to Dundee's Lake and dropped them off, again admonishing them about guns. "No, sir," they reassured him. "Your .38 with blanks is gonna be the only gun out here."

"If it's not, I want you to call it off immediately. Understand?" the man instructed. The boys nodded.

An hour later, a jeep came down the turnrow and parked a hundred yards from the lake. From their vantage point in the alfalfa, the two conspirators watched the other four Jakes walk around the end of the lake and to the blind by the cottonwood. They were too far away to make out the words, but every now and then the high pitch of Rookie's voice would carry to them. "Motor-mouth," Birdlegs grinned.

Soon the callers were apparently situated, for the big spotlight flashed on and swung around to survey the area. Then even the small flashlight went out, and they again heard the Rookie's voice, this time raised in protest. After nearly fifteen minutes of darkness and silence, the agonized squeals of a crippled rabbit pealed out from the blind.

"Let 'em do it a coupla times," instructed Heater.

Twice more the rabbit cried out, and then Birdlegs cut the recorder to low volume and punched "play." Heater jumped involuntarily as a panther squalled. "Um. Scared me and I knew about it," he muttered.

Momentarily, they saw a glimmer from the small flashlight, and recognized Perfect's voice in remonstrative tones. The rabbit squeals started once more. "Let 'em do it again," whispered Heater.

This time, Birdlegs turned the volume up a little.

Once again, the crippled rabbit squealed. The Heater nudged Birdlegs and held up his stake, as the operator of the tape player turned the machine to full volume. "Here goes!"

In the blind, Perfect was in charge of both caller and spotlight and was ready. As the loud scream started, he flipped the light switch and yelled, "There he is!"

The Rookie was crouched just in front of the other three, and had decided to take dip of snuff to calm his nerves. He had opened a brand-new can when the scream began, seemingly right in front of the blind, and he glanced up to see two fierce red eyes burning into his own. When Perfect yelled from right behind him and fired the .38, it was too much. He bolted for the jeep.

In bolting, he unconsciously flipped the snuff can over his shoulder. Right into the faces of Perfect, Deadeye, and Boateater.

These latter two were in the act of bolting themselves, and Perfect, seeing the panic beginning just as planned, couldn't control his mirth. He started to burst into laughter. But the actions of bolting and laughing require deep breaths in order for participation to be to the fullest degree. Deadeye, Boateater, and Perfect sucked in full breaths — of snuff.

The Rookie was out of the blind at full gallop when the first explosive sneezes began behind him, just as the panther screamed again. He had never experienced a panther attack before, but the choked yells, wheezing, and sneezing from the blind in conjunction with the fourth and fifth panther screams, sounded much like one, he imagined. Under the impression that he was the sole survivor, he lined out for the jeep like a greyhound·

The fifth scream had not come from Birdlegs' tape player. Rather, it had sounded from less than fifty yards behind the two boys lying unarmed in the alfalfa field. The Heater looked at Birdlegs, who was looking back at him. "Did you hear that?" they whispered at the same time. Before either answered, the panther screamed again, closer.

Luckily, the tape recorder's strap was draped across Birdlegs' shoulder, or it would have been left. The two Jakes sprinted toward the jeep themselves. They rounded the lake just in time to hear the engine crank and see the lights flash on as the vehicle roared away in a cloud of dust.

Puffing, wheezing, and snorting, the other three Jakes came running up with the small flashlight. "Where you guys . . ." Boateater started, then the beam of light swept across the tape player. "Uh-oh, we been had!" he began again, his face contorting in anger.

"Hey, wait, y'all!" the Heater threw up his hands in protest. "We *did* start it, but . . ." He was interrupted by yet another scream. "But we're all here now!" he exclaimed. "That's real!"

Perfect grabbed the flashlight and pointed it down the dirt turnrow. "Well, I ain't gonna stand here an' talk about it!" He spoke grimly. "No tellin' where our jeep is by now. Prob'ly Omaha. Let's put some distance 'tween us an' that cat!" They all began trotting down the road, keeping close together and glancing back often. "We can get my big light tomorrow," Perfect puffed.

Two sets of eyes watched them go as the Duke flipped his recorder to "off." Wacky Mack shook his head. "That was mean, Duke," he rasped.

"Aye know," was the reply. "Served them right, did it not?" He took a drink.

*   *   *   *   *   *   *

The Rookie's last lesson almost had tragic consequences. That year, the State granted hunters a fall turkey season in an area that included the Woods. The Jakes greeted the news of the ten-day season with appropriate enthusiasm.

The Heater was blinded in at the base of a big cypress at the edge of the Swamp, calling about every ten minutes. The other Jakes were scattered across the Woods as usual, including the Rookie, who was hunting by himself that morning. The newcomer's patience had worn thin after the first hour, though, and he arose and began slipping along the Swamp edge, where the ground was soft enough to deaden his steps. He looked and listened eagerly for turkeys, which he had observed many times before while hunting other game.

Soon he heard a hen call, and paused to get a better direction on the sound. The call was repeated and Rookie, not sure of his own calling, and uncertain how far away the turkey was, decided to get closer. Using his new-found skills, he sneaked along from tree to tree silently in the damp earth.

When the hen called again, he was surprised at how close it seemed, and froze behind a pecan tree to search the Woods in front of him. Once more he heard the sound, and now he located it just beyond a large cypress tree nearly sixty yards ahead of him. Hens being legal that season, he raised his shotgun, wondering, "Will this thing shoot that far?" and waited for his quarry to walk around the side of the tree. Sure enough, there was a movement, and the Rookie fired.

The Heater had thought a couple of times that he had heard something behind him. Moving as cautiously as possible, he eased his right hand out for support and leaned over to see if a turkey was slipping in. Fortunately, he was still in the act of turning his head when the shot boomed.

Pain seared his arm just below the elbow, and a blow to the head stunned him only momentarily. He jerked back behind the tree bellowing "Hey! Hey! Heeeyyy!!" The hand that he raised to his forehead came away bloody and, as he looked, blood welled up from his forearm. "Some durn sonuvabitch shot me!" he muttered, then proceeded to point this out to the party responsible. "You sonuvabitch, you shot me!"

"Who's that?" came a high-pitched shout that Heater recognized. Once again he reached to touch his forehead, just above the eye. While he *was* bleeding, he realized the wounds were glancing cuts from the number six shot, not entrance holes that indicated pellets in his brain. Knowing he was not mortally wounded, he chose an agressive retaliation that gave vent to his anger. "RrrrAAARRRgggg!!!" roared the Heater, and jumped to his feet.

"Who's that?" the Rookie said again, and he got his answer. Cap off to reveal a bloody, snarling visage, the Heater charged around the cypress tree, gun at port arms. As the shooter stepped out from behind the pecan, the shootee raised his own weapon.

"You sonuvabitch, you better run!" came the agonized bellow, just before the blast. Bits of bark and small limbs flew from the pecan tree just above his head, and the Rookie dropped his gun, spun, and fled.

"RrrrAAAAARRRRggggghhhh!!!" The Heater roared his war cry and charged in pursuit.

The Rookie was faster anyway, and fear lent wings to his heels. The distance began to increase rapidly between the two hunters, and was probably seventy-five yards when another shot boomed and the Rookie felt pellets striking his backside. He screamed and jumped clean over a sycamore top that most full-grown whitetail deer in flight would have gone around.

While he was as mad as a wet hen, the Heater had not lost control. He was well aware of the damaging range of number six twelve-gauge magnum shells, and knew that the Rookie was wearing a heavy hunting coat with a double-lined game pocket that covered his vitals from shoulder blade to mid-buttock. By aiming low, he reckoned that the only area where a pellet might penetrate the boy's jeans was between his knee boots and the lower hem of the coat. Heater was enraged, but in the midst of his red-hot anger there was an ice-cold control center telling him, "We're gonna teach this guy a lesson!"

"RrrrAAARRRgggg! Boom!" The Jake and his shotgun roared, the brush top audibly taking the brunt of the load right behind the runner. The range was increasing, but then the Rookie glanced over his shoulder and hit a grapevine, tumbling head over heels. The Heater rounded the brush top to see his assailant just rising, poised for a second like a sprinter in the starting blocks. Range reduced to seventy yards, the boy fired again.

Had the jeans not been drawn tight across his thighs and bottom, the Rookie probably would have escaped the assault with no penetration. But even at that distance a half-dozen of the pellets still had enough energy to come through his jeans and lodge just beneath the skin. Their force and his own terror collapsed him to the ground. As his pursuer charged roaring in for the kill — undoubtably with fixed bayonet — the Rookie vomited in fear and rolled onto his back to make a last-ditch plea for his life.

The Heater fired his last shot (unplugged guns were legal for turkeys) into the air over his quarry, bringing sticks and leaves down into the terrified boy's face. "I'm sorry! I'm sorry!" the Rookie squealed, just short of tears. But repentence was apparently not going to save him.

A few years before, Uncle Bubba had served a term as District Attorney, and had prosecuted several "hunting accident" cases. The Jakes had heard him holding forth several times on the subject: "A man who shoots, but is not absolutely sure of what he is shooting at and consequently injures or kills another man, should be held just as guilty in the woods as in the city!" The Jakes had been taught this, and now one of them was fervently teaching the lesson again.

The Heater, blood trickling down his face and right arm, stood over the Rookie, who now cried, "You shot me, too!"

With awful countenance, the victor pitched his gun to one side, drew his belt knife, brandished the six-inch blade in the air, and roared, "RrrrAAARRRgggg! Yeah! An' now I'm gonna gut you out and *eat* you!"

The Rookie fainted.

The other Jakes, attracted by the shots and yells, arrived in time to prevent the Heater from carrying out his stated intentions. Perfect accompanied him back to Camp for first aid while Birdlegs retraced the scene of battle to collect discarded guns and gear. Boateater and Deadeye eventually roused the Rookie and led him into Camp just as Perfect was popping a second pellet from under the skin on Heater's forearm. The wounds on his forehead were just deep scratches, but the one through his eyebrow bled profusely.

"Don't put the knife and tweezers up yet," Deadeye

142

drawled. "We gotta dig some outa Rookie's butt!"

The Heater smiled coldly and reached for the instruments. "My pleasure," he said. "I'm gonna enjoy this."

Silently, the Rookie dropped his pants and boosted himself face-down over the cypress log. Boateater stepped to the other side to help hold the patient when the wincing started. As the budding physician sterilized the blade again, he spoke almost gloatingly. "I just want you to know this is gonna hurt you a lot more'n it's gonna hurt me!"

This proved to be true, but the patient stood it well, for the six pellets were barely under the skin. When the operation was over, and the area was well painted with iodine (the doctor had disdained mechurochrome. "Doesn't sting enough!"), the Rookie gingerly stood and pulled his pants back on. His voice was not trembling just from the pain as he spoke.

"I'd like to stay, but I know how you must feel about me. I'll leave if you want me to, but . . ." he stuck his hand out to Heater, "please forgive me. I've learned my lesson. I wouldn't have shot you for the world!"

The other Jakes nodded silently to the Heater over the Rookie's shoulder, deferring the decision to the one who had been victimized. Slowly the Heater nodded his head and accepted the Rookie's hand.

"Okay, you stay," he said. "And I wasn't really gonna eat you!"

The wild dog population had been building steadily, in spite of the fact that the Jakes and the landowners stayed on watch for the canines. They destroyed several a month during the hunting seasons, but it was still an undeclared war, as opposed to a declared war. As Deputy Don was to put it later, "They just hadn't never made us mad yet."

However, that fall open hostilites had to be declared. Both

the Duke and Papa Jake lost several cows and calves to wild dogs, and one night on a coon hunt, Scotch and Soda came upon a pack gathered around a bitch in heat. Before the Duke and Uncle Bubba could reach the scene, a dozen males-in-attendance had jumped the blueticks. Scotch was killed and Soda was so severely injured that he had to be put to sleep.

A small pack got into Deputy Don's fowl yard one night and ran amuck. Unlike their wolf kinsmen, wild dogs seem to kill for the fun of it, not just for food. Two thirds of the flock were either killed by the dogs or crippled too badly to survive. Three nights later, probably the same pack returned and got into the hogpen. Two shoats were savaged, but the old sow and boar took their toll of the intruders, and Deputy Don was sleeping lightly, too. Five of the pack never made it back to the Woods.

These incidents and others increased the resolve of the hunters to alleviate the problem, yet their attitude was still "If I see a dog, and nothin' else is around, I'll shoot it." Certainly no one was going to take a chance at scaring a buck or a gobbler off by banging away at non-domestic canines. Even Wacky Mack began to carry a rifle in addition to his usual pistol, but none of them were actually hunting for the dogs, they were just on the lookout for them while hunting other game.

This was to change.

At least a couple of times a month, Baby Sister was making horseback rides to "the ly-berry," as she referred to it in conversation. Papa Jake and Other Mother were still the only ones who knew of these visits, and Papa Jake had sought out Wacky Mack to "be sure she ain't botherin' you." The veteran had shook his head.

"She ain't botherin' me none. You oughta be prouda that girl for readin' so much."

One fall afternoon, Baby Sister was loping along on Polly, headed for "the ly-berry," and was at the edge of the Woods directly behind Deputy Don's

place when a pack of wild dogs burst out of the trees, snarling and barking. The girl screamed and the horse began kicking and pawing in self-defense, sending two of the canines limping back to the Woods. Terrified, the pony wheeled and stampeded, the maddened, howling pack right behind. The dogs were just considering giving up the chase when Polly stepped in an armadillo hole and stumbled. Though she didn't quite go down, her rider did.

Baby Sister took the fall on her shoulder and rolled, somersaulting to her feet with barely a bruise. Normally Polly would have stopped for her to remount, but today they were both panicked by their pursuers. Baby Sister ran screaming behind the horse, but she wasn't fast enough. The pack caught her.

Undoubtedly it would have been a fatal encounter but for Sugarpie. Deputy Don's wife had been planting turnips in the garden when the attack occurred, and at the first barks and screams had charged to the rescue as fast as her bulk could go. Fortunately, Polly's flight had been toward the garden.

Baby Sister had gone down under the pack's initial surge, and that could have been the end of it, but for two things: half the dogs were still chasing the horse; and the girl was clothed in riding boots, heavy jeans, gloves, and a corduroy jacket. She managed to get in a couple of good kicks, keep her face covered, and struggle back to her feet swinging, kicking, and screaming. She had just gone down for the second time when Sugarpie arrived.

"Haaaawww, stay with 'em, chile! Haaaawww, stay with 'em!" the woman bellowed encouragement. She plunged into the fray laying about her with the hoe, and the first two blows split skulls. Baby Sister took heart and regained her feet, but now the half of the pack that had gone after Polly was returning. Sugarpie's hoe handle broke on the third lick, though it opened up the recipient right behind its rib cage. With one arm the woman pulled the girl to her, while with the other she swung her three-foot club. A half-shepherd leapt from behind and locked its fangs into Sugarpie's buttock. Screaming and flailing, she tore lose, just as another cur charged in to rip her leg. The flailing hoe handle broke again, but just then a shot boomed. Deputy Don was on the way!

The lawman was an excellent pistol shot, as was to be expected, and he had run to the house for his .357 magnum revolver when the first sounds of the attack reached him where he was repairing the hogpen fence. Shooting into the massed pack, he disabled nine dogs with his six shots, and the canines could not stand against this assault. The survivors turned tail, leaving their wounded.

With a crying, bleeding female under each arm, Deputy Don hustled straight back to the patrol car. He knew that if he ever let Sugarpie sit down, it would be almost impossible for him to lift her by himself. His charges collapsed into each other's arms in the back seat while he dashed into the house for an armload of towels. Upon his return, he found that his wife had somewhat recovered from shock and was peeling off Baby Sister's ripped, bloody jacket.

"How 'bout it?" he asked, handing her the stack of towels.

"Just get us to the hospital! They can sew me up, but this girl's bleedin' bad up under her arm. Crank the car!" She began applying towels to wounds, staunching the flow of blood.

Deputy Don had his siren and flashers going before he was out of his own yard. "Headquarters, this is Deputy Don," he spoke into the microphone. "I got a 'mergency! Get Doc McClendon to stand by at the hospital. I'm comin' in . . ."

Baby Sister opened her eyes that evening to see her father and mother, Doctor Mac, and Wacky Mack standing around the hospital bed. She was stiff and sore all over, and observed that a tube was taped to her left arm, just above a cast. She felt so weak that she didn't even try to raise her right arm, and her throat was painfully dry when she tried to speak. Doctor Mac leaned over with a glass of water and a straw. After a sip, she was able to force out, "How's Polly?"

Other Mother began to weep anew, but Papa Jake stepped forward to pat his daughter's hand. "She's okay. Mack brought her in."

The pony had come trotting into her usual destination, Wacky Mack's yard, while the man was splitting firewood. Eager for human reassurance, she had walked right up to him, and he was examining her when he heard Deputy Don's siren.

Still holding the axe, Wacky Mack had vaulted aboard Polly and headed for his neighbor's house, full of fear. There, the open door, a towel dropped on the front steps, and drops of blood in the yard led him back to the scene where dead and dying dogs, the broken hoe, fragments of Sugapie's dress and Baby Sister's jacket, and the girl's riding hat had told the story.

He had returned to Don's and called the sheriff's department dispatcher, who filled him in on the known details, for the deputy was still en route to the hospital. Mack had called Papa Jake, who had only just received a patched-in call from Deputy Don. The veteran had locked the house, strode to the corn crib for a croker sack, shouldered the axe, and grimly led Polly back toward the field of battle. He knew that Doc would need the canines' heads to check for rabies. He had taken time to clean up afterwards, and arrived at the hospital with his grisly load just as Baby Sister was being wheeled into Recovery. Wacky Mack felt totally, unconsolably, guilty.

Doc McClendon was speaking matter-of-factly to the girl. "Honey, you're going to be okay. I had to put sixty stitches in you, but most of them won't show, and I tried to be real neat on the ones that will. The worst place was right under your left arm, and you lost some blood there. Your left wrist had a slight fracture, too; either from a bite or the fall, I couldn't tell which. We'll leave that cast on for a couple of weeks, but I won't keep you in here but a day or so. Got any questions?"

The girl indicated that she needed another sip of water, after which she asked, "How's Sugarpie?"

"She's just down the hall, and said she'd come see you when you woke up. I had to put you to sleep to sew you up," he said apologetically. "She had to have nearly as many stitches as you did, but hers were mainly on three bad cuts and tears. She won't be comfortable sittin' down for a while," he observed. "Y'all were both awfully lucky."

He turned to the adults. "Let's let her get some sleep now," and led the way out into the hall. There, he said to Papa Jake, "Mack's brought the dogs' heads to test for rabies. I'm sure there won't be any, but it'll set our minds at ease. Let you know tomorrow. But y'all better do something about those packs."

Wacky Mack nodded. "T'morra." He looked at Papa Jake. "Meet me at the Jake Camp at daylight. Bring Bubba. I'll have Duke. Shotguns, rifles, pistols. Plenty ammo." He turned to stride down the hall, then wheeled and spoke to Other Mother. "I'm sorry."

She smiled and stepped forward, surprising everyone by enveloping the bearded man in a hug. No one else heard what she whispered to him. "It's not your fault!"

        *   *   *   *   *   *   *

After he returned from the hospital, Wacky Mack gathered all his gear together in his jeep and drove around to the Jake Camp. Uncle Bubba was at their fire, having driven in to inform the boys about the attack on Baby Sister. The two adults included the Jakes in their plan of battle for the morrow. The bearded woodsman unrolled an aerial map of the Woods.

"They gen'rally run at night an' lay up in th' day 'til late afternoon. Three main restin' an' dennin' areas here . . ." he indicated the overgrown log dump near Dundee's Lake where the Heater had been attacked, the Locust Thicket on the other end of the Woods where Perfect had missed Ole Cow-foot, and a small island in the Swamp close to where Baby Sister's assailants had been.

"Talked to Duke from th' hospital. Wind's been from th' east early an' it's dry. He an' Big Gus're gonna set th' old log dump afire in th' mornin'. Diesel fuel t' start it." The veteran's voice was becoming hoarse; none of his audience had ever heard him speak so long before. "We'll set up t' get 'em comin' out. Bubba, take Perfect an' Deadeye t' th' north. Heater, your daddy's comin'; you an' him an' Birdlegs spread out west. An' me an' them," he indicated Boateater and the Rookie, "will cut 'em off from th' Canal an' Swamp."

His voice was so scratchy that Deadeye got up and went to the ice chest to get a canned drink for him. Wacky Mack nodded and took a sip gratefully. "Unplugged shotguns — I brought some buckshot — an' .22 rifles. Lotsa shells in my jeep. If they come after you, climb a tree." He leaned back. "Questions?"

"How 'bout th'other two places?" Birdlegs asked.

"One at a time. We got all day," Uncle Bubba took up the discourse from the hoarse veteran. "Now, y'all be damn sure you know *exactly* where the man next to you is; and nobody gets up and goes chargin' around. Stay put and be sure of your shots. Shotguns if they're close, rifles if they aren't, and keep plenty of extra shells close. Be sure what you're shootin' at is a dog. I don't care if Ole Cow-foot comes boilin' out right at you; we're just huntin' wild dogs." He looked at the Rookie. "You hear?"

"Yes, sir!" the newest Jake was emphatic. The other boys nodded.

"See y'all in the mornin'," Uncle Bubba stood. "You comin', Mack?"

The veteran shook his head. His voice was barely audible. "Nah. Thought I'd stay here. If th' Jakes'll let me."

The hunters were in position the next morning when the

Duke and Big Gus drove up to the east side of the old log dump. There was very little dew, and sure enough, the light breeze was from the east. In the back of the pickup was a hundred-gallon tank, and the farmer drove slowly along the edge of the brush while Big Gus stood in the back operating the hand pump and aiming the fuel hose. Diesel spurted twenty feet with each stroke of the pump, soaking the dry growth. At the southeast corner, Big Gus fixed the nozzle into its spout and reached into the cab for a box of kitchen matches. As the Duke turned the truck and started back down the edge, Big Gus struck and flipped matches. Thick black oily smoke curled up behind them and the fire began to spread, drawing more breeze as it fed itself.

The first shots were not at fleeing dogs. Birdlegs was kneeling by a sycamore watching the dense thicket a hundred yards away when he caught a movement out of the corner of his eye. Three dogs were trotting by at thirty yards, unaware of the ambush and headed toward their usual stronghold. The Jake downed one with his first shot, a second with the third shot, and crippled the third cur with his last shotgun blast. The dog limped into the thicket just as the clouds of smoke began to ascend from the opposite side of the log dump.

There had been some speculation around the fire the night before as to the wild dog population, but most of the guesses were way off. Even Wacky Mack, when pressed for an answer, had said "Aww, seventy-five or eighty."

Boateater was being facetious when he estimated "a hundred an' twenny," but his guess was closest. Thanks to the efforts of Stumpy Olson, the small-town dog catcher who had been keeping his pound population down by releasing his charges in the Woods nine miles away (and thereby pocketing some of the food allowance), the total number of wild dogs in the Woods had grown to one hundred forty-two before Baby Sister's attack.

Sixty-one of them were homeported in the old five-acre log dump thickness.

As the flames spread, dogs began to make their escape in all directions, except east into the flames. Shotguns boomed and rifles cracked. Only Deadeye never got a shot, which of course led to later accusations of "sleeping on watch." A pack of six charged Perfect's direction and he killed four with his shotgun before they reached him. Fortunately, Uncle Bubba saw that his son had gotten too far from his rifle and extra shells in the excitement, and he came running to help. He shot the two mongrels as they snarled and bit at Perfect's heels, so the boy suffered only one gash, just above the boot-top.

This was the only human casualty, though. When the fire had burnt out and the hunters tallied their kill, thirty-six canines were dragged up to be piled and burned with the rest of the diesel fuel. Birdlegs, having had a head start, was high man with eight. Although no one could be sure of the exact total, they also counted up at least fifteen that got away but were badly crippled. Wacky Mack vowed to follow these up later, "but now load up an' let's head for th' Locust Thicket," the leader directed.

They detoured by the Jake Camp for root beer, coffee, and the sweet rolls that Papa Jake had thought to bring, and to tend to Perfect's wound. The Jakes were beside themselves with excitement and re-enacted the battle over and over. Birdlegs even had the adults laughing as he mocked Deadeye's war cry: "Hhrroonnk, hhrroonnkk!" he snored.

"I don't like you any more. Take me home," Deadeye grinned.

The plan was slightly different for the attack on the Locust Thicket. The Jakes surrounded the dense grove while the four adults invaded it to both ambush and drive. Big Gus waited on the other side of Muddy Slough in the Duke's pickup with a scope-sighted 30.06 in case some of the dogs swam the Slough and crossed the newly-planted wheat field.

Wacky Mack knew from his trapping observations that the dogs holing up in the Locust Thicket often used the nearby beaver dam to cross the Slough. He placed the Heater and Deadeye there, and the latter made up for earlier that morning. Of the twenty-six dogs that flushed from their thorny residence, fourteen attempted to cross the dam, and not one succeeded. Seven more were killed by the others, and three who escaped were badly crippled, including one that Big Gus rolled at a range of nearly two hundred yards.

The raiders returned to the Jake Camp for lunch before their planned attack on the little Swamp island. To the men it was a nasty, bloody job that had to be done, and their guilt at not having tackled it sooner was what drove them. To the Jakes it was war without someone shooting back, and as young men throughout the ages have done, they reveled in the supposed glory of conflict. Perfect bravely limped around Camp wearing his wound as proudly as a medal, and the other boys were more than a little envious.

As the plans were laid for the final assault of the day Wacky Mack pointed out the need for extra care, "since some-a th' cripples an' survivors from Deputy Don's prob'ly laid up on th' island."

"Wish Deputy Don was here now," the Heater ventured.

"Let Don alone," Wacky Mack rasped. "He's doin' good at his own job, I 'spec'!"

And he was. Both Mack and Deputy Don had known for a while that Stumpy Olson had been releasing strays in the Woods, but neither had been able to catch the dog catcher red-handed. At the hospital last night, though, the two had discussed the need for action based on circumstantial evidence. The lawman had volunteered.

Just before noon, he walked into the dog pound after the assistant had left for lunch. Stumpy was alone, stuffing a huge wad of tobacco into his mouth when Deputy Don walked in. The dog catcher's greeting was familiar, one lawman to another.

"Howdy, Don. How's tricks? (spit!)"

"Not too hot, Stumpy. Say, you 'member me askin' you not to dump no more strays down in our Woods, 'bout a year ago?"

The man squinted speculatively. "Ya ain't never seen me dumpin' none, have ya? (spit!)"

Deputy Don's .357 magnum, pointed between Stumpy Olson's eyes, made a chilling sound as the hammer clicked back. The eyes crossed.

"I ain't *got* to, you low-life sonuvabitch. If I catch one more stray out there in my Woods, I'm gonna blow your wormy brains right through this concrete-block wall." The pistol barrel was pushing so hard into the man's fleshy face that the wrinkles in his forehead creased around the front sight. "You understand?"

The dog catcher gulped to answer and swallowed the chaw of tobacco. Fear helped control his stomach, though, as the relentless barrel backed him into the concrete wall. The pressure seemed to bore into his skull.

"If I ever catch you outside the city limits on my side-a town, I'm gonna shoot you down like a rat!" Deputy Don promised. "My wife an' li'l girl were mauled yesterday by your damn dogs an' I'm a mind to kill you now while there ain't no witness." The dog catcher began to weep, and fouled his pants in fear. A strangled moan came from his clenched teeth.

Abruptly, Deputy Don wheeled, holstered his pistol, and strode angrily out. Stumpy Olson stood as if still pinned to the wall and vomited again and again down his front. Half an hour later, when his assistant returned from lunch, the stench in the pound was unbearable. Stumpy took the rest of the day off.

Deputy Don returned to the Woods in time to participate in the day's last assault. The hunters waded through the knee-deep waters silently and took the island pack by complete surprise. Of twenty-three dogs, nineteen were killed outright, and two more were crippled so severely that they drowned before reaching solid ground.

In twenty-four hours, the wild dog population in the Woods had declined by seventy-seven percent.

When Wacky Mack strolled into Baby Sister's room that night, no one knew him at first; he wasn't wearing camouflage. Nodding to the girl's parents, he suggested, "Why don't y'all go get somethin' t' eat an' a good night's sleep? I'll watch."

The woman smiled her thanks and bent to kiss her daughter. "'Night, Baby. See you in the morning."

As the door closed behind them, Mack pulled his chair close to the head of the bed and rasped at his charge, "Lissen good, now." Under his arm was a leather-bound volume which he opened, clearing his throat. "'It was seven o'clock of a very warm morning in the Seeonee Hills when Father Wolf woke up'. . ."

When his voice gave out, the girl was asleep.

*   *   *   *   *   *   *

After the excitement of The Great Dog War, it was hard for the Jakes to settle back into normal campfire routine. But deer season began, and memories of their Day in Combat began to fade. Perfect's wound healed, and he missed a big eight-point buck on opening day. The Heater and Birdlegs both bagged bucks early in the season, and Deadeye, after sleeping in one morning while recovering from a light case of flu, killed a nine-point that walked right by Camp.

"Nuthin' to it," he declared. "Got up at eight, had a root beer by the fire, picked up my rifle, took a rest on the cypress log, an' shot 'im in the neck. Wish I felt well enough to help y'all field-dress 'im. But Rookie needed to learn anyway. Here, son, don't cut too far up on the neck. I might mount this'un." All this was spoken from his (aptly-named) director's chair by the fire.

There were still a few encounters with wild dogs, but no one was ever threatened. Birdlegs and Boateater watched six cross a beaver dam on Muddy Slough one evening and slip into the Locust Thicket. The boys were hunting wood ducks, but hurriedly took the plugs from their shotgun magazines and reloaded. While Boateater lay in ambush at the dam, Birdlegs circled the Thicket and walked in from the west, yelling. It worked like a charm. The dogs trotted out in single file to escape the way they had come. Boateater let the first two get on the dam before rising to fire. He killed five dogs with five shots, and Birdlegs came racing around the thicket in time to down the remaining cur.

Wacky Mack borrowed one of Uncle Bubba's Labradors the first week she came in heat, and invited the Heater and Perfect to accompany him one weeknight. They tied the Lab to a tree, sat back with a spotlight, and began to bark in imitation of a pack themselves. Between dark and eleven, they killed five strays and crippled two more that came eagerly to the noise and smell.

The bearded woodsman hunted wild dogs relentlessly for the next month, with some help from the Jakes and the other landowners. The night of the JakeFest he drove up in his jeep, got out, and ambled to the fire with a box under his arm. The boys had invited Baby Sister this year, and she sat on a canvas chair, feeling like a queen. Wacky Mack bowed suitably and handed her the box. "Proud t' announce th' only canine in these Woods now!" he declared with just a trace of pride.

In the box was a five-and-a-half-week-old bassett puppy, all ears and tongue. Matter of fact, "He's all ears!" was what Baby Sister squealed. And "Ears" he became. The pup investigated everything in Camp, singed his tail on a hot brick by the fire, turned over the water cooler, and finally crawled up in the hollow log, wet on the Rookie's sleeping bag, and went to sleep. His new owner was hopelessly in love with him by the time Papa Jake took them home.

"What was that for?" the Heater asked Wacky Mack a trifle jealously, after his father and sister had left.

The veteran glanced over the edge of his coffee mug at the brother. "Like gettin' back on a horse when it throws you. She jus' got mauled by dogs. If she don't get used to 'em again quick, she might grow up scared of 'em."

The Heater fell silent, suitably impressed by the importance of the gift and the length of the speech. Besides, he figured, he could train Ears to run deer and rabbits.

This was not the only gift presented at the JakeFest. Uncle Bubba had done a little law work for a client who was low on cash, and took an almost-new 30/30 Winchester in trade. He brought it home and showed it to Perfect, remarking, "I don't know what I'll do with it. You and I have four deer rifles between us."

Perfect instantly had an answer as to the final disposition of the lever-action carbine. The Rookie had been using guns — all his hunting gear, really — borrowed or handed down from the other Jakes. He nearly cried that night when they presented him with his very own.

He did cry eight days later because of the new rifle. He

was sitting on a cottonwood stump when Ole Cow-foot came wading out of the Swamp and stopped to shake, less than thirty yards away. Rookie coolly shouldered the 30/30 and levered five shells through it — without ever pulling the trigger! It was a classic case of buck fever, worthy of even Perfect. Disdainfully, Ole Cow-foot strolled on off into the Woods.

Around the fire that night, Rookie told his story to the mixed disgust, amusement, and sympathy of the other Jakes. "He was so big!" the boy indicated an immense set of antlers with his arms above his head. He paused, then continued his observation, "And you know, every one of those shells turned a little flip right in front of my face!"

*　　*　　*　　*　　*　　*　　*

That next night, as the Jakes were eating supper, a skunk came ambling around the side of the cypress log and was less than fifteen feet from the fire when Boateater saw him. Half-chewed chili and crackers sprayed over the whole assembly as he choked, "Ahu, ahu, a-hack!! A skunk!!"

Of course, no one wanted to yell and disturb their visitor's tranquility at such close range. Nor did anyone want to make any sudden moves. Except for Birdlegs, seated on the opposite side of the fire, everybody else was within the danger zone should the skunk decide to spray. However, the varmint sat down to regard its hosts, only four steps behind the Heater's back.

Slowly, the two boys farthest away from the fire laid down, and on elbows, heels, and backsides, scuttled casually back to the tent. Even more slowly, the pair of Jakes next closest to Deadeye and the Heater, who truly felt "under the gun," laid gently down and came crawling on their bellies around both sides of the fire to join the first two escapees, leaving their frozen companions.

"What'll we do now?" asked the Rookie, safely out of range.

"Let's shoot it!!" Birdlegs suggested, his enthusiasm quietly growing as Boateater nodded concurrence.

Eyes still glued on the skunk, the Heater enunciated calmly but coldly, "I . . . will . . . kill . . . you." No one doubted that he would, especially the Rookie.

"Okay, smart guy, you say so," Birdlegs, out of range, was content to discuss matters at length. Deadeye looked like he was about to fall asleep, but the others noticed that he had gradually lowered his plate to the ground.

"Heater," Deadeye whispered without moving.

"Yeah."

"Let's make like a shepherd and get the flock outa here."

"Fast, or slow?"

"Reeeaaalll ssllooooww."

"If he moves, stop unless I holler go."

"Your call," agreed Deadeye.

The skunk was distracted by a flea on its flank, and while its head was turned, the two Jakes moved on hands and knees around the fire and into the shadows of the tent where the others stood with bated breath. "Great moves!" complimented Perfect.

Their visitor rose from its scratching and casually investigated the base of the cypress log. "Hey! What if it goes up in there?" Boateater exclaimed.

"Ssshh! Don't scare it!" Birdlegs said. "We gotta do somethin', guys!"

It was decided that they would divide into three teams, one boy with a shotgun and one with a garbage bag and shovel. The plan was for the closest pair to arrange both annihilation and disposal. One pair would come around from each end of the log and one pair would remain by the tent in case the animal moseyed that way.

Their problem with this solution was that no one wanted to be in charge of the disposal. The Jakes knew that if a skunk was shot in the head or the spine, it supposedly could not raise its tail to spray. Therefore, at the shot, the boy with the garbage bag should be perfectly safe to quickly step out and scoop the dead animal into the plastic bag. Once the top of the bag was securely closed, they would not have to worry about any post-mortem reflexes, for any smell would be contained by the bag. That was their theory.

The Jakes paired up for the operation and two of the three pairs chose shooter and bagger by the "eeny, meeny, miney, moe" method. There was no need for this with the other pair.

"Ain't no way I'd trust you shootin'," the Heater said.

"I'll bag," agreed the Rookie meekly.

As luck would have it, when they put their plans into operation, the Heater eased around his end of the log to view the skunk, again seated unconcernedly less than ten feet away. "Get ready," he whispered to the Rookie, who nodded, garbage bag in hand and old entrenching tool clutched in a sweaty palm.

The Heater's shot took the skunk in the head, apparently rendering it rigid. The Rookie rushed out at the boom, bent, and was rolling the varmint into the open bag when the violent convulsions started. The bag closed over at least half of the spurting spray.

But the rest took the Rookie full in the face and chest. To give him credit (and the Jakes did!), he did not release the top of the plastic bag.

"Go! Go! Go!" Boateater yelled. "Get it outa here!"

Gagging, stumbling, but valiantly holding the bag tightly, the boy headed out into the Woods. Perfect had the presence of mind to grab a flashlight and run alongside to guide him at least a hundred yards away from Camp; but not too close alongside. Finally he puffed, "Far enough! Bury 'im here!" From a distance of thirty feet, he held the light while Rookie dug a shallow grave. As the boy was filling in the hole, Perfect too began to gag. "Here's the light," he called, and pitched the flashlight. "I'm goin' back to Camp!"

When the miserable Rookie came dragging back to Camp, the other Jakes had begun to implement de-toxification procedures. They had the stinking boy strip, downwind of the tent, on the other side of the sweetgum tree. Using water drained from the ice chest, they pitched him soap and a wet towel to lather with. The fact that it was about forty-five degrees and the Rookie was bathing in ice water didn't evoke any sympathy. When the ice water gave out, they sparingly used drinking water from the cooler and collected all the toothpaste in Camp for him to scrub with. Next, they turned to canned drinks and catsup.

By now the Rookie's teeth were chattering. But he still smelled of skunk. The Heater began to open cans of sardines and drain the juice off. After three hours, the Rookie was beginning to turn blue — a smelly blue.

The other Jakes drew straws, and Boateater got the job of driving the stinking naked boy to the barns over a mile away and hosing him down. Two towels and an old sleeping bag were in the back of the jeep. Later in life, the Heater would wonder what medicinal properties there were in either the skunk juice or the cures that kept the Rookie from dying of pneumonia; he never even caught cold!

Back at Camp, they had rigged an old ground cloth as a makeshift tent between the fire and the cypress log. "Ain't nooo way he's sleepin' in the tent!" drawled Deadeye.

Sad, smelly, cold, and resigned, the newest Jake caught the Heater's eye before the latter entered the tent for the final time. "Even?" he asked.

"Even," grinned the Heater.

*   *   *   *   *   *   *

The High School Chorus and Glee Club, of which both Perfect and Birdlegs were members, gave several concerts just prior to Christmas. One of these was on Friday night, and therefore the two Jakes were late for the Jake Camp, not even leaving town until after eleven.

The basketball teams were participating in a Holiday Tournament sixty miles away and no school bus was available to transport the singers, so Burly Shirley, the Band and Choral Director, had arranged for several of the older students to drive loads of singers in their cars to the mall where they were performing. Perfect and Birdlegs were in a car with four senior boys, and Smilin' Jack had insisted on stopping by The Push and Pull Drive-in on the way back for "a burger and a brew."

Perfect quietly abstained and ordered a root beer, but Birdlegs wasn't fixing to back down in front of the older boys. Besides that, he was thirsty. He chug-a-lugged his first-ever beer to the cheers of the seniors. "Tastes jus' like horse pee smells an' looks," he thought. And ordered another. He drank four beers and ate a double cheeseburger with every-thing, just like the big boys.

This was no real problem, for Perfect had Uncle Bubba's Bronco at the school to drive them back to the Woods. Birdlegs was serenading the town with a "joyful noise" as Perfect pulled out of School Street and turned onto the almost deserted highway.

Almost deserted; for across the highway in the Episcopal Church parking lot sat Officer "Marvelous Marv" Burt Marvin, deep in gloom. His fiancee had picked this day to give him back not only his ring, but the gifts he had already placed under her family's tree. Marvelous Marv was not in the mood for gay carols sung by loud, happy, youthful voices. The po-liceman had no Christmas Spirit at all; more like Halloween.

Besides that, Perfect, seeing no traffic for a mile either way, came to only a "rolling stop" as he turned onto the highway. He was in a hurry; the Jake Camp was calling.

Marvelous Marv cranked the patrol car and radioed his intentions to stop a traffic violator. He didn't switch on his flashing lights at first, thinking that he might follow unobser-ved for a few minutes to note behavior deserving of more charges. Mentally, he licked his lips: "failure to stop," "reck-less driving," "speeding," "DWI." It would help his own feelings no end to make some other human being miserable tonight. The old saying "Misery loves company" was about to be proven once more.

Before the policeman could get a clocking on the Bronco, though, the vehicle turned off the highway onto a blacktop road. This increased his anger, for the highway looped around the town from east to west and was within the city limits for three more miles, whereas the Bronco was out of the city limits within a quarter of a mile on the blacktop. He flipped both flasher and siren switches and stomped it.

However, Perfect had stomped it too, before noticing the flashing lights behind him. As a matter of fact, he had become caught up in Birdlegs' Christmas Spirit, and the two were harmonizing quite pleasingly on an up-beat version of "We Three Kings of Orey and Tar." The Bronco's performance was illustrative of the music's beat, leading Marvelous Marv to another, more obvious, conclusion. Perfect never even heard the siren until he stopped singing to allow Birdlegs to take the solo on "Frankencense to offer have I."

Marvelous Marv was licking his chops. So far he had "all of the above," plus "fleeing to avoid arrest." If he played it right, he might be able to add "resisting arrest," and maybe even get to use his nightstick or pull his gun. So Sandy wanted to date around for awhile, huh? He'd teach these dudes to mess with his girl. He just hoped there would be a Billy Badass in the Bronco for him to vent his displeasure on.

Speak of angels and hear wings flapping.

As Perfect pulled over, Birdlegs became aware of the siren and the red-and-blue flashing lights of a city policeman. Yet they were nearly a mile outside of the city limits on a lonely blacktop road. The Jake was indignant. "Hey, he's got no jursidiction out here!"

Before the Bronco was fully stopped, Birdlegs was out the door and around the side of the truck to point this out to the patrolman. "Hey, you've got no jurisdiction out here!" he roared in the cop's face.

Marvelous Marv had attained the height of five-foot-six with his elevator shoes on; just one more reason to hate the world, especially tonight. He also hated onions, and though Birdlegs was shouting from five inches above, the policeman could tell the boy had not only had onions on his double cheeseburger but had eaten nearly half of Smilin' Jack's double order of onion rings.

And had several beers. Marvelous Marv reached for his

.nightstick and handcuffs, smiling with satisfaction. He hoped Sandy had been considering this tall youngster as a suitor. "You're under arrest!" he informed Birdlegs with relish.

"What!!" More beer and onions for Officer Marvin. Perfect, just now getting out of the Bronco, was greeted by the sight of his companion, face down across the hood of the police car, being handcuffed by the short, mad cop.

"Wha'd we do?" the driver asked, interrupting the reading of the suspect's rights.

Irritated, Marvelous Marv turned to the boy threateningly. "You stay outa this and you won't get in trouble!"

"But wha'd we do?" Perfect repeated. Birdlegs tried to stand erect, but was pushed back across the hood.

"Try drivin' drunk, for starters," answered the cop.

"But I'm not drunk! I haven't even *had* a drink!"

"Yeah, but this kid has!"

"But he wasn't drivin'!"

"Well, I reckon he was!"

"No, sir. This is my daddy's Bronco!"

"I don't care if it's Henry Ford's Bronco. No one drives drunk around here!"

"But I wasn't drivin' drunk!"

"No, *he* was! And I'm gettin' tireda your lip, kid. You want cuffs, too?"

Perfect, who never got mad, got mad. "*Read* my lips," he enunciated. "I . . . was . . . driving! . . . Not . . . him!"

"Okay, that's it!" Marvelous Marv jerked out a second set of handcuffs and poked this second Billy Badass menacingly in the chest with his billy club. "Hold out your hands, boy. Or I'm gonna work you over so your mama won't even know you!"

Such was the scene that was illuminated by the Duke of Dundee's headlights. No one had noticed the pickup approaching. The tall farmer stopped and offered assistance. "Problems, officer?"

"I got it under control," growled the policeman. "These two smart-alecks are gonna spend the rest of the night in jail."

"May Aye inquire as to the charges?" asked the Duke.

"None-a your . . ." Marvelous Marv began, then stopped.

162

This guy talked like a lawyer. "Well, we'll start with DWI, reckless drivin', flight to avoid arrest, and resistin' arrest," he stated officially.

"But Mr. Duke! *I* was drivin' and I ain't had a drop! He claims I wasn't drivin', but I was. Honest!"

"Quite right, officer. This young gentleman *was* driving, for Aye saw them as they left town. Why were you two in town so late?" the man asked.

"School Glee Club concert . . ." Perfect started, but Marvelous Marv cut him off, brandishing his club.

"Shut up, you! Now listen, Mister. I don't know who you are, but . . ."

The Duke drew himself up to his full six-foot-three-inch height and towered over the cop. "Obviously you do not. Suffice it to say that Aye consider myself a colleague of this young man's father, who is a former District Attorney and one of the best barristers in the State. Since Aye can testify that you have falsely arrested the passenger for driving, there may be some question, not only in a jury's mind but also the chief's, as to exactly *who* has been drinking tonight! As a matter of fact," the Duke leaned down into the shorter man's face and breathed deeply, "Aye can now testify that Aye smell liquor on your breath, Patrolman . . ." he leaned farther to squint at the name tag on the policeman's pocket.

Marvelous Marv knew he had painted himself into a corner. Not only did this tall man talk like a lawyer, but the second kid's daddy was a former D.A. He began to unlock the handcuffs, muttering under his breath, "Oh, for the days when lawyers drove Cadillacs and Continentals." At least then one could tell an attorney by the vehicle. If this dude was bluffing, he couldn't afford to call it. "Awright, you guys, get outa here. But if I ever catch you again . . ."

They were already running for the Bronco, tossing "Thanks, Mr. Duke," over their shoulders.

The policeman turned to the tall man, who regarded him frostily. He put as much threat into his voice as he dared, trying to save a little face. "Mister, I didn't catch your name, but I'd swear you've been drinkin' a little . . ."

With a withering stare, the Duke of Dundee replied, "Certainly; and not just a little! Some of us must drink quite a lot in order to more effectively confront the incompetence of our public officials!" He tipped his hat. "A pleasant evening to you, officer."

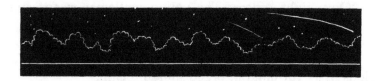

The second night behind a cold front is often crisp and so clear that one can almost reach out and touch the stars. It was on just such a night that the Jakes came rolling into Camp late, having spent the first part of the evening at a New Year's Party at Crazy Sharon's house. As the jeep pulled up under the sweetgum tree and the Heater switched off the engine, Perfect suddenly exclaimed, "Look!"

He pointed into the sky, and the others saw a volley of shooting stars that seemed to be so close that "Shoot-a-mile! looks like they're bouncin' off the tree limbs!" observed Birdlegs.

"I heard 'em talkin' on TV last night 'bout some meteor shower," said Boateater. "Reckon that was it?" The Jakes began to unload themselves and their gear.

"Naw, dummy," Deadeye drawled. "A meteor shower lasts all night. Looka-there! More of 'em!"

The Heater was piling wood on the usual campfire site when Perfect stopped him. "'Fore you light it, let's watch awhile," he suggested.

It is possible that many city dwellers never get a true impression of the heavens until they get there (assuming that true city dwellers would be admitted to the Pearly Gates; the Jakes had their doubts), because the city lights outshine their heavenly competition. Unless one has frequent access to a planetarium, the next best situation is to be in the countryside and completely away from any other light source, including campfires.

"What're you gonna do, freeze to death?" The Heater was somewhat pragmatic at times.

"Aw, man, we can just wrap up in sleepin' bags and watch for awhile," Boateater pointed out. After all, he was the Jake with The Official Information. "Man, that's pretty!" he breathed as another spray of heavenly sparks glowed across the clearing.

The boys spread ground cloths by the unlit pile of firewood, slipped into their sleeping bags, and lay back in order to watch the interplanetary fireworks display without craning their necks. "Toe-tal-lee awesome!" exclaimed the Rookie, almost prayerfully.

And it really-and-truly was. In addition to the meteor showers, Deadeye showed a surprising knowledge of the stars, planets, and constellations. In his quiet drawl, with the baying of hounds as a musical background, he pointed out both Dippers, Orion, the "Seven Sisters," Venus, and other heavenly bodies. He showed so much knowledge, in fact, that Birdlegs became suspicious. As the instructor showed them Sirius, the Dog Star, Birdlegs balked. "There ain't no Dog Star! You're jus' hearin' the Duke's hounds an' makin' all that up!" As if to back him up, the new blueticks, Gin and Tonic, audibly turned their chase toward the Jake Camp.

"Okay, then, *you* tell us what it is!" The Rookie sided with the quiet, confident professor.

"Well . . . I don't know," muttered Birdlegs.

"There ya go," shrugged Deadeye wisely.

The Jakes were lying in total darkness, talking quietly, when suddenly they were hailed: "Hallo, the Camp!" They recognized the Duke's voice.

"Yes, sir," Birdlegs called back, reluctant to break the spell.

The Duke of Dundee strode into Camp and stopped in bewilderment. "Good Lord, Father Phil! They all are completely stoned!" He snickered and punched his companion playfully on the arm. "Aye don't mean 'stoned' in the Biblical sense, of course. Aye mean 'stoned' in the current definition of journalism and literature." The boys could see that their friend was "three sheets in de wind with de fourth 'un flappin'!" as Big Gus often said.

165

"Aw, we ain't stoned," protested Perfect. "We're lyin' here watchin' the meteor showers."

"The what?"

"Look up yonder," Deadeye pointed, and the two men turned to gaze skyward. They were rewarded by a spattering of fiery dots over the sweetgum tree.

"Beautiful," nodded Father Phil.

"Aye'll be damned!" the Duke said, and sipped from his pint bottle. He remembered his audience. "Begging your pardon, boys. Phil."

The minister grinned. "Let's rest here awhile and watch with the boys, Duke," he suggested.

"Grand suggestion." The farmer tapped Birdlegs with his toe. "Share your ground cloth and blankets, young man. You've not been eating onions and drinking beer again, have you?"

The Heater moved over and offered half his sleeping bag, zipped out, to Father Phil. Both men lay down, the Duke carefully removing his remaining two bottles from his pockets. Almost immediately, they were treated to the best shower yet. "I'll drink to that," Duke muttered, and did so.

The Rookie picked up the Jakes' conversation back where it had been interrupted. "So what makes it do this?"

Deadeye was more reluctant to speak with grown-ups present, but in their silence, finally did so. "Waaalll . . . th' Earth's rotatin' around the Sun in our solar system; an' ever' now an' then some meteorite or asteroid belts come by at the same place we are . . . an' . . . we can see 'em."

"But where'd they come from?"

The silence stretched out once more until Deadeye answered again. "Reckon God made 'em."

The heavens flashed and sparked again and a couple of the boys shivered, but not from the cold. "Pretty one," whispered Boateater.

"How do you feel about the Big Bang theory, Phil?" asked the Duke.

"Do you really want to know, or are you just agitating in front of the boys?" the minister's teeth shone as he grinned at his long-time hunting companion.

166

"What's that?" asked the Rookie.

"Basically, the belief that some great ball of matter exploded billions of years ago, hurling this planet and all those other bits of light out there to settle into their natural orbits and paths," the Duke explained.

"Where'd the ball come from to start with?" queried Heater.

"How'd it come to explode?" Perfect wanted to know.

"And what . . ." Deadeye began when the man interrupted.

"Hold it! One at a time!" the Duke protested. "Aye never said Aye believed in it anyway!"

Father Phil laughed. "Agitator!" he kidded.

"So what do you believe?" asked Rookie.

"A great many people subscribe to the traditional Creation Theory of the Bible." The Duke paused to take another sip.

And during the pause, in a small voice, the Rookie asked, "What's that one say?" There was an amazed silence.

The minister wisely let the Jakes carry the ball. His companion, realizing he was in over his head, shut up. Venus glittered warmly, perched on a limb in the sweetgum. Another shooting star arched across the velvet blackness.

"You ain't read it in the Bible?" Birdlegs demanded. In the Southern boys' experience, this level of ignorance was impossible to achieve.

"Never been to church," the Rookie, in the darkness, was not aware of the impact of his statements on the other Jakes. He had been here nearly five months, and not one of them had even thought to ask. In halting tones, embarrassed by the presence of his preacher, Perfect explained the Creation story, with the helpful comments of the other boys.

"How's that better than the Big Bang theory?" asked the newly-enlightened one when the story ended.

The Duke chimed back in, since he had brought it up originally. "Well, a great many scientists . . . Phil, your smugness comes audibly to my attention. This is your balliwick. Say something!"

Father Phil smiled. "Duke, you're wearing a Rolex watch, aren't you?" He didn't need to see the nod in the darkness to continue. "This universe of ours works even better than a good watch, doesn't it?" Again, he continued without verbal agreement. "Now, if you took that expensive watch apart piece by piece, and dropped all the pieces in that bucket over there, how many times . . ." he repeated deliberately, ". . . how *many* times would you have to shake that bucket and dump it out before a perfectly assembled and running watch would reappear? A million times? A billion?" He lapsed into a satisfied silence.

"But there are natural laws that govern . . ."

"Commanded by whom?"

"And men made the watch."

"Men made by whom?"

As another series of showers winked out, the Duke was saved by the sounds of Gin and Tonic barking "bayed" at the edge of the Swamp. He took another sip and rose quickly. "Tally-ho! The quarry awaits! Good night, gentlemen."

As the two men strode off into the darkness, the Jakes saw a flashlight beam snap on and heard the Duke's protesting tones. "Father, you are blinded by legends and traditions. If you consider..."

They heard Father Phil laugh. "Duke, you could think more clearly if you'd lay off . . ." The voices trailed off in the dark distance.

"Wanna light the fire monster?" the Heater asked.

"No!" five answers came at once.

"Guess if we stay up awhile, we can sleep late, huh?" he observed.

"That'd be good," the Rookie said.

The Heater noticed the new kid seemed to be developing a slight drawl.

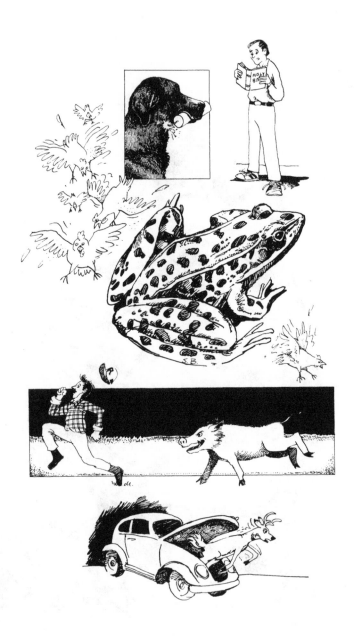

PART IV: AGE 16

Late spring and early summer that year were wetter than usual, and in one way, this was good for the farmers' crops. In another way, however, it caused problems seldom encountered in two generations in the area. In the past couple of years beavers had quietly colonized most of the nearby waters, and now the abundant rainfall gave Nature's Engineers a chance to show their talents. They did so with enthusiasm.

As the farmers' crops began flooding in unaccustomed places, they of course sought out the culprits, and declared war. As the saying goes, "there are few problems that cannot be solved by an appropriate charge of high explosives." By regularly dynamiting the dams, the field-flooding was mitigated, and the beavers were kept in a state of high employment. A dam blown one morning would be nearly as good as new by the next day. Then it would be blown again.

As the normal summer dry season came along, the danger of flooding passed and the blasting ceased. Both beavers and dynamiters took a well-deserved break. The intact dams then served a needed purpose in Nature's Plan: the ponds provided water for all manner of wildlife.

One afternoon the Heater and Deadeye were walking the upper part of the Canal not far from the houses with a couple of rakes and a croker sack. Some of the shallower ponds were beginning to shrink with the summer heat, and the boys were gathering crawfish. The big ones, when purged, would go into the boiling pot, while the little ones were to be kept in the wet sack for a jug-fishing trip on the River that weekend. They also kept the bullfrogs and the larger fish that they raked up. The "trash" fish and the snakes were disposed of.

They were accompanied by one of Uncle Bubba's Labradors, a male that the man had not been able to sell from the last litter. Pepper was nine months old, headstrong, and, of all things, gunshy. Even the appearance of a .22 rifle was enough to send the retriever cringing back into the kennel, so he seldom tagged along with the Jakes, as they were usually armed. Today was an exception.

The boys had raked out two shallow ponds with very little success, and were detouring around a deeper pond when Deadeye pointed to an object near the middle of the dam. "Is that what I think it is?" he drawled.

"Aw-Riiiight! Dynamite!!" the Heater exclaimed.

It looked like the stick of dynamite, fuse intact, had been shoved halfway into the dam, and then had not been lit, or perhaps the fuse had gone out. Papa Jake had gotten into the habit of blowing this particular series of dams by starting downstream, placing a stick, lighting the fuse, and striding on to the next one. He was usually several dams upstream before the first one blew. Apparently he had not checked behind himself the last time.

"Hey, let's blow the dam!" Deadeye suggested.

The boys had the means available to do this. A couple of years before, the Jakes had visited the Army-Navy Surplus Store in town for the purpose of rigging up their own survival and hunting belts. They each had a military webbed belt from which hung several pouches, a canteen, and a sheath knife. One of the pouches on each boy's belt contained survival gear—fishhooks, nylon line, a small whetstone, Band-aids, a "space blanket," antiseptic, a couple of packs of the new "survival food" ("You know what that stuff tastes like?" Boateater had asked. "No; an' don't tell me!" Birdlegs had answered), a small snakebite kit, and matches in a waterproof container.

The Heater had his belt on, matches included, and he had a more practical idea. "Naw, man. Let's go fishin' with it!"

Though it too had begun to shrink, the deeper pond they stood next to was big enough to have some decent-sized fish still in it.

"How do you do that?" asked Deadeye. "Won't the fuse go out?"

"Naw, it's got nitro or somethin' in it."

"Won't it tear up the fish?"

"Well, if it was right on toppa one, I guess it would. But mostly, the concussion kills 'em all over the pond an' they float up to the top. Might even be a good-sized bass in there." The Heater was sorting through his pouch for matches.

"I dunno." Deadeye wasn't enthusiastic. Unlike Heater, he had never seen dynamite used before.

"C'mon, candy!" snorted the experienced Jake. "We'll fill that ole sack up pronto!"

"Well, let's get way the heck away from it," grumbled Deadeye. "I bet it'll blow that ole stinkin' mud a hunnerd yards."

"We'll run up in the trees after I throw it," Heater agreed. He looked at the fuse. "Wonder how long that'll burn?"

"'Bout two seconds." Deadeye was certainly caught up in pessimism today. He began moving toward the trees.

The water level had shrunk from seepage and evaporation until there was a space of over twenty yards from the edge of the water to the nearest tree, with about fifteen feet of slimy, sloppy, evil-smelling mud around the pond. The boys retreated almost to the shade of the trees and the Heater hefted the stick of explosive. "You're gonna hafta throw hard," his companion warned, his voice again showing a degree of reluctance for this project.

He got a disgusted stare in return from the District III All-Star first baseman. "Get serious, man!"

Taking a deep breath, the Heater struck the match and held it to the fuse.

It caught instantly in a shower of sparks, which scared both boys into thinking the explosion had begun prematurely. Instead of drawing back as if for a throw from first to home plate, the Heater flipped the stick hurriedly, as if to the pitcher covering first on a bunt attempt. It didn't help that the dynamite stick wasn't nearly as heavy as a baseball. Fuse sputtering, the dynamite splattered in the mud just short of the water.

"Playtime!" thought Pepper.

"You dummy!" Deadeye fussed. "You didn't even get it to the water! There's plenty-a fuse." This was easily apparent now. "Run get it an' . . . Pepper! No!"

"Hey, you dumb dog! Get away from that!" the Heater screamed. "DON'T BRING THE DAMN THING BACK HERE!!!"

Deadeye wheeled, mumbling an expression he had heard his father use: "Feets, don't fail me now!"

"Pepper! No, Pepper! No! Pepper!..." the Heater was interupted by his departing comrade's warning.

"The fool's bringin' it back!"

The young Lab had been bred to retreive, and here he saw an opportunity to accomplish his purpose in life without the hated explosions that accompany gunfire. He carefully picked the stick out of the mud and loped back toward the thrower, hoping they could play this game for awhile.

However, the thrower was obviously interested in playing other types of games today. Tag, for instance.

At the point where these games were being played, the Canal bank was almost twenty feet high, with a grown-up ditchbank and trees on each side. The Heater and Deadeye dropped sacks and rakes and headed up the bank, which was at a sixty-degree slope. Deadeye set a record pace with his slight headstart, but it wasn't enough. Fear is a wonderful propellant.

"Huuunnng! Huuunnng!" Deadeye heard a strange high-pitched moaning seemingly gaining on him. Considering the present situation, he assumed that it must be the sound a dynamite fuse makes as it fizzes down to the lethal point. He scrambled desperately up the bank as the sound grew closer and closer. His first sobs were bubbling forth when the Heater passed him on all fours, nearly at the top of the bank. "Huuunnng . . ." moaned the Heater, eyes rolling, spittle visible on his lips.

Casting a glance over his shoulder, Deadeye observed that Pepper was still bounding playfully behind them, accepting this pursuit as a game instead of a real chase. It was the fact that

Deadeye could not see the fuse at all that was responsible for helping him catch his comrade. They topped the bank neck-and-neck, the retriever about ten yards behind.

"Split up!" Deadeye gasped. Having scaled the steep bank, the Jakes were quick to assume normal, human, two-legged motion.

Arms and legs pumping, the Heater was pulling ahead again. Abandoning his moan, he answered, "Split up your-self!"

Fortunately for the boys, the blast was just below the edge of the bank they had just topped. Either place would have been equally unfortunate for the dynamite-toting dog.

The explosion lifted the pair off their feet and flung them into the brush of the ditchbank. Deadeye, being lighter, flipped in the air and landed upside down in an ironwood shrub. One ankle wedged in a crotch and he hung stunned, head and shoulders on the ground. The Heater sailed, arms outstretched, to a belly-flop landing on the ditchbank. He was knocked breathless and lay almost unmoving, drawing in hoarse shuddering gulps of air.

Heater recovered first and finally sat up, checking all his bodily parts. Finding none missing, he tried to stand, sobbing with relief at his success. At first he thought Deadeye was dead, but then he saw his hands move to feel for his glasses. Weak and shaking with relief, it was all the Heater could do to lift and un-wedge Deadeye's ankle and release his friend. They sat together at the base of the ironwood, drained.

Finally, Deadeye asked, "You look yet?"

A shake of the head was the only reply.

"Want to?"

Another shake.

Painfully, Deadeye stood. "But we gotta. We gotta bury 'im."

Heater nodded, sighed dejectedly, and began to move. Their task didn't take long.

It is not at all unusual for male dogs allowed to run free in the country to be gone for a couple of days. It was three days later when Uncle Bubba stopped by to see if anyone had seen Pepper. "Hate to lose a dog, even a gunshy one," the man

opined. "But if y'all haven't seen him around, I don't know. Sometimes folks drivin' by will just pick up a good-lookin' friendly dog for a pet. That'd really be better anyway. I don't think I'd ever have made a gun dog out of him."

The Heater wanted to make his uncle feel better. He nodded his head and spoke seriously. "I'd quit lookin' for 'im, Uncle Bubba. Somehow I just know ole Pepper got picked up."

There comes a time in any male's life when suddenly he realizes that females are different — in a new, mysterious, stirring way — and may be pursued as such. Nay, *should* be pursued! Heretofore, girls were variously regarded as boys with long hair whose weird bodily development prevented them from skinny dipping; or as sweet-smelling goddesses on pedestals to be worshipped from afar, lest a buddy should discover one's secret crush on a senior cheerleader or Nyoka the Jungle Girl and tease unmercifully; or as just plain nuisances; or (and this was much closer to God's plan than the Jakes knew) as just friends with different interests in life.

With some boys, these stirrings make themselves known earlier; with some, later; and some are pushed into early recognition by well-meaning parents. This is a mistake, for whenever the awakening comes it is there for the rest of the male's life, with few exceptions. Better to simply let nature take its course and drop The Net of Enslavement to Feminine Pulchritude upon the unwary male at the intended age.

Sixteen was that age for the Jakes.

Several sets of parents sponsored a back-to-school barn dance for the tenth-grade class that fall, and Birdlegs became the first Jake to formally recognize the faint stirrings that encourage pursuit. He asked Crazy Sharon to go to the dance with him.

Actually, Birdlegs was not the only one to encounter this

non-understood desire to be alone with a girl, but being impetuous, he was the first to verbalize it to the object of his affections. And, as the bravest of the Jakes, he deemed the prize worthy of the expected harrassment. Though the Heater and Deadeye continued happily in their ignorance, Perfect had thought to ask Cuddly Carrie but could not overcome his natural caution; and Boateater, who had suppressed these stirrings for some time, had intended to ask . . . Crazy Sharon! It was a tribute to his patience that Birdlegs survived the teasing from his fellow Jakes during the week before the dance.

The event was to be held in the big dairy barn belonging to The Space Ace's father. In addition to owning a dairy, this gentleman also managed fruit and nut orchards, hay and silage crops, and a chicken-and-egg operation. It was this last enterprise that provided the sport on the night of the dance.

In a last-ditch show of rebellion against these strange emotions, the four Jakes without dates vowed to "do somethin'." The Rookie, not being in school, was not included in their plans. On the pretense of "jus' seein' if there was anything we could do to help clean up," the Heater and Perfect paid a visit to the Space Ace a couple of afternoons before the dance. Giggling and prattling along without ceasing, the girl showed the Jakes around her father's complex, unsuspectingly helping them to "case the joint."

The night of the dance, the four conspirators showed up in Heater's jeep, with burlap bags and four ski masks hidden behind the back seat. The dance was to last from eight 'til twelve, with a half-hour intermission beginning at ten. For the first hour the four boys acted normally, Perfect and Boateater even dancing a few times while Heater prowled the sidelines and Deadeye made a nest in the hay and went to sleep.

At nine o'clock, however, the Jakes slipped outside separately and met at the jeep. Quickly donning their masks, they grabbed the croker sacks and trotted through the darkness to the henhouse, where the fowl were roosting.

If one is careful and silent, a sleeping chicken can often be lifted from its perch and inserted into a dark sack without being particularly disturbed. The Jakes worked carefully and silently, but quickly.

There was an unattended outside staircase on each side of the barn, leading to the hay-filled loft overlooking the dance floor. Up each staircase went a pair of boys, each boy holding a croker sack of muffled chickens. They spread out to the four sides of the loft, watches synchronized, waiting until exactly fifteen minutes before intermission. This was when the sponsoring parents would be the busiest, bringing out punch and refreshments while insuring that no early-maturing couples slipped out into the darkness for privacy.

With those harmonious sounds emanating from the bandstand, none but the four Jakes noted the Heater's whistle. The sacks were untied, each boy keeping the top closed with a foot. On signal, four chickens were pulled by their legs from the darkness and rudely introduced to the lights and noise of their first barn dance.

It is amazing how far one can throw a live chicken if one holds it by the feet and swings it in an arc a couple of times before releasing it. The Jakes chose this method to acquaint the first four chickens with their new environment. In a flapping shower of white feathers, the unfortunate first four fowl flew forty feet out before starting to descend toward the dancers, most of whom initially equated this new show with the band's special effects.

Still far enough back from the loft edge to be unobserved, the Jakes only swung the second set of chickens once, and the third set they just flipped, so that the first dozen chickens reached the floor at about the same time but at different points. They then emptied their bags as quickly as possible, sailing cackling hens helter-skelter over the railings. The dance floor below was in bedlam as the Jakes headed breakneck down the outside stairs, still unidentified as yet.

Screaming girls and shouting boys were pouring out of the main entrance, accompanied by chaperones, chickens, and band members. The drummer, caught up in his own rhythms, had panicked when a flapping, squawking fowl had suddenly sailed into the midst of his enclosure. Half of the percussion section was scattered across the bandstand by his distraught departure, and he ran slap over both keyboard and keyboardist.

Three of the four punchbowls were dropped in transit, and

the one already in place had a white chicken land squarely in the middle of it. Cranberry juice was the punch's basic ingredient, and the hen emerged from its dunking a peculiar shade of red. It then proceeded to impart to the town kids the meaning of the saying "Mad as a wet hen!"

Boys chased chickens, boys chased girls, chickens chased girls, chaperones chased anything that ran before them. The outside darkness was not the only sanctuary. The bandleader, already well-oiled, regarded the scene with a jaundiced eye and decided "I need a drink!" He then climbed the ladder to retrieve the bottle of whiskey he had hidden in the loft during the afternoon set-up. After things had settled down somewhat, Coach Fuzzy climbed the ladder to find him totally snookered in the hay. A further search turned up three more bottles and a stash of "left-handed cigarettes." With all this evidence, a chaperone meeting was hurriedly called. The blame for the entire incident was assigned to the band, which was banned from all subsequent school-related appearances.

Discarding their ski masks, the Jakes easily blended in with the mob outside and got off scot free. They even gained a measure of applause from the adults by coming up with several burlap bags and organizing a chicken-catching team to return the poultry to the henhouse. Three chickens were fatally injured (one by the drummer), and the newly-red hen quit laying for a month.

It was quite a memorable dance, even for those without dates.

Not long after the barn dance, an almost revolutionary change occurred at the Jake Camp. Although Baby Sister had graced the campfire a few times and Other Mother had been invited twice, they were considered "family." Now, the talk was of "outside" women. The dance had been universally proclaimed a disaster by all concerned and the Jakes, with two JakeFests under their belts, were boastful of their own talents as host.

"If I was to give a party, I wouldn't give no *dance*," Boateater spoke scathingly. "I'd throw a *real* party, with hot dogs an' hamburgers an' marshmellers an' root beer . . ."

"An' Perfect playin' git-tar, an' singin', an' ghost-story tellin' . . ." enthused Birdlegs.

"An' a full moon, with the hoot owls hootin' an' the screech owls screechin' . . ." Heater chimed in.

"So the girls'd get scared an' snuggle up so you could smell their perfume an' stick your head in their hair an' go . . . Whhhoooooooooooooo!!!" Boateater howled at the moon and the other Jakes joined him.

"Hey, let's give a party out here an' invite some girls!" Birdlegs was the one to put their thoughts into words.

"Aw, you couldn't get any girls to come out here in the Woods!" the Rookie said scornfully.

As has been noted before, scorn didn't sit well with Birdlegs. He jumped to his feet, incensed, jabbing with the green willow stick on which he had impaled his hot dog. "Ha! A lot you know! I could have a hunnerd girls out here if I wanted to. You ain't even from here! You don't know these kinda girls! If I gave a party out here, they'd love it!" He was punctuating his sentences with stick jabs, the hot dog perilously close to falling into the fire.

"Waal, I dunno. I . . ." began Deadeye, but the orator cut him off.

"That's right, you *don't* know!" Birdlegs had begun rising on tiptoes as the stick waved up and down, making his points. "But I know! *I've* had a date! Have *you* had a date? No! Have *you* had a date? No! Have *you* . . ." He made the rounds of his companions, emphasizing their ignorance and his own omniscient experience. "No! *Nobody* else has had a date! And I *know!*" But by now he had forgotten what it was he was supposed to know.

"Know *what?*" asked the Heater, who as yet did not know what it was he didn't know. Either the question or the hot dog finally falling off stopped the discourse.

"I don't know," admitted Birdlegs. "Whatever we were . . . oh, givin' a party out here. I know the girls would come!"

"Who?" Deadeye tried again. "You don't know a hunnerd girls."

"Well, I know enough for us!" was the reply. "You wouldn't know what to do with one girl, much less a hunnerd."

"Okay, let's do it!" Perfect uttered his first words of the night on the subject.

The logistics took a couple of weeks, but they did it. The Jake Camp was cleaned up better than it ever was for a JakeFest, and the weather cooperated beautifully with an early cold snap. That Friday night was clear and just crisp enough for the fire to feel good. From somewhere toward the lower end of the Swamp, the musical baying of Gin and Tonic echoed faintly. Hoot owls hooted, screech owls screeched, and just after the girls arrived a bobcat squalled three times across the Woods toward Deputy Don's place. It was starting out great, Birdlegs thought. "Thank you, God," he breathed, looking up at the twinkling stars.

He, Deadeye, Rookie, and Perfect had gone ahead to complete preparations, while the Heater and Boateater waited for the girls at Papa Jake's. The boys in the Woods had heard the high-pitched laughter and excited squeals as soon as the two jeeps turned off the gravel onto the Woods road. The Rookie was somewhat shy, but all the other Jakes had been raised with

Crazy Sharon, Cuddly Carrie, and Space Ace. They were old friends with a new meaning. Baby Sister and her spend-the-night guest, Ice Cream, had also been asked.

The only newcomer was the redheaded girl whose parents had moved to town just before school had started. She was tall, long-legged, and graceful. It was said she could dunk a basketball, and had been a starter the year before for her former school. Leapin' Lena was Crazy Sharon's second cousin, and the Jakes' long-time friend, who was now blossoming into a dark-haired beauty, had brought the new girl along.

They had a ball. Cuddly Carrie and Ice Cream had just the right touch of feminine nervousness about the dark, the Woods, and the strange sounds during the silent "Listen!" periods. The Space Ace babbled unconcernedly away, giggling when she wasn't talking; but Leapin' Lena noticed that she stopped just short of getting on anyone's nerves. Crazy Sharon and Baby Sister were as matter-of-fact as always; everybody was their friend, except that Crazy Sharon had only met the Rookie once before. However, after ten minutes of conversation, he felt like he had known her all his life.

Leapin' Lena was a little abashed at first, her cousin being the only one present she knew. She thawed quickly when Perfect brought out his guitar, though. She also played, and had a pleasing alto voice. The new girl and Perfect were instant hits on duets, switching back and forth on the guitar. She promised to bring her own, "next time."

Somehow — this first time, anyway — there was no open competition for attention that so often develops to ruin such mixed outings. None of the boys made fools of themselves trying to show off, and none of the girls were vampish. In spite of being two years younger, Ice Cream and Baby Sister were treated as equals, and though vaguely awed and appreciative, it made them feel ten feet tall.

When the Duke of Dundee and Father Phil drifted into Camp to pay their respects, the Duke, though obviously "under the influence," was so courtly and mannerly that all the girls fell in love with him. To requests of "do us a poem, Duke," he recited some verses from the *Rubiyat*, including, of course, "a jug of wine, a loaf of bread, and thou, singing beside me in the wilderness." His popularity was damaged somewhat, however, by his encore of Kipling's "The Female of the Species." He was pelted with marshmallows by the females in the audience, and only rescued by the "treed" baying of Gin and Tonic. Father Phil led him away into the night, to the strains of "Comin' Thru' the Rye."

The Jakes ended the evening by telling ghost stories, Rookie pulling out a new one that Aunt Florrie, who owned the boarding house, had told him. It concerned the mysterious disappearance of a group of boys visiting a haunted house, with the sole survivor being found stark raving mad and beating on the tin roof with a blood-stained hammer. But before he could deliver the punch line, Rookie was interrupted by a "clank, clank!" from the direction of the road.

"What was that?" the storyteller asked, more for confirmation than identification.

"Clank, clank," moved closer.

"Sounds like . . . ahammeronatinroof!" Ice Cream rushed the words together nervously.

"C'mon, you guys," said Crazy Sharon.

"Clank, clank." Louder and closer.

The hairs on the back of the Heater's neck began to stand up. He joined them, moving toward the tent. "Hey, we're all here," he pointed out. "I'm gettin' a gun!"

"Clank, clank!" sounded again, and now they could hear a series of rhythmic thuds as well.

"This ain't funny," warned Boateater.

Even the Space Ace was frozen in silence. The Heater raised his rifle. A huge bulk loomed in the darkness, and the clanking and thudding sounds were almost upon them.

"S-s-s-stop this!" stuttered Leapin' Lena. Perfect heard the safety on Heater's rifle "snick" to off.

And Deputy Don's milk cow stepped into the firelight, her bell clanking. The thudding of her hooves ceased as she stopped to regard the breathless humans at the fire. Both Ice Cream and Cuddly Carrie nearly "jumped out of their skins" when the cow mooed loudly.

Shouts, squeals, and nervous laughter frightened the lost cow and the Heater and Birdlegs had to run to catch her, leaving the other Jakes to proclaim their innocence. It was hard for the girls to believe that the boys had been just as frightened as they had.

That broke up the party, but on a good note. Birdlegs and Heater took Ice Cream and Baby Sister with them in one jeep to lead the cow back around to Deputy Don's. Perfect and Boateater loaded the other four girls into the second jeep and carried them back to Papa Jake's house, where Crazy Sharon's parents had stayed for supper and waited afterward to transport the girls back into town. As she disembarked, the Space Ace giggled and voiced all their thoughts. "That was great! Let's do it again!"

The Rookie and Deadeye finished cleaning up Camp, and threw some more wood on the fire. As he settled back in front of the blaze with a canned drink, Deadeye felt A Wise Saying coming on.

"Y'know," he drawled, "sometimes girls are fun to mess around with!"

*　　*　　*　　*　　*　　*　　*

School always began each morning with the students in their homerooms for roll call, after which they made the Pledge of Allegiance. Then from the loudspeaker system in the office came the day's announcements, a short Bible Reading, and a prayer. Prior to the middle of the Jake's ninth-grade year, the policy had been for each homeroom to rotate the Bible Reading and prayer among the students. Now, however, one senior would go to the office and read the assigned verses each morning for a week, changing on  Wednesday mornings. This new policy had been initiated because of the Heater, but it was actually Perfect's fault.

184

As usually happened under the old system, the Heater had forgotten that he had Bible Reading Duty one morning in homeroom, and had been flustered when The Great Green G had called on him. He stood at the front, flipping through the pages while the teacher finished marking her roll book, and was grateful when Perfect passed him a note that said "Song of Solomon 7:7-9." He had just found the page when the Great Green G nodded impatiently. "Go ahead."

The Heater cleared his throat and galloped right in:

'You are stately as a palm tree, and your breasts are like its clusters. I say'...

He hesitated as he realized what he had just read to the class, but his initial thought was to gloss it over by rushing on.

'I say I will climb the palm tree and... lay hold... of its b-br-bran-ches'?

The Space Ace began to giggle, and now the Heater recognized the trap he had stepped into. Cheeks flaming, he glanced up at Perfect, who was innocently taking in The Inspired Word, as read by his cousin. Before that cousin could whisper, "I'm gonna kill you!" the Great Green G cleared her throat ominously.

"Ahem! . . . Continue."

The tortured boy's eyes returned to the page and he mumbled,

'Oh, may your breasts be like . . .'

"We can't hear you!"

Heater looked beseechingly at the teacher, eyes pleading to somehow be let off the hook. Even Crazy Sharon was trying to stifle laughter. Snickers and muffled giggles came from all over the room. Except from the innocent, interested Perfect and the Great Green G, whose face was set in stone.

She was a five-foot-one, two-hundred-ten-pound, fifty-eight-year-old spinster English teacher, and she was relishing the moment. "We cannot hear you. Please repeat that last sentence. And stand up straight. Don't mumble. And don't rush. Remember," (Deadeye, at the back of the room, thought she must look just like the cat who ate the canary) she emphasized, "be respectful during the reading of the Holy Word."

The Heater shuddered and continued:

'Oh, m-may your b-b-breasts b-be like clusters'
(a deep sigh) 'of the vine.'

Once more the youth cast a supplicating look at the
teacher, begging for mercy with pain-filled eyes. Instead, she
responded with even more cruelty, pointing a finger demurely
at her own chest and pantomiming "Me?"

The Heater collapsed into acceptance of his fate. As the
class roared with laughter, he deadpanned finishing the Reading and sat down, stone-faced. Prayer was dispensed with in
the ninth-grade homeroom that morning.

Perfect wisely refused to leave the room during recess
under the pretense of speaking to Burly Shirley, who had just
taught health class, about a Glee Club number. By noon the
incident had become a school legend, and suddenly the Heater
was the object of admiring comments from even the seniors.
Smilin' Jack shook his hand and asked for the chapter and
verse, obviously wishing he had thought of it himself. By the
time school was out, the Heater had completely forgiven —
nay, was even grateful to — his cousin.

However, it took less than a week for Coach Fuzzy to
implement a new policy, and the culprit only avoided a licking
by pointing out, "But, Coach! It's in the *Bible!*" The Heater's
Bible Reading spawned a flurry of Biblical research, and in the
few days afterward, even the sixth graders were treated to so
much begatting and going-into that the principal put his foot
down and instituted the practice of one senior each week
reading Assigned Verses over the loudspeaker from the office.

The readings for the new school year had begun in Exodus
and had reached the end of the seventh chapter that Friday
before the weekend that the Jakes helped the Duke of Dundee
drain his lake. Friday's reading had caused quite a stir at
school. Once each month the city purged the water systems
with an extra-heavy dose of chlorine, and the resulting particles
of (purified) rust and algae caused the water to run reddish for
about an hour afterward. When the Bible Reading had been
about the waters of Egypt turning to blood, and then at recess
the faucets had spouted red, it put The Fear of God into even
Charley Garbage, the janitor.

The Jakes were laughing about the incident as they drove

down the Duke's turnrow Saturday morning. The coontail moss had become so thick that fishing was almost impossible during summer and fall, so the farmer had decided to partially drain the lake, poison the moss, then pump back up and restock. He had invited the Jakes to come shoot snakes and bullfrogs, and to catch the larger bass, crappie, and catfish that would be stranded by the draining.

The moss harbored a lot of bullfrogs, and the boys quickly collected enough big ones for several suppers. But there had obviously been a tremendous hatch that summer, for the dwindling waters were literally alive with younger bullfrogs, most too small to harvest for their legs. They ranged from about toad-sized to nearly twice toad-sized.

And Perfect was the Bible scholar; he later considered the idea to be A Revelation From God.

"Hey!" he suddenly yelled, bubbling with unaccustomed enthusiasm. "Guess what Exodus chapter eight is about!"

The question seemed so out of context with their surroundings that everyone stopped in their tracks to try to think where the train of thought had come from, and where it was going.

"C'mon, guess!" Perfect was hopping up and down in the mud, holding the .22 aloft in his left hand, his right raised in a triumphant fist.

"Errr . . . Plague of . . . Blood. . . . Umm . . . Plague of Frogs!!!" the Heater finally yelled.

The Jakes were beside themselves, especially after Perfect suggested it was a Revelation. Deadeye had to explain it to the Rookie, but by then the Heater and Birdlegs were in the jeep and headed for the barns to get croker sacks. "Ohboy-ohboy-ohboy-ohboy-ohboy . . ." Birdlegs' voice faded into the dust clouds behind the vehicle.

They were back in ten minutes. The Duke watched in amused bewilderment for half an hour, then went to fetch Papa Jake. "You remember when you made me accompany you to watch those damn boys chase rabbits? Well, you are not going to believe this until you have seen it!"

The Jakes got to school bright and early Monday morning. Perfect had talked Uncle Bubba out of the Bronco, for

Heater's jeep couldn't hold all the pulsating croker sacks. As the two country Jakes pulled into the parking lot, Birdlegs and Deadeye joined them in the former's jeep. Boateater and the Rookie were already waiting in the pickup. Rookie's old second-hand Volkswagon Beetle sat across the street in the Catholic church parking lot.

"Charley Garbage just unlocked," Boateater advised them. "He oughta be headed for the men's room for his mornin' constitutional. No one else is here yet."

"Let's go!" ordered Perfect.

There were two wings in the school building, each housing three classrooms on each side of a central hallway. Four more classrooms and the administrative offices opened off of the end hall that joined the two wings. Up and down these three halls of the main building were rows of metal lockers, one assigned to each student.

But while there was a locker for each student, there was not a student for each locker. The Baby Boom was over, and about one locker in every ten was vacant.

There was still a little drippage from each sack, though the Jakes had hung them up Saturday night and thoroughly hosed off all the mud. Five boys grabbed two sacks each, holding them well away from their clothing, while Perfect followed with a large towel to wipe up any tell-tale drips. Deadeye and Boateater turned down the first wing, and Birdlegs and Heater trotted for the second. Perfect stopped the Rookie at the middle hall, and pointed to one locker on each side. "Quick!" he hissed.

The Jakes had rigged the sacks with a piece of wire at the bottom, so they could be hung upside down from the coat hooks in the vacant lockers. The top of the sacks were closed with twine tied in a slip knot, a four-foot piece of string dangling loose. After hanging the sack from the coat hook, the boys carefully led the end of the twine through the vent at the top of the locker and taped it there with a short strip of clear tape. They then shut the no-longer vacant lockers and noted the numbers.

Less than five minutes after splitting up, the Jakes were back together in the parking lot. Charley Garbage, still seated for his "constitutional," wasn't even through the morning funny papers.

"Okay, now," Perfect was instructing the Rookie, "numbers 13, 51, 80, 96, 111, 132, 144, 175, 202, an' 249. They're written down on this sheet. When you hear the second bell ring, walk up to th' end door of the high school wing. You can hear the loudspeaker from there. When the Bible Readin' starts, there ought not to be anybody in the halls. C'mon in an' get the first four. Jus' pull the string an' open the locker as you go by. Be sure you wait 'til they start prayin' before you go into the middle hall, 'cause they could see you through th' office winda 'less they've got their eyes closed. Pull those two you an' I did, then hightail it down the junior-high wing gettin' those four. Then you're right out that end door next to your Beetle, an' gone."

"Got it!" the Rookie shivered in anticipation. He was not as familiar with practical jokes as the rest.

The Heater stuck out his hand, and as the Rookie grasped it, the others laid their palms across the first two.

"No sweat!" Boateater said.

"No chokin'!" warned Birdlegs.

"Let's get 'em, gang!" exclaimed the Heater.

As the school Jakes began to get their books together and other cars began to arrive in the parking lot, the Rookie had an awful thought. "Hey," he said. "If I do this during prayer, is God gonna be mad?"

"Man, are you kiddin'?" Boateater answered. "God *told* Moses to do this. You're jus' like a Saint, doin' what's in the *Bible!*"

The conspirators split up to casually lounge in the vicinity of the frogs' lockers, lest a careless student should open the wrong one. But there were no mishaps. Hearts pounding with hard-to-conceal anticipation, they waited almost until the "tardy" bell to crowd into homeroom. Soon the senior boy who had the Bible Reading that day intoned:

> 'But if you refuse to let them go, behold, I will
> plague all your country with frogs; the Nile will
> swarm with frogs which shall come up into your
> house, and into your bedchamber and on your

bed, and into the houses of your servants and of
your people'. . .

Unconsciously, Boateater began squirming in his seat, until
the Great Green G tapped her ruler on the desk and glared at
him.

"Let us pray. Oh, Lord, . . ." the senior continued.

He finished his prayer, and Coach Fuzzy's voice came back
over the air. "That is all. Homeroom is dis . . ." A piercing
scream interrupted him, and the students all heard "Damn!
What the Hell . . . ?" before the loudspeaker went dead.

"Somethin's wrong in th' office!" Perfect exclaimed, and
bolted for the door before the Great Green G could stop him.
Half the class was close behind him. The same thing was
happening in every other homeroom, and as the students
entered the halls, pandemonium reigned.

To say that there were frogs everywhere would not be
entirely accurate, but to say that there were frogs more places
than there weren't would be reasonable, under the circumstances. And these frogs had been sacked for over thirty-six
hours, so they were extremely active.

Women's fashions, ever fickle, were that year condoning
everything from mini-skirts to ankle-length full-cut dresses.
Many of the young ladies, upon entering the halls, were to find
that a cool frog jumping straight up into the inner sanctums of
a full-cut skirt produced unexpectedly stimulating reactions.
Two senior girls, one junior cheerleader, and the eighth-grade
history teacher were so stimulated, in fact, that they ripped off
their skirts right in the middle of the hall and went flying bare-
legged into the nearest ladies' room.

With all the uproar, it was a simple matter for the Jakes to
join the rush and unobtrusively shut ten open lockers.

Coach Fuzzy was hoarsely shouting "Fire Drill! Fire Drill!"
into the loudspeaker. Most of the students were headed
outdoors anyway. Burly Shirley, who was a Pentecostal, took
the situation quite literally, and had her ninth graders kneel for
prayer in their schoolyard assembly area. Charley Garbage
tripped the fire alarm switch when Coach Fuzzy began yelling
"Fire Drill," and then the town sirens added to the din. When
the police cars and fire engines arrived, Coach Fuzzy gave up

and used the police chief's bullhorn to announce that school would recess for the day. Buses ran before noon, and those children whose parents could not be contacted were allowed to use the gym facilities for the rest of the day.

Several older boys volunteered to stay and help clear the school of this mysterious plague of frogs. Some of the farm boys even had croker sacks stashed in their vehicles. Or somewhere. Sixteen boys remained to perform this task better suited for youngsters than adults anyway, and Coach Fuzzy showed his appreciation by treating them to lunch at Charlie Pignatelli's Pizzaria. Television crews were present before the boys left the school, having sacked probably ninety percent of the surviving frogs. Many had been squashed flat.

Father Phil and two other ministers were called in for consultations at an emergency School Board meeting that evening, and random telphone polls revealed that no other school in the area had, in the past few weeks, incurred the Wrath of God. At least not to the extent of full-fledged Plagues (the reddish water was viewed in a new light). Of course, no other school had been reading in the seventh and eighth chapters of Exodus, either.

The Board Vice-President maintained that it was an expensive gag, and finally made a motion to declare it as such and punish the perpetrators. But the Board President refused to even ask for a second, much less call for a vote. As he pointed out, "If it *was* a gag, and we vote it ain't, then we're fools in God's eyes. If it *is* a plague, and we vote it ain't, we're gonna get worse than frogs. If it *was* a gag and we catch 'im, we'll have to prove it, and this has already made national TV. Some-a them hot-shot lawyers'll get into it, and we'll be *famous* fools for gettin' after a kid who turned loose a few frogs in school."

"And . . ."

"A *few* frogs!" Coach Fuzzy interrupted. "There musta been ten thou . . ."

The gavel banged him out of order and into silence. The President glared and resumed his discourse. "And if it *is* a plague and we vote it is, we'll be fools for havin' to vote on what's in the Bible!" He paused. "In other words, we'll be fools any way we go except home. And I'm goin' there!" He rapped his gavel sharply on the table. "Meetin' adjourned until the regular weekly meetin'. . . . But Coach," he eyed the principal levelly, "you watch what the hell you read in the mornin'!"

He chose the Beatitudes.

Late that night, Papa Jake came into the Heater's room and woke the boy up. "You didn't tell me about the trouble at school today, son."

"Trouble?" the Heater bluffed, rubbing his eyes.

"Trouble. As in 'you're in trouble!'" his father said.

"Yes, sir." Humility seemed to be called for.

"I saw y'all catchin' all those frogs on Saturday, and I can add as good as the next guy. How in the hell did y'all manage to do that?"

Sometimes it's best to throw oneself on the mercy of the court. The Heater did so now. He told the whole story, even down to the dark blue lacy panties that the eighth-grade history teacher was wearing. Finally he fell silent. His parent was weeping, and not from sorrow.

"Well, good luck. I hope they don't find out, 'cause I'll undoubtedly have to hire a lawyer. I'll tell the Duke to keep his mouth shut, too. But, dammit, y'all stay out of trouble for awhile!"

Heater changed his mind about volunteering information on the barn dance. "Yes, sir!" he nodded.

Papa Jake paused at the door after flipping out the light.

"Dark blue lacy bikini panties, huh?" he checked, just to confirm the original information.

"Yes, sir. Mostly lace, really."

The father closed the door. "Boy's grownin' up!" he muttered, still laughing.

With the wild dog population having been totally wiped out for a year, the Woods gained another game animal. Apparently the canine predators had been preying heavily on the feral hogs, so the Jakes had rarely seen one. Now, however, the pressure was off and the number of hogs increased to the point that Papa Jake encouraged the boys to hunt them. The meat of a young wild hog during a fall when there is a good crop of pecans and acorns is "tender, sweet, and hard to beat," as the saying goes.

The Jakes killed a couple of shoats and barbequed them over coals of sassafras wood, and the results convinced them that this was deserving of the main course at the next JakeFest. Accordingly, a hog hunt was scheduled for the Saturday before deer season opened.

The Rookie was still working for the construction company while living at Aunt Florrie's Boarding House, and had saved enough money to buy himself not only a shotgun, but also a .357 magnum revolver. After all, in a small town, a sixteen-year-old boy who talks funny and has quit school has a limited number of options as to how he can spend his money. The boy was proud of his new pistol, and showed up for the hog hunt with the .357 by his side.

Pal and Polly were pressed into service for the purpose of locating the porkers. Perfect and Birdlegs had ridden the ponies down to the Woods Friday evening, tethering them beyond the sweetgum tree, which upset Boateater no end the next morning. He had latrine duty, and felt strongly that this contribution caused an unwarranted increase in his duties. The residue certainly qualified, though; he couldn't argue with that. As the Heater, who had cooking duty, pointed out, "If it was chocolate cake, it'd be my job to clean it up, but . . ." Grudgingly, Boateater dug another hole.

Birdlegs and Perfect rode off early in opposite directions to make a fast circuit of the Swamp and report back, for the Jakes knew that a herd of hogs would lay up close to wherever it had fed during the night. Perfect found a large patch of freshly-rooted ground on the back side of the Woods not far from the little Swamp island where they had ambushed the wild dogs. Birdlegs galloped back to tell the rest of the Jakes to drive the jeep around to Deputy Don's house and come in from there, since it was so much closer. The Rookie spun the cylinder on his new revolver as the Heater cranked the jeep. "Ah cawl this mah 'hawgleg,' 'cawse this is whut Ah shoot hawgs with," he bragged, exaggerating Deadeye's drawl.

The two horse-riding Jakes had tied up their mounts and were waiting impatiently when their four comrades came walking down the slope from Deputy Don's. "C'mon," beckoned Perfect, who had already scouted the herd's whereabouts. "They're layin' up on The Island."

Because high-powered rifles and pistols were involved, it was deemed unsafe to surround the island as they had done for the wild dogs. Therefore, they waded out and approached the Island silently in a line abreast. The Rookie was in the middle, and it was he who sighted the first pig, a medium-sized black-and-white shoat. The young hog snorted in surprise as it flushed from a palmetto clump, then ran twenty feet before it turned to see what it had run from. The Rookie dropped into a crouch, aiming with both hands. The .357 boomed and the shoat went down, squealing and kicking, while hogs of all sizes and ages erupted from all over.

The herd was composed of an old boar and two big sows, one sow having just weaned her brood of eight shoats, while the other sow had whelped her litter of a dozen piglets only ten days before. These panicked little piggies came squirting out from beneath an elbow bush at Rookie's shot, right in front of Boateater and Birdlegs. "Catch piggies!" exclaimed the former, and instantly the two rifles were leaned against trees as the pair charged after the squealing babies.

Whose mad Mama was on the way.

Birdlegs dived and caught a piglet in each hand and had risen to show his prizes to his comrade, who had one trapped beneath his jump, when he heard an angry adult pig squeal behind him. His feet started moving before he cast a glance over his shoulder, but Boateater was already in front of him. Right off the end of the island the sow chased the two boys who had terrorized her brood. In waist-deep water they were able to evade her, though they had to abandon their catches, which splashed away with only eyes and snouts showing, as hogs swim.

Perfect and Deadeye each dropped a shoat, but the Heater was behind a cypress tree when the herd flushed and was unable to shoot. Deadeye's pig was crippled and he ran to finish it off, joined by Perfect. The Heater came sprinting up to join them as they heard the .357 boom again. All three Jakes froze, ringside spectators to The Rookie's Great Hog Chase.

The huge boar had jumped out at the first shot, and as the shoat went down, the sire realized the full implications of the gunfire. The herd chieftain took flight for the other side of the island. But the Rookie had seen him.

Long legs pumping, the newest Jake charged after the boar, pistol held aloft. He would almost catch up, stop, aim at the galloping tusker, fire, miss, and chase again. The three boys watched wide-eyed as the hog stayed just in front of the Rookie. Until he ran into a brush top.

Cornered, the boar wheeled to face his pursuer. As the hog braced himself, the Rookie slammed to a stop and stuck the pistol nearly between the enraged eyes, scant feet away. "Die, hog!" he bellowed, and pulled the trigger.

"Click!" said the hammer, falling on a spent shell.

There was time for the watchers to etch the scene in their minds — the Rookie, arm outstretched, pistol unwaveringly fixed on the boar's head; the hog, tusks and eyes gleaming, gathering his muscles for his turn at pursuing. Then the tusker roared. "Rrrooooiiinnnkkk!!!"

Revolver held aloft in one hand, knees nearly touching his chin with each step, the Rookie spun and started back from whence he had come, the snorting, grunting hog intent on mayhem right behind. The newly-pursued spied his fascinated comrades. "Shoot 'im! Shoot 'im!" he yelled.

The Jakes had already thought of this, but the boar was too close behind. And gaining!

"Climb a tree!" called Perfect.

"Turn sideways!" was the Heater's advice.

Dropping his fickle pistol, the Rookie headed for a hackberry limb. He almost got both legs out of the way before the gleaming tusks slashed by below him. The boar skidded to a stop and was wheeling to slash again when three rifles cracked almost simultaneously. The tusker went down kicking, heart-shot.

Still hanging from the limb by both hands, the Rookie looked fearfully at the others as they ran up. "He got me, I think," he said, voice quavering. Sure enough, bright red blood trickled onto the leaves beneath him.

"Waal, c'mon down, Tar-zan," Deadeye reached up to steady his wounded companion. One leg nearly folded when the Rookie dropped to the ground. Perfect stepped up to grab his other arm, as the Heater indicated a seat on a nearby fallen log. They eased him down to sit, and Heater began unlacing the short leather boot while Deadeye retrieved the empty pistol and Perfect trotted off to find Birdlegs and Boateater.

"Boy, he got you good!" A gash nearly five inches long started just over the boot top and ran diagonally across the calf to behind the knee. Heater drew his knife and finished slitting the pants leg after removing the boot. Blood flowed freely and the wounded one twisted his leg to try to see for himself. It looked almost an inch deep in the middle.

The Heater felt the hamstring tendon at the back of the knee. "This might hurt, but I needja to bend your leg, then straighten it all the way out," he ordered. The Rookie did so, with no apparent impairment. They checked the ankle's flexing with the same results. Heater's hands were slippery with blood when Perfect, Birdlegs, and Boateater hurried up.

"Son of a three-toed, bare-backed berry picker!" Perfect exclaimed. Boateater whitened and turned away. Birdlegs knelt down; as usual, he was inspired by the challenge.

"Shoot-a-mile! Whadda we do now?" he queried. "You ever put in stitches before?"

"Ohhh, no!" the Rookie cried.

"Jus' kiddin'! Jus' kiddin'!" Birdlegs assured him.

The Heater regarded everyone in the party with a critical

eye. All of them had waded the murky Swamp waters up past the knee, and both Boateater and Birdlegs were wet above the waist. All their shirts were sweat-soaked and sprayed with mosquito repellant, for it had not yet frosted. "Has anybody got anything on that's clean enough to bandage with?" he asked hopefully.

Deadeye had a small, relatively clean handkerchief in his shirt pocket. "To wipe off my glasses," he explained, offering it to Heater.

"Survival kits?" Perfect voiced the thought, reaching for his own.

"Great idea!" the Heater agreed. "S'pose a coupla you leave your kits here an' wade on back to get the horses. We can't let 'im wade outa here, an' I betcha we can't carry 'im. I might have an idea."

Perfect and Boateater undertook to return for the horses as Heater began to go through the survival kits. Each one had a small plastic bottle of antiseptic, but large Band-aid patches were the biggest bandaging material available. The medicinal Jake laid out his materials. "Turn over an' lie on your stomach," he ordered the Rookie.

He poured most of one bottle of antiseptic on Deadeye's handkerchief and sponged off his own hands and the Rookie's leg, after first rinsing most of the blood off with water from his canteen. He then picked two full bottles and nodded to Birdlegs and Deadeye, indicating that they were to hold the leg outstretched. Unscrewing both caps, he took a breath, said "Hang on" to the patient, and poured the contents of both bottles into the gaping wound.

"AAAARRRggghhh!!!" screamed the Rookie.

"Yell if you want to," Heater said mildly.

After a minute the burning lessened, and the patient threatened weakly, "I'm gonna kill you!" The Rookie-holders leaned to help at the medic's next instructions.

"Take this lighter and sterilize these," he handed Birdlegs two six-packs of small brass fishhooks, "and use your match to sterilize these," he pulled a set of fingernail clippers from his pocket for Deadeye. As they performed these tasks, he poured more antiseptic over his own fingers, holding the bottle with his wrists. He held out his hand for the first fishhook, grasping it by the eye of the inch-long shank.

Placing his fingers at the top of the cut and squeezing it together, the Heater stuck the point of the hook through the skin on one side of the wound and, working as quickly as possible, brought the point through the skin on the other side of the gash. The barb prevented the hook from pulling back out. With the fingernail clippers, he then gripped the base of the shank and bent it across and under the barb. He sat back and admired his handiwork. "Whatcha think?" he asked.

Rookie, still face-down, just groaned, but Birdlegs and Deadeye regarded him with new respect. "You thinka that yourself?" Deadeye wanted to know.

"Do it!" Birdlegs handed Heater another sterilized hook. The wounded one moaned and bit his wrist.

The sixth hook was being bent and the bleeding was almost stopped when Wacky Mack appeared. The Jakes had never seen him surprised before, but he definitely was now. "What th' hell're you doin'?!?" he demanded hoarsely.

The Heater was taken aback, but Birdlegs answered quickly, having just sterilized what seemed to be the last hook needed. "Hookin' 'im up!" he said matter-of-factly.

"With fishhooks?" This was a Wacky Mack that none of them had ever seen before.

"Well, it's stoppin' the bleedin'! We had to do somethin', an' nobody had anything clean for a bandage." The Heater sounded defensive.

"How you gonna get 'em out?" The bearded man bent to examine the wound closely.

"Clip the shank in two and pull it out by the barb end," the medic was confident about that part. "Jus' like I get fishhooks out now. Like Doctor Mac got out Boateater's." He began to slip the last hook through to close the bottom of the gash. The blood was barely oozing out now.

"Well, I'll be damned." Wacky Mack shook his head. "You okay, son?" he turned his attention to the Rookie.

The victim rolled his eyes. "I'd have to get better to die!" he moaned. "Aaiiigh!" he croaked as Heater, finished, poured the rest of the antiseptic over the wound.

"Next!" announced the doctor, as the sloshing sounds of Pal and Polly neared.

Wacky Mack turned to Birdlegs and Deadeye. "C'mon, you two. I'll help dress those hogs. We'll keep one horse here t' pack 'em out on." As an afterthought, he reached into a pocket and pulled out two clean bandanas, handing them to the Heater. "Tell Doctor Mac I want 'em back," he warned.

"Fishhooks!" Doc McClendon exclaimed. "What the heck made you think of that?" The physician examined the leg closely as the Heater related the details of the injury and subsequent operation. Finally, he began to paint the area around the wound with even more antiseptic. "Well, it's a good job. Lots of doctors use staples now instead of stitches anyway, and this is about the same thing. Tell you what," he addressed the Rookie, "I'm going to shoot you up with antibiotics and bandage this real good. If there's no infection by Monday, we're home free. "Now, for the important thing — did you kill the hog?"

Doc McClendon right then received an invitation to The Third Annual JakeFest.

Actually, there were more or less two JakeFests that year. At the regular one, the Friday after Thanksgiving, the usual men-folks came, plus Doc McClendon and Father Phil. The Duke got roaring drunk and almost met his match in poetry-quoting as Doctor Mac also got well-oiled and spouted a great deal of Browning and Bobbie Burns. Then the two men cooperated and traded lines from Shakespeare's *Julius Caesar* and *A Midsummer Night's Dream*. The doctor had such a good time that he promised the Jakes "twenty-five stitches and two casts, all free, to be claimed at any time during the next year" in return for another invitation.

There was no way the men could eat all of the barbequed pork — the boar and the three shoats — so, under the guise of "not wastin' any meat," the Jakes made plans for the next night, too. They asked the girls again.

Word had gotten around school after the first females-at-fireside session, and plenty of girls would have volunteered had they gotten the chance. However, the Jakes stayed with their previous choice of girls: Crazy Sharon, Cuddly Carrie, Space Ace, Leapin' Lena, and of course Baby Sister. The only newcomer to the fire was the A+ blonde that the Heater had dated a couple of times who was also Perfect's oft-time science lab partner. Since the time that she had poured nitric acid in with sulphuric, she had been known as "Mad Mel."

It had been cloudy all day, but the rain held off just long enough. By the time the youngsters had finished supper, the rumble of thunder could be heard in the southwest. From where they were, deep in the Woods, they could not be sure how fast the storm was approaching, so the boys suggested that preparations be made to break camp before everyone got wet. After Perfect and Deadeye doused the fire, the lightning in the towering thunderheads was the principle illumination and the girls marveled at how beautiful the heavenly display was. The Rookie looked at Boateater. "Hey, 'member the meteor showers?"

"Aw, man! What a great idea!" Boateater exclaimed.

The Woods were in a topographical depression, with the Swamp as a center, of course. The Jake Camp was a half-mile north of the Swamp, where the ground began to rise again, and the trees blocked most of the sky to the south and west. However, by going back out to the gravel road and then through the Woods to the southern rim of the depression, the Jakes and their guests had an unobstructed view of the southwest. They all disembarked at Muddy Slough and sat on a couple of ground cloths that Perfect had thrown in the jeep.

The front was coming in slower than they had anticipated; yet because of that, it was more majestic. When the bluish lightning flashed, they could see the cloud tops flexing, building, massing for Nature's assault. Thunder boomed and the youngsters shivered.

"Why does it make you feel kinda cold an' queasy at the bottom of your stomach?" Mad Mel asked slowly.

"And the shivers run from the bottom to the top of your spine?" added Cuddly Carrie.

"Makes me cold an' clammy across the toppa my chest," the Rookie whispered.

"That's my pet king snake. I wondered where he'd gotten off to." Birdlegs ducked as six people threw dirt clods at him for breaking the mood.

The next Tuesday, a lanky senior called The Splinter caught the Heater aside after school. "Look," he said belligerently, "I understand you've got ideas about Mad Mel."

"Not particularly," was the reply. "But if I did," and this was delivered in the same tone as he had been addressed in, "I wouldn't care 'bout checkin' it out with you!"

The Splinter was a wide receiver on the football team, and a pretty good one. "Well, I'm tellin' ya, sport. Back off," he warned.

The Heater was on his way to a fall semester pitchers-catchers clinic and did not have time for a confrontation, but neither was he going to back down. Angrily, he rejoined, "Hey, bite my butt, stupid! I'll date any girl I wanna date. I ain't had a date with Mad Mel in a while, but if I ask her it'll be up to me an' her, not you!"

"Don't lie to me! You took her out Saturday night!" the senior claimed.

"I never did! I didn't even . . . oh, yeah. I know what you're talkin' about. But . . ."

"But, but, but. Sounds like a motorboat. If I catch you out with her again, your momma won't even know you," Splinter shook his fist in Heater's face.

In the face of anger, make him mad, the Jake thought. "Well, hide an' watch, hot-shot, 'cause I got a date with her Saturday night," he bluffed. Behind him, Blue John, the catcher, opened the dressing room door.

"Hey, Heater, c'mon!"

Splinter grabbed the younger boy's shoulder as he turned to leave. "All right, smarty. If you ain't chicken, see you Friday night in the church parkin' lot. Bring a box to take home all your teeth in!" Heater jerked loose and stomped away.

On the way to school the next morning, he related the incident to his cousin. Perfect shook his head. "That's a big buncha meatheads that run together. You better take a backup crew."

By Friday evening, the Jakes were all in attendance at the gym as the pitchers and catchers finished and headed for the showers. Matter of fact, there were a good number of students still hanging around the school; a fight between a senior and a sophomore over a girl was exciting stuff. In reality, of course, the fight wasn't over a girl. As with most fights, it was caused by one person trying to impose his will on another.

As they undressed to shower, Blue John remarked to Heater, "You know ole Splinter thinks he's a hot-shot with that karate junk, don'tcha? Fights with his feet a lot."

"Didn't know that."

"Yeah. Jus' be ready. He don't fight fair." The catcher patted him on the shoulder. "Good luck!"

Many baseball players, especially catchers and infielders, wear a protective piece of equipment referred to as a "cup." Though the Heater was at this special fall practice to improve his pitching, he had had to do some catching as well; as on any team, there were more pitchers than catchers. To guard against wild pitches and bad hops, he had worn a cup, just like Blue John. An idea dawned. He pulled his jeans on over his cup.

The Heater had a habit too of taping his glove hand; just several loops of adhesive tape around the hand to deaden the impact of a couple of hundred throws a day back from the catcher. Now, instead of stripping the tape off, he stepped over to the equipment locker and added a couple more strips to the taped hand and also taped his throwing hand. His knuckles were completely protected by several layers of tape.

It was almost dark when the Jakes left the gym walking toward the parking lot. Their leather jackets were beginning to get outgrown in places, but they all had them on. They almost swaggered, hands in jacket pockets, as they rounded the corner of the school and approached the parking lot.

Boateater stopped and stared. "Good Golly Greenwood! Must be a hundred people there!" Actually, there were only twenty-eight.

"No sweat." Birdlegs had a smug look on his face, and never broke stride.

The Splinter stepped forward as the Jakes approached. He wore jeans, a tee shirt, and unsoled leather moccasins. He was stripped for battle, bouncing on his toes. The Heater removed his jacket and shirt and handed them to Birdlegs, whose jeep was parked close. The tall boy walked to his vehicle, unlocked it, and laid Heater's clothes on the seat.

There was the usual amount of sneering and posturing that takes place before such scheduled events. Through all of it the Heater faced the Splinter, staying barely beyond arms' length with fists on hips and legs spread strangely. He taunted the senior, seeming to swagger in one place, pelvis thrust forward. Finally Splinter went into action.

His first move was to kick Heater squarely between the legs. Normally this is a good move in any fight, as it renders the foe breathless and helpless for a few moments, if it doesn't end the fight altogether then and there.

It did end the fight.

The Splinter broke his his big toe and two bones in his foot. To the amazement of the gathered crowd, the Heater smiled contemptuously and offered, "Wanna try again?"

But Splinter obviously did not. He was bent over in pain, holding his foot. Heater stepped forward and uppercut him with a taped fist. The senior spun and landed face-down on the concrete.

That's when the Heater blew his cool.

He landed astraddle the Splinter's back, knocking the wind out of his fallen foe, and grabbed the boy's hair in both hands. Splinter's face and the concrete began a contest to see which was the hardest.

203

"Hey!" yelled a senior halfback. "He's gonna kill 'im!" The crowd surged forward.

And Birdlegs jumped from his jeep with a shotgun. At its boom, the crowd fell all over itself backing off and the Heater stopped and ducked, thinking himself the target. The Splinter was beyond caring.

Birdlegs stepped forward coolly, yet knowing the blast would bring a patrol car soon. "You through?" he asked Heater.

Shaken, not from the unexpected gunfire but from the realization of his own temper, the Heater stood, flexing his fists. "Yeah," he said. The Jakes began to move toward their vehicles.

"Hey," the senior halfback said again, "that wasn't fair."

"Hey," Birdlegs smiled ominously, "we don't fight fair!"

As so often happens after a little success, the Jakes got cocky. One of their number not only had whipped a senior, but they had stood down half the football team. Girls all over school took notice of the group of tenth graders, and the girls with whom the Jakes were special friends became just a tad possessive. The boys developed a slight swagger, even Perfect, and Boateater took to walking down the junior-high wing once a day so the little kids could have their fair chance at adoration.

They stayed out later. They dated, and even kissed a girl or two. They drove fast, and had races on roads where they shouldn't have. They drank beer, and a couple graduated to whiskey. Three of them even tried marijuana cigarettes. In the words from an old high school yearbook, their motto became "live fast, die young, and have a good-looking corpse!"

Three of them almost made it.

Birdlegs, Boateater, and the Rookie had triple-dated one Friday night, and were on their way back out to the Jake Camp, having stopped for a bottle of rum — Rookie had a fake ID. They had already consumed several beers at the dance intermission, and later someone had spiked the punch with vodka. They caught the drive-in at Charlie Pignatelli's Pizzaria right before closing time and purchased three fountain drinks. Pouring half the drink on the ground, they refilled their cups with rum and headed for the Woods, singing.

Boateater had forgotten Deputy Don's story about Don L.

Birdlegs was driving seventy-five miles an hour when he unexpectedly reached the "T" intersection at the 3-Way Store. Suddenly, he had two choices: straight ahead across Farmer Jordon's harvested cottonfield, or try to make a right-angle turn at seventy. Fortunately, he selected the first. At least he didn't roll.

Also fortunately, the roadside ditch was shallow. Though the jeep bucked severely and left the ground twice, it crossed the ditch and continued out across the field, bouncing over the rows. It had rained the night before, and this too was an advantage, especially for the Rookie. Sitting in the back of the open jeep, he was catapulted up and out when the vehicle jumped the ditch. He turned a complete flip in the air and landed on his rump, splattering mud for thirty feet. Except for having bitten his tongue, he was unhurt.

Birdlegs was applying full brakes, but it was having little effect. Both his and Boateater's heads bounced back and forth from dashboard to windshield to seatback. Then a front tire blew and the jeep began to skid. Finally, the mud built up in front and stopped the vehicle, fifty yards out into the field of bare stalks.

When the Rookie ran up, both occupants of the wreck were unconscious. He determined that they had regular pulsebeats, though the driver was breathing funny, and made sure that there was no arterial bleeding. He knew better than to try to move them. He cut the switch off, raised the hood to assure himself there was no danger of fire, and checked his pockets to be sure he had change for the public telephone at the 3-Way Store. Stone-cold sober, the Rookie ran through the muddy field to the blacktop and turned toward the store, a half-mile away.

Uncle Bubba drove the slippery road through the Woods to the Jake Camp at two in the morning to deliver the news to the other three Jakes. Boateater had a severe concussion and had used up most of Doctor Mac's free stitches on his head and arms. Birdlegs had broken his wrist and three ribs, partially collapsing one lung, and had used up the rest of their allotment of free stitches. The Rookie had two stitches where he had bitten through his tongue, and also complained of a terrible headache. Whether that was from hangover, impact, or stress was unclear, but Doctor Mac went ahead and admitted him with the other two.

"Indications are that he was drivin' drunk, and that is a damn-fool thing to do!" Uncle Bubba emphasized his point by pounding his fist on the hood of his Bronco. "Well, they're lucky, though. Y'all go on back to sleep, but c'mon in 'bout nine in the mornin'. Visitin' hours start at ten."

Both Birdlegs and Boateater were still very woozy when the rest of the Jakes came in the next day. The Rookie was feeling okay physically, but mentally he was awfully low. After all, he had been the one who bought the rum with a fake ID. Deputy Don had already been in for an early official visit, and by the time he saw Perfect, Deadeye, and Heater, the Rookie was willing to plead guilty and go to the firing squad rather than face his companions' parents.

"Hey, you didn't twist their arms!" the Heater tried to console him.

"But I'm a dropout; I'm not from here; they're gonna blame me anyway!" the Rookie wailed.

"There it is," Deadeye drawled in agreement.

Perfect gave Deadeye a dirty look. "Aw, you ain't to blame, Rookie. We all are. We've had a wild hair up our rear for over a month now. I knew better. So did you. So did they. Main thing is, everybody's gonna be okay. We'll just have to learn from this an' settle down."

Deadeye was in an agreeable mood today. "That's right. Really, for the last month, ain't none-a us had walkin'-around sense. Heck, I even tried one-a them li'l ole left-handed cigarettes!"

"That I gave y'all!" The Rookie had another helping of guilt.

"Right again," Deadeye nodded.

The Rookie was saved by Other Mother's entrance into his room. "Rookie, Doctor Mac says he'll let you go today if somebody will check you over the weekend. Why don't you plan on spending the night at our house and going to church with us tomorrow?"

"Yes, ma'am." Little did the Rookie know that, loaded with guilt, he would "walk the aisle" at the invitational hymn and join the church that next morning. "I'll get the Heater to drop by Aunt Florrie's and get me some clean clothes." The boys left the hospital after Doc McClendon's visit.

Saturday night, Boateater and Birdlegs had recovered somewhat when the other four Jakes visited. As Rookie had surmised, he absorbed most of the blame for the incident, especially from Boateater's mother. However, the parents were preparing to leave when the four Jakes walked into the room, so after enduring some scathing comments and murderous looks, the coast was finally clear. As his mom left the room, Boateater grinned and shrugged an apology at the Rookie. "Sorry, man."

"S'okay. Looks like I better get used to it."

Boateater shrugged again. "Better you than me!"

At that point, the door opened and Father Phil, Wacky Mack, and the Duke of Dundee walked in. They had of course talked with Doc McClendon and Papa Jake or Uncle Bubba. They not only knew the condition of the hurt boys, they knew how they had attained that condition. Their reactions varied.

Father Phil was smilingly sympathetic, yet gently disapproving. Though neither of the boys was of his flock, they often attended his services and youth activities, and he also considered them personal friends. Without a sermon — indeed, with few words at all — the minister got his message across.

Wacky Mack was blunt, as usual. He shook each injured boy's hand and announced, "Glad you're gonna be okay. Coulda been a helluva lot worse. Y'all're damn fools!" The veteran then sat down next to the Rookie and gripped his hand so tightly the boy winced. Perfect overheard the man growl in a raspy whisper, "Dammit! Wha'd I tell you 'bout them sonsabitchin' left-handed cigarettes!" The Rookie looked like he was going to cry.

It was the Duke of Dundee who was openly enraged, however. Veins bulging, neck corded, face red, he towered over the beds and began to lecture. He did not spare the other four boys, either. He shook his finger in all six faces, tongue-lashing all and sundry, magnificent in his anger. Finally, spent, he croaked almost like Wack Mack in his last admonition: "Aye am glad you are alive and uncrippled. But, for God's sake, *DON'T drink and drive!!!*" With that, he stomped to the door. Father Phil and Wacky Mack rose to leave too, rather awed by the performance.

The Duke held the door for the other men, but just as they stepped out into the hall, Birdleg's voice stopped them.

"But, Mr. Duke," his tone was aggrieved and slightly injured. "You do it, don'tcha?"

There was no answer as the three men continued their exit and closed the door behind them, so none of the Jakes saw their friend's reaction. Father Phil thought the tall farmer was having an attack as he clutched his chest and staggered against the wall. But as the minister and Wacky Mack moved to his aid, the Duke of Dundee threw his head back so hard they heard it thump on the concrete-block wall. In an agonized whisper, he choked out, "Sweet Jesus! They have been looking at me!"

And the Duke quit.

He quit cold turkey.

He went through his cabinets and poured brandies, bourbons, vodka, rum, gin, scotch, wines, and liqueurs down the kitchen sink, shocking algae that had lived in his drain lines and septic tank for years. He connected a hose to the beer keg in its special cooler and drained the draft beer into the yard where Gin, Tonic, and the new bluetick puppy, Tequila, got happily polluted. He cleaned out under the seats of his pickup and car. Even the bottles locked in the file drawer at his farm office and shop were broken into the trash barrel, the liquor running down into old used oil and air filters. This Saturday-night flurry of resolute activity kept him up until three o'clock.

He arose Sunday, showered, dressed, and went to church for the first time in years. After church, he visited the hospital and apologized to the two Jakes for his tirade the night before. He was still there when the rest of the Jakes came in, excited about Rookie's joining the church. Crazy Sharon, Baby Sister, and Leapin' Lena trooped in right behind the boys, and soon the Duke was quoting poetry. Deeming the occasion worthy of Robert W. Service, he did "Dan McGrew" and "Sam McGee" before a nurse stuck her head in to warn them about the noise.

"And he ought not to be laughing like that, either," she said of Birdlegs.

Parents arrived, and then Father Phil and Doc McClendon came by on their rounds. "This is more folks than I usually get at Sunday night services," the minister observed mildly. Whereupon the Duke grandly offered to treat everyone to supper at Charlie Pignatelli's *if* they all went to night services to see the Rookie baptised.

"*You're* comin' to the Baptist church?" Father Phil was mockingly incredulous.

"Surely it will be safe? Aye assumed that you would not be preaching at a baptismal service," was the rejoinder.

"Anytime three of us Baptists get together, one preaches, one listens, and one passes the plate!" the minister warned.

The Space Ace, Mad Mel, Cuddly Carrie, Blue John, Rapid Robert, Ice Cream, and most of the Jakes' parents joined the crowd at church and Charlie Pignatelli's that night. The Duke picked up the tab for $104.22 when the party broke up. He drove home humming "Comin' Thru' the Rye" and "My Bonnie Lies Over the Ocean." As he swung into his driveway, he broke into "Auld Lang Syne," and went in to have a drink.

There was none.

It was a long night.

Fortunately, Uncle Bubba and Papa Jake drove over the next morning to thank him for supper. The Duke informed them of his resolution and subsequent craving, and his desire to do it himself and why. The three drove into town to tell Father Phil, who had worked closely with Alcoholics Anonymous. "It's gonna be tough, Duke!" the preacher warned.

Coon hunting helped. The men enlisted Deputy Don and Wacky Mack, and every night during the week, one or two of the men would be out in the Woods with the Duke and his dogs. Deputy Don borrowed some Black-and-Tan hounds from his cousin in an adjoining county to join Gin, Tonic, and Tequila. Father Phil bought a rangy young Catahoula hound which was reputed to be a coon dog, naming him "Holy

Ghost" because of his spooky white eyes. However, it turned out that Holy Ghost had been running coons only because no hogs were available; when he happened upon the feral pigs in the Swamp, it became apparent what purpose he had been bred for.

"That Holy Ghost is in Hawg Heaven!" Deputy Don joked to the Duke and Father Phil after the third time the Catahoula had to be pried loose from a porker's ear one night.

The Jakes were pressed into service over the weekends and again over the semester break. The Duke lost weight, lost sleep, became haggard and gaunt, but in the night-time Woods there was activity he loved, companions who cared, and no bottles. During the week of semester break, there was a Jake campfire every night, and both Rookie and Deadeye found that they loved the thrill of stumbling through the night after the hounds. During rest times around the fire, they all observed the Duke's shaking hands and morose moods, but Father Phil and Wacky Mack had told them why the man was going through his hell. The night that Boateater and Birdlegs returned to the Jake Camp, the Duke cried like a baby. And the boys understood.

Of course, the coon hunting could not be an every night thing, not over weeks and weeks. Had it been, the Duke might have made it. But his companions had jobs, duties, school, other things to do. The dogs had to be rested. Even though it was off-season, the Duke himself had obligations during daily business hours. And so, after nearly six weeks of abstinence, the Duke paced until after midnight one Tuesday and decided he couldn't stand any more. He had to have at least one drink. Pulling on a jacket, he stomped resolutely to the truck and started out of his hundred-yard-long driveway.

A muddy jeep with a canvas top was parked across the end of the drive next to his mailbox. Incredulous, the thirsting farmer stepped from his truck and walked to the jeep door. Wacky Mack peered out at him, a sleeping bag zipped halfway up his chest. Not sure whether to be angry or not, the Duke of Dundee asked slowly, "Have you been here all this time?"

"Nope," his friend answered, squinting in the headlight beam. "Jus' when you need me."

The Duke backed up the driveway and returned to his house. He slept like a baby.

And made it.

The Jakes had been taught never to waste game, and therefore one evening when the Rookie was driving out to the Woods, and the car in front of him hit a deer but kept going, the boy pulled to the side of the road at the scene. Perfect, in the passenger seat of the VW convertible, exclaimed, "It's a li'l ole spike buck!"

Apparently the deer had jumped out into the side of the passing car, which knocked it back into the ditch. Though the season was over, it seemed a shame to leave that much good meat to rot. "Waal, let's take it home and dress it out," Deadeye drawled. It was a tight fit, but the buck was small enough for them to close the front trunk on it.

They were pulling into Perfect's driveway when the first bleating sound was heard. At first, they thought the Beetle's horn was stuck, but when Rookie punched the button, there was a slightly different tone. Then the kicking started.

"Son of a three-toed, bare-backed berry picker! That deer's alive!"

It was very much alive indeed, and obviously wanted out. "What're we gonna do?" asked the Rookie. The little car was bouncing with the buck's efforts to free itself.

Perfect thought fast. His mother was gone, so the garage was empty, though Uncle Bubba's Bronco was parked by the basketball goal, indicating that he was home. "Pull up into the garage," the boy ordered Rookie.

It was a one-car garage, but there was plenty of room for all the other things garages accumulate. Two garbage cans for garbage, one more for fat pine kindling, and a fourth one full of pecans, lined one wall. Gardening tools, sprayers, and flower pots sat next to an old metal cabinet crammed with paint, yard and garden chemicals, and home-repair paraphanalia. A three-horse and a ten-horse outboard motor sat on their racks. An old storm door was propped up against the wall, and two bicycles leaned against it. The riding lawnmower and wheelbarrow were parked on the same side as the garbage cans. A rack of baseball bats and equipment was next to the back steps. The family's Continental fit with barely room to open the doors on each side, but there was plenty of room for the Rookie's VW.

"Now what?" the driver wanted to know. The deer was bleating strongly now, and its kicks were rocking the car. "Hurry up, man! He's gonna wreck my car, and it ain't even paid for!"

Perfect leaped from the vehicle, motioning for Deadeye to follow. He jerked two baseball bats out of the rack, handing one to his companion as he instructed the Rookie, "Now, you open the trunk an' we'll hit 'im with the bats."

Deadeye backed off. "Ohhh, no! I ain't fixin' to hit no live deer with no baseball bat!" The buck bleated and kicked.

"C'mon, candy! He's already been run over by a car an' been closed up in the trunk of a Volkswagon! How dangerous can he be?" Perfect was confident. "Jus' hit 'im in the head when he pokes it out. Unlock it, Rookie."

Deadeye stepped up, grumbling, "I bet we're gonna get in trouble for this!"

The Rookie unlocked the trunk, but the deer did not stick its head out.

Some pitchers throw fastballs at over ninety miles an hour, and even though the pitcher's mound is sixty feet from home plate, many batters cannot connect with their target. According to later testimony from Deadeye, "that damn deer came outa that car doin' a hunnerd miles an hour!"

At six feet, neither batter came close.

Deadeye's bat hit the spare tire and bounced back, catching Perfect, who had missed deer, car, and everything, in the back of the head as he followed through. One Jake down.

The deer bolted from the trunk, bounced off the wall, and slammed into the metal cabinet, knocking it over. By this time, Perfect was going down and Deadeye was recoiling with his bat. He never got it up. The buck caroomed off the falling cabinet and ran slap over the boy, knocking bat and glasses flying. Two Jakes down.

Down the line of garbage cans crashed the panicked deer, sending garbage, kindling, and nuts flying all over the garage. Its hooves hit the front of the wheelbarrow, and that implement flipped up onto its wheel, one handle striking the deer's nose as had been planned for the baseball bats to do. The buck turned a backflip onto the garbage cans again, and in regaining its feet, knocked over the only one still standing. Deadeye sat up just in time to see the deer charging him again. The boy jumped toward the back steps, but hit the rack of baseball equipment. His fall onto the steps was padded by the gloves, and two dozen balls rolled free.

The animal rounded the Volkswagon, where the Rookie was still perched on the trunk in awe, slipped on a baseball, and would have fallen to the concrete floor if Perfect hadn't been there first. That Jake was knocked back down into a rapidly-spreading puddle of paint and roofing tar that had spilled from the overturned metal cabinet, which the flailing hooves now drummed on.

All this happened in maybe fifteen seconds. Inside, Uncle Bubba threw his paper aside and leaped up, exclaiming, "What the hell!"

On, on, pressed the buck, smashing into the bicycles, feet lashing at the entangling spokes. The storm door toppled just as the deer cleared it, and the falling glass door hit the Rookie right in the top of the head. The glass broke, knocking the boy from his perch and into Deadeye, who was trying to rise again. Three Jakes down.

The three-horse motor went crashing from its rack as the spike exited the garage, free once more. Just then, Uncle Bubba jerked open the door, stepped squarely on a baseball on the top step, and would probably have broken his back had he not landed on top of Rookie and Deadeye.

"What the hell's goin' on here!!!" he roared, regaining his feet. Uncle Bubba was seldom angered, but the total destruction of his garage in so short a time accomplished that emotion. "What the hell're y'all doin'?" he bellowed again at the three rising Jakes.

Dripping paint and tar and holding the back of his head, Perfect started to explain. "Daddy, that deer . . ."

"*WHAT* deer?!?!" screamed his furious parent.

That spring, the young men's fancy turned not only to turkey hunting, but to love. The Heater had fallen pretty hard for Mad Mel a few months earlier, and it had caused some friction that he didn't understand. Crazy Sharon, whom he considered a long-time good friend, had begun to treat him rather coolly. Boateater, who had always thought Crazy Sharon hung the moon, lately seemed to take offense at any and everything the Heater said or did. Perfect had developed his own case over Leapin' Lena, and had little time for cousins or friends. Birdlegs became almost malicious in his teasing while the Rookie, left out of any romancing, developed a chip on his shoulder. Their Jake Camp, even with turkey season going on, became a test of endurance and patience.

Toward the last weekend, the Heater finally killed his first turkey of the season, a jake. All the rest of the Jakes had killed at least two birds except the Rookie, and the gobbler he had bagged was the biggest anyone had seen in years. Its twelve-inch beard looked thicker than most paintbrushes. When Heater walked into Camp that Saturday, a little before noon, with a fourteen-pound jake that they had to hunt for the beard on, there was general laughter.

As the afternoon wore on, the jocular remarks about "How thick was the shell?" or "Musta been a helluva shot, gettin' one that little without hittin' the mama too" began to wear on the Heater. Then when Perfect casually remarked that he wouldn't be in Camp for supper because he had a date, Birdlegs changed the emphasis of the teasing to the subject of women. Boateater and the Rookie picked it up, including a not-entirely-imaginary affair between Deadeye and Cuddly Carrie, and finally even Perfect let it get under his skin. He and Boateater engaged in a shouting match that ended, just short of blows, when the Heater pointed out to his cousin that he had been "actin' like a boy dog sniffin' around a girl dog in heat!" Perfect's reply was a blow that caught the Heater totally unexpectedly and almost knocked him into the fire.

The other Jakes jumped up to separate the cousins before any more blows were passed, but Boateater took a slap on the cheek intended for Perfect and replied in kind. Furious, the Heater swung at random and bloodied Birdlegs' nose. Deadeye retreated from the brawl and tripped over the dutch oven, spilling the venison stew into the fire. When he started to laugh, Heater broke loose and tackled him, sending the pair of them into the tent, which of course collapsed. Perfect screamed in rage and rejoined the fight.

Women sure complicate life sometimes.

The combatants finally separated, the Heater in a towering rage. He stuttered, spit, cussed, and almost foamed at the mouth. "Out! Out! Get outa here! These are my daddy's Woods, an' I want y'all outa here!!" He spat bitterly. "I'll bring your damned ole stuff out tomorrow! Jus' get outa here! I don't ever wanna see y'all again!"

The other boys quailed in the face of this tirade. Their guns were in the jeeps anyway, and they piled into Birdlegs' new one, leaving Heater his. With sullen looks they drove away. No one spoke.

The Heater drained some of his anger by kicking branches into the fire and breaking up some more to pile onto the blaze. He strode to the sweetgum tree for a root beer, drained it in

one continuous swig, and jerked out another to drink more
leisurely at the fire. When he turned from the ice chest, a voice
rasped, "Bring two." Wacky Mack sat by the cypress log as if
he had been there for hours.

It took the boy a while to get another bottle, and it seemed
a long way back to the log. His steps dragged. Had the man
heard all of the fight? Was he as at fault as his guilty feeling
indicated? The Heater handed Wacky Mack his root beer and
sat down in silence.

And that silence stretched and stretched and stretched.
The man and the boy stared at the fire and drank their root
beers in sips. It was a contest to see whose could last the
longest, as if as long as there was liquid in the bottle neither
would have to speak. The Heater won; Wacky Mack finished
first. The man sighted through the neck of his brown bottle at
the glowing coals and finally broke the silence.

"You're wrong, y'know."

Heater knew, but bluffed. "Howzat?"

Wacky Mack used the toe of his boot to shove a small log
farther up into the fire. "Y' can't treat friends like you been
treatin' 'em."

"How come? They treated me like that."

"Naw. They're jus' reactin' t' th' way you been lately. You
been ignorin' friends jus' like a fella can't have girlfriends an'
friends, too."

"Well, if they act like mine, he can't."

Wacky Mack stood and walked around the blaze, pushing
the unburnt stubs of logs and branches into the coals. Finally
he sat back down. "Son," he rasped, "most likely you'll date a
coupla dozen other girls an' fall in love four or five more times
'fore you end up marryin'. Then again, maybe this'un's th' real
thing. Either way, you figger on givin' up huntin'?"

"No, sir."

"Figger you'll be gettin' outa th' house for weekends, or
maybe even a week, t' set around a fire like this an' hunt
turkeys or deer or ducks th' next mornin'?"

"Yes, sir."

"Who with?" the man let the question hang in the firelight
until the boy had to answer.

"My friends." The reply was grumbled.

"Who's that?" Again, the query dangled almost visually before them. The screech owl called its quavering, shivering cry. A pecan log popped, sending sparks flying into the air. The two stared into the fire, both seeing faces.

"Lemme tell you a story, son," Wacky Mack finally sighed when the Heater couldn't answer. Having said that, he stood and pitched another couple of logs onto the fire, then walked to the ice chest for more root beers. He handed one to the boy, seated himself against the log, and took a swig. Staring moodily at the fire, he began.

"Never knew my dad. Mom run off with another man when I was 'bout six. Stayed in two or three orphan homes 'til I was 'leven. Some of 'em beat hell outa me. Lived with a foster fam'ly a coupla years. But I was too damn mad alla time, so that didn't work." The man sipped at his drink to relieve some of his hoarseness. It didn't help much.

"Lived on th' road a coupla years. Jus' left th' foster fam'ly. Ridin' my thumb; ridin' the rails; mostly shank's mare." He patted his thigh. "Saw a lotta th' country. Drank a lotta whiskey. Smoked some dope. Bad stuff. Messes with your brain." The voice was so coarse it almost set the Heater's teeth on edge.

"Got inta some trouble with th' law out West. Rinky-dink stuff, really. Wrong crowd. Judge gave th' lot of us a choice: jail or service. Lied 'bout my age. Joined th' Marines. Turned seventeen in Vietnam."

There was such a long pause that the Heater finally turned his gaze away from the fire and was about to ask "What happened?" when Mack took another sip and began anew. This time there was an edge of pain to his words, not from the coarseness but from the content.

"First friend I ever had was in th' Nam. Big guy. Cooter could handle a machine gun like you do a .22. Laughin'. Always laughin'." Then, wonderingly, "Even made me laugh." The boy looked sideways and his companion caught the glance. "Huh! I usta laugh," Wacky Mack declared.

"We were bein' lifted outa a hot L-Z. I got hit in th' leg an' they threw me in a chopper." The words sounded as if they were being dragged forcibly from the bearded lips. The Heater couldn't tear his sideways glance from his friend, who stared into the fires of his own private hell. The voice was like fingernails being dragged across a blackboard.

"Somebody's *always* gotta be last. Aw, God! An' th' best always put others first. Cooter was laughin' an' firin' that sixty when Sarge an' Rebop pulled me away from th' perimeter." The voice finally failed.

"What happened?" The Heater couldn't wait.

A long swig of root beer helped renew the tale in a whisper. "They couldn't get 'im out."

The pair gazed at the flames for a long while before Wacky Mack sighed and began again. "Went back for another tour. Lookin' for 'im, I guess. Platoon sergeant. Got real close to the L-T. College kid, trusted everybody. Lung-shot on night patrol. I was carryin' 'im on my shoulders, runnin', when NVA mortars hit. They said he blocked mosta th' shrapnel." The pain was so evident that the Heater sneaked another look to see if the man was actually bleeding.

"Nearly three years recuperatin'. Did some college on th' G.I. Bill. Th' therapy nurse was a sweet li'l thing. I fell for her. Asked her t' marry me. Ring. Lookin' at houses. Talkin' t' preachers. Whole nine yards. Two weeks 'fore th' weddin', she eloped with a Navy doctor bein' transferred t' D.C. I didn't even know for three days. I came here."

Wacky Mack's whisper was barely audible. The Heater had to strain to catch some of the words over a distant owl hoot. Just as the boy decided that the story had ended and opened his mouth to speak, the scratchy whisper began again.

"Son, th' only three friends I ever had I lost. Made up my mind. Never let anybody close t' me again. But that's no way t' live." The man turned toward the boy and his eyes glowed redly, reflecting the firelight.

"Boy, you don't 'preciate what you got with this bunch. God! You got no idea how many times I've laid out there in th' dark, jus' baskin' in the warmtha y'all's friendship. I've followed y'all around. Not spyin', jus' . . . I felt pulled by a spirit I never had." The whisper loudened for one final, painful surge. "I stayed in my shell. But now, from watchin' y'all, I

218

know I was wrong. Most men would give their right arms — both arms, even — for what you've got. DON'T SCREW IT UP!!"

The man slumped back against the log, spent, knees drawn up, hands dangling across them, head bowed. The Heater made a conscious effort to breathe again. After maybe five minutes, he stood and walked to the cypress log, bent, and rummaged for the jar of Vaseline that had been there since just after the tick incident. He walked over to his turkey and stripped a handful of the smaller feathers from the legs. Depositing these items in the jeep, he made as if to vault in himself, when a thought struck him. He turned and walked to the man by the fire, who was still motionless.

The Heater put one hand on Wacky Mack's shoulder and squeezed. With an insight beyond his years, he grinned slightly and whispered, "Didn't work, did it? You came outa your shell an' you let us get to mean somethin' to you. Right?"

The man shook his head briefly, then sighed and nodded. "Reckon so."

"I gotta go see some folks," the Heater stated.

"I know."

"You be here when I get back?"

"I'll be here," Wacky Mack whispered.

The Heater stopped his jeep in Perfect's driveway and flipped on the dashboard lights so he could see his face in the rearview mirror. Working quickly, he smeared a thin coat of Vaseline on his chin, cheeks, and upper lip. Then he carefully arranged the small black leg feathers against the sticky covering. Wiping his hands on his jeans, he shifted into gear and pulled up to the garage.

Perfect had just walked into the house. His mood had not been conducive to a fun date, and he had sense enough to realize it. He had told Leapin' Lena about the fight and she had understood. "Go see 'im," she had advised as he left her house. When Perfect opened the door at Heater's knock, his remaining anger vanished into incredulity.

"What the heck is on your face?!" he gawked.

Heater grinned through the feathers. "It's crow. Found an ole dead one by the side-a the road, so I've been eatin' crow. It ain't so bad. Thought I'd come by an' eat some here." He held up his hand and turned serious as Perfect started to speak. "No, wait. I was wrong tonight an' I'm sorry as I can be. Will you forgive me?" He held out his hand.

Perfect grinned and grasped it. "Well, okay. Long as I ain't gotta kiss you or hug you." He laughed at his cousin's face. "You wanna come in an' wash that off?"

Heater shook his head, "Nope. I gotta go to four other houses. Thanks for bein' a friend." He turned to go.

Perfect was still slightly unbelieving, but could come up with no other explanation for the black feathers. "How much did you eat?" he asked curiously, stopping his cousin.

The Heater didn't crack a smile. "I ate the whole sonuva-bitch!!!" he declared.

PART V: AGE 17

The weather that summer was especially hot and dry, and the Jakes spent a lot of time at their old swimming hole. The fact that they had introduced girls to the pleasures of Life In The Woods occasionally complicated matters.

For instance, there was the time that Crazy Sharon and Baby Sister were out riding Pal and Polly and decided to visit the Jake Camp. As they loped along the Woods road, a chorus of yells and laughter from the direction of the Canal attracted their attention. The ponies made little noise as they turned from the road and plodded through the Woods, and since it was obvious to the riders what the occasion for the commotion was, they didn't make any noise either. The girls approached the Canal unheard and unseen.

It was quite evident that the Jakes were skinny dipping. Only one was actually in the water.

The Heater was on the end of the diving limb; Boateater was climbing the tree to join him; Birdlegs had just swung from the bluff; Deadeye was waiting for the swing's return; Rookie floated in an old inner tube, arms and feet dangling in the water. Perfect was the only boy who was submerged, and thus protected from the mounted watchers.

"One, two, three, go," muttered Crazy Sharon.

"Hellooo, Jakes!!" pealed out in girlish tones.

The Jakes panicked. Birdlegs forgot to let go of the swing and swung all the way back to the bluff naked — where he got off the swing, turned, and dived into the water. Deadeye sat down on the bank with his back to the girls. The Heater froze on the limb until Boateater shoved him off and jumped behind him. The Rookie flipped over too quickly, and he was temporarily wedged in the inner tube. For a brief moment he was trapped underwater, his white rump shining in the center of the black inner tube.

Perfect never lost his composure. "Howdy, ladies," he greeted, tipping an imaginary hat. "Y'all c'mon in, the water's fine."

The Heater surfaced and glimpsed the visitors. "I'm gonna kill you!" he vowed to his sibling.

"She made me do it!" Baby Sister giggled, pointing at Crazy Sharon.

Birdlegs heaved the first mudball at the riders and the other Jakes quickly followed suit, mud being their only available defense. The girls wheeled the ponies and galloped away, their laughter echoing through the open Woods.

"RrrrAAARRRgggg!!" roared the Heater. "I'm gonna kill 'em!"

Perfect was still treading water in the middle. "Nah," he advised. "Don't get mad. Let's get even."

It was Deadeye who provided the means for revenge. He still had his summer job as a lifeguard at the community club pool, having graduated to the regular noon-to-closing shift. Several of the girls had been agitating him to convince the club manager to keep the pool open after dark. Leapin' Lena brought it up one afternoon when the temperature had climbed to above the one-hundred-degree mark.

"This concrete's so hot you could fry eggs on it! Why don't y'all let us come out here at night, when it's comfortable?" the redhead complained.

"Waal, I *did* check that out," Deadeye drawled from his perch. "I might could fix it up, but you couldn't tell anybody else."

"How?"

The swimming pool facilities were situated at the west end of the community club complex. The tennis courts, which were sometimes used at night, were located on the east end. Each had its own parking lot and locker room. In addition, the courts were located close to the road, while the pool was toward the rear of the sprawling clubhouse-bar-dining room-dance hall building. Hedges, a rose garden, and a patio dining area behind the clubhouse also screened the pool from the courts. So, being almost a hundred yards away from the lighted tennis courts, the darkened pool area was completely private unless someone purposely went over there.

Eyes invisible behind his prescription sunglasses, Deadeye answered Leapin' Lena's question. "There's a few couples of adults that like to come out here skinny dippin' at night an' they pay me to help set it up. Can't tell you who," he hastened as the girl's eyebrows shot up, "but I could do the same for y'all," he offered.

"Whadda you do?"

"Waal, on nights when nuthin's goin' on out here, if they pass me the word, I leave the pool cleanin' ladder," he pointed to a ten-foot rubber-coated aluminum ladder with arms on the top which leaned against the equipment shed, "hooked on the inside of the fence right where the service road comes by." He pointed now to the west side of the eight-foot board fence. "Then they just park on the service road outa sight, bring a step ladder for the outside, an' climb over the fence an' skinny dip. I get the pool ladder the next day an' nobody ever notices. I could do the same thing for y'all," he repeated.

"Grown-ups skinny dippin'?" Leapin' Lena wasn't sure whether to be suspicious or scandalized.

Deadeye began closing the trap. "Gotta skinny dip. I hafta treat the pool ever' night 'fore I close up with muriatic acid. That stuff'll eat up cloth, but ain't strong enough to hurt anything on folks." The boy was playing it low-key. He leaned his head back and closed his eyes. "Jus' lemme know. Y'all ain't gotta pay me. Wake me up if somebody starts drownin'." Having planted the seeds, he went to sleep.

Two days later, Leapin' Lena and Crazy Sharon approached the lifeguard just before closing time. "What if we wanted to swim tonight?" the redhead asked.

Deadeye shrugged, put the skimmer down, strolled over to the shed, picked up the pool ladder, and hung it over the west-side fence. He came back and began skimming surface trash and leaves, never saying a word.

Crazy Sharon regarded him suspiciously. "So what's this junk 'bout skinny dippin', 'cause the acid will eat up cloth?"

Deadeye shrugged once more and put the skimmer down. He stepped over to the equipment shed again, reached in for a gallon jug, and poured some of the fluid from the jug onto a corner of the towel around his neck. He replaced the jug and walked back to the girls, wordlessly holding out the towel. The wet corner was smoking slightly, and small holes began to appear in the cloth.

"Dadgum! That won't hurt us?" Leapin' Lena exclaimed.

The boy sighed reproachfully, turned and strode back to the shed. He again pulled out a jug, poured some fluid on his hand, and walked carefully back, offering the girls some of the liquid in his palm. Deadeye had been prepared; the girls had not noticed that he had used different jugs. He spoke for the first time. "Might bleach out your hair a little. I'd wear a swimmin' or shower cap." He rubbed the liquid on his arms to demonstrate that it was harmless. "This stuff's s'posed to dissolve bacteria in the pool. Most cloth is dyed with bacterial agents. An' some-a these new suits are made entirely of syn-thetics," he observed wisely as he picked up the skimmer again.

"How do we know you won't spy on us, or tell?" the pretty brunette demanded.

Deadeye looked properly hurt and pointed to the girls' bikinis. "Heck, I see alla y'all near'bout ever'day next to nekkid anyway. I'm used to it. Don't bother me none. An' as for tellin'," he looked at Leapin' Lena, "had you ever heard 'bout the grown-ups skinny dippin' before?"

She shook her head.

"An' did I name names, or tell you when?"

Another negative indication.

"Besides, there ain't any night lights out here, 'cause they'd attract bugs that would be all in the pool the next mawnin'. If it's too dark to see, what difference does it make?" He began skimming the pool again, dismissing them with, "Jus' drive out here late at night an' see how dark it is yourself. But I ain't leavin' the ladder if I don't know for sure."

Crazy Sharon was still not convinced. "Don't call us, we'll

call you," she remarked.

The next Tuesday, Deadeye was approached by Leapin' Lena again. "We wanna try it tonight," she said nervously. The boy shrugged and gave a thumbs-up signal, never moving from his sprawl in the elevated seat.

When he closed up that evening, he hung the ladder on the fence and doused the pool with an extra-heavy dose of chlorine. He didn't want it heavy enough to hurt anyone, but he did intend for the water to have a strong chlorine scent and sting the eyes more than usual. He stored all the other equipment and locked up, then drove straight home and called the Heater.

It was nearly midnight, and the two boys hidden in the hedges between the pool and the silent golf course had just applied the third coat of mosquito repellent when Deadeye observed, "Car comin'!"

Actually, it was a truck. The Space Ace's father's old pickup drove slowly by the community club complex and continued down the blacktop away from town. A few minutes later it came back by, this time driving without lights. The third time, the old truck pulled into the swimming pool parking lot, but as the boys held their breath it slowly circled the gravel lot and pulled back onto the asphalt road.

A fourth time it came by, and this time it parked in the lot while two of the occupants got out and walked down the service road. Leapin' Lena was easily recognized because of her height, but the boys had to guess the identity of the other. "Gotta be either Crazy Sharon or Mad Mel," was the Heater's opinion. "Not enough bosom for the Space Ace. She's prob'ly drivin'." After checking the area, the two girls ran giggling back to the truck, the sound carrying to the hidden Jakes.

The old truck drove out to the asphalt again, down the road to the unoccupied tennis court parking lot, and turned around there to start back. "Aw-Riiiight!" exclaimed the Heater.

Sure enough, the truck parked on the service road alongside the fence and the engine was switched off. For fully five minutes, no one disembarked. Finally the passenger door opened, and by its brief light the boys saw Crazy Sharon and Leapin' Lena get out. The driver was on the far side of the truck from the watchers, but as Deadeye said, "Gotta be Space Ace; it's her truck." With the pickup doors closed, there was not enough illumination for the Jakes to see, and they could barely follow the shadowy figures' progress.

Metal scraped on metal, and Deadeye surmised, "Must be gettin' the ladder out." He had no sooner said that than a girl was briefly silouetted atop the fence in the mile-distant lume from the town lights. "Leapin' Lena goin' over," he exulted.

All three girls crossed the fence, and soon the first splash was heard, with accompanying squeal. "You wanna sneak up an' peek?" Deadeye could barely withstand the urge.

"Naw. Let 'em alone this time. If it works, they'll be back for a longer time." The Heater wanted this hook to be sunk deeply. His theory was correct about the first time. Less than ten minutes later the three girls, clad once more, came scampering back over the fence. Amid giggles and squeals, they quickly put their step ladder back into the truck and sped away. The two Jakes stood. The Heater held out his hand. "Good job. I think we got 'em. Jus' don't say a word to anybody else. Lemme know when they wanna go again." The two boys turned to trot across the golf course to where the Heater's jeep was parked.

Two nights later, the girls arranged another session. From their concealment in the golf course hedge, the Jakes were able to determine that four girls crossed the fence. Perfect was along this time, and he identified his science lab partner. "That's Mad Mel, all right."

Again the boys stayed hidden while the girls swam and frolicked for nearly an hour. "Next time," grinned the Heater triumphantly. The Jakes began to finalize plans as they walked across the golf course.

It was Sunday afternoon when Crazy Sharon informed Deadeye that they wanted to use the pool late again. On the Sabbath, the club closed at five p.m., and Deadeye was seemingly reluctant to agree. He finally let the girl talk him into it, however. In actuality, he was gloating; this gave the Jakes more time to plan. He called the Heater.

The Jakes were in full attendance for night church, and all went to Deadeye's home afterward. Each one of them had a complete change of clothes with him, totally camouflaged, and Deadeye even pulled out his camo face paint from turkey season. As they smudged black, green, and brown grease on their faces, the lifeguard explained the plan, for some were not aware of the pending operation.

"Okay, I think this's the best way," the drawl almost disappeared as the general addressed his troops. "The ladder's on the shallow end side, an' they'll prob'ly be in the deeper water. We always chain up the patio tables an' chairs at night, since the time somebody chunked 'em all in the pool, an' they're here — by the corner of the shed." He was sketching a rough map on the flyleaf of his Sunday School book.

"I figger they'll put all their suits an' towels on that clump of tables an' jump in," Deadeye went on. "They won't hardly see one guy slippin' over the fence, 'cause the lights of town are th'other way. Heater an' I figger one guy slips in, crawls around th' edge of the shed, eases their stuff off the table, an' crawls back out with it. Then we take the pool ladder out behind us. With the tables an' chairs chained up, there's no way for 'em to get out. Good?"

"We gonna watch?" The Rookie seemed eager.

"Naw," said the Heater. "Then we set off the burglar alarm." He chuckled maliciously.

"The burglar alarm?" Boateater was mystified.

"Right," nodded Deadeye. "There's a two-minute delay from the time it rings at the police station 'til it rings at the club. The cops will be here about the time the girls hear the alarm."

"Good Golly Greenwood! Y'all're really after 'em!" Boateater sounded doubtful.

"Aw, man, they'll just laugh an' take 'em home!" Birdlegs said. He looked at the Heater and Deadeye. "I'm your inside man."

"There it is," Deadeye grinned.

Again it was nearly midnight before the girls showed up. This time there were five. The presence of Cuddly Carrie caused Deadeye to voice a protest. "Hey, guys, maybe we . . ."

"Shut up, candy!" Boateater muttered.

When the gaiety inside the fence indicated that the time was right, the Jakes approached silently. Birdlegs' eyes gleamed whitely as he shook hands all around, then pulled on a watchcap. He was up and over the fence like a snake.

Deadeye had been right. The towels and suits were on the tables grouped at the corner of the shed. Birdlegs couldn't resist looking at the splashing girls, but they were all in the dark deep end. The Jake hadn't been inside the fence more than five minutes when a camouflage laundry bag was boosted over to the other boys and the silent one slipped back over the fence, teeth and eyes shining in a grin.

They lifted the pool ladder over to the outside of the fence and then the Heater trotted to the clubhouse's west entrance. He slid his pocketknife across the crack at the top of the door where Deadeye had shown him. There was a tell-tale click.

Officer Marvelous Marv was just leaving the Push and Pull Drive-in when he received a call from the dispatcher to "check out possible break-in at community club." The dispatcher wasn't excited. About two dozen homes or businesses around town had burglar alarms, and the police department averaged about one false alarm a night, more during thunderstorms or periods of high humidity, like tonight. Marvelous Marv had just started his first shift after a two-week vacation, however, and he was properly enthusiastic.

The Jakes saw the patrol car speeding toward the community club, running without siren, flashers, or even lights. The patrolman knew that the two-minute delay would give him a chance to catch an unwarned burglar, and a bust on his first night back in town would impress the Chief no end. The car swung through the east-side parking lot without stopping, turned into the main drive of the club, and looped that area without seeing anything suspicious. Then it whipped into the swimming pool parking lot.

Since Space Ace's truck was parked by the service road, Marvelous Marv did not see it at first, and had made a circuit of the deserted lot before he caught a glimpse of it in his rear-view mirror. He slammed on the brakes, killed the engine, rolled out of the car, and sprinted for the vehicle, almost hidden in the shadows. He knew the alarm would sound in seconds.

It did.

The Jakes were having trouble muffling their mirth as they anticipated events from their hiding place. The cop was only halfway across the parking lot when the alarm went off. It wasn't a particularly loud alarm, just a high-pitched beeping that automatically cut off and reset after five minutes.

The five nude girls in the swimming pool squealed with fright and headed for the table where their suits and towels had been. Their clothing's absence elevated the squeals to shrieks, and these sounds were further increased to full-fledged screams when the ladder was discovered missing. Cuddly Carrie and the Space Ace burst into tears. Mad Mel had a sudden premonition and vented her frustration in a roar of rage. Leapin' Lena jumped to grasp the top of the wooden fence while Crazy Sharon stooped to lend her cousin a boost. The redhead was silouetted from the waist up above the fence when Marvelous Marv, running toward the source of the noise, switched on his flashlight.

The cop stopped in open-mouthed shock. "Great Balls of Fire!" he exclaimed. Officer Marvin had never won any awards for accuracy.

Leapin' Lena dropped back behind the fence blushing all over, though no one could tell in the darkness, and a new chorus of terror and frustration arose.

Marvelous Marv reached a not-un-obvious conclusion. "Great Balls of Fire!" he repeated. "Some girl's drownin'!" He dropped the flashlight and raced to the rescue, performing an event never taught at the FBI Academy: The Thirty-Yard Full Undress Sprint. Tossing cap, unbuckling gunbelt, untying shoes, unbuttoning shirt, and unzipping britches, Marvelous Marv was down to his boxer shorts by the time he reached the ladder.

The Jakes jumped to a conclusion themselves. "It's Marvelous Marv! An' the sonuvabitch is gonna *rape* 'em!" The inherent difficulties for even a well-trained officer in raping five totally-panicked, but otherwise quite healthy, seventeen-year-old girls in a concreted pool enclosure with a burglar alarm going "beep-beep-beep!" never occured to the boys.

Birdlegs and Boateater were by far the fastest of the Jakes, and the former got a head start. The girls' screaming and crying prevented the policeman from hearing the boys' approach, and he had just attained the top of the stepladder and reached to vault over the fence when Birdlegs jerked the ladder out from under him. Marvelous Marv vaulted head-first into the top board of the fence and bounced over, landing stunned but otherwise unhurt in a pyracantha bush.

Perfect had the camouflage laundry bag with the girls' suits and, thinking quickly, he flipped it over the fence. "Get your clothes on!" he hissed over the beeping alarm. Having seen the policeman's fall, the Jakes gave him up for dead. The question was: could they get away with his murder? Birdlegs still held the ladder, overwhelmed by the apparent consequences of his action. Deadeye ran for the fence behind the shed to retrieve the pool ladder.

"Don't you come in here!" Mad Mel said threateningly over the beeping as the girls sorted through the mixed bathing suits in the darkness. The Heater had grabbed the step ladder from Birdlegs and was setting it up to mount.

Deadeye came racing back with the pool ladder. Crazy Sharon's top was at the bottom of the jumble of suits and towels; she was the last girl decent when the pool ladder was shoved over the fence. "Hurry!" Perfect called.

At this point, the Jakes heard one of the most wonderful sound of their young careers. Marvelous Marv moaned.

"Hurry!" Perfect called again. "He's alive!" The five girls scampered out and the Heater went over into the pool enclosure to check the policeman. The man's fall had been cushioned by the pyracantha and, except for a knot on the forehead, the Heater couldn't find any physical damage. The cop was beginning to moan again and stir as Birdlegs dropped over the fence also.

"He's okay except for a knot on the head, and he's comin' to. Let's get outa here!" The Heater grabbed the camo bag from the ground, removing the last trace of evidence, and went up the ladder. "C'mon!" he called as he stepped from the top of the fence to the step ladder.

The Idea That Would Save The Night hit Birdlegs, "like a

bolt of lightnin' from Heaven!" as he later claimed. Smiling, he pulled off the policeman's socks and boxers, and almost ran up the rungs as the man moaned again.

Marvelous Marv cursed as he rolled naked from the pyracantha's clutches and hit the ground next to the concrete. He was rising slowly to hands and knees when Birdlegs pulled the pool ladder back outside.

The girls were already in the truck, waiting for their ladder and the opportunity to tell Birdlegs in absolute sincerity, "We're gonna kill you for this!" The other Jakes had been quick to give the actual raider all due credit. But as the truck began to roll, the urgency in Birdlegs' voice stopped it.

"Wait!" he ordered as he grabbed the door handle. "Gimme some panties and a bra!"

"Some WHAT!!!" Crazy Sharon exclaimed, but the Space Ace responded automatically to the tone of command. As a country girl, she made it a summer practice to keep a change of clothes in a beach bag behind the truck seat in case of a supper invitation after swimming. She quickly pulled out the demanded garments.

"Your name on 'em anywhere?" he asked. As the girl shook her head, he slapped the truck. "Go, then! Go!" Away went the vehicle, the echoes of the ladies' sentiments still hanging in their dust:

"We're gonna kill you!!"

Deadeye had already run to the police car. As a long-time club lifeguard, he knew the usual police reaction to the community club burglar alarm. He keyed the microphone and tried to speak in imitation of Marvelous Marv. "Club's okay. False alarm."

To his relief, the bored response came back. "Roger. Resetting." The beeping ceased, within thirty seconds of doing so itself automatically.

Deadeye looked up from the car to see the other Jakes bearing down on him, all carrying various articles of clothing. "What the Hell?" he asked. Birdlegs' grin could indeed have been worn comfortably by the proprietor of that region.

"Put that there, an' that there, an' those here, an' these li'l ole things go right here!" Birdlegs orchestrated the scene carefully. As a final thought, he sprinted toward the trash can at the corner of the golf cart shed and came racing back with an armload of empty beer cans. The other boys began to grin with sudden understanding. "Y'all ready?" Birdlegs asked with satisfaction.

"Ladder?" Deadeye raised his eyebrows.

"Hedge behind the shed," Perfect answered.

The Jakes started across the golf course at a trot, headed for their vehicles.

Marvelous Marv almost lost his badge in the investigation that followed his being found stark naked in the pool at the community club by rookie patrolwoman Mary Wheeler. Ms. Wheeler had already stopped at the parking lot to investigate the empty patrol car, which was littered with empty beer cans and a carefully-arranged pile of police clothing. She also testified that the panties and brassiere displayed prominently on the dashboard had caught her eye, the size of the latter garment casting considerable doubt on Marvelous Marv's contention that he had been the victim of malicious teenagers. His haste to rescue the drowning girls had also precluded his being able to produce an accurate description of the truck. Only the waitress at the Push and Pull Drive-in saved the policeman's job. At that, there was initial speculation that she was the woman involved, but she was cleared (and so was Marvelous Marv) by excusing herself for a moment from the Chief's office. She retired to the ladies' room and returned quickly with a 32B.

All suspicions allayed, the policeman was reinstated after a three-day suspension.

Six weeks later Marvelous Marv married the waitress and they moved to Montana, where he took over as a small-town marshal and they lived happily ever after.

A new mall opened on the south side of town just after the
Jakes started their junior year, and it contained a four-screen
cinema. Previously, movie lovers had had only one choice for
weeks at a time, so the initial success of the new picture show
was quite impressive. However, the large numbers of vehicles
left unattended after dark led to an increase in crime. A small
group of youthful delinquents from a nearby low-income
housing project were the main offenders, and their age caused
law enforcement problems.

A new youth court judge, a nephew-in-law of the govenor,
had recently been appointed for the district. He was rather
young himself, and prided himself on being a "progressive."
He constantly criticized the law officers' practices as "heavy-
handed," and took precautions to insure that any and all
possible real or imagined infringements on the rights of the de-
fendants were meticulously notated. Gang members quickly
learned that a neat and polite demeanor in court would be rewarded, at least the first three times, with a suspended sentence. Young Judge Owen Moore soon became known as
"Judge Open Door."

The reaction of the law enforcement officers at first was
anger, but the first few explosions in the courtroom resulted in
stiff fines for contempt. This in turn caused such resentment
that the officers began to mete out at least some measure of
justice upon arrest, which of course led to charges of police
brutality. Judge Door's former law partner filed suit against
several officers, Deputy Don being one of the first. Predicta-
bly, the police and sheriff's departments soon adopted a "Why
bother?" attitude, especially on complaints from the mall area.

Then the Jakes were personally affected by the crime wave.
Boateater's mother had her purse snatched. A side window was
broken out of Deadeye's car and his tape collection was stolen.
Crazy Sharon and Leapin' Lena were chased back to their car
one night after the show by three boys shouting obscenities.
The top was slashed on the Rookie's old convertible.

The boys and girls sat around the Jake campfire and discussed the situation on several nights. Vigilante justice seemed
called for, and exotic schemes were proposed, along with even
more exotic punishments. The weekend after the girls had

been chased, Crazy Sharon was especially imaginative.

"You know what I'd do if I caught those guys that chased me?" she asked.

"Naw, but I hope it'd be just as serious as what they'da done to y'all!" Birdlegs growled.

"Well, I'd strip 'em nekkid an' hang 'em by their hands an' feet between two trees out here," The girl was relishing the thought. "An' I'd let the mosquitoes eat 'em alive!"

"Good Golly Greenwood! Wouldn't that be tough!" Boateater exclaimed.

"Boy! I'm glad she ain't mad at me!" the Heater observed to Perfect.

"Oh, but I am," the pretty brunette said sweetly.

The Jakes shuddered. Perfect squinted in attempted recollection. "Hey, who was that guy who wrote about all the stuff th' ole Indian squaws used to do?"

Deadeye got up, reached into the log for his can of fogger insecticide and sprayed the outskirts of Camp again. Repeated hourly, this ritual kept the Jake Camp tolerable in warm weather.

Leapin' Lena picked up her guitar and looked at Perfect. "Speakin' of bugs, you 'member all the words to 'Blue-tail Fly'?"

So the moment passed, but the conversation would be remembered.

The very next weekend, a highly-touted war movie began at the mall cinema, and the Jakes crowded into Perfect's Bronco after supper to catch the late show. When they exited the movie, machine-gun fire and mortar bursts still ringing in their ears, they were greeted by the sight of shattered glass. Parked purposely right in front of the cinema, the Bronco's driver's window had nevertheless been broken completely out. The radar detector was gone from the dashboard. "My fuzzbuster!" Perfect cried.

They phoned the police from the mall, but it was nearly forty-five minutes before a patrol car showed up. Yawning, the officer jotted down a few notes and said, "Never find it. Hope insurance will pay for your window. By the way, your tag expires this month." The policeman waved and drove away.

"Go!" hissed Heater.

Three dark-clad figures in ski masks, one of them swinging a baseball bat, suddenly blocked the alley in front of the escaping pirates. On one side of them was a fence; on the other a line of parked cars. The pirates split up.

As one dodged between a Ford van and a Lincoln, a fourth darkly-dressed figure appeared in the gap, from the direction of the parking lot. Another was closing fast with a baseball bat. The kid decided to run over the unarmed Perfect as the lesser of two evils. He was wrong. Boateater ran up with his cord and blindfolds.

The second pirate almost made it over the fence, but the Heater leapt and grabbed him by the most available hand-holds — his back pockets. Rookie held his bat ready, unable to swing without endangering Heater. The pirate had reached into his pocket for his switchblade knife when the three Jakes had appeared, blocking the alley. Feeling himself being pulled backward off the fence, he flicked the blade open and slashed behind himself in panic.

But the boy's jeans were old and worn, and the pockets ripped off just before the knife reached Heater's hands. That Jake fell back, still holding the pockets, just as a ten-inch blade swung back and down. Blood spurted from the pirate's left buttock.

"Watch out! A knife!" the Rookie yelled, and swung the bat. It connected with a satisfying "crack" and the pirate disappeared over the fence, head-first.

"C'mon! We got one!" hissed Boateater, who had run to help, arriving just in time to see the kid escape over the fence. The Heater realized he was holding not only pockets, but also a wallet and hair pick. He stuck these items into his own pockets and raced to the truck with Birdlegs and the Rookie. Less than a minute later, the three vehicles were headed out of town, three Jakes and a bound and blindfolded fuzzbuster pirate in the back of Boateater's truck.

Deputy Don was returning to town, finishing the three-to-eleven p.m. patrol, when the three Jake vehicles passed him, headed for the Woods at a high rate of speed. "Them boys gonna get into trouble, drivin' thataway," he muttered. But it was too close to the end of his shift for him to pursue them. He continued to the sheriff's office and was signing out when he overheard the dispatcher putting out an alert to the patrols.

"We have a report from the city police of a possible kidnapping of an eighteen-year-old male from the South Mall parking lot by persons unknown. Suspects are believed to have left the scene in several vehicles, headed south or east. Be aware of suspicious activity. Over."

Deputy Don did not have a lot of formal education, but he was an excellent lawman. "What're them damn boys up to now?" he growled. Hurriedly he finished his report and left, grumbling that he was going to have to be awake a while longer.

It did not help the deputy's state of mind to have to walk a half-mile into the Woods, either. But once he began the jaunt, he was glad he had decided to check on "them damn boys." Faint hoarse screams reached his ears before he was halfway to the Jake Camp, and became louder as the lawman approached the Camp. Puffing and sweating, Deputy Don was forced to slow down and walk the final hundred yards. By now the screaming had subsided to an insane moaning interrupted by shrieks and curses. The deputy was totally unprepared for the sight that met his eyes.

Four Jakes sat around the campfire with root beers, laughing tauntingly. Barely visible back in the Woods toward the Swamp were the Heater and Birdlegs, performing some type of operation on a blindfolded and naked young male, who was stretched out and bound by his wrists and ankles between two small pecan trees. As the lawman watched incredulously from the shadows, the two Jakes stepped back laughing. The nude kid's newly-shaven head caught a slight gleam from the firelight forty yards away. The Heater and Birdlegs walked back toward Camp gleefully. Behind them the prisoner squirmed and bucked, moaning all the while.

Deputy Don stepped from the shadows and was almost at the fire when the first Jake saw him, for the boys' attention was riveted on the writhing nude. "What the *hell*'re y'all doin'!?" the lawman hissed, holding his finger to his lips for silence.

It was Boateater who had seen the man first, and he recovered from his surprise. "Dispensin' justice!" he replied. "This is one-a the bunch been stealin' stuff an' chasin' girls over at the Mall. We caught 'im in th' act!"

"You know they got kidnappin' charges out on y'all?" Deputy Don was not being entirely factual.

"Nobody saw us! . . . 'Cept that one that got away," the Heater's voice trailed off.

"Yeah, an' he's in the hospital claimin' some other gang slit 'is butt open an' whupped 'im an' broke 'is ankle. An' robbed 'im, too."

"Aw-Riiiight!" The Heater and the Rookie shook hands. Dropping his voice, Heater added, "But we didn't rob 'im. Here's his billfold. It pulled off in my hand. I ain't even looked in it."

The nude captive in the Woods screamed.

"What're y'all doin' to *him?*" Deputy Don wanted to know.

"We're gonna let the 'skeeters eat 'im," Perfect said calmly.

"Wha'd y'all shave 'is head for?"

"'Cause there was too much hair. Lotta 'skeeters were buzzin' around and couldn't find a place to eat." Birdlegs had had the idea to provide more dining area and was rather proud.

"Y'all can't do that! That's takin' the law into your own hands. I oughta run y'all in yourselves. Y'all in wuss trouble than he is!"

"Judge Door would jus' turn 'im loose! He's even got you for arrestin' 'em in the first place. The law don't even care that this guy prob'ly stole my fuzzbuster." Perfect was disgusted. "Well, he's payin' now!"

Deputy Don could stand it no longer. He had to grin. "You whippersnappers really oughta get a medal for this. But if they was to catch y'all — whooo-eeee!!" he whistled. "That damn judge! Y'know, I'd love to see somebody doin' him an' that sumbitch of a podnuh of his like this!" He turned serious. "This fella seen y'all?"

"No, sir," came the answer. Perfect went on to explain about the ski masks and the blindfold.

"You sure ain't no way he can identify none-a y'all?"

Again he was assured.

"Okay." The deputy became businesslike. "Right now, we gotta get this guy outa here 'fore he knows where he's been an' who had 'im there. What we'll do is this: y'all cut 'im loose an' tie 'im back up an' put 'im in your jeep. Carry 'im out to my car an' we'll put 'im in the trunk. Then I'll make a run to the River an' turn 'im loose over there, still blindfolded an' hands tied. Time he gets back home his own mama ain't gonna know 'im. But first," he paused to let the fuzzbuster pirate scream again, "y'all got another root beer?"

Nearly an hour later, they cut the pirate down and followed the lawman's instructions. As he closed the trunk on the whimpering figure, Deputy Don smiled and shook hands all around. "Y'all done good." He shook his head. "Just don't do it no more!"

Back at the fire, the Jakes had opened another round of root beers when Perfect made A Wise Saying. "Y'know," he said, "there's a lotta satisfaction in seein' justice carried out!"

Saturday morning two weeks later, Perfect didn't even get up until after ten. The night before had been Homecoming, and Crazy Sharon had been crowned Queen. Birdlegs and Boateater had been her escorts, and the Homecoming Dance after the football game had lasted until two a.m. The Heater had even gotten a bid for the Rookie from Queen Sharon, so the Jakes had not been in Camp that night.

Uncle Bubba was just hanging up the telephone when Perfect came downstairs yawning and rubbing his eyes. "Mornin', son," the man greeted rather absently. "Good time last night?"

"Yes, sir." The boy poured himself an orange juice and began sorting through the cereal cabinet. When he turned around he noticed his father was still standing by the phone, rubbing the scar on his chin, as was his habit when perplexed or in deep thought. "What's wrong?" he asked, pouring milk into the bowl.

The man shook his head. "Strange. The County Attorney says Judge Door and his ex-partner claim they were workin' late yesterday evenin' and some armed men in ski masks kidnapped 'em. They say they were stripped and held prisoner for hours and tortured before bein' turned loose. But they were picked up just across the county line at a cat . . . at a house of ill repute, about three this mornin'. A deputy brought 'em in for disturbin' the peace, public drunkenness, and indecent exposure." The man shook his head and grinned slightly. "Only thing is, the Judge's Cadillac was in the . . . er, house's parkin' lot, and their clothes were inside the house."

"How come he called you?" Perfect wanted to know, around a mouthful of cereal.

"Knew I used to be District Attorney, and wanted some advice on how to handle it. He said the sheriff told him that the preliminary investigation showed no evidence to support the kidnappin' claim, and he thinks they just got caught with their britches down." He laughed. "Literally, I mean!"

"Serves 'em right," Perfect munched. "How were they tortured?"

"He said Doc McClendon examined 'em and couldn't find any signs of it. Just some faint chaffin' around their wrists and ankles, but they coulda got that in the cat . . . er, the place they were found. Other than that, he said they looked just like anybody else who'd been runnin' around outside at night, nekkid—the mosquitos 'bout ate 'em alive, and . . . Son! You okay?" He stepped over to slap his choking boy on the back.

Perfect waved him off, coughing. "I'm okay," he finally managed in a strangled voice. "Jus' got one-a those dried dates or somethin' stuck in my throat." He motioned at the cereal.

It was after lunch when Perfect drove the Bronco down to the Woods. Someone *had* used the Jake Camp. The ashes were still warm.

*   *   *   *   *   *   *

The construction crew that the Rookie worked with was hurrying to finish a remodeling job on an office building before the late-fall rains set in. While removing some old sheetrock in the basement, the youngster discovered a large tank and called it to the attention of the foreman. Upon investigation, that worthy came to the conclusion that it had been the fuel oil tank for the out-dated heating system that had been replaced with modern units almost thirty years before. A stick inserted through the top bung tapped on a dry bottom, and when the rusted drain plug was finally removed, nothing drained out. The tank had been empty for years.

It was too big to pass through the existing doorways, and the foreman ordered an oxy-acetylene torch so it could be hauled away for scrap. "We'll cut it up and haul it out in sections," he declared.

But even though the tank had been empty for years, decades of holding fuel oil had allowed the inside to be permeated with fumes. The foreman had been cutting with the blue-white flame of the torch for less than five minutes when the tank exploded.

The foreman was killed instantly, as was a second man standing between the tank and a bricked section of wall. The Rookie and two other workers were blown across the room. One of the men suffered a fractured skull; he died two days later in the state hospital. The other's spine was severed; he was paralyzed from the chest down and was sent to the state facility to begin rehabilitation.

The Rookie was the only blast victim to be admitted to the local hospital. His hands and face were burned, and one ankle was broken. "But it's his eyes I'm worried about," Doc McClendon confided to Father Phil. "All we can do is keep him bandaged up for nearly six weeks before we know whether he'll be able to see okay again."

Time weighed heavily on the boy's hands in the hospital. He was frightened; he was in pain; he itched but couldn't scratch. His hands were bulkily bandaged, as was his head, in ointment-soaked dressings. Though he had plenty of company in the afternoons after school, there was nothing to occupy his time during the other twenty hours of the day. He obviously couldn't watch television or read, nor could he operate a portable tape recorder. The Rookie became irritable and restless, and Doc McClendon was afraid it would affect his recovery.

"We've got to figure out some way to keep the boy quiet,

Phil," the physician told the minister a few days after the accident. "If he keeps disturbing those bandages, not only will it slow the healing process, but it may cause an infection. Put your mind to it."

Two nights later, Father Phil and the Duke of Dundee hailed the Jake Camp on their Friday night coon hunt. The two men gratefully accepted mugs of hot chocolate from the Jakes, and nodded when Crazy Sharon offered to fix them hot dogs. "Since Aye abstained from liquor, Aye seem to require more and more to make it through a coon hunt," the Duke complained. "It may even be that Aye *need* to drink to continue to hunt!"

"'Course it might be that coon huntin' drove you to drink in the first place," Deadeye observed.

"Hey, we'll jus' keep lotsa hot dogs for you!" the Heater promised, grinning.

As they ate, Father Phil thought to bring up Doc McClendon's fears about the Rookie. "He's got no family here, nobody but you all. And the only time he's quiet is when some of you are around, Doctor Mac says. Any suggestions?"

There was a full Jake Camp tonight, and the boys and girls began to discuss the situation as they toasted marshmallows. Perfect and Leapin' Lena strummed guitars, and the rhythm reminded the Space Ace of the JakeFest. "Hey, he loves to listen to y'all singin' an' Mr. Duke recitin' poetry. Why don't we record some-a that?"

Father Phil approved, but pointed out, "He can't work a tape recorder. He'd probably love some music from by the fire, but a nurse would have to cut it on and off and flip it. And remember, we're talking about a month to six weeks."

"We oughta record the JakeFest, though. That's a good idea," said Birdlegs. "But it doesn't solve the problem durin' the daytime when we're in school. Tell you somethin' else, too," he waved the charred marshmallow on his stick at his audience. "We're fixin' to get cramped for time after school, y'all. Junior Book Reports come up this six weeks."

"Good Golly Greenwood!" Boateater exclaimed. "That's right. Smilin' Jack used to say that was the toughest thing in high school. All those books to read an' get tested on!"

"Hey! What if . . ." The others saw the faraway glimmer of an idea in Heater's eyes. "What if . . . Hey! What if we started a readin' program for 'im? Durin' school! An' got outa the Book Reports!"

"Do what?" Mad Mel wasn't the only one confused.

"You're outa your gourd," Deadeye snorted.

"Naw, I ain't!" the Heater waxed enthusiastic. "We could set up a rotation between us for nearly every hour of every day. Our class schedules are different anyway. We could get outa English, study hall, phys ed, an' maybe some other classes to go to the hospital an' read durin' the day. An' since we'd be readin' to the Rookie, the Great Green G wouldn't hafta test us to see if we cheated an' just read the notes." The boy was leaning forward, talking earnestly now.

"We'd kill a buncha birds with one stone! We'd keep Rookie quiet, read the books, skip the tests, and . . . get outa school some-a the day." His eyes swung to meet Father Phil's. "All we need is an adult to go see Coach Fuzzy an' the Great Green G."

The Duke chuckled and accepted a marshmallow from Baby Sister. "Hoist on your own petard, Phillip. And rather neatly, Aye might add."

No one else spoke, all eyes riveted on the minister. "I think I hear those dogs barking 'treed,' Duke," he suggested.

The farmer cocked his head and smiled. "No. Sounds to me like the Heavenly Choir singing 'How Are You Going to Get Out of This One, Phil?'"

Father Phil laughed and stuck out his hand to the Heater. "Deal. You put it on paper and talk to me after church Sunday. If it's good, I'll talk to Coach Fuzzy."

"Aw-Riiiight!!" the kids cried.

Father Phil had done a good job of selling Coach Fuzzy, and now the principal was explaining the concept to his skeptical English teacher. "It'll be good for the boy, good for our kids, and good for the school. Just think, this could mean national publicity!" he concluded. "*Good* publicity this time."

"But the kids would be out of school for several hours a day," the Great Green G protested. "And how do we know they'll really be reading to him?"

The administrator grinned slowly. "I know how we'll get the results. We'll test the kid they're readin' to. I've always maintained that the measure of a good teacher is how much her students learn. Get a list of the books each kid is gonna read, and make up a good basic test on each one. If a kid fails to communicate, we can pull that one out of the program after a coupla weeks. Whadda you think?"

"We'd have to give the test vocally, wouldn't we?"

"So? I'll get Phil to help, and I will too." The man stood. "I think we oughta give it a try. If it doesn't work, we can stop it, but we owe it to the students. I've talked with them all, and they're enthusiastic; and enthusiasm counts for a whole lot."

"I bow to your judgement. However, tell them to see me about which books to read," sighed the Great Green G.

After lunch, the Heater came by her room to talk about the books. The teacher couldn't help but notice that the boy wrinkled his nose after reading her suggested list. "You have objections to my list?" she asked primly.

"Well, Miz G," the boy said slowly, "you don't know the Rookie, but he's only got an eighth-grade education. An' that was in California," he added condescendingly. "We gotta read 'im stuff he'll understand. And also stuff he'll enjoy. 'Member, he's laid up blind for six weeks. Some-a these books are depressin' as . . . heck."

"I take it you are suggesting 'Oh, oh. See Jane run' books? Possibly getting down to the reader's level, too, right?"

The Heater grinned. "Yes'm. We talked about that one, but I don't wanna get 'im excited 'bout Jane, not in his condition. But Birdlegs did suggest th' one 'bout 'See Spot. See the ball. See Spot chase the ball.' He likes that one, an' you'd be s'prised at how good he can read it!"

The Great Green G stifled a grin. "I'll be in charge of the sarcasm, thank you. All right. Bring me a list of ten books *you* want to read him, and we'll compromise. If possible."

The Heater had study hall in the library with Perfect and Crazy Sharon that next period. Just after school ended, the three walked into the English teacher's class with a list. "Hard to get it down to ten, Miz G. We didn't realize there were so many good books." The Heater handed her a list in Crazy Sharon's looping handwriting. "We tried to pick from different fields, and we didn't put down any that you already had on your list."

The Great Green G read aloud. "*Huckleberry Finn, The Call of the Wild, The Spirit of the Border, True Grit, By Valour and Arms, Penrod and Sam*; I am familiar with these and consider them classics. But *Illusions, The Old Man and the Boy*, and *The Green Berets?* And the Bible? Do you know how long it would take to read the Bible to this boy?"

"Jus' parts of it, ma'am," Crazy Sharon protested. "An' we'd get a modern translation so it'd move pretty good. This guy never went to church until he came here."

"An' we think Robert Ruark's a classic outdoor writer. It's just outdoor writers get overlooked 'cause all the city folks think they ain't got no deep messages or anything," the Heater explained.

"Don't have any deep messages," the teacher corrected.

"An' one-a our best friends went through the Vietnam War," Perfect pointed out. "An' we're gonna get the Duke of Dundee to come in a coupla times a week to quote poetry."

"The Duke quotes poetry?" sniffed the Great Green G.

"Yes, ma'am. Service, Kipling, Tennyson, Burns; you name it. He's trained to be an actor," Perfect assured her.

The teacher made her decisions. "Very well, we'll use this one, this one, and this one of yours; and this one and this one of mine. The Bible is extra, and I would suggest beginning the day with an hour of that." She began jotting notes in her elaborate, almost artistic handwriting, always done in green ink. "Give me a schedule of who reads what when, because you will have to work your school absences with the office. Not less than an hour of any work at any one sitting, and you'll have to see Doc McClendon about a schedule so you won't interfere with the hospital staff. At the end of two weeks, I will come to the hospital and test the boy myself to assure that you are doing your jobs." She scrawled a great green "G" across the top of the paper, the sign of her approval.

"Test the Rookie?" Crazy Sharon asked, not sure she had heard correctly.

"And if he fails, so do you," was the answer, dripping sweetness.

Perfect was bold. "An' if he makes an A?"

The teacher was trapped, but gracefully surrendered. "So do you!"

"Aw-Riiiight!" she heard the Heater exclaim from the hall as they left.

"I've never seen anything like it!" Doc McClendon declared to Father Phil that next Sunday afternoon when the minister made his hospital rounds. "We had to move the Rookie to a semi-private room because so many of the other patients wanted to listen to the readings. Now we just pull the curtain across the middle of the room and we've got chairs in the half next to the door. One of the nurses checks in to be sure they're being quiet. I was going to discharge Boy Chile Meadows Thursday, but he begged me to let him stay until Baby Sister finished *Illusions.*"

"But how's the boy doing?" asked Father Phil.

"Sleeping like a baby at night, quiet during the day. It's working like a charm. The other night Cuddly Carrie was reading *Spirit of the Border* right before bedtime, and the kid told me he was so tired of dodging Indians he couldn't help but sleep!"

"Yeah, he said his arms ached and he was almost seasick after Birdlegs quit for the night halfway through *The Old Man and the Sea* Friday." The minister shook his head. "Did you know a couple of them missed the campfire to come read to him?"

"Not all of it," the doctor grinned. "The Duke recorded that session in the Woods and brought it up here. Heck, I even stayed and listened. He was doing poetry, and Perfect and that tall redhead were singing with Mack playing the harmonica. . . . By the way, they're coming up here tonight for a jam session. Mack too. I'm giving them that end waiting room and we're taking all the patients that want to go."

"I'll stop by after church," Father Phil promised.

The next Friday afternoon, Coach Fuzzy and the Great Green G spent three hours at the hospital. Mona the Moaner had agreed to sit in on the last afternoon English class, which came during an off-period in her history lessons. The Rookie had been nervous at first, but Coach Fuzzy's relaxed manner put him at ease. By the time the testing was over, the boy was actually enthusiastic, going into more detail than the Great Green G really intended. As they left, the principal chuckled. "How'd he do?"

The English teacher was a trifle flabbergasted, but would have died before admitting it. "Well enough," she responded primly.

"Well enough to keep it up?"

"For a while."

At the end of the six weeks, Doc McClendon had the eye specialist present as the Rookie's dressings were removed for their daily change. After nearly an hour's examination, the man pronounced his verdict. "If he'll be careful for another couple of months, I think he'll be good as new. No strain, dark glasses, and these drops," he scribbled a prescription on a pad, "ought to do the trick. I'll drop over once a week if you'll let me know when."

Three nurses wept when it was announced that the Rookie would be discharged soon.

At his "final exam" with the Great Green G (whose visits had become regular), the boy asked shyly as he saw her for the first time, though through dark glasses, "Miz G, what would it cost for me to get you to tutor me in the afternoons for a little while?"

She was taken aback, but recovered well. "I would have to think about it, but we could work it out if you were serious. As a matter of fact, I have a few things that need fixing around the house. Perhaps we could trade out."

"I'm serious. I'd love to learn to read like the other kids. Ain't those swell books?"

"Aren't those swell books," the teacher smiled.

"Yes, ma'am. Aren't those," repeated the Rookie obediently.

*   *   *   *   *   *   *

The Rookie had only been out of the hospital a couple of

weeks when Crazy Sharon and Leapin' Lena paid him a visit. The pretty brunette came right to the point. "'Member when you said you hoped to one day be able to repay us for readin' to you?"

The boy nodded. "An' I meant it, too."

"Well," the redhead declared, "the day has come. But you gotta swear you won't ever tell!"

The Rookie swore, only slightly apprehensive.

As happens every so often, there had been a spate of Unidentified Flying Object reports during the past two weeks, capped by the testimony of a foursome of campers in Missouri. The two couples claimed that a huge flying saucer had descended upon them with blinding lights, crackling noises ("like lightning"), and a strange ray that temporarily paralyzed them. They were examined by weird rubbery-looking little beings, and finally released unharmed. This had been the Number One topic of discussion during the weekly current events period in Mona the Moaner's history class.

When Crazy Sharon and Leapin' Lena began to tell the Rookie what they had in mind, the boy tried to stop them. "Wait! You're askin' me to go against my friends!" he protested. "I can't do that."

"Of course you can," the redhead smiled sweetly. "You swore, didn't you? No crawfishin', now."

"We'll stop before anybody goes too far," Crazy Sharon assured him. "Besides, you promised. And we're your friends, too. Aren't we?" She put just the right amount of doubt and hurt into the last phrase, and Rookie's resistance melted.

"Okay," he surrendered.

It just so happened that the other Jakes had been invited to accompany the Duke of Dundee to a regional coon hound field trial. Doc McClendon had vetoed the Rookie's going, but all the other boys were leaving after school Friday for the hundred-mile trip, planning to return to the Jake Camp about dark on Saturday evening. Saturday morning, the Rookie went to the Woods with six jean-clad young ladies.

They were met at Camp by Wacky Mack, for Crazy Sharon had learned of Baby Sister's "ly-berry priv'leges" at the veteran's home and of his apparent affinity for her. She and the younger girl had paid a horseback visit to the log cabin Wednesday afternoon, explained their project, and asked for his help. The man was no match for the two of them, and had finally agreed. "Oughta be fun," he had rasped.

Crazy Sharon knew what she wanted done and the general directed her troops, leaving the technical details to the Rookie, Wacky Mack, and Mad Mel. Since the boy had not fully recovered, the man did most of the climbing. Leapin' Lena, Baby Sister, and the Space Ace were quite agile in the trees and a great deal of help. Cuddly Carrie served as general "go-fer."

A couple of hours after noon, tired but expectant, they were ready for the late lunch provided by the girls, and a trial run. The portable gasoline-powered generator that Wacky Mack had provided cranked on the first pull, and made little noise. One by one, the Rookie flipped on lights, amplifier, microphone, keyboards, reverberator, and electric fence convertor. The little power unit hummed happily along, and both males nodded. "It'll handle the load," the Rookie assured Crazy Sharon.

Wacky Mack walked to his jeep and returned with a roll of camouflage netting. As he and the Rookie began to drape it around their "control station" located about twenty yards behind the woodpile, the man spoke sternly to the girls. "Now y'all gotta promise t' stay back outa sight 'til I give th' word. When they get inta Camp, they're gonna take care-a business y'all don't need t' watch, okay?"

The girls nodded, and Space Ace giggled. Crazy Sharon gave final instructions. "Wear warm clothes, 'cause we're gonna hafta sit quiet 'til they sack out. Then Mr. Mack an' Rookie will run the wire around Camp for the 'lectric fence an' we're ready."

"You're sure the 'lectric fence won't hurt 'em?" asked Baby Sister.

Wacky Mack shook his head. "Nah. It's on low. Jus' scare 'em."

Leapin' Lena put a hand on the Rookie's shoulder. "How're you feelin'?" Crazy Sharon also turned questioningly to him.

The boy grinned. "Better'n I've felt in a coupla months."

He shook his head. "An' prob'ly better'n I'm gonna feel for a couple more. They're gonna *kill* me for this."

Wacky Mack shook his head again. "Nah. I'll make it right."

"We will, too!" the girls chorused.

And then Leapin' Lena and Crazy Sharon each kissed one of the Rookie's cheeks. The boy blushed, open mouthed.

Wacky Mack growled, "See. Toldja if you'd burn that damn mustache off, th' girls'd like you better!" Then the man made an unprecedented offer. "Tell you what. We only got a coupla hours. S'pose you girls get your stuff together an' c'mon over t' my place. Rookie'll go with me now. I put a stew on 'fore I left. We'll have supper an' come back together."

Baby Sister graciously gave up her exclusive. "Y'all'll love it. He's a good cook, too."

Though Crazy Sharon knew what the invitation meant, she was smart enough to play it casual. "Okay with everybody? . . . See you guys in about half an hour, then."

It *was* a great venison stew. And neither Leapin' Lena nor Mad Mel had ever eaten hoe cakes before.

An exhausted band of Jakes arrived in Camp that Saturday night. They had managed only three hours' sleep in the past thirty-six hours and had walked over hills, slogged through marshes, crossed creeks, fought thickets and canebrakes. "Mr. Duke," Birdlegs had complained as they piled into the super-cab pickup for the trip home, "I don't mean any disrespect, but if I was gonna be a coon hunter, I'd be forced to take up drinkin'!"

The boys wearily disembarked from the jeep under the sweetgum and unloaded the water cooler and ice chest. "Son of a three-toed, bare-backed berry picker!" Perfect exclaimed. "I'm gonna sleep 'til school starts Monday!"

They had stopped for supper on the way home, so no one was hungry. "Y'all even wanna build a fire?" asked Boateater.

"All I want's a sleepin' bag," the Heater sighed. "I ain't even gonna check for snakes."

Deadeye had already checked the tent for insects and had found none. "If y'all're gonna build a fire, I'll spray. But if we're jus' gonna hit the hay, I'll let it go tonight."

"Shoot-a-mile, let's sack out," Birdlegs stooped and began pulling sleeping bags out of the hollow cypress.

And so, twenty-five minutes after they had arrived in Camp, the five boys were snuggled into their sleeping bags in the tent. The Camp was in darkness.

Ten minutes later a chest-high, one-strand electric fence was in place around Camp on previously-installed insulators and the Rookie was slipping back toward the canebrake to get the girls. They waited another ten minutes before implementing their plans.

Crazy Sharon leaned close between Rookie and Wacky Mack. "Ready?" she breathed. Her voice quivered with excitement.

Basking in the faint scent of her perfume, the Rookie hesitated to reply, but his companion whispered, "Go ahead."

The two large ice chests brought in earlier in the day were opened, and the Space Ace and Mad Mel donned rubber gloves to remove the smoking contents. The dry ice, provided by the shipping department of the poultry operation, had been broken into chunks by the Space Ace before she had filled the ice chests. Now the two gloved girls tiptoed around the outskirts of Camp tossing fist-sized pieces of the stuff all over the area. Soon an eerie mist eveloped the Jake Camp.

The Rookie grasped the microphone, nervously trying to recall his old California accent. The Space Ace was barely able to contain her giggles as she scrambled back behind the netting, removing her gloves. Wacky Mack grasped the power unit's pull cord and glanced at Crazy Sharon. Her eyes gleamed in the moonlight. "Go!" she whispered. Wacky Mack pulled and the Rookie and Mad Mel began flipping switches.

Suddenly the Jake Camp was illuminated even brighter than day by four powerful overhead spotlights. Smaller, softer blue and red lights blinked in a circle around the larger blinding lights, as if to mark the perimeter of a vessel overhead. Crackling, popping, staticky sounds filled the air along with a humming similar to a gasoline-powered engine. Beams of light shone from all sides of the Camp at ground level. Had all this not been enough to wake the exhausted Jakes, a booming, reverberating, strange-sounding voice announced in unearthly tones: "EARTHLINGS!!! DO NOT BE AFRAID!! WE WILL NOT HARM YOU!"

Reactions inside the tent varied.

Boateater and Birdlegs, clad in long johns, were out of their bedding and peeping out of the tent flap within seconds of the initial illumination. The Heater and Perfect sat up, not willing to believe their eyes and ears. Deadeye grabbed his glasses and retreated into the depths of his sleeping bag, quite possibly the most sensible thing to do under the circumstances, since all their weapons were still in the jeep.

"EARTHLINGS!!! DO NOT BE AFRAID!! COME OUT OF THE TENT!"

It didn't occur to any of the Jakes to wonder how an alien being knew that a tent was a tent. "Good Golly Greenwood! What're we gonna do?" quavered Boateater. Ominous noxious-looking smoke from the spaceship's exhaust covered the clearing. Lightning flashed and glittered blue and red. Thunder boomed.

"EARTHLINGS! COME FORTH!!" gargled the strange voice.

"I'm gone!" yelled Birdlegs, and bolted from the tent.

The Heater and Perfect joined Boateater at the tent flap as their comrade made his break for freedom. But as he sprinted for the Woods there was a boom, a crackling, and a flash; and then Birdlegs screamed and staggered backward into the clearing.

The Alien warned the Jakes amidst the angry noises, "DO NOT ATTEMPT TO ESCAPE!! WE DO NOT MEAN TO HARM YOU! YOU MUST ALL STAND IN FRONT OF YOUR TENT! . . . NOW!!!" was the order.

The three boys ventured trembling out of the tent, joining Birdlegs, who was shaking with fright. "Th-th-they shot me wi-with . . . a ray gun or somethin'!" he stuttered, teeth chattering.

"YOUR COMRADE WILL BE INCINERATED IF HE DOES NOT OBEY!!!"

One warning was enough. The Heater and Perfect reached into the tent and dragged Deadeye out, dumping him to the

ground just as if the sleeping bag was a sack of baseball equipment. That Jake stood reluctantly, adjusting his glasses.

"EARTHLINGS! DO NOT BE AFRAID! YOU WILL
BE TAKEN INTO THE SPACESHIP ONE AT A TIME TO
BE EXAMINED! IF YOU DO NOT RESIST YOU WILL BE
RELEASED UNHARMED! RAISE YOUR RIGHT HAND
IF YOU UNDERSTAND!"

Perfect had to help Deadeye get his hand up. The Heater
raised his left hand. Birdlegs, who had already felt the sting of
the Death Ray, raised both of his.

"TURN TO YOUR RIGHT AND FORM A LINE
ABREAST!"

The boys obeyed, not questioning the Alien's knowledge of
military manuevers. This manuever had been a prerequisite to
Wacky Mack's participation. It positioned the boys in a row
facing away from the girls.

"WE WILL BEAM YOU UP TO THE SHIP ONE AT A
TIME FOR INSPECTION! YOU WILL BE ENCASED IN
DARKNESS AND YOU MUST STAND PERFECTLY STILL
WITH YOUR EYES CLOSED DURING INSPECTION!
DO YOU UNDERSTAND?!?"

"Yes, sir!" the Heater, Perfect, and Birdlegs blurted.
Deadeye and Boateater nodded dumbly. Fists clenched by
their sides, Adam's apples working, the Jakes awaited their fate.

"REMOVE YOUR CLOTHES!!"

Never have five sets of long johns been removed so quickly.

"CLOSE YOUR EYES AND REMAIN PERFECTLY
STILL!"

"Good luck, guys," choked the Heater.

Wacky Mack switched off the generator. For several
moments all five Jakes stood at attention in the darkness —
even the ones that peeked saw only the encasing darkness
promised by the Alien. Each felt the probing eyes from that
blackness and sensed unknown presences in the suddenly-silent
night.

Until a half-dozen of those presences, after almost two
minutes of silence, screamed in girlish voices, "Hellooo,
JAKES!!"

Wacky Mack had to take on-the-spot command to prevent

a massacre. Once the Jakes had dived back into their clothes (and Deadeye was still standing stark naked when the other four were fully re-clothed), their efforts at retaliation knew no bounds. The Heater and Birdlegs were especially vehement, and not only about the girls' part in the fraud. The Rookie also came in for some dire threats.

Acting quickly, Wacky Mack threw some wood on the firesite, pitched some gas on the pile, and flipped a match to start it. The sudden blaze momentarily halted everyone's actions, and the veteran made a call to order in his loudest effort. But before his "Hey! Lissen up!" was completed, he interrupted himself with a strange hacking noise, clutched his chest, and sank to the ground, still hacking. In mutual concern, boys and girls ran to their friend's aid. The Heater put his arm around the shaking shoulders, noticing tears in the man's eyes.

"Mr. Mack! What's wrong? You havin' an attack? Get 'im somethin' to drink, y'all. Mr. Mack! What's . . ."

Wacky Mack clutched his young friend's shoulder, gasping for breath. "Dummy! Some doctor you're gonna be! Hell-damn, I'm jus' laughin!" And he lay on his back by the fire, holding his sides and continuing the strange noise.

The Heater looked in wonder at Crazy Sharon, whose lips began to part in a grin. Leapin' Lena chuckled and punched Perfect in the ribs. The Space Ace could hold back no longer, and burst out in a fit of giggles. Cuddly Carrie began to laugh at the expressions on the Jakes' faces. Baby Sister rolled on the ground with Wacky Mack.

Boateater was the first Jake to crack. He pointed at the Rookie mock-threateningly. "You get latrine duty for six months!"

"It'll take six months jus' to clean up behind y'all tonight!" Mad Mel laughed.

"An' you'll have to wash Deadeye's sleepin' bag!" Baby Sister whooped.

"Warsh, hell!" that worthy snorted. "*Burn* that sucker!"

Wacky Mack had almost stopped hacking, but this exchange started him anew. Perfect and Boateater joined him. All the girls were howling with laughter. The Heater signaled

257

to Birdlegs and the two walked to the sweetgum tree, where they picked up the whole ice chest of root beers and brought them back to the fire. "You did look funny when that Death Ray hit you. What was that?"

"Electric fence wire." The Rookie had not yet dared smile.

"Death Ray!" gasped Cuddly Carrie, and the merriment began anew.

The Heater grinned at Birdlegs and heisted his root beer in a toast. "If ya can't lick 'em . . ." And he collapsed with the rest of the crowd.

Birdlegs regarded the Rookie solemnly for a moment, then stuck out his hand. "Great joke. I owe you." He threw his arm around the other's shoulders and they were the last to join in the laughter.

Wacky Mack finally wore slap out and just quit. As the merriment waned, Perfect shook his head at the man. "I don't think I ever heard you laugh before," he said wonderingly, gasping for breath.

"Don't think I have, in at least fifteen years," was the rejoinder. "Didn't hurt near'bout as much as I thought it would." But the voice was as rough as a wooden boat being dragged across the gravel road by the bridge.

Birdlegs stood and walked to the hollow log. "Might as well get somethin' to eat," he remarked, rummaging through their food supply. "Ain't anybody gonna sleep for a while, after that!" He found marshmallows and crackers in one tin, and hot chocolate mix in another.

The Heater filled the tea kettle with water to boil, while the Rookie and Deadeye went to break off some limbs to toast with. As they walked into the darkness, the others heard Deadeye ask, "Is that damn Death Ray still on?"

Cheese, hot dogs, and buns were in the ice chest with the drinks, and the Jakes managed to come up with a full meal. "Look at us," Boateater observed. "Servin' these girls like queens, after they've jus' pulled The World's Dirtiest Trick on us!"

"Oh, no!" Leapin' Lena protested. "The World's Dirtiest Trick was when y'all lured us into skinny dippin', an' then tricked us an' Marvelous Marv!" She proceeded to tell Wacky

Mack the story, with proper embellishments. The man had another hacking spell and wiped tears from his eyes.

"Awright, I'm gonna tell y'all The *Real* World's Dirtiest Trick. *If* you swear never to tell anybody about it . . . or about this one, either." The Heater spoke with such authority that the girls nodded.

"Besides," Crazy Sharon said seriously, "y'all never told anybody else 'bout the skinny dippin', an' I 'preciated that."

"Okay, Jakes?" The Heater received nods of approval. "You swear, now?" he faced the girls. More nods. "Okay. You 'member the Plague of Frogs? Well . . ." He told the story, and when he finished there wasn't one of them who wasn't laughing.

Wacky Mack finally stopped hacking and wiped his eyes again. He looked pointedly at his watch. "Late," he rasped. His voice reminded the Heater of the night of the JakeFight. "Carry me out t' where my jeep's hid. Get th' spaceship stuff together. T'morra evenin' we'll get what's in th' trees. Supper for ever'body at my place t'morra night?"

There was a chorus of agreement, and as the Heater drove off with Wacky Mack, the girls shared with the boys their wonder at being invited to the log cabin earlier. All the gear was boxed and stacked by the sweetgum tree when the two jeeps returned, and was quickly loaded.

The Space Ace hated to leave. "Can't we jus' have one more marshmeller?" she begged.

The man nodded. "One more while I tell y'all somethin'." He seemed to be thinking deeply as the youngsters settled down by the fire. "I need t' thank y'all," he growled and sipped at another root beer. "Y'all taught me t' laugh again, but you taught me somethin' else. Somethin' I wish I'd known a long time ago." He paused to rest his throat, then continued. "Me an' most other folks in th' world ain't ever caught onta th' fact that males an' females can be friends — good friends — without romance or sex bein' involved. Don't ever lose holda that. Friendship is friendship. Sex, age, color, wealth, education don't make no never mind!" His voice was almost too weak to be emphatic. He tried to speak again, stopped, took a swig, and tried again. He finally forced out,

"Thanks." Then he turned and began to walk away into the Woods.

"Er . . . your jeep's here, Mr. Mack," Crazy Sharon called.

The reply was a harsh croak. "Need t' walk. Boys'll drive y'all."

Boateater stood, but Heater quickly pulled him back down and yelled softly at the man's back, "No, sir! We ain't drivin' no girls home. You're gonna hafta come back an' do it yourself." The others stared at him curiously, but he waved them to silence.

The camouflaged figure stopped, barely visible and facing the darkness. Then Wacky Mack turned and strode back to the fire.

The Heater thought he might have misjudged and gone too far. He stood, slightly nervous, to face the man.

Who placed a hand on his shoulder and whispered, "Tryin' t' run again, wasn't I?"

A grinning nod was his answer.

Wacky Mack drove the girls back to Papa Jake's house, and their rollicking midnight chorus of "God Bless the Jeep Driver" awakened every household they passed. They didn't care.

A new coach had come to the school that year. Coach Fuzzy's responsibilities as principal had grown so that he could not do justice to any collateral coaching duties, and the School Board had hired an applicant from the southern part of the state. His job was defensive football coach, physical education teacher, soccer coach, and girls' basketball coach. Though Burly Shirley, in addition to her band and choral duties, was a fine phys ed and health teacher (she was also a weight lifter, and her upper arm and shoulder structure resembled a man's), she had a dismal three-year record as girls' basketball coach. So she had been replaced in this position.

Coach Roach was one of those agressive-type individuals who is always right and always pushy. His bushy eyebrows almost met his bristly black hair, cut in a flattop, and his head was thrust eternally forward from his shoulders to add to his agressive appearance. His black mustache hairs stuck almost straight out, "like a hog's bristles," Leapin' Lena had observed. Yet the man's won-lost record had been impressive at his former schools, and that was what counted, not his physical appearance.

The new coach had bought a home on the back side of the same block where Boateater lived and had lost no time in dropping a few hints around the neighborhood that he and his wife were "swingers." His wife was a blonde with very fair skin and bright red lipstick on lips that seemed to always be slightly pursed. She had also been hired, to teach history, and had an aggravating habit of considering dates, places, and names with an audible hum. She would never have said, for instance, "Columbus discovered America in 1492." Her classroom lecture sounded more like "Mmm . . . Columbus discovered America in . . . mmm . . . 1492." She had quickly become known as Mona the Moaner.

The Jakes had had little contact with Coach Roach during first semester, though after girls' basketball started they quickly picked up on the fact that Leapin' Lena had a violent dislike for the man. It was early spring when the Jakes ran afoul of him.

There is usually a short period of time when it seems nearly every high-school sport is being practiced at once. The tournament season was just winding down for both boys' and girls' basketball; spring football training had begun; and practice had started for the spring sports of baseball, tennis, track, and soccer. Perfect and the Heater played baseball; Boateater and Birdlegs ran track; and Deadeye was a tennis player. With turkey season also in April, spring was a busy time for the Jakes.

One afternoon Deadeye, Crazy Sharon, and the Space Ace were returning to the gym from the courts and rounded the corner of the building to hear Leapin' Lena's voice raised in protest. The Gaper and Hamburger, leaving the gym after football practice, had stationed themselves at the exit as this last member of the girls' basketball team left. By standing close together, the boys playfully forced the girl to squeeze between them, and Hamburger had taken the opportunity to get an extra squeeze in on the redhead. When she turned to slap her assailant the Gaper grabbed her wrists from behind, and Hamburger leered toward her, hands raised like paws. Deadeye stepped around the corner to view this scene. He didn't hesitate.

His tennis racquet's handle broke, but it was for a worthy cause. The left side of Hamburger's face bore the marks for three weeks, and for the rest of the school year the students called the fat boy "Waffle."

The Gaper shoved Leapin' Lena aside and went for Deadeye, disregarding the Jake's glasses. Though partially blocked by the racquet handle, the blow knocked the smaller boy down, and both football players stepped forward to stand over him. Just then, Heater and Perfect, returning from baseball practice, rounded the corner. Their reactions were instantaneous.

The rest of the baseball players were willing to let the conflict continue uninterrupted; but then the tracksters began arriving, headed for the showers, Boateater and Birdlegs at the forefront. Seeing two Jakes wrestling the bigger boys, and another rising while removing his glasses, they joined in the fray. As the Jakes had long ago been instructed, "Don't fight; and don't fight fair."

With five-to-two odds, even considering the size of the two, it was over quickly. A crowd of students were cheering their favorites on when the soccer team, finally excused from practice, came trotting in, led by Coach Roach.

The new coach was not acquainted with the Jakes' close friendship, nor did he care to hear the particulars about what began the conflict. All he cared about was the fact that his first-string safetyman and his right tackle were being hammered bloodily into submission by five boys in an obviously unfair fight. He waded in, shoving Jakes right and left, to rescue his gridiron stars.

"Good God! Look at you!" Coach Roach bellowed. "What the hell happened to your face?!?" He was speaking to Hamburger, but the Gaper could just as easily have been the subject, having been propelled into the corner of the gym door with some force. "All right! Into my office, alla you guys!" All protests were shoved aside as the seven combatants were ushered into the nearby coaches' quarters.

There, justice was speedily dispensed, according to three basic judgements: one, the Gaper and Hamburger played football for Coach Roach; two, this pair had very obviously taken severe physical punishment already; and three, the five-to-two odds had been unfair. The Jakes were lined up and given ten licks each with the two-foot-long paddle the coach had made himself for such occasions. Smoldering with righteous anger, the five friends left the office, planning revenge for their blistered behinds. Coach Roach had made the Jakes' Bad List.

At the Jake Camp that Saturday, it was suggested that they use the same treatment as had been used on the fuzzbuster pirate. But Coach Roach was an extremely strong person, so this was ruled out. "Durn! He prob'ly knows karate an' all that other stuff!" the Heater grumbled. And then Crazy Sharon, who along with Baby Sister was paying a horseback visit to the Camp for lunch, related the confidence that sealed Coach Roach's fate.

"The sonuvabitch did WHAT?!?!" Birdlegs exclaimed angrily.

"Now, don't you tell her I told you this," the girl emphasized. "But Lena almost quit the team, she was so upset. He was tapin' her knee before practice, kneelin' in front of where she was sittin' on the bench, and you know how loose those uniform shorts are. He just ran his hand right up inside her britches leg. Said his hand slipped!" she snorted.

"And all the girls know he started off the season makin' 'em practice without their bras. Said it gave 'em 'more freedom of movement.' Burly Shirley got that stopped!" Baby Sister contributed.

Perfect's jaw muscle was twitching on the left side, betraying his anger. Through gritted teeth he growled, "He's gotta go!"

Deadeye and Boateater nodded as the Heater spoke. "Okay, that's it. If there're ways to get to 'im, you girls let us know. But startin' now, that sonuvabitch is dead meat. He's crossed the Jakes!" He solemnly held out his hand. The Rookie stepped around the glowing coals to grasp it, and the other four leaned forward to add their hands to the stack.

"Go get 'em, y'all!" Crazy Sharon encouraged. "If you need us, holler!"

The Jakes nodded and began to plan.

The Heater was the first to get a shot at Coach Roach. As he pulled out of his driveway one morning early in the week, he caught sight of a three-foot-long chicken snake stretched along the top rail of the decorative split-rail fence. It was a tight fit getting all of the snake in Baby Sister's lunch box, but they managed it. Her lunch went into Heater's sack and they sped to school, arriving well before the "homeroom" bell.

Coach Roach was not in his office, nor were any students around to notice the boy entering the room. The top drawer of the desk became the snake's new temporary sanctuary. The Heater left undetected.

Blue John was in the Coach's homeroom, and related the scene to his pitchers at practice that afternoon. Pointing across the practice field, he brought the soccer coach's bandaged wrist to their attention.

"He was runnin' his mouth as

usual, an' jus' reached inta the drawer for his roll book without lookin'. Musta laid his hand right on that snake. Anyhow, he slammed the drawer shut, 'fore the snake could get out. But he didn't get his hand out first!" The catcher spat, unprofessionally as yet — he had to wipe his chin — and laughed. "Coach couldn't make up his mind. He wanted his hand out, but he wanted that snake in. Jus' jerkin' an' slammin', jerkin' an' slammin', jerkin' an' slammin'. Hollerin' to beat the band alla time; we all thought he was havin' some kinda fit. With that metal lock bolt that sticks up a little chewin' his ole wrist to pieces. It looked like hamburger meat when he finally got it out!" He spat dribblingly again. "Says he's gonna kill whoever did it when he catches 'em."

Birdlegs and Boateater struck next. The former went horseback riding a couple of afternoons later and was reminded of an old trick he had once heard Uncle Bubba and Papa Jake laughing about. He obtained a paper bag and scooped it half-full of brand-new, smoking-fresh manure from the milk cow's stall. Then he drove to Boateater's house.

The two Jakes, following their elders' descriptions as well as could be remembered, wadded up some tissue paper and placed it on top of the manure. Then Boateater snitched a can of lighter fluid from his dad and got a box of matches from the kitchen. Just at dusk they went across the back yard and down the alley that ran behind the two rows of homes, to hide in the hedge behind Coach Roach's driveway.

They had not figured on a long wait, and they were correct.

The girls' team was playing in the final tournament of the season and the Jakes knew that their game was scheduled for the four-to-six p.m. time slot, because all other sport practices had been cancelled after school. Therefore, they were almost sure that the coach would come home soon after dark. Soon they heard the loud exhausts of the little sports car as it turned into the alley and seconds later Coach Roach swung into his driveway.

"Bbbrrraaappptttt!!!" the little car roared before lapsing into silence. Birdlegs nudged Boateater as the driver swung jauntily from his vehicle. Obviously he had won the game.

As the man walked to his porch Birdlegs quickly tore away

the top of the bag, leaving nothing but the tissue paper above the manure. The door was just closing behind the coach when the boys sprinted from the bushes and ran to the porch. Birdlegs set the bag right in front of the door as Boateater sprayed lighter fluid on the tissue. Then the latter poised with a match while the former raised his fist to knock. "Ready? Go!" hissed Birdlegs, and he beat frantically on the door that the homeowner had just walked through. Boateater lit the tissue and the boys ran.

"Fire! Fire!" Coach Roach, just unbuttoning his lime green sports coat, heard the cry and the pounding on his back door and ran to open it. Something had indeed blazed up, but was dying down momentarily. The man hastened to extinguish the flames.

He stomped them.

Now, Coach Roach was a classy dresser, especially for his ball games. Tonight he had on, in addition to the lime green jacket, light yellow pants and white buck loafer shoes. This is not the recommended dress for stomping fires. Nor manure.

The first stomp sent jets of foul-smelling material as high as his crotch. The second stomp, with the other foot, was good enough to get the stuff waist-high. It also splashed Mona, who had come running down the hall. Finally, the natural slickness of the matter caused him to slip and fall, covering the backside of the lime green coat. Birdlegs and Boateater were already in the latter's back yard, but they could hear Mona the Moaner's wails and Coach Roach's curses quite well.

But he did put out the fire.

The very next day it was Deadeye's turn. The waffle marks on Hamburger's face and Deadeye's broken tennis racquet had led Coach Roach to the inescapable conclusion that the smallest Jake had caused the fight. As punishment, he had decreed that the boy must clean the Visitors' dressing rooms during the basketball tournament.

The first day of the tournament the coach had not been at all pleased with the job Deadeye had done on the toilets. Therefore, having no idea of Birdlegs' and Boateater's prank, the Jake had planned an incident that would make quite an impression on his inspector. He skipped study hall during last period to work on cleaning the bathroom facilities.

Coach Roach burst in about the time Deadeye was finishing up. The man was clad in yet another fancy suit of clothes, having incinerated the unlucky outfit of the day before. He was naturally in a bad humor, and warned, "This bathroom better be spotless, or you're in for it!"

No commanding general ever took such pains to find something wrong, but stall after stall, the commodes were spotless. Until he reached the last one. The porcelain was sparkling, except for a blob of brown just bigger than a silver dollar halfway between the rim and the water. "Is that what I think it is?" Coach Roach was fit to burst.

Deadeye was laconic. "Waal, Coach, I don't know what *you* think it is, but I know what *I* think it is."

The man was infuriated. "Boy, if that's what I think it is, I oughta make you eat it!"

Deadeye leaned over, adjusting his glasses. "Waal, it sure looks like it." He reached forward and came up with a dollop on his finger. "Feels like it, too." As the horrified coach watched, he held his finger under his nose and sniffed. "Kinda smells like it."

Then the moment of glory. Deadeye stuck his finger in his mouth and slurped. "Yep, tastes just like it!"

Coach Roach threw up all over his fancy outfit and ran retching from the room.

Deadeye took his jar of peanut butter and went home, whistling.

A late cold front was forecast to come blasting through that Sunday night, and two of the Jakes got an unexpected call to help their nemesis. Perfect had gone home with Boateater after church and the two were covering plants in the yard when they heard the coach's car approaching from a block away. As the loud auto whipped into the alley, the driver waved at them briefly and continued to his home.

Five minutes later, Coach Roach came walking down the alley and hailed the two Jakes. Butter would not have melted in his mouth, as the saying goes. "How you boys doin'? Say, Mona's wantin' to do the same thing for her shrubs. Reckon y'all might have some-a that roll left over and might help me cover hers? Ole Coach sure would be obliged."

The Jakes were working on the next-to-last japonica, and would obviously not use all of the roll of plastic. Agreeably, Boateater shrugged. "Sure, Coach. Be right down."

As the man strode away, Perfect looked at his comrade and winked. "Talk about luck! Jus' let's keep our eyes open."

They covered several bushes under Mona the Moaner's direction, and then she suggested that several houseplants and potted ferns probably should be brought in. Coach Roach and the two boys started on that, and as Perfect carried a scheffelera into the den, he asked, "Ma'am, could I use your bathroom a minute?"

"Sure. Mmm . . . right down the hall," she said as she moved to direct the placement of a fern in the kitchen.

Perfect needed just one glance into the bedroom to see that his idea was plausible. He had remembered the time when a visiting preacher and his wife had spent the night at his house and Uncle Bubba had somehow gotten the dual controls switched on the electric blanket. The couple had been haggard the next day, and the boy could still hear the conversation around the breakfast table:

"Fran would barely wake up feeling cold, and she'd turn up the control on her blanket. Ten minutes later I'd be burning up, and I'd turn my control down. A little while later she'd come up for air, freezing, and turn her dial up. I'd throw my covers off and turn the thermostat down. Then I'd be freezing, without my covers, and pull them back over me. Ten minutes later I'd be burning up again. And she'd be snuggling up to me, trying to get warm, which just made me hotter! We finally got up and figured out the problem about four a.m. I never spent a worse night in my life!" The preacher had been emphatic.

It took Perfect exactly twenty-three seconds to slip into the bedroom, dive under the bed, and switch the blanket controls.

Ever since the Plague of Frogs, Coach Fuzzy had insisted on a Monday Morning Devotional and Prayer Breakfast for his faculty. Not only were Coach Roach and Mona the Moaner twenty minutes late for the breakfast the next day, but the entire faculty heard him berating her as the couple hurried down the hall. "Well, it's your damn fault! If you weren't so damned hot-blooded, I coulda got some sleep last night! . . . Mornin' y'all. Sorry we're late."

They looked, as Coach Fuzzy later remarked to the Great Green G, "like Death warmed over."

And Mona the Moaner's nickname took on new meaning.

The noise made by Coach Roach's little sports car was not particularly objectionable during working hours. But the neighbors on the block had grown tired of hearing the loud exhausts roaring through the alley after bedtime, especially since most houses' bedrooms faced away from the street, toward the alley. That week, Boateater approached the Heater with a possible solution to the problem.

Papa Jake had been tearing down the older abandoned tenant houses on the farm at the rate of two or three a year for the past several years. Each of these houses had been built up off the ground on concrete blocks which were about three feet high. Boateater had seen stacks of these old foundation blocks around the barns, and he asked Heater to bring him one when he came to school the next day.

The old block weighed well over a hundred pounds, and it was all Boateater could do to pick it up and walk with it. But he brought it home that afternoon late and carried it around behind the garage, unseen by his parents. There he painted it with a can of flat black spray paint he found in the storeroom, turning the block over so that both ends were covered well. Then he went in to supper and homework.

By bedtime, the boy had still not heard the tell-tale exhausts of the coach's car, and he took a quick stroll to insure that every neighbor whose driveway opened off of the alley was home for the night. The only one missing was the Mayor, and as Boateater was returning across his back yard, he saw the

Cadillac turn into the alley. Grinning in anticipation, he told his parents "Good night" and went to his room.

As soon as he heard his parents retire, the Jake eased his window open and removed the screen. He slipped quietly outside and darted through the shadows to the garage. The paint had been represented as fast-drying, and sure enough, not a smudge showed as the boy ran his hand over the block. Grunting, he picked the block up and staggered across the yard with it.

Two doors down an elderly widow had a huge fig tree on the back of her lot which blocked the beam from the streetlight, throwing a shadow across the alley. This blackness was only one house away from the coach's driveway. Knowing the man always entered the alley from behind his own corner lot, Boateater situated the block on its side in the middle of the alley with the smaller end facing the direction Coach Roach would come from. Satisfied that the black block was invisible in the black shadow of the fig tree, the boy retreated into the widow's hedge and settled down to wait.

He had to wait over an hour, for Coach Roach had been "tutoring" a senior girl known as Rhonda Roundheels tonight. These sessions usually lasted late; and though Mona the Moaner sometimes participated, she had not been present this time. It was almost midnight when Boateater heard the sound of the little car approaching from down the street.

"Bbbrrraaapppttt . . . bbbrrrooommm!!" roared the exhausts as the driver downshifted, slowed, turned, and accelerated once again into the alley. Then there was a scraping, grinding noise and a "Bbbrrrooommm, bbbrrrooommm!" as the engine raced. Being a front wheel drive, the little auto stopped as the front wheels left the alley's gravel, the front bumper resting on the concrete block. "What the hell?!?!" the driver bellowed.

The coach leapt from his vehicle and stomped around in front of it, cursing quite colorfully as he saw the problem. "What kinda damn town would . . ." he began. Then he had an idea. "By God, the Mayor oughta see what his damn street department does!" So saying, Coach Roach stormed down the alley to the house where the Cadillac was parked and began banging on the back door. Lights began to flash on in bedrooms up and down the block.

It took all the strength Boateater could muster to lift the little car slightly and shove it backwards off the foundation block, but his adrenalin was pumping. He grasped the concrete and, with a mighty heave, managed to get it onto his shoulder. Keeping to the shadows, he staggered through the widow's yard and across the street. The little creek that flowed through town paralleled this street, and a footbridge crossed the creek right in front of the widow's home. There was a muffled splash as the block hit the water. Freed of his burden, Boateater raced home and was in his room by the time the irate Coach was ushering the equally-irate Mayor down the alley to the little car.

The resulting argument, at the top of the two men's voices, brought six more neighbors into the alley. Before it was over, the coach had been declared either drunk or crazy, and was beginning to believe the latter himself. The incident was reported rather heatedly to Coach Fuzzy that same night by three different callers, including the Mayor. Coach Roach was placed on disciplinary probation and had to write letters of apology to every neighbor on the block.

He also had mufflers installed on his sports car and began parking on the street in front of his house.

Coach Roach was addicted to chewing tobacco, and at the Jake Camp that Saturday night, the Rookie made the remark that he had seen the man at a promotional tobacco giveaway in the mall that morning. The boy still used snuff, and he had gone to the mall himself to try the new brand and receive some free samples. "That guy musta got a dozen packs," he declared. "Bet he don't hafta buy tobacco for another month."

But the Heater had opened several of the coach's drawers trying to determine where to hide the chicken snake. He smiled ominously. "Betcha he does."

Charley Garbage habitually opened all the doors early in the morning, including the gym, where the coaches' offices were located. Early Monday morning the Heater slipped into the gym while the janitor unlocked the other school buildings, and made his way unobserved to Coach Roach's office. Since there had been a soccer match Saturday afternoon, the boy figured that the coach might have stashed his tobacco supply, and he was right. Two packs had already been opened for sampling, one labeled "Mild" and the other "Regular." The Heater pulled a box of red pepper from his pocket and sprinkled the contents quite liberally into the pouches, shaking them and finally mixing it in with a finger. Satisfied, he replaced the packs.

But as he started out the door, he saw to his horror that the occupant of the office was just entering the gym himself. There was no other option; the boy retreated into the office and quickly closed the door, stepping behind it. He crossed his fingers, but to no avail. Coach Roach opened the door and walked in.

As in many school buildings, the doors here opened to the inside and toward the corner. Heater was lucky; the coach did not shut the door behind him.

The student did not even know of Coach Fuzzy's Monday Morning Faculty Devotional and Prayer Breakfast, or he would never have planned his prank for this day. The short devotional was rotated among the teachers, and today was Coach Roach's turn. In light of the recent midnight altercation in the alley, Coach Fuzzy had suggested that the coach speak on the Third Commandment: "Thou shalt not take the name of the Lord thy God in vain." At that, the principal had been tempted to assign the Seventh Commandment, for rumors were beginning to surface about the coach's dalliance with Rhonda Roundheels and a couple of other ladies around town.

As the Heater cowered behind the door, he heard the coach muttering various appropriate phrases that he recognized as being rather sermonistic. Less than five minutes passed before the man said audibly, "That oughta do it." The boy heard the desk drawer open and close, not knowing that the coach had just replenished his tobacco supply. The door closed behind Coach Roach as he headed for the cafeteria and his devotional. Gratefully, the Heater peeked out, assured himself that the coast was clear, and fled.

The faculty met half an hour before school on Mondays,

had coffee and doughnuts, and then sat with second or third cups while the ten-minute service was held. As was his habit, Coach Roach had a couple of doughnuts with coffee and then placed a chew in his jaw after he finished eating. It made no difference that he must speak this morning; he could talk around the wad in his mouth. "Disgusting habit!" Burly Shirley observed to the Great Green G, as usual loud enough for most to hear. Since all the coaches chewed, she made that comment several times a day.

The speaker turned a chair around at the head of the table, put one foot in it, propped elbow on knee, and leaned forward to speak. "Folks," he proclaimed, "our devotional today is on the Third Commandment, 'Thou shalt not take the name'. . ."

Suddenly his eyes bulged and a gurgling sound emanated from his throat. Then, "Gaaahh! Putooee! Putooee!" he gagged and spit, spewing tobacco and juice half the length of the table. "Goddamn! Hellfire and damnation! Somebody..."

And Burly Shirley hit Coach Roach.

It was bad enough that he had spit tobacco on her blouse and one arm, but he had also taken the name of the Lord her God in vain, and the Pentecostal lady would not stand for that. Her fist caught him on the jaw in a most unlady-like punch, all her weightlifter's strength behind it. Coach Roach hit the floor, out cold. He later swore that his foot had slipped off the chair, and he was knocked unconscious when his head hit the floor.

His job was not lost, however. Coach Fuzzy, a chewer himself, agreed that the coach's tobacco pouch contained enough red pepper "to knock a mule on its butt." And subsequent investigation revealed that still another pouch had been tampered with.

The facts cut no ice with Burly Shirley, though. In righteous indignation she marched out, drove home, showered, changed clothes, and reported back to school at ten o'clock, just daring the principal to dock her pay.

Instead, he gave her a small bonus that pay period.

The night of the Senior Prom arrived, with fully half of the high school in attendance in the gym, in addition to numerous assorted guests from other area schools. The Jakes had conspired with the girls in what they hoped to be the crowning blow for Coach Roach. The Rookie had gotten a bid from Mad Mel, and once again he used his fake ID to buy liquor. But this time it was for a good cause.

The Jakes divided up the vodka into easily-hidden half-pint bottles and set themselves to the task of spiking the punchbowl at the adult table. Had they but known, the boys could have saved their money, for several of the male teachers and chaperones, Coach Roach included, had brought their own spiking materials.

Crazy Sharon, Mad Mel, and Leapin' Lena had flasks in their purses, and each took the opportunity early in the prom to offer a cup of spiked punch to Rhonda Roundheels. They then managed to get together with the older girl about an hour into the dance and the Space Ace suggested they stage a contest between themselves to "dance Coach Roach under the table." Rhonda quickly agreed to participate in the rotation. After that, it was just a case of Cuddly Carrie signaling to the bandleader, her cousin, as to when to play slow dances. For nearly two hours Rhonda Roundheels danced nearly every slow dance with Coach Roach, and nature took its course.

Students were forbidden to leave during the hour-long intermission, but adults could come and go as they pleased. Coach Roach took pains not to be seen as he and Rhonda slipped out the Visitors' dressing room outside door, to which he had a key.

But he was observed. The Rookie was not a student, so he was allowed to leave, though he could not come back in. He had left and stationed himself in the shadows next to the parking lot. He watched the coach and the girl hurry to the sports car, which had its top down on this warm spring night. As they backed out of the lot, the boy ran to his own convertible and followed the couple, driving the Beetle without lights.

The school was on the outskirts of town, and the baseball field, with its fence lined on the outside with weeping willow trees, was only a couple of hundred yards down the road. The side of the field away from the school had long been a favorite parking place for couples, and the alcohol-fueled passion of this couple was too strong for them to make it any farther. The Rookie smiled as he watched the sports car whip into the parking lot and pull up under the trees. He swung the Beetle to the side of the road and got out, shucking his party clothes there in the dark. He pulled on jeans, a dark sweater and cap, and tennis shoes, checked his pocket for the valve stem wrench he had placed there earlier, and picked up a wire coat hanger from the back seat. Silently, he circled the fence toward the coach's car.

Coach Roach and Rhonda Roundheels had wasted no time. Before the engine had been switched off the girl was in the back seat, removing her striking scarlet dress. She had her panty hose off before the man was in the back seat; and by the time he had untied his shoes she was completely nude, her garments draped across the front seat. She threw herself on the coach passionately, laughing at his grunting efforts to disrobe as she kissed him and rubbed herself against him. The Rookie, thirty feet away in the shadows, was panting and sweating himself at the scene in the moonlight.

Yet he watched closely as the man's clothing was flipped from back to front seats: lemon yellow sport coat, light blue slacks, tie, shirt, undershirt, shorts, and finally, socks. The two heads disappeared from his sight. On hands and knees, the Rookie crept toward the car.

His first task was the hardest, yet the occupants of the car paid not the slightest bit of attention. Shielded from the passionate pair in the back seat by the vehicle's oversized headrests, the Jake reached a long arm in from each side of the car and filched every piece of clothing except shoes from the front seats. He had brought the coat hanger to straighten out for this purpose, but the two lovers were too single-minded to notice anything. Quickly, he bundled the garments under his arm and scuttled back to the trees.

Valve stem wrench in hand, he returned to the car and crawled around it, loosening the stems on each tire until he could barely hear the air coming out. He anticipated that the car would not be called upon to move for some time. He had only one close call. As he adjusted the last tire, the feminine cries of passion suddenly increased and the car lurched. Rookie looked up to see Rhonda's upper body thrust over the side of the convertible, not three feet from his head. But the girl's eyes were closed tightly; and then she cried out and seemed to melt back down into the seat, where masculine sounds became more dominant.

"Gee, I'm sweatin' more'n they are!" the Rookie whispered as he made the sanctuary of the willows again. As much as he hated to leave the show, he gathered up the bundle of clothing and sprinted silently down the road to the Beetle. He was back at the school tapping on the designated dressing room window about twenty minutes after he had left. Birdlegs opened the window, eyebrows lifted questioningly. The Rookie gave him a thumbs-up signal.

"No sweat," he started, and then chuckled. "Correction. Lots of sweat, even me!" He passed the pilfered clothing through the bars and stuck his hand through for a round of handshakes. "Good luck, you guys!"

"Great work, Rookie!" the other Jakes whispered in excitement. The window closed and the boy walked back to his Volkswagon. However, he didn't leave. He decided to stay and see the rest of the show.

Like many gymnasiums, this one also doubled as a theater for assemblies and school plays, so a stage was built on one side of the court and bleachers on the opposite side. The heavy curtains stayed closed unless the stage was in use. The electrical control panel for the curtain, stage lights, and sound system was on one side of the stage. The only regular use of the stage was by the home economics class, which taught sewing and modeling. Several full-sized mannequins used by the class were moved to the wings during assemblies or plays. The Jakes made their way to the darkened stage with the bundle of clothes, and went behind the curtain to meet the waiting girls.

"Hey?" called the Heater quietly.

"Over here," Crazy Sharon answered, and flashed a light from her purse-sized flashlight. "You got 'em?"

"Bullseye!" Birdlegs grinned, holding out his bundle. "Rookie done good!"

"Hurry!" Leapin' Lena was businesslike. "Intermission is half over." She was pushing out one of the mannequins, while Mad Mel shoved the other.

Working quickly, they slipped the lemon coat and blue slacks on the male dummy and the scarlet dress on the female. The mannequins were then postioned center stage, just behind the curtain. As a final touch, Boateater hung the brassiere and bikini panties from the outstretched hands of the male, and gave the female Coach Roach's tie and polka-dot boxer shorts. "Aw-Riiight!" grinned the Heater, viewing their work.

Perfect took the flashlight and ushered all the others off the stage. "Hurry and mingle!" he ordered as he turned back to the control panel. He located the "Stage Lights" and "Curtain" buttons. Taking a deep breath, he punched them in that sequence and ran.

The crowd on both gym floor and bleachers was startled by the sudden lighting and the receding curtains. At first, no one recognized the significance of the two figures on the stage, until two feminine voices (never positively identified) screamed "Coach!" and "Rhonda!" almost simultaneously.

Coach Fuzzy finally came to his senses and stormed, livid, up to the stage, but Perfect had made good his escape. By now, the whole crowd had recognized the scarlet dress and lemon sport coat. A quick search of the offices proved fruitless, but a math teacher came running in to inform the principal that the coach's car was not in its parking space. Mona the Moaner burst into tears as the crowd ran from gym to cars.

Some witnesses later swore that a small foreign convertible was parked by the side of the road as the cars began to depart the parking lot, and that this car's lights flashed on as it sped toward the baseball field. Those who followed said they saw brake lights go on and headlights go off just past the ballfield, leading them to believe it had turned there. A line of cars wheeled into the baseball parking lot.

There was indeed a small foreign convertible under the willows.

Rhonda Roundheels, with only a month to go, was allowed to graduate. Coach Roach was fired on the spot.

The front slipped up on the Jakes. It had been bright and starry when they went to bed, but by daylight it was sulky and still. The distant rumble of thunder could be heard not only in the southwest, but also in the west and northwest. They had planned on a bass fishing excursion to Dundee Lake since turkey season was over, and as Boateater pointed out, "Bass'll bite when it's thunderin'." Sitting by the fire waiting for the coffee to boil, they began to rig their rods.

By the time Heater had finished making coffee, however, the higher tree limbs were beginning to sway back and forth with windy gusts; but there was no breeze at ground level. In fact, the cookfire smoke hung in Camp, making their eyes itch. Thunder boomed continually now, much closer, but their vision to the west was blocked by the trees. Perfect voiced his thoughts, "Sounds like it's gonna storm. Maybe we oughta hold up. I don't wanna be on the lake when it's lightnin'!"

"Reckon we oughta head on in?" Deadeye asked.

"C'mon, candy! Scareda gettin' wet? You ain't gonna melt!" Birdlegs snorted.

The treetop-high wind moaned eerily and the branches began to thrash, yet still no breeze stirred the smoke from the fire. The Rookie felt a cold chill and actually looked behind him.

"Y'all feel that? Spooky!"

The others were used to the fast-moving fronts of this area of the South, but the Rookie had only migrated three years ago, and he was still rather uninitiated to the vicissitudes of Mother Nature. The Heater had felt the chill too, though, and raised his eyebrows. "Might be some hail in this 'un."

Lightning flashed constantly now—not the booming bolts that shook the ground, but glowing lines that criss-crossed the clouds and soft furry-looking green-yellow balls that winked and winked again. In spite of the lightning's illumination, however, it was growing darker.

"Maybe we oughta pack it in, guys," the Rookie suggested. "Or at least drive out to where we can see what's comin'."

Somewhere close the top snapped out of a tree and crashed to the ground. The world took on a greenish cast.

"Talked me right into it." Perfect stood and beckoned.

"Help me get the tent down."

Then the wind just quit dead. In the sudden stillness, the sullen air seemed almost too heavy to breathe. Boateater had always a low-pressure sensitivity, and now he felt hairs began to stand up on the back on his neck. "This is not good," he warned.

Birdlegs sprang to his feet and ran to the sweetgum tree. "Lemme look an' see what's goin' on!" he cried as he began to climb. From the tree's upper crotch, one could see over the top of the woods and view approaching clouds. The Jakes had many times used this "Crow's Nest," as they called it.

"Careful!" called Deadeye, moving to help Perfect with the tent. Heater, Rookie, and Boateater began making preparations to break camp. They were halted by Birdlegs' exclamation:

"Good God A'mighty!! A tornado!!"

"Right, man," Boateater was not scornful, but he definitely didn't want any kidding around about this.

"No, really! It is!" The scout's voice was high-pitched. "Boilin' up, blacker'n night!" He sounded as if he were broadcasting; indeed, he was.

"It's movin' like it's goin' south of us. Gettin' bigger. Jus' missed the locust thicket. Oh, no! What about Deputy Don's place? An' Wacky Mack's? We better try to warn . . ." He began to descend, the words spilling out. Then he suddenly stopped, transfixed.

"Another one! Two more! Comin' at *us!*"

There was no doubt whatsoever in anyone's mind. Birdlegs had barely raised his voice on this last warning, yet the sounds cut like a knife.

"Do it! Do it! Go!" yelled the Heater, galvanized into action.

The wind hit with a rush, almost ripping the tent fabric from Perfect and Deadeye's hands as they tried to fold it. The Rookie ran for the jeep. Boateater looked up and bellowed in sudden consternation. "Get the hell down outa that tree!"

The yell jarred Birdlegs from his slack-jawed rigidity, and he almost dropped from his perch, hand-over-handing like a monkey. The wind blast whipped the words from his mouth: "Go! Go! It's nearly here!"

Limbs broke and crashed around the Camp. The scout hit the ground and grabbed the Rookie by the collar, jerking him from the jeep. "Too late for that!" he roared. "It's comin' down our road!"

"The log!" cried Boateater. "Get in the log!"

The tent jerked away from the two Jakes' hands and flew almost straight up. The Heater seconded Boateater's suggestion and began shoving gear farther back into the cavity. A hackberry was uprooted and crashed into the huge sweetgum, the larger tree holding the smaller one from smashing down on the jeep.

The log was nearly fifteen feet long with a cavity at least three feet in diameter. With all their gear shoved to the middle, three Jakes squirmed in feet-first from each end as the roar of the approaching storm crescendoed with the sound of a runaway train. The Rookie, atop the Heater's and Birdlegs' backs, screamed, "Look at the fire! It's goin' straight up!"

Indeed, ashes, coals, and burning brands joined leaves and dust, swirling around in a circle and spiraling upward. Perfect braced knees and elbows against the cypress as the wind sucked at him. "Hang on!" he yelled to Deadeye, who clung to his and Boateater's backs. He shut his eyes and began to recite, "Yea, though I walk through the Valley of the Shadow of Death . . ."

Trees snapped and crashed around them. At one point it was darker than night. The roar was deafening, and Boateater felt his ear drums pressured as if during a takeoff in an airplane. His scream was not heard by either of his two companions, inches away.

Lightning exploded much too close for comfort, and their refuge trembled and shook as it had not done since the storm that had brought it to earth half a century before. Hailstones as big as baseballs drummed all over Camp, one raising a knot over Birdlegs' ear as it bounced into the log. Rain followed the hail; sheets of rain, at times almost horizontal, blowing into both ends of the log.

Finally it was over. The awful roaring noise ceased, replaced by the gentle patter of rain. The Heater was the first to open his eyes. "Hey? Everybody okay?"

"I am not believing that!" The Rookie was emphatic, in his fear reverting to his California accent.

"Son of a three-toed, bare-backed berry picker!" Perfect finally breathed. "You still there, Deadeye?"

"I'm here, but my glasses're gone. Y'all don't go to movin' around an' step on 'em."

Except for the knot above Birdlegs' ear and Boateater constantly working his jaw, trying to pop his ears, the Jakes were healthy, if wet. Still almost in shock, they slithered out of the log and stood unbelieving in the midst of the destruction. They did not feel the drizzling rain as they wandered in a daze around the once-familiar area.

"I ain't b'lievin' this!" whispered Boateater. Perfect found Deadeye's glasses snagged in an ironwood forty feet behind the tent site. The lenses were unbroken, but one earpiece was missing.

Birdlegs suddenly remembered the scene from the Crow's Nest. "Hey, what about Deputy Don an' Wacky Mack? That's where the big funnel was headed."

The old sweetgum still stood, sheltering the jeep, but the road was criss-crossed with trees and obviously impassable. "We'll have to walk out anyway," observed the Heater. "S'pose you two," he indicated Perfect and Deadeye, "go on back to the road. I know Daddy an' Uncle Bubba will be down lookin' for us if they ain't been hit. Y'all can tell 'em we're okay an' get 'em to pick us up at Deputy Don's or Wacky Mack's. We'll head thataway across the Woods to see if they got hit an' need help."

Birdlegs moved toward the jeep. "Better take the .22's an' any axes or hatchets with us. No tellin' what we'll hafta go through, an' I know this'll bring some snakes out."

Perfect and Deadeye removed their rifles from the jeep and headed west. "See y'all in a while," the former called. "Be careful!"

Boateater looked around at the wreckage of their Camp and snorted. "Huh. 'Be careful,' he says. Right!"

It took over an hour for the four boys to make it across the Woods to Deputy Don's, normally a forty-five minute journey from the Jake Camp. To their relief, the closer they got to the edge of the Woods, the less destruction there was, and when they finally broke into the open they could see the house was still standing. They trudged through the muddy field and found Deputy Don and Sugarpie working doggedly to remove the remains of the small barn. Pitiful grunts and moans sounded beneath the boards, and the man said grimly, "Had a cow, calf, an' two hogs in there. Betcha the cow's dead."

He was right. The four Jakes pitched in and had the rubble off the animals quickly. Both hogs seemed healthy, but the calf was unable to stand and having trouble breathing. The lawman carried it tenderly to his car and laid it in the trunk. "I'm gonna run 'im to the vet's. Y'all wanna ride?"

"We're gonna check on Wacky Mack," the Heater said. "But if you see Perfect, give 'im a ride home so Daddy'll know we're okay."

"Damnation! I plumb forgot about Mack. Oughta have my tail kicked! Alla them big trees 'round his house, too!"

"Go ahead on with that calf. We'll check on 'im," Birdlegs assured the man.

"All right. But get Sugarpie to call me on my radio if anything's wrong down there. I'll be right on back after I get this calf to town." Deputy Don accelerated down the road.

As the Jakes approached the log cabin, there didn't seem to be any obvious damage. Some limbs had been ripped from the huge old trees, but they could only see one tree that had been uprooted, toward the back of the lot. "Hellooo!" Boateater yelled as they came near. There was no answer.

Only when they mounted the steps to the porch did they notice the fallen tree across the back corner of the home. The roof had been smashed down onto the porch by the oak. While the Heater pounded on the door, Rookie, Birdlegs, and

Boateater walked the length of the porch to the corner to inspect the damage.

"Reckon it hurt th' inside-a . . ." Birdlegs was saying, when a horrible gasping croak stopped him.

"Mister Mack!" the three cried at once. The Heater came running.

The bearded woodsman had apparently been standing on the porch when the tree had crashed. He was pinned to the porch decking by one of the bigger limbs across his chest. "He's breathin' funny," the Heater proclaimed, "and there's a little blood comin' outa his mouth. Maybe broke ribs? Punctured lungs?"

"We gotta get this damn tree off 'im — NOW!" declared Birdlegs. "What . . ."

The Rookie took off around the corner toward the man's jeep. "Jack an' winch!" he yelled over his shoulder.

They positioned the vehicle's jack under the tree trunk close to the man's body while the Heater drove the jeep around to face the smashed corner. Another oak grew close enough to winch from, though it took a dozen throws to get the cable over a main limb. Boateater pulled on the hook while the Heater paid out cable, and finally there was enough to loop around the trunk. With the Rookie jacking and Heater winching, the tree was inched up enough for the other Jakes to gently pull Wacky Mack clear of the wreckage.

Boateater was the fastest, and as soon as the man was free, he said, "Gone to call an ambulance!" and sprinted out of the yard and down the road toward Deputy Don's, the nearest telephone. Birdlegs hurried inside the cabin for blankets while the Heater examined the unconscious man for further injuries. Rookie, as long as the tree's weight was up off the decking, pulled some cypress blocks from under the porch and braced the trunk up.

With Wacky Mack covered and nothing else they could do until the ambulance arrived, the three boys released the cable, repositioned the jeep, and winched the oak clear of the porch. It crashed to the ground just as the first wails of the ambulance siren were heard.

Doc McClendon came into the waiting room, still in his

operating attire. He was a little taken aback at the crowd. Six
Jakes, four girls, and seven adults waited anxiously. "He's not
out of the woods yet, but I think he'll make it. Six ribs were
broken, one lung punctured and collapsed. Hip joint's rup-
tured and his pelvis is fractured but still in place. You boys did
well to keep him flat and not try to bring him in in his jeep.
He took a lick on the head too, but it's nothing he won't get
over. He's damn lucky y'all got there when you did, though."

Deputy Don was weeping. "I wasted more'n a hour foolin'
with that damn barn, an' him layin' down there under that
damn tree!" Sugarpie wept with him.

Both Birdlegs and the Heater put their arms around the
deputy's shoulders. "Wouldn'ta made any difference anyway,
Deputy Don," Birdlegs assured him. "You couldn'ta got it off
'im by yourself."

The Heater nodded. "And nobody else coulda got that
ambulance out so quick after Boateater got you on the radio.
Y'all musta been drivin' seventy-five miles an hour."

"Eighty-six," corrected Deputy Don flatly.

"Hey!" exclaimed the Rookie in relief. "Great idea! We
can start 'im a readin' program, an' the Duke can come in an'
quote poetry, an' Perfect an' Leapin' Lena can sing to 'im,
an'..."

"Do you want him to recover, or are you just trying to
finish him off?" kidded the Duke of Dundee.

Doc McClendon looked around at the crowded waiting
room. "Y'all want to hear something ironic? Here y'all are
worryin' about him, and you know what he asked me when he
came to?" He paused while they all shook their heads.

"He said, 'Doc, do you know if the Jakes are all right? I saw a tornado headed toward their Camp and I was just going out to check on them when the damn roof fell in on me!'. . . That's what he said," the doctor related.

HOME SWEET HOME

Part VI: Age 18

The Rookie had recovered to the point that the eye specialist said he could return to work on a limited basis. But the construction company was working on a job out of town, and the boy didn't feel that his old Beetle would make the round trip on a regular basis, so he began to look for other jobs. He was hired by Birdlegs' father to work at the lumberyard.

One of his first projects was to rebuild the corner of the porch roof at Wacky Mack's house. Papa Jake had suggested a weekend project by friends and neighbors, and Birdlegs' dad not only donated the materials, he paid a couple of his men to help. All the Jakes were there, of course; as were the Duke of Dundee, Uncle Bubba, and Deputy Don; and Big Gus and June Bug had come with Papa Jake.

Sugarpie fed the men barbeque for lunch and steak for supper. Uncle Bubba went back for seconds that evening, exclaiming, "Lordee, Don! Do y'all eat like this all the time?"

The lawman rejoined, "Not hardly. Just right after a barn falls on one-a my cows."

The girls had come out in the afternoon to serve lemonade and cookies, and stayed to clean up behind the men, who were finished before dark. After supper the adults left, but the boys and girls stayed for a while and built a bonfire of the unsalvageable lumber and pieces of the now-chainsawed oak tree. It was Baby Sister who had The Great Idea.

"You know what we oughta do?" she asked retorically. "We

oughta decorate this place an' throw a home-comin' party for Mr. Mack when he gets out."

The suggestion was received with enthusiasm by all present and assignments were meted out. It was voted not to invite the grown-ups. "Jus' us kids," Boateater declared. Even though Wacky Mack was pushing forty, the kids did not consider him a "grown-up."

Boateater and Perfect checked with Doc McClendon the next afternoon, and he gave them a tentative date of two more Saturdays for the veteran's release. Twice they had almost lost Wacky Mack; once when his lungs collapsed right after admission, and again when he contracted viral pnuemonia. "My guess is that he'll never fully recover. He had too much old damage to his lungs," Doctor Mac told Papa Jake in confidence. "He'll have to be real careful from now on. Matter of fact, if it was winter-time, I'd keep him here three more weeks."

School had just let out for the summer, so the youngsters had plenty of time to spend on the party. The girls were doing most of the cleaning and cooking, so the Jakes busied themselves with catching enough bass to skin and charcoal broil for the main course. They also had to chainsaw their way back through the Woods to the Jake Camp, with Big Gus following on Papa Jake's small farm bulldozer. The jeep was in running shape, but the windshield and right front fender were smashed. The sweetgum and hollow cypress log were fine.

On Thursday night before the party, Birdlegs' father asked his son, "Y'all know you've got two reasons to celebrate Saturday for, don't you?"

Birdlegs thought, but had to reply, "No, sir."

"Yeah. Saturday is the Rookie's eighteenth birthday. He's the first Jake to come of age."

"How'd you know?"

"He had to fill out some insurance forms at the lumber yard. My liability won't cover employees unless they're eighteen or will be within six months. I knew he was close, so I checked to be sure."

Birdlegs got on the phone. This part of the party was going to be a surprise.

About four o'clock Saturday afternoon, Perfect, Baby Sister, and the Rookie arrived at the hospital in the Bronco. The girl carried a fresh change of clothes from the log cabin. Doc McClendon released into their custody a thinner, wan Wacky Mack who moved as if he were slightly hunched. "Now you be careful," the nurse fussed at her former charge. "Otherwise, you'll be back in here!"

The veteran's raspy voice was little more than a whisper now. "God, I hate hospitals!" he said as the group moved down the front walk toward the vehicle.

Perfect drove the ten miles to the log cabin slowly, for it was obvious that each bump caused his charge pain. They detoured carefully down the newly-bulldozed road into the Jake Camp to show the man the damage to the Woods, and stopped for a few minutes at Deputy Don's to show him the new barn. Finally the Bronco pulled into the driveway in front of the log cabin.

"Home, Sweet Home!" muttered Wacky Mack. He was reading the huge banner that hung the length of the porch.

As the man stepped from the vehicle, a bevy of boys and girls suddenly burst from the cabin. The rest of the Jakes, along with Crazy Sharon, Leapin' Lena, Mad Mel, Cuddly Carrie, and the Space Ace all crowded around him, the girls bearing garlands of flowers. Wacky Mack made as if to get back into the Bronco. "Back t' th' hospital!" he kidded.

The Heater and Birdlegs returned to the grill in the back yard while Boateater and the Rookie proudly showed off the repaired porch corner. "I was here?" the veteran asked. The two boys demonstrated how and where they had found him, and how they had gotten the tree off of him and the porch. Though it had been told again and again during his hospital stay, he had to hear the now-famous tale of The Great Boateater Race just once more.

Baby Sister finally broke in tactfully. "Mr. Mack's exhausted. Let's get 'im inside."

"Jus' get me t' one-a those rockers," he pointed to the chairs on the porch as he clutched her shoulder. "Been inside too long."

They served supper on the porch, and after the plates were cleared, the Heater and Deadeye approached Wacky Mack with a gift-wrapped box. "Mr. Mack, we want you to know how much we 'preciate you." Deadeye spoke formally as the Heater presented the man with the box.

Wacky Mack sat motionless for a full minute, the present resting on the rocker's arms. It seemed as if he was almost afraid to touch the box. Then he reached out with two fingers to pull on the bow. He unwrapped it so carefully that Birdlegs only half-jokingly assured him, "It's not a bomb."

It wasn't.

It was a brand-new leather jacket with the word "Jake" embroidered over the left breast pocket. Wacky Mack just sat and looked at it in the box, shaking his head.

"Well, durn! Do you like it or not?" the Heater finally broke the silence.

"Yeah." It was barely a whisper.

Crazy Sharon and Baby Sister took the man by the arms and gently urged him to stand. Still occasionally shaking his head in silence, he shrugged into the new jacket. He didn't speak until he put his arms around the two girls' shoulders and hugged them. "You kids!" he croaked. Then he raised his arms as high as he could without pain. "I'm proud to be a Jake!" was the loudest thing he had said in a month, easily. The kids cheered.

As the leather-clad man sat back down and began a round of hand-shaking and careful hugs, Crazy Sharon clapped her hands. "Time for dessert, girls!" she called. The Heater winked at her and nodded as she went inside.

When the door opened again, Perfect and Boateater suddenly threw their arms over the Rookie's shoulders and swung him around to meet the emerging girls. Baby Sister held a chocolate cake with a single candle and "Welcome Home, Mr. Mack!" lettered in red icing. Behind her, Space Ace and Cuddly Carrie carried an ice chest full of homemade strawberry ice cream. Leapin' Lena followed with plastic bowls and spoons, while Mad Mel brought paper plates and plastic forks. Last came Crazy Sharon with another cake, upon which blazed eighteen candles. It too was lettered with red icing: "Happy Birthday, Rookie!"

Birdlegs conducted the traditional birthday song for the blushing boy as the girl held the cake so he could blow out the candles. The Space Ace had planted two trick candles on opposite sides of the cake and Wacky Mack had to stifle a laugh as Rookie huffed and puffed in vain from side to side. Finally he caught on and pinched the wicks, grinning. "Y'all used to always do stuff like that to me," he complained good-naturedly.

Then Boateater produced a second box, identical to the first, and presented it to the birthday boy. "Happy birthday from all of us," he said simply.

The Rookie looked at the present and glanced at the empty box next to Wacky Mack's rocker. "Aw, naw," he shook his head.

Perfect punched his shoulder lightly as he stepped back. "Aw, yeah."

"Aw, naw," the boy repeated.

"Pull 'im up a rocker," the man ordered. When the Heater did so, the celebrant collapsed into it as if his knees were weak. "Aw, naw," he said for the third time.

Baby Sister had finally held Wacky Mack's cake close enough, but still had to help the man blow out the candle. She and Crazy Sharon now set their burdens on the table, where the other girls had already put their stuff. "Well, open it, dummy," the younger girl urged.

The jacket was identical to Wacky Mack's, even down to the word "Jake" over the pocket. It had cost the other kids a little more each, since there was one less to share the expense, but the expression on their friend's face was worth it. "Thanks," he breathed reverently as he put it on.

Deadeye was the only Jake who could still wear the jacket originally given to him by Wacky Mack just over four years ago. Now he went inside and came out with it on. He posed with Wacky Mack and Rookie for a moment, then sighed and shook his head. His jacket was still good, but it was worn, tight across the shoulders and obviously beyond zipping. He began to shrug out of the leather.

Which Leapin' Lena noticed had been slightly altered. Instead of the boy's name over the pocket, now there was simply "Jake" in newly-embroidered letters.

"This ole thing's too good to just throw away," he drawled casually, and held it out to Cuddly Carrie. "See if you can wear it." She could.

The Heater had slipped inside unnoticed, and now he stepped back onto the porch with an armload of leather jackets. "We thought y'all might could get some more good outa these," he also spoke casually. "Leather lasts a long time, an' we only got two or three years outa these." He handed cleaned jackets, one patched, all with "Jake" now embroidered over the left breast pocket, to Crazy Sharon, Mad Mel, Baby Sister, and the Space Ace. To Leapin' Lena he apologized. "We didn't have but five, an' all of 'em were too short for you. Hope you understand." She grinned and nodded as the other girls tried theirs on. Crazy Sharon's eyes glistened.

Wacky Mack excused himself to go inside. He was back in only a moment with an almost-new jacket that matched the others except that it was not embroidered. Shrugging, he handed it to the redhead. "Got a special deal on a half-dozen when I got y'all's, so I had one for me," he explained. "Can y'all get it embroidered?"

Perfect nodded. "Yes, sir." The girl quickly donned the obviously seldom-worn jacket. It was only slightly too large. She kissed the man on the cheek and he blushed. Tears gleamed in her eyes, too.

The Heater grinned and took out his pocketknife. "Now we gotta initiate alla y'all. Hafta slit your wrists an' lick everybody else's blood an' say The Jake Pledge an' . . ."

"How 'bout we jus' serve y'all cake an' ice cream 'fore it melts," Mad Mel snorted, turning toward the table.

"Hey, thanks, you guys," Crazy Sharon said softly.

As the Rookie was handed his dessert, he cleared his throat and spoke seriously. "Lemme tell y'all somethin'. You've got no idea how much tonight means to me. Do you know that in all my life, no one ever gave me a birthday party before?"

Boateater was puzzled. "They don't have birthday parties in California?"

· "I came from a broken home. Nobody cared." The other youngsters were clearly unbelieving and thought the Rookie was kidding, until Wacky Mack cleared his throat.

"He's bein' straight. Me, too," he rasped. "Until t'night, nobody ever gave me a party." He waved a forkful of chocolate. "My first cake."

"Well, durn!" the Heater declared. "When's your birthday? We'll do it again."

"Couldn't stand it. I'd get fat," was the reply.

It was just after dark when the kids finished cleaning up and deposited the trashbags in Boateater's pickup, which had been hidden around back with the Heater's jeep. "We ain't gonna stay late, Mr. Mack," said Birdlegs. "We don't wanna tire you out on your first night outa the hospital."

The man offered his hand. "Thanks, kids. You got no idea what this meant t' me."

"Bet I do!" The Rookie grinned as he shook the hand.

Wacky Mack squinted up at him speculatively. "You might. By the way. Doctor Mac said I might oughta get somebody t' stay with me th' first few days. You be int'rested?"

The boy was taken aback, but Birdlegs clapped him on the shoulder and answered for him. "Sure he would. Jus' gimme your keys an' we'll bring your Beetle an' some clothes out tomorrow."

Three weeks later, the Rookie canceled his room at Aunt Florrie's Bording House and moved in with Wacky Mack.

Dove season arrived that fall, and Papa Jake had allowed the Jakes to prepare a hunting field for themselves. Game and Fish Commission regulations tried to work hand-in-hand with normal agricultural practices, and doves usually were attracted in huntable numbers to fields of newly-planted wheat. The Heater and Birdlegs, however, seldom did anything halfway. They planted in their five-acre Jake Field approximately the same amount of wheat seed that a farmer would plant on the whole lower forty.

A week before the season opened, Papa Jake happened to see a light plane circling the corner of the Woods where the boys were planning to dove hunt. Upon investigating, he saw the problem himself and surmised that the plane had been a game warden surveillance team. He considered it rather obvious that the amount of wheat and doves were readily visible from the air.

The man sent Big Gus on a tractor to disk the field and reprimanded his son rather warmly that evening. "Now y'all won't be able to hunt it the first weekend of the season," he declared. "According to law, you can't hunt it for ten days after the baiting problem has been corrected. That means no hunting on the Jake Field until the second weekend."

But the little field had swarms of doves on it, and the hunting was not really good on the other fields the first weekend. The temptation was too great. The afternoon of the first day, the Jakes decided to check out the Jake Field. "Just in case," they took their shotguns.

Birdlegs had to go back to Papa Jake's house for more shells, so the Heater and Perfect went on ahead in the jeep and the Bronco, carrying the rest of the Jakes and several of the girls. The Jake Field was almost a mile and a half away from the gravel road down an extra-rough turnrow. The other youngsters had barely had time to reach the field when Birdlegs returned; but as he approached the turn-off from the north, a line of traffic came around a curve a half-mile away, headed toward him. The boy jammed on his brakes as the first pickup in the oncoming line turned onto the rough turnrow that led to the Jake Field.

Horrified, he watched as five pickup trucks with the state Game and Fish Commission insignia on their sides headed toward his unsuspecting comrades. Birdlegs thought quickly and turned his jeep around in the middle of the gravel road.

He had one chance to warn the Jakes. Since the road the wardens had taken was so rough, he might be able to go faster and get close enough on the Duke's turnrow. In a cloud of dust, he sped down the gravel road toward the Duke's place. The Jake Field was just across the little creek from Dundee's Lake, and Birdlegs knew that the Duke's turnrow was wide and smooth. At sixty miles an hour, he swung onto this turnrow and stomped it.

The other Jakes heard the fast-approaching vehicle and its

tooting horn and Perfect walked to the edge of the narrow, shallow creek to investigate. He feared Birdlegs' jeep would flip as it skidded to a halt.

"Wardens! Wardens!" Birdlegs cried. "Comin' in from th'other way! Throw your guns an' shells in here quick!"

"But we ain't even shot!" Boateater called, though as Heater later said, "We prob'ly would have."

"Don't matter! Do it! Do it!" exclaimed Perfect, pitching his shotgun and shell vest across the stream to Birdlegs. "Hurry!"

Ninety seconds later, the jeep was headed back down the Duke's turnrow at only a slightly slower pace than before. The Rookie and Deadeye, who had waded the creek to ride back, clutched the dashboard in fear.

Five minutes after that, a dozen wardens closed in on the baited field to catch three young men relaxing under three separate shade trees around the edge of the field with three young ladies. The couples were unarmed.

Birdlegs' Ride became nearly as famous as Boateater's Race.

The second weekend of the season they could legally hunt the small Jake Field, and Saturday all of the girls were along. The temperature and the action were both hot, and several of the boys were shirtless. Boateater was one of these, and he was stationed on one side of the small square field. He shot one dove that glided almost to the center of the open disked ground before falling. The boy ran out to retrieve the bird.

But just as he knelt to pick it up, another flock of the gray darters swooped into the opening from the Woods. Boateater stayed stooped, so as not to spoil someone else's shot. Then, just as he started to stand, a flight came in from the north. He crouched again.

He missed the pair that came by him, and paused to reload. Once more he moved as if to return to cover at the side of the field, just as Birdlegs yelled, "Watch!" A trio of doves had slipped in over the Rookie's corner. Boateater bent down again.

The boy had not noticed that he had been standing in a fire ant bed. The insects had rebuilt their home after Big Gus's disking of the field, and were in their normal bad temper concerning this new invader.

A fire ant's philosophy counsels stealth before an attack in force. The first troops went up the boy's pants leg and were halfway between knee and crotch when the second wave swarmed up over his boottops and dug in. Suddenly Boateater's legs were on fire with ant bites.

The Jake threw his gun to the ground and screamed, beating his legs. It was quickly obvious that this defense was not entirely sufficient. This was also not a time for modesty.

Shamelessly, Boateater dropped his camouflage fatigue pants down to his ankles and bent over right in the middle of the open field, beating and brushing at his bare legs. His agonized yells indicated that at least some of the first wave of ants were getting close to tender areas. The boy's companions all rushed to help.

Now, Crazy Sharon had, in jest of course, given both Boateater and Birdlegs sets of cute little men's bikini underwear for Valentine's Day that spring. They were white with pretty little red hearts and a message across the back: "Kiss my Valentine!" And Boateater had his on this second weekend of dove season.

Birdlegs was a little bit jealous, but not for long. The girls all agreed that the things were so attractive that all the Jakes received sets.

The Heater had bought a small sports car that summer. He had always been a fast driver, but a good one. Yet there is a lot of difference between fast in a jeep and fast in a small car. The Jake began to get a reputation for speed. As Big Gus told Papa Jake, "Dat boy don't know but two speeds: stopped, an' lak a bat outa Hell!"

Papa Jake cautioned his son, to no avail. He fussed at him, but it did no good. After one apparently close call, the man lost his temper and chewed the boy out. A week later, he took the car keys away from the Jake. But it was harvest season and farming precluded him driving an almost-eighteen-year-old high-school senior everywhere he needed to go. So Papa Jake gave the keys back with a warning. He might as well have been speaking to the wind.

The Heater grew resentful of his parents and, like Boateater a few years earlier, became rebellious. Relations around the household were, as Baby Sister told Crazy Sharon, "like waitin' for a case of dynamite to go off!"

One Friday night the Heater and Perfect were absent from the Jake Camp, having gone to a fall weekend baseball clinic at a nearby college with the rest of the team. Just after supper, the other Jakes were surprised to see Papa Jake come driving up in the old jeep.

"Hope nothin's wrong?" Birdlegs voiced all their fears.

The man held his hands up in front of him. "Aw, naw. Jus' visitin'." He strolled to the fireside as Boateater leaned into the hollow cypress for a folding chair. "Thanks, son," he said as he accepted a canned drink from the Rookie.

"How's Mack doin'?" he asked the boy.

"He has coughin' spells, but he's gainin' weight an' gettin' around pretty good."

There was a short pause. Then, "Y'all do any good today?"

"We killed half a dozen squirrels between the time we set up Camp an' dark," Boateater replied.

"Oughta be good in the mornin'. Wanna spend the night an' hunt with us tomorrow?" Birdlegs offered.

Papa Jake shook his head and took a long swig of his drink. He stared into the fire for a long moment as Boateater raised his eyebrows at Deadeye, who shrugged his shoulders. Finally the man spoke. "Boys," he said slowly, "I got a problem and I'm not sure what to do about it."

Again there was a short silence, then Boateater queried, "Yes, sir?"

Sighing, Papa Jake came out with it. "It's the Heater. He's drivin' too damn fast, but I can't tell 'im a damn thing. I'm scared he's gonna hurt somebody. Or even break his own damn neck and take one-a y'all with 'im. I just can't get through to 'im."

No one said anything for at least a full minute, then Deadeye admitted, "Waal, sir, he scares me, too."

Birdlegs shoved a burning branch into the fire and spoke, "I know what you mean. I drive too fast myself, but he's way faster'n I am."

The Rookie made a stab at being faithful. "But he's a good driver. 'Cept for goin' too fast, he's not careless or a show-off."

"Yeah, but . . ." Boateater shook his head. "You gotta think about what might happen. A blowout, fishtail, or another driver that's drunk or stupid . . ." He looked at Papa Jake. "You're right. Whadda you want us to do?"

"I dunno. Talk to 'im? Whadda y'all think?" He was obviously at the end of his rope and the Jakes realized that.

Birdlegs nodded. "Okay. We'll try. We'll kick it around tonight an' talk to 'im or beat 'im up or somethin'."

Papa Jake stood and shook hands with the four boys. "Thanks." He grinned slightly as he returned to the jeep.

That Tuesday evening the man was sitting in front of the fireplace reading the newspaper when the Heater walked up and clapped him on the shoulder. "Hey, Daddy."

The father glanced over his glasses, and the son smiled and ducked his head in imitation. "Hey, I'm gonna slow down," he said.

"I'd 'preciate it."

"Yes, sir. 'Night."

And he did.

Speed was not the only problem the Jakes had with driving that fall. Poor judgement also gave them some troubles.

There was the weekend they planned a co-ed rabbit hunt — the traditional kind, complete with hounds. Birdlegs brought

his pack of mini-
ature beagles early
that Saturday
morning, and they
planned to hunt
the Locust
Thicket.

The problem
was, it had rained
over two inches
the night before.
Water ran well
over the beaver
dam that the Jakes usually used to cross Muddy Slough. Normally, this would just have meant that the boys would hike the
half-mile from where the gravel road crossed the bridge, but
they knew this was impossible for their feminine companions,
and made mention of this fact.

"You think we can't walk half a mile jus' 'cause we're *girls*?"
Crazy Sharon asked belligerently.

"No," Birdlegs replied reasonably, "we think you *won't* walk
half a mile, in the *mud*, 'cause you're girls."

"So, are we goin' home?" Leapin' Lena also sounded reasonable. And hopeful.

"Nah, we'll put 'em in four-wheel drive an' go in on that
old turnrow along the bank of the Slough," Heater declared.
"Daddy won't mind."

"I dunno. That's awful muddy," Perfect cautioned.

"C'mon, candy," Boateater taunted.

"Yeah, don'tcha wanna have any fun?" Birdlegs scoffed.

"Naw. Jus' don't wanna push," Deadeye pointed out.

"I don't like rabbit meat that much anyway," Mad Mel
opined.

"You reckon these jeeps will pull that much mud?" the
Rookie ventured.

The two jeeps were parked on the gravel, alongside the
culvert where the muddy turnrow met the road. Birdlegs
slapped his vehicle and exclaimed, "Man, my ole jeep'll go as
long as the water ain't above the windshield!"

Baby Sister was doubtful. "Even if we got down there, won't it be too wet to hunt?"

"Hey, c'mon!" Birdlegs was vehement. "I done brought my li'l beagles out here an' ever'thing! Even if we jus' let 'em run an' listen, it's gonna be fun! You ain't gotta kill nothin' to have fun huntin'!"

So saying, he cranked his jeep and shifted into four-wheel drive. The half-dozen little dogs began to bark, sensing imminent release from their small cage on the tailgate. "Lead the way!" he called to the Heater.

"Hang on!" came the reply.

They nearly made it to the Locust Thicket.

The first jeep's rear wheels skidded sideways at a point where the turnrow dipped just below the edge of the ridge. Before the Heater could regain control, he was sideways and blocking the road.

Birdlegs had to try to swing around him, and did so, narrowly missing the front bumper. However, one wheel hung in a subsoiler rut and pulled him into the field also. Mud flew in all directions as the two jeeps spun their wheels. And sunk deeper into the mud.

"RrrrAAARRRggg!!" roared the Heater as he switched off his motor. His bellow was echoed by several of the girls.

Both vehicles were unloaded to lighten their loads, but that didn't help. The Jakes tried to winch from one jeep to the other, but that only pulled them closer together and left no room to turn them around into the road again. Nor was there anything else to winch from; trees at both the Locust Thicket and Muddy Slough were too far away. After being splattered with mud several times, the girls moved out of range, sitting on the ice chest and dog cage to watch the operations.

They tried jacking the jeeps up and placing branches under the wheels, slogging a hundred yards for the limbs. They tried digging new ruts and paving them with more branches. They pushed forward, backward, sideways. Birdlegs kicked his. Heater asked the ladies to cover their ears while he cussed his.

It had been ten-thirty when they got stuck headed for a two-hour rabbit hunt. They ate lunch, still stuck, at twelve-thirty. At one Perfect and the Rookie left, slogging north across the wheat field toward the barns a mile and a half away. It was two-thirty when they knocked on Big Gus' door and asked him to come rescue them with a tractor. It was three-thirty before both jeeps were pulled back onto the torn, rutted turnrow facing back toward the gravel road.

The Jakes chained Heater's jeep behind the tractor and hooked Birdlegs' to the back of the front jeep with the winch cable. Muddy, bad-tempered, and exhausted, they loaded everything and everyone back into the open jeeps just before the rain began again.

As the tractor started pulling the two loaded vehicles down the sloppy turnrow toward the gravel road, Crazy Sharon turned to Birdlegs and asked sweetly, "Are we having fun yet?"

With Wacky Mack's injury making the veteran unable to be in the Woods as much as before, the Jakes found a new problem to cope with. Poachers began to invade the Woods, and while it was not particularly hard to catch them, the youngsters were not at all comfortable with these confrontations with grown-ups.

The Jakes now ate supper at Wacky Mack's at least once a week and sometimes spent the night there, rolling sleeping bags out on the floor in front of the fireplace. One night the Heater brought the subject of the poachers to the man's attention. "There's not enough game in the Woods for ever'body that wants to come in there an' hunt, Mr. Mack. Y'all've taught us not to be greedy, to only take good shots, an' to follow up on cripples; but some-a them guys blast away at everything they see. An' when we catch 'em, they're men an' we're just kids. What can we do? How'd you keep 'em out?"

The man coughed — a juicy-sounding cough — and shook his head. "It's tough," he rasped. "My advantage was reputation."

"How's that?" The Rookie was puzzled.

"Whadda y'all call me, to yourselves?"

"Sir?" Birdlegs pretended not to understand.

"C'mon. What?" the veteran demanded.

Perfect grinned. "We call you 'Wacky Mack,' sir."

"Why?" Still a demand.

"Waal, we thought you'uz a li'l weird at first," Deadeye explained.

"Sometimes I still think that," Boateater teased, and the man threw a sofa cushion at him.

"That's how I kept 'em out. Dog 'em, jus' spooky like. They never knew what I was gonna do. Made 'em so nervous they couldn't hunt."

"We can't do that, though," protested the Heater. "We're jus' kids an' they know that."

"Boy, when I was your age . . ." the veteran muttered, but then broke off. "You're right," he agreed. He thought a moment and suggested, "How 'bout Deputy Don?"

"He said jus' come get 'im, but he's on patrol a lot. Even if he was home, how're we gonna get a poacher to wait while we run get a sheriff's deputy?" Perfect was a touch sarcastic.

"Could tie 'im t' a tree an' let th' 'skeeters eat 'im," Wacky Mack winked.

"How'd you . . . Never mind. Can't do that. There was an early frost an' the 'skeeters are gone," Perfect grinned.

"Lemme think on it," the man said.

It had indeed been an early winter, and though duck season didn't open for a month, there were a goodly number of ducks already in the Swamp and on the Canal. One poacher in particular, a man the Jakes called "Sneaky Pete," would park his truck next to a bridge a half-mile below the Woods. Then a partner would drop him off at the bridge across the Canal just above the Woods. Sneaky Pete wore stocking-foot waders and had a camouflage-draped inner tube and, wearing swim flippers over old sneakers, he would float the length of the Canal through the Woods. Moving silently down the stream with such a low profile, the man killed ducks by the sackful. He also took squirrels, rabbits, turkeys, and an occasional deer, for he carried several buckshot shells for just such opportunities.

The Jakes had seen him several times, but when they accosted him, the man simply flippered by in silence, safe in the waters of the Canal and Swamp. Though Deputy Don met Sneaky Pete at his truck several times, the man had always cached his illegal kill; and since he was not on posted property when caught, the lawman could take no legal action.

Then, the week before deer season opened, the Heater heard a voice close to the edge of the Swamp. The Jakes were scattered across the Woods squirrel hunting that morning, and Heater had earlier heard a series of .22 shots from the direction he now heard the voice. Curious, he moved in silence toward the noise. It was definitely one voice, holding forth in a monologue. "What the hell?" Heater muttered.

As he advanced, the voice became clearer, and he could make out words and phrases. "So beautiful . . . I wish . . . take you right . . . so soft . . ." Now Heater could hear a sob at intervals. "Hurt you . . . so wonderful . . . I'd have loved" — the sobbing again — "I promise I'll . . . never, never . . ." The Heater stepped around a cypress trunk to see Perfect sitting on the damp ground at the edge of the Swamp.

"What's wrong?" the boy asked as he reached his cousin. Then he saw Ole Cow-foot.

Perfect turned a tear-stained face to the Heater and patted his dead companion. "He's dead," he wept. "He'd been gutshot with buckshot an' he crawled up here. I put him outa his misery." Perfect stroked the huge old buck's neck. "Ain't he big? Magnificent! But some sonuvabitch . . ." he broke off crying, and hugged the deer that had been a legend for so long.

The Heater sank to his knees in awe, grasping the heavy antlers. He counted fifteen points. "Oh, God, he was fine! I can't believe that . . ." And he too cried for the fallen monarch.

"Sneaky Pete floated the Canal yesterday," Perfect said. "He did it. I know he did it. An' I'm gonna *kill* the bastard. I'm gonna KILL 'im!!" he suddenly roared, scaring the Heater half to death.

"An' I'll help you, gladly. But right now . . ." the boy pulled out his knife grimly. "Let's go on an' dress 'im out."

That night at the Jakes' fire, the boys discussed ways to handle the situation. "I betcha he's killed a hunnerd ducks, an' the season don't even open 'til next month," Birdlegs growled.

"You can't jus' wait at the bridge for 'im all the time, though," Boateater pointed out. "He'd jus' drive on by if he saw us."

"Y'all don't forget we're in school 'cept on weekends, too," Deadeye said. "And Rookie's workin'."

"Well, it can't keep on like this," the Heater declared. "Even if I gotta stay outa school a week."

"Hey, what if we took turns?" Perfect spoke slowly. "We know he's gonna come in early, right? So if we each take one mornin' next week, we'll only be a coupla classes tardy. That won't hurt much. We could even talk to Coach Fuzzy."

"Yeah, but even if we catch 'im, we can't do nothin'. He'd jus' wait'll we were gone an' come back." Boateater blew at his flaming marshmallow. "So whadda we do?"

"Wanna go ask Wacky Mack?" queried the Rookie.

"Waal, we done that," Deadeye drawled. "All he told us was we hafta act crazy."

Perfect slammed one fist into his other hand. "I got it! An' it's jus' crazy enough!"

"Waal, lay it on us."

Perfect did. Birdlegs and the Heater were enthusiastic, exclaiming, "Aw-Riiiight!" Deadeye took off his glasses and began polishing them in silence. Boateater shook his head dubiously. The Rookie was the only one to voice his fears.

"But what if we slip up an' he dies?"

Perfect was grim. "We won't. But if we do? . . . I hope he suffers as much as he made Ole Cow-foot suffer!"

It was Heater's day that Tuesday morning. He drove to the Jake Camp before dawn, having told Papa Jake that he was "doin' some extra scoutin' 'fore deer season." It was the same excuse Perfect had given to Uncle Bubba the day before. Perfect had agreed to pick up Baby Sister for school.

Just after sunup, the Heater heard a shotgun boom from the Canal. "Ahuh. Upstream from the ole swimmin' hole," he muttered. He picked up his scope-sighted .22 rifle and left Camp at a trot. At the spot where the Canal met the edge of the Swamp, the Jake crawled up behind a big cottonwood. As he made himself comfortable for the wait, a shotgun spoke twice just over a hundred yards upstream. "Aw-Riiiight!" the boy breathed.

As he watched, three wood ducks swam into sight just out of range downstream, feeding out of the Swamp into the Canal. An idea occured to him and the Jake grinned maliciously.

Soon the object of his wait hove into view. The Heater was surprised at how effective the camo-draped inner tube was. There was not even a ripple on the water when Sneaky Pete came slowly down the Canal. Not only was the man camouflaged, but his gun was even made invisible with camo tape. With his weapon lying athwart the tube, arms crossed over the gun, head on his hands, the man's contraption looked like a small pile of sticks and leaves dislodged from a beaver dam. "I gotta try that," thought Heater.

Camouflaged himself, the Jake lay unmoving and unseen as the man floated by. After he passed, the scope-sighted .22 eased forward and the Heater focused his attention where the man's was—on the three wood ducks downstream. Sneaky Pete was only twenty yards from the ducks when they flushed, and not quite forty from the Heater, who timed his shot perfectly.

The shotgun boomed twice, killing two ducks on the water and the third as it flew. Sneaky Pete flippered toward the ducks, his attention given to reloading, and was picking up the first one when he realized that he was sinking. He always carried a few cold patches for emergency repairs, but suddenly he was aware that this was no thorn-snagged slow leak. He dropped the duck and flippered frantically for the nearest bank, holding his gun aloft.

For a few seconds after the head disappeared the shotgun was still visible, but it was dropped when Sneaky Pete's head broke the surface again, gasping for breath and from the cold water. Thrashing and kicking, he made it to shore. Laboriously, the poacher disentangled himself from the deflated tube, its camo netting, the burlap game bag that was strung out behind him, and his soaked hunting coat.

From the pockets of the coat he extracted not only the patches, but also a thermos and a pint bottle which he placed on a log next to the small hummock he had swum to. Sneaky Pete was across the Canal from the Heater and almost fifty yards distant, when he turned the tube around to investigate the hole. The Heater couldn't hear what he said, but the man certainly said something.

The Jake looked through the four-power scope and saw the bewildered man poke both index fingers into the holes that lined up diagonally through one side of the tube. The boy swung the crosshairs past the tube and lined up on the pint bottle. He squeezed.

The shattering of the bottle and simultaneous curse from its owner muffled the slight crack of the .22. Sneaky Pete jumped to his feet and looked wildly around, but nothing moved. "Hey!" he yelled, but no one answered. "What the hell's goin' on?!?" the Heater heard clearly. He smiled and moved the crosshairs to the thermos bottle.

That next Friday night, the Duke of Dundee and Uncle Bubba walked into the Jake Camp just as the boys were finishing supper. Tequila and Coffee, the new bluetick pup, had jumped a bobcat and the coon hunters had to travel far and fast to pull the hounds off the trail. The men nodded gratefully to the root beer and squirrel and dumplings offered by the Jakes.

The Duke looked at Rookie. "Aye understand that Wacky Mack has fully recovered and is up to his old tricks."

"Howzat?" the boy asked.

"Some character waved me down on the road one day last week and asked me to give him a ride back to his truck. He looked awful, and was blue with cold. Wearing old tennis shoes over stocking-foot waders that were ripped in several places." He took a bite of squirrel. "Mmmm, good! Anyway, he claimed Wacky Mack had shot his boat out from under him, or some such damn thing. Said he nearly drowned, lost his gun, then got lost in the Swamp, running from Mack shooting at him. Downright petrified, Aye would venture to say." He sipped his root beer. "Know anything about it?"

The Rookie grinned. "Well, you know how Mr. Mack is! He never said a word about that!"

The JakeFest that year was held at Wacky Mack's cabin, and attended by a much smaller crowd than usual. There were several reasons for this: for the first time, it rained on the night of a JakeFest; also, Mr. Boy Chile Meadows had passed away that day, and most of the adults went "calling" on the family that evening; and to make matters worse, Deputy Don had patrol. The owner of the cabin was the only grown-up present.

Naturally the conversation turned to the recently-deceased. "Whatcha reckon they'll do with that big ole house?" Deadeye asked from where he was sprawled on the floor.

"Prob'ly sell it," Boateater remarked, toasting a marshmallow in the fireplace.

"Betcha they'll tear it down." The Rookie knew something about old buildings. "Bet it's 'bout to fall down anyway. Cost too much to fix it up."

Perfect grinned at Leapin' Lena. "Ever hear this'un?" He began to strum. "'This ole house once knew my children, this ole house once knew my wife'. . ."

The redhead picked it up. "'This ole house would groan and tremble'. . ."

"I bet it's haunted!" exclaimed the Space Ace, interrupting the singers before Wacky Mack could get his harmonica out.

"Aw, bull!" snorted Birdlegs.

But the girl was insistent. "I heard they closed off the top two floors an' never let anybody go up there. He had all those sisters that died before him, too. Betcha they're all mummified in the upstairs rooms, like in that scary movie."

"Hey, let's go see!" proposed Heater.

That next week, talk of The Haunted House was all over school, accompanied by the Jakes' boasts of "We ain't scared!" Saturday night would tell the tale.

The Jakes were not the only practical jokers in school. While listening to the Space Ace rattling on about ghosts, skeletons, mummies, and other assorted Denizens of Spookdom, the Gaper nudged Hamburger. "Let's go check it out tonight."

The old three-story house about two miles out of town had once been a mansion, but hard times had fallen upon it. Relatives had removed all the furniture during the weekend after the funeral, and now it was just a hollow shell. Only Mr. Boy Chile had occupied it the past sixteen years, and he had spent most of the last four years in and out of the hospital and the nursing home.

As the two boys explored the upper stories with their flashlights, it soon became apparent why the top floors had been closed off. The roof leaked. In several rooms the ceiling plaster had fallen, and patches of rot and mildew on the old tongue-and-groove floors showed in the beams of their lights. But there were no skeletons or mummies, and no ghosts showed themselves.

Hamburger grinned. "Man, I'd hate for those guys to be disappointed. S'pose we help 'em thrill the girls?"

"Whatcha gonna do? Hide in a closet an' jump out an' holler 'Boo!'?" asked the Gaper.

"Could. But you 'member that story the Heater loves to tell 'bout the crazy guy tappin' on the roof with a blood-stained hammer?"

"Yeah," nodded Gaper.

"Well, what if we brought a ladder and went through that trap door up there," he shined his light straight up, "and beat on the roof? They'd mess in their britches!" chuckled Hamburger.

"I got a ladder," the Gaper smiled.

Saturday night was a suitably spooky night for investigating a haunted house. Cloudy, moonless, and threatening, the skies revealed bolts of lightning in the west, and the muttering rumble of thunder promised storms. The Jakes, accompanied by Crazy Sharon, Baby Sister, Cuddly Carrie, and the Space Ace, drove up to the gloomy old house in Deadeye's parents' van. Leapin' Lena had an out-of-town ball game, and Mad Mel had flatly declined, stating, "I ain't goin' in no haunted house!"

It certainly looked haunted, they decided.

"How you wanna do this?" asked Boateater nervously. "All together?"

The Space Ace vetoed that quickly. "Somebody has to stay here to go get help if we don't come back out. You know that," she reproved.

"I'll stay!" seven voices said at once.

"Aw, c'mon, candies!" Birdlegs scoffed. "Me an' her'll go up by ourselves." He grasped Crazy Sharon's hand.

She quickly jerked it away. "No, you an' her won't, either. Not by ourselves!"

The Heater suggested, "Let's flip coins. Odd goes, even stays; half and half. Cut the inside light on." He pulled out a handful of coins. "Y'all flip. Me an' Birdlegs are in the first five for sure."

Depending on how one looked at it, Deadeye, Cuddly Carrie, and the Space Ace either won or lost. They gained the privilege of going in first. "I don't think I want to," Cuddly Carrie ventured. "Doesn't somebody else . . ."

"Trust me. You'll love it!" Crazy Sharon assured her.

Armed with flashlights, the first five left the van and moved to the front of the home. The Heater and Birdlegs ran up the steps, but once on the porch their enthusiasm began to wane. They politely waited at the front door for the other three. "Ready?" Birdlegs asked as he pushed open the door.

"They're in!" the Gaper whispered to Hamburger, who was already on the roof. The taller boy went up the last three rungs on the old wooden ladder and closed the trap door quietly behind him. Each of them held a hammer. They moved away from the trap door, careful to stay out of sight of the van. Kneeling, they began a rhythmic tapping on the old asphalt roofing.

Inside, the Jakes heard nothing above their own echoing footsteps and voices. They gave only a cursory look to the first floor, for the Space Ace had pointed out "The skeletons and mummies are always on the upper floors."

The second floor revealed nothing more threatening than rotten flooring and sagging ceilings. "Rookie's right. This sucker's 'bout to fall in," Birdlegs observed. Up the creaking stairs toward the third floor went The Brave Five.

The pair on the roof were beginning to get impatient for some sign that their haunting tapping was attracting attention. They increased the volume, not realizing that the muffling asphalt roofing and the creaking stairs prevented their victims from hearing the pounding. Only after the boys and girls were all on the third floor could a muted thumping be heard.

"What's that?" Cuddly Carrie moved closer to Deadeye.

"Jus' thunder," assured the Heater. "Hey! Look at these old newspapers on the walls!"

The Gaper and Hamburger were just above the old gabled window that was next to the stairs. Through the smashed panes, the larger boy heard his energetic hammering dismissed as "jus' thunder" by Heater, and it made him mad. "They want loud poundin'? I'll give 'em loud poundin'!" the fat boy whispered. So saying, he stood and began jumping up and down on the roof. "EeeYYYAAAhhh!" he emitted his version of a ghostly scream.

Hamburger weighed two hundred fifty-five pounds, which is a fine weight for a defensive tackle. It is somewhat less than ideal for a roof-jumper, however. The fat boy hit a spot that had leaked for years and thus was rotted. He literally "went through the roof."

Standing so close to the gabled window, the Jakes initially assumed that the ghostly screamer was crashing through the window and focused their lights in that direction. They almost missed the sight of Hamburger dropping fifteen feet into the same story of the house they now occupied, but when they realized their natural mistake and swung inboard with their lights, there was indeed a ghostly apparition doing the scream- ing.

As he had made his hole and fallen through it, Hamburger's white sweatshirt had been jerked over his head by the splintered boards around the hole. The Jakes' lights now shined on a ghostly whiteness — skin below the shoulders and sweatshirt covering head and raised arms. The five youngsters stood petrified as the shrieking phantom appeared in mid-air descent and then disappeared through the floor.

For the floor beneath the leaky roof was also rotten, and Hamburger's weight had built up no little bit of momentum.

"Shoot-a-mile!" Birdlegs yelled over the screaming of the ghost and the girls. "What the hell was *that?*"

"A ghost! Go!Go!Go!" The Heater headed for the stairs, knocking Deadeye aside and chivalrously grabbing Cuddly Carrie. Birdlegs jerked the Space Ace toward him and followed the first pair.

Deadeye's light was knocked from his hand and smashed, but he saw his companions' lights headed downstairs as he stag- gered from Heater's blow. He recovered his balance by shoving against a thin, hard object in the dark, and raced toward the descending beams yelling, "Wait for me! Wait!!"

The object was a wooden ladder. It clattered to the floor, leading Deadeye to the conclusion that he was being chased by a skeleton. Fear lent wings to his feet and he caught the other four as they reached the bottom of the stairway, headed for the door.

The ghostly screams were on the first floor with them, and the kids burst through the door and off the porch, never touch- ing the steps. Boateater already had the van cranked and

Rookie held the door open. Deadeye was the first in and Heater came last, yelling, "Go! Go!Go!GO!!"

The tires threw gravel twenty feet as the van shot out of the driveway, and the storm broke behind them.

At church Sunday, and again at school Monday, the Haunted House was the talk of the town's youth.

Hamburger was excused from phys ed for two weeks, having mysteriously sprained both ankles over the weekend. The Gaper had an awful cold, which is not unusual for someone who spends four hours on a roof in a rainstorm.

Each of the Jakes, except the Rookie, had a large package under the tree that Christmas and they knew what the boxes contained. To tell the truth, they rather expected Wacky Mack to give them new JakeJackets, and Christmas morning they were not disappointed. But also in each box was a little card with "My cabin, 3:00 p.m., Christmas Day" scrawled on it. They phoned each other to find that all had similar instructions, so Birdlegs picked up Boateater and Deadeye, and met Perfect and the Heater at the gate below Deputy Don's house. They drove together to the log cabin.

The five identically-jacketed boys knocked and the Rookie, similarly-jacketed and grinning from ear to ear, opened the door and shouted "Chris'mus Gif'!" Laughing at the youngster's having adopted this old Southern custom, even down to mimicking Deputy Don's accent, they entered shaking hands and exchanging thanks for presents. The owner of the cabin sat by the fire coughing, as he did so often now. The little cedar tree that they had cut and decorated a week ago at the party here with the girls glittered in the corner. The piles of wrapping paper around it testified that Wacky Mack and the Rookie had had a wonderful first Christmas together.

The Jakes posed for the man, thanking him for their new jackets, and he in turn showed them the book he was reading — a present from Deadeye. The Rookie served mugs of hot chocolate as Wacky Mack motioned to the boys to sit.

"I asked y'all over t' tell you somethin', an' t' thank you," he rasped, then paused to cough. He took a sip of hot chocolate. "I've thought a lot this past six months. An' I reckon I owe y'all a lot." He paused again, and Perfect wondered briefly if he had stopped simply to breathe.

"You owe us, Mr. Mack?" Boateater was puzzled.

"Yeah. Y'all slipped in on my blind side, I guess, but y'all... gave my life meanin'. An' purpose, too." There was another hesitation while he sipped from the mug, holding it with both hands. "Y'all prob'ly never realized it, but y'all showed me that life ain't jus' gettin' by. It's 'bout givin' more'n you take. Y'all ever think 'bout how much y'all give?" Wacky Mack began to cough, and the Rookie had to take the mug from his hand before it spilled.

"Not very much." The Heater spoke to fill the vacant space.

The man wiped the corner of his mouth with his bandana. "Naw, y'all do, too." The voice had almost a gargling tone at the start of the sentence. "An' y'all take a lot. But y'all get what you take 'cause you've given. Unnerstand?"

It was obvious from their faces that they did not. Wacky Mack shook his head in frustration at not being able to get his point across. "Like them jackets. Y'all knew what was in them boxes 'fore you opened 'em. But y'all got 'em 'cause y'all gave th'others when you didn't hafta." The coughing interrupted him. When he spoke again it was barely more than a whisper. "I'm sayin' life, friendship, love, whatever; th' more you give freely without lookin' for nothin' back, th' more you're likely t' get."

"Waal, I dunno. I can 'member when you gave us a lotta stuff an' a lotta lookin' after, an' all we ever gave you was a lotta trouble."

The veteran grunted. "Huh. Reckon y'all did too. I laid out b'hind that ole log many a night, liss'nin' an' learnin' what friendship is. Watched y'all doin' stuff t'gether. Watched y'all take this boy an' make somethin' outa him. Watched . . ." Once more he was interrupted by a coughing spell.

The Heater took over. "Mr. Mack's sayin' he started lookin' out after us 'cause he liked what he saw. And that he felt like he was part of . . . that he was a Jake, a long time 'fore we knew he was around us."

The Rookie picked it up. "An' y'all took me in when you coulda jus' left me for dead," he grinned at Heater. "Or worse, for a hophead or somethin'. Y'all gave me somethin' to shoot for."

"But only 'cause you came over on your own to help start my truck," Boateater pointed out. "So you gave an' we took, then we gave an' you took... Oh, I see what he's talkin' about."

"An' wasn't nobody keepin' score!" Perfect declared.

"That's it!" Wacky Mack's voice was stronger than before. "Nobody kept score. Y'all see?"

Birdlegs felt A Wise Saying coming on. "So, friendship is not keepin' score. That's why you got us over here?"

"Yep. Now go home. Merry Christmas." Wacky Mack nearly grinned as he picked up his book.

Two days later the veteran drove himself in to see Doc McClendon. The physician was disturbed by the sounds in the man's chest and checked him into the hospital. Not quite thirty-six hours later, Wacky Mack died.

The conference room at Uncle Bubba's office was hardly big enough for the crowd that the attorney had summoned New Year's Eve morning. The youngsters were slightly awed and bewildered, for as Boateater had exclaimed, "We didn't do nothin'! Why do they want us?" Yet all six Jakes were present, as well as all the girls: Baby Sister, Crazy Sharon, Leapin' Lena, the Space Ace, Mad Mel, and Cuddly Carrie. Papa Jake and Other Mother were there, as well as Perfect's mother and both of Birdlegs' parents. One parent from each of the other families had been asked to attend, and only Cuddly Carrie's had not been able to come. Deputy Don and the Duke of Dundee were already sitting in the back corner of the room.

In his best "cultured" voice, as Perfect called it, the lawyer directed the adults to the chairs against the wall while the youth he seated at the table, Jakes on one side and girls on the other. Then he took his place at the head of the table and called the meeting to order.

"As most of you know, we are assembled here for the reading of The Last Will and Testament of the individual we all knew as 'Wacky Mack.'" He took off his reading glasses and glanced at the line of adults. "As his attorney for several years, I can assure you that he had assets that were not readily visible to the casual observer. Without going into detail, let me just say that Mack had a regular disability income from his military service for the past twenty years. Yet he lived off the land, so to speak, and invested most of the money. Except for the log cabin and a few vehicles over the years, he had very little in the way of major expenses."

He put his glasses on again and began to skim down the document. "There is a trust involved, of which my brother and I," he nodded toward Papa Jake, "are trustees, and we need not go into those details as yet. Duke," he looked up over his glasses, "you and Don are asked to accept the role of trustees of Mack's real estate and real property, consisting of the home and approximately eighty acres of woodland. This land trust is set up for a period of seven years, with a payment of ten thousand dollars a year to be divided between you as is mutually agreeable. There is also an ample reserve for expenses, such as taxes, maintainance, and home improvements as deemed necessary." The two men nodded as the lawyer glanced over his glasses again.

Uncle Bubba's tone became less formal as he directed his attention to the youngsters at the table. "You kids — minors under the law — are the beneficiaries of the bulk of... Wacky Mack's estate. Uh-uh, now!" he held out his hand to Baby Sister, "No crying. Not now. Control your emotions and let me get through first. Then you can cry." He smiled sympathetically.

"Now, I don't know whether you boys — Jakes, as the Will

refers to you — were aware of it, but Mack owned his land free and clear. Homesteaded it, which is unusual these days. This land is left to the six of you jointly, with the provision that if one of you decides not to continue his association with the others, his share is to be divided among the remaining Jakes. It cannot be sold unless every single one of you were to agree. Do you understand?" Dumbly, the boys nodded.

"The home is bequeathed to you six young men in the same manner, with the exception that the Rookie shall have the right to permanent residence there until he is twenty-five years of age. However, this permanent residence shall not be to the exclusion of any of the other five — under reasonable circumstances." He glanced at his own son, removing his glasses. "In other words, if Rookie's there sleepin', studyin', whatever, you couldn't come bargin' in at three in the mornin' with a bunch of drunken fraternity brothers from college. Do you see my point?"

"Yes, sir!" Perfect nodded empathetically.

"If there is a dispute about 'reasonable circumstances,' then the two trustees," the attorney pointed toward Deputy Don and the Duke of Dundee, "will have final judgement." He looked around the table before putting his glasses back on. "However, I don't foresee the problem occurrin'. Better not."

He went back to the document. "In addition, the Will provides a trust fund for each of you boys, to remain under control of the trustees," here he pointed at himself and Papa Jake, "until you all are twenty-five years of age. The amount of each trust is . . . twenty thousand dollars."

"Shoot-a-mile!"

"Good Golly Greenwood!"

"Son of three-toed, bare-backed berry picker!"

"Apiece?" was Deadeye's mother's question.

"Yes, ma'am," Uncle Bubba answered reprovingly.

"I ain't b'lievin' this!" the Heater whispered to the Rookie. Then he noticed the boy was weeping silently.

"There are additional trusts provided for, that I shall discuss with the appropriate person at the appropriate time." The attorney now turned toward the girls.

"Now, for the fairer sex. As you know, Mack had quite an extensive library, including many collector's volumes." He held out his hand to Baby Sister. "It's yours."

"Oh, no!"

"Oh, yes. You may leave it in place under the care of the trustees, or you may remove all or part of it at your pleasure. Keep it, sell it, give it away, start a library, whatever you want to do." He smiled. "It's yours."

"He knew!" the Rookie's exclamation interrupted the proceedings.

"Beg your pardon?" The lawyer was taken aback.

The Rookie spoke directly to Baby Sister. "He knew this was comin'. I didn't realize what he was doin', but for the past few months, he'd been gettin' down a coupla dozen books every night an' signin' 'em. He was gettin' 'em ready for you!"

At this the girl burst into tears. As Crazy Sharon put her arm around the younger girl, the Heater elbowed Rookie. "Hush, man. You're gonna break everybody else up!"

"I'm sorry," the boy apologized. "It just hit me what Mr. Mack was doin'." He looked at Uncle Bubba. "I'll shut up." He pulled a bandana handkerchief out of his pocket and offered it to Baby Sister.

While the meeting was momentarily disrupted, the attorney reached down and picked up his briefcase. From it, he extracted six small velvet bags, each of which had a small tag on it. As most lawyers do, Uncle Bubba had a flair for the dramatic. Holding the bags, he stood and walked behind the row of girls. As he reached her, he called each girl's name and placed a bag on the table in front of her, instructing, "Wait to open it." Then he sat back down, deliberately reclosed the briefcase, and deposited it on the floor by his chair before turning back to the table.

"These are not part of Mack's estate. They were gifts that he entrusted to me to give to you at my discretion, and I have the proper documentation to satisfy any tax questions. Young ladies, please accept these gifts as a token of Wacky Mack's esteem for you. You may open the bags."

Emeralds, rubies, and sapphires appeared on the table. They were big stones, pendants set in gold. There was an awed hush.

Uncle Bubba spoke casually. "If I were a bettin' man, I'd bet those stones were obtained in Southeast Asia, and I'd bet

317

they entered the country illegally. But that's been too long ago to worry about now. I would also bet," his voice lowered, as if he was speaking to himself, "that you ladies are collectively holdin' well over one hundred thousand dollars' worth of jewelry in your hands. At least by some appraisals."

"Shoot-a-mile!"

"Good Golly Greenwood!"

"Son of a three-toed, bare-backed berry picker!"

"I ain't b'lievin' this!" the Rookie spoke to Heater, who nodded, speechless.

From the back of the room, Deputy Don whistled in a barely audible tone.

Crazy Sharon's father exclaimed, "She can't take that!" His daughter not only held a large ruby pendant, but matching ruby earrings. Baby Sister had a set of sapphire earrings to match her sapphire pendant, and the rest of the girls each held a pendant of red, green, or blue hue.

"She either takes it now, or I'll take it back and hold it for her twenty-first birthday." The attorney was brisk. "And furthermore, it is a conditional gift. It may not be disposed of or encumbered in any way until the recipient is twenty-five years of age." He sounded official again. "Do you understand, girls?" They nodded, each involved in putting on her pendant.

Uncle Bubba put his glasses on and returned to the Will. "I was to read one part to you before this hearing is closed," he said. "Ahem. I am quoting here. 'I never had kids of my own. After the past few years, I never felt like I needed any more than you all. Mind your folks, drink your milk, say your prayers, and every now and then remember old Wacky Mack!'. . . As executor, I declare this estate hearing closed."

The Rookie had not brought enough bandanas.

*   *   *   *   *   *   *

As is usually the case, the last five months of high school passed far too quickly, in a mad rush. The Jakes were so caught up in the whirl that one of them, Boateater, didn't even make a single turkey hunt that season. This Jake's aforementioned speed took him to the District and Regional track meets, and eventually to the State Finals, where he tied the record for the 400-meter run. Several colleges vied for his abilities, and visits to their campuses were squeezed into his already crowded schedule. He made very few Jake Camps that spring.

Perfect made only two or three more. He and Birdlegs had captured the lead male parts in The Senior Musical Dramatic Presentation, *West Side Story*, opposite Leapin' Lena's female lead. With baseball season also demanding his time after school and on weekends, even Uncle Bubba rarely saw the boy. Perfect and Cuddly Carrie were also battling it out for Valedictorian, and college representatives called on these two, as well as Crazy Sharon, with offers of academic scholarships.

The Heater was involved with baseball season, too, and several colleges had approached him with athletic offers, necessitating campus visits. Birdlegs' time was taken by the track team as well as his Senior Play co-star singing duties. Deadeye and the Space Ace won tennis meets at different levels, up to the State Quarter-Finals. Crazy Sharon, in addition to playing on the tennis squad, was elected Miss High School and subsequently participated in area beauty pageants as contestant and celebrity. Mad Mel's science project took her all the way to the State Competition, surprisingly accompanied by Baby Sister, whose off-the-wall experiment with alcoholic mice captured the judges' fancy even though this was her first year of high-school competition.

In addition, all of the seniors had college visits and decisions to make; Senior Term Papers to research, prepare, and write; and the inevitable Senior parties, proms, and class get-togethers. All had at least bit parts in the Senior Play; most were involved in the high-school annual staff; and they all sent out invitations, got presents, and had to write thank-you notes. They were busy youngsters, doing what had to be done.

The Rookie got lonesome and contracted a terrible case of the melancholies. He had just lost Wacky Mack and now seemed to be losing *all* his friends, all at once. He said as much to the Great Green G at the end of one of their tutoring sessions. She understood.

"No, they've not forsaken you. They are only caught up in a system that has functioned like this for decades, and will probably get worse in years to come." She eyed him speculatively. "It's called 'growing up,' and you're going to have to face it yourself soon."

"Whatcha mean?"

"You are going on nineteen years old. Do you intend to live in the Woods and work at the lumber yard all your life? Not that there is necessarily anything wrong with that, but it *is* a decision you must make. What is your goal in life? What is your potential? What must you do to reach that potential?" She paused and thought for a moment. "As a matter of fact, that is your homework assignment for the next lesson. Write me a paper stating what you intend to do with your life."

That was Tuesday afternoon. The next afternoon, Baby Sister rode by the log cabin on Polly to find the Rookie hard at work. While she knew that he had been taking lessons from the Great Green G, the girl had never seen him this enthusiastic about an assignment. They talked until dark, and he ended up following her home in Wacky Mack's jeep to be sure she made it safely.

At his Thursday session, the Rookie had his answer ready for his tutor. "I wanna be a teacher, I think. If I can. I think I know the value of an education an' can maybe get that idea across to students who might be havin' trouble an' thinkin' 'bout droppin' out. I dunno what I wanna teach, but I'm gettin' to where I love readin', an' I can do lots of things with my hands." He wanted a reaction. "Whatcha think?"

"I think you will probably never teach English," his tutor said sarcastically. "I also think," she said seriously, pausing for emphasis, "that this is not a practical goal unless you renew your pursuit of the educational process."

"Yes'm, I know that. So, how do I go about it?"

The woman thought for a moment. "There is a test you can take to get into college even if you haven't finished high school. Let me check and I'll have all the details for you next week."

Coach Fuzzy helped his English teacher gather all the information and forms she needed for the General Educational Development Program. After they had discussed all the details thoroughly, however, the Great Green G sat in silence for a moment, obviously considering something. Finally she spoke.

"Frank, I am an old woman," she began.

Coach Fuzzy was only a couple of years younger than this lady himself, and he protested. "Not *that* old, Miz G!" he said. "We're not even to the stage where they refer to us as 'Mature Adults' at church, yet."

"Nevertheless, I am unmarried and have no illusions that I will ever be otherwise. I enjoy my job, this school, this town, and these kids. I have decided that I wish to do something of lasting benefit. I have a little money saved up that I will never use, and who would I leave it to?"

"Well, I don't . . ." The uncomfortable principal was grateful for the interruption when the Heater knocked on the door.

"'Scuse me, Miz G. Hey, Coach. Ma'am, you asked me to bring you this stuff about the Rookie? I wrote down all I knew an' got some stuff from Uncle Bubba. He wanted to know why you wanted to know, so I told 'im. Hope that was okay? An' he's got a letter in here to you." The Heater was in a hurry to get to baseball practice and all this information poured out like water from a bucket. He deposited some papers on the desk and turned to leave.

"One moment, please," the Great Green G said, halting the student. "I need to speak to you about a Term Paper."

The Heater was suddenly concerned. "What's wrong with my Term Paper?" he demanded.

"Nothing is wrong with your paper. I would not have dreamed that there was so much trivial knowledge afoot concerning the Abominable Snowman. It is one of your companions that concerns me."

"Err . . . yes'm?"

She pulled a paper from her desk drawer with Birdlegs' name on it and showed it to the boy. "This young man has woefully neglected his work to participate in other school and extra-curricular activities, some of which involve the pursuit of a certain young lady and a certain wild fowl that belongs in a barnyard."

The Heater grinned. "Yes, ma'am. He's doin' that."

The Great Green G fixed him with a direct stare. "If this Term Paper is not up to decent standards by next Monday, the boy will fail English."

Coach Fuzzy felt like a fly on the wall, and knew he was not included in this conversation. The boy exclaimed, "Aw, Miz G! You can't do that! Then he couldn't sing in the Play, or even graduate! Does he know this?"

"He knows, but he has gotten so far behind that I do not believe he can catch up by himself."

"So what can I do?"

"He must have a B on his Term Paper to pass," the teacher declared.

"A B! He can't do that good!" the boy protested.

"He must have a B on his Term Paper to pass," the lady repeated.

"I don't see how he'll ever . . ." He was interrupted by her third repetition.

"I said 'He must have a B on his Term Paper to pass.' *Do you understand?*" Her gaze was level, uncompromising.

Suddenly the Heater grinned. "Yes, ma'am. I think I understand now. Err . . . what subject?"

The Great Green G dropped her gaze to the paper and nodded, "Quarter horses," she stated.

"Yes'm. Bye, y'all." The boy turned to go, but he stopped, turned back, and walked around the desk. "Thank you, ma'am," he said, and bent quickly to kiss the woman on the temple. Her ruler clattered against the door facing behind him as he escaped into the hall, his laughter echoing with his footsteps. The Great Green G blushed.

Coach Fuzzy chuckled. "Did I just hear what I think I heard?"

Had the Jakes been assembled, they would have judged their English teacher's reply worthy of A Wise Saying. "There is more to education than passing Senior English," she remarked primly.

The principal spread his hands. "Aw, absolutely!"

"Now, as I was saying before we were so rudely interrupted, I would like to make some lasting contribution here. You will need to take care of the details, but I would like to set up a scholarship fund for a deserving student each year, based on their appreciation of an education and their ability to communicate that."

"I take it you're not talkin' about an 'egghead award,' but all-around education including participation in school activities?" the man observed.

"And the appreciation of that, plus . . . well, you know the young man I've been tutoring in the afternoon a couple of times a week?"

"Of course. I helped work out that deal at the hospital, re-member?" he reminded her.

She pointed at the forms. "And do you know what started him on the road to this?"

Coach Fuzzy shrugged. "I guess you. You've been tutor-ing him for over a year."

"No. It was those children reading to him. They awakened him to the value of an education, without really meaning to."

"I think I see what you want," the principal nodded. "Tell you what. I'll draw it up and check it out with you before I take it to the School Board." He stood and grinned. "Do I get three guesses as to the first recipient?"

She blushed again and tapped her cheek. "I think even a broken-down old coach could figure that out."

He laughed. "Good choice. I'll work it up this weekend and let you see it Monday. Oh, yeah, how much? Two-fifty? Five hundred?"

"I think a thousand dollars each year would be a good fig-ure."

The man was shocked. "Whoa! Don't bite off more'n you can chew. A scholarship of a grand a year would take an en-dowment of . . ." he figured silently, "about twelve or thirteen thousand the first year."

She nodded. "As I said, I'm getting old. I've been teaching for almost forty years, and I've lived alone in an apartment. I've saved money, but now am faced with what to do with it. Do you have a better solution?"

Coach Fuzzy shook his head appreciatively. "A thousand bucks for one little kiss. . . ."

She saw the look in his eye. "Frank, I've just been kissed for the first time in twenty years, and I could not stand it twice in one day. . . ." She blushed as Coach Fuzzy leaned over the desk. "Frank, I'll have you brought before the Board on sexual harrassment charges if you . . ."

But he did, and she didn't.

It was Baby Sister who picked up on the fact that the Rookie was feeling left out. Once she mentioned it, though, the Heater almost instantly understood. "Well, durn! I never thought about it, we've all been so busy lately. An' him jus' losin' Wacky Mack this winter, too. Whatcha think we oughta do? Not but two weeks 'til graduation, but we've got a little time now. Senior Play was over last week, an' baseball an' tennis this week. Term Papers are over, an' the State Finals track meet is this Saturday."

"Why don't we have another JakeFest Party for graduation?" was the girl's suggestion. "Last one it rained, an' Mr. Boy Chile died. An' Mr. Mack was sick."

"Hey, maybe Rookie will know whether he passed the GED test by then! An' we could have a real graduation party for him, like we've all been havin'!" The Heater was enthusiastic. "I could find out from Miz G if he passed, an' maybe even make it a surprise party."

His sibling had obviously given it some thought already. "I even know when we can do it. Next Sunday night."

"Sunday night is church night."

"Not that Sunday night," she reminded him. "None-a the churches in town have services that night 'cause it's y'all's Backache service at five o'clock."

"Our *what* service?"

"Your Backa . . . whatever. When they preach at the seniors," she said.

"Oh. Baccalaureate service, dummy."

"Oh, yeah? Well, spell it, dummy," she retorted.

The Heater only paused for a moment. "Never mind, dummy. If we gotta go to Baccalaureate, how're we gonna have a party in the Woods?"

"Because, dummy, the service is over by six, an' it doesn't get dark 'til after seven-thirty. We could set everything up that afternoon an' y'all could change clothes after Backache an' still be in the Woods 'way 'fore dark."

Years ago, Papa Jake had had a second phone line installed.

"You call the girls?" Heater grinned.

"On my way!" was her reply.

By the time school was out the next afternoon, they had it all arranged. As Baby Sister climbed into Perfect's Bronco for the ride home, she asked her brother, "Wha'd Miz G say about the GED?"

"Durn, she had to call near'bout to Washington, D.C., but she found out he passed." The Heater frowned and turned to their cousin. "You know, she wanted to know was Uncle Bubba gonna be there. Said be sure an' tell 'im the Rookie passed the test, but wouldn't tell me why. How come?"

Perfect shrugged, never looking from the road. "Shoot. You askin' *me* why the Great Green G does somethin'? But I'll tell Daddy. All th'other grown-ups comin'?"

The Heater grinned. "Said they wouldn't miss it. Father Phil's even gonna say a few words. But I told him *just* a few," he hastened to add.

They drove a mile in silence before Perfect spoke. "*Damn*, I wish we were gonna have some harmonica music!"

The weather cooperated beautifully. A slight cold snap came through Saturday night, so the fire felt good after sunset on Sunday. The Duke had provided steaks for supper, and even offered to cook them, but the Heater had turned him down. "No, sir. Then this would be a DukeFest, not a JakeFest."

Perfect and Leapin' Lena brought out their guitars while Heater and Rookie grilled steaks ("Ole dead cow meat," Rookie grinned at his companion), and Birdlegs joined the guitarists on several songs from their Play. They finished with "Tonight" and Deputy Don wiped an eye afterward, commenting, "Thought I heard a mouth organ a coupla times on that 'un!"

Deadeye, reclining against the log, drawled, "Me, too." The firelight reflected off of his glasses, and Crazy Sharon couldn't see his eyes to tell if he was kidding.

The Space Ace giggled and punched Mad Mel, pointing at the old sweetgum. "Remember the Spaceship?"

"Awright!" warned Boateater. "You start tellin' 'bout that, an' we'll tell about y'all skinny dippin' with . . ." Cuddly Carrie clapped a hand over his mouth.

Papa Jake was puzzled. "Spaceship? I never heard . . ."

"Ain't fixin' to, neither!" growled his son, squinting threateningly at Space Ace.

"Aye propose a treaty," announced the Duke. "Nothing told at this campfire tonight will be repeated before you Jakes are twenty-five." He looked at Uncle Bubba for confirmation. "That way, the statute of limitations will have run out on all your crimes. Consider that you all are going to leave us this summer, and chances are very good that we will never have an opportunity like this again." To support his own proposal he observed, "It took very nearly a year for me to find out about those painted armadillos, for instance."

"I agree," Uncle Bubba voted, and looked mock-seriously at Deputy Don. "Sir, as The Presiding Officer of the Court, do you swear that nothing these young innocents tell us tonight will ever be used against them in a Court of Law?"

Deputy Don raised his right hand. "Indubidibly, I does!" he answered solemnly. " 'Fore God an' Father Phil."

The minister grinned. "And I promise to say a special prayer for repentance and forgiveness of the whole group — after I have heard all their confessions."

"And I'll tend to anybody that goes into shock, apoplexy, or fits of laughter," said Doc McClendon. "So give, you all!"

Crazy Sharon began. "Well, the Spaceship idea started after the Jakes played The Second Dirtiest Trick in the World on us girls . . ."

"Oh, Lord," Father Phil whispered to the Duke of Dundee. "Can't wait to hear what The First Dirtiest Trick was."

The Heater shook his head at the Rookie and moved the steaks back from the coals.

His instinct was right. It was a late supper, indeed, punctuated by more stories and laughter. The adults were warned several times, "Now, y'all said you wouldn't tell."

The original purpose of The Spring JakeFest was almost forgotten until Uncle Bubba rose after supper and walked toward his Bronco. He returned with a package and a file folder, asked the Rookie to stand, and handed him the package. "What's this for?" the boy asked as he unwrapped it.

It was a robe and "one-a them funny li'l flat-topped graduation hats!" as Baby Sister described it. The Rookie was mystified when Perfect and the Heater stood also and held the gown for him to put on. "What is this?" he asked again, as Crazy Sharon adjusted the cap and tassle on his head.

Uncle Bubba reached into the file folder and presented the boy with two pieces of paper. "Son, you have passed the GED test, and I am proud to award you not only this certificate for your attaining a high-school equivilency education, but also a copy of your other trust fund."

The Rookie stood open-mouthed. "Sir?"

"There was another trust set up by Wacky Mack, but I could not reveal it until now. He wanted you to further your education, but only if you began that process on your own. There is enough in that trust to assure you of a college education, but it only went into effect upon the earning of this GED certificate." The attorney held out his hand. "Congratulations. Now, I believe Father Phil has a few words to say for your graduation service."

The minister rose and offered the awed cap-and-gown-clad youngster his chair. "Never preach to anybody that's standing up," he grinned. The Rookie collapsed into the seat, nearly in shock, as Father Phil cleared his throat.

"I'm not going to talk long," he began. "Most of you have already heard me speak once tonight. But you young folks around this fire have come to mean an awful lot, not only to me, but to a whole group of adults. And to each other. I've — we've, rather," he indicated the group of men, "along with one who isn't with us in person tonight — have seen you all grow up together as friends. We've seen you hurting: physically," he nodded toward Doc McClendon, "spiritually, and even," he grinned, "legally. Yet still you kept your friendship intact. We've seen you fight, we've seen you play, we've seen you laugh, we've seen you love.

"We've watched you grow from children into young adults. Were we at war, we would probably see at least one of you disabled or buried within the year. I thank God we are not. When Wacky Mack, as you called him, was your age, he was in a hospital bed recovering from wounds that eventually contributed to his dying. I pray that you will not experience war.

"You Jakes have known fear, pain, sorrow, laughter, love,

327

anger, and heartbreak. You've seen the world both ugly and beautiful, and you have an appreciation and a perspective of both. You've been through an awful lot these past few years, and you've managed to keep your feet on the ground and your friendship secure. I pray that you will continue to be friends the rest of your lives, even though you face a separation at this point in your relationships."

A pecan branch popped in the fire, sending sparks flying head-high. Father Phil grinned as the Rookie made sure none had landed on his robe. "I love all of you, and I look forward to a lot more JakeFests, even though you'll all be pulled in different directions these next few years.

"But bear this in mind: you are at the end of your youth, on the threshold of young adulthood. As we've heard here tonight, you've certainly made these past few years a lot of fun. Don't let these next few years — the last of your youth — slip by. Don't waste them! For after college comes job, marriage, mortgage, children, duties, responsibilities; and then suddenly, you wake up old one day.

"Don't misunderstand me here. I don't mean for you to go wild. I simply mean that if you live right, the next four years will be more fun than any others of your life, before or since!" The minister finished, somewhat shaken by his own vehemence, as was most of his audience. "God bless you," he concluded.

The Duke stood clapping and walked to the Bronco, returning with a bottle of champagne. "Aye do not need to warn you about this stuff," he announced, pouring a little into each of the extended paper cups, "but Aye would like to propose a suitable toast to the lot of you. And then..." he glanced at the Rookie, "Aye would like to hear the truth about a certain coach who left rather suddenly. There's a rumor going around..."

Holding his cup carefully, Birdlegs leaned back against the cypress log between Deadeye and Boateater and spoke softly, directing his question at Perfect. "Did I understand Father Phil to say that the next few years will be more fun than the last few?"

But it was the Heater who answered, and with A Wise Saying: "Huh. There ain't that much fun in the whole wide world!"

THE

JAKES!

CPSIA information can be obtained
at www.ICGtesting.com
Printed in the USA
BVHW040026281021
620053BV00002B/9

9 780961 759148